The Serpent

D1391019

Other titles by Neil M. Gunn published by Souvenir Press

Novels: The Drinking Well
          The Green Isle of the Great Deep
          The Grey Coast
          Morning Tide
          Young Art and Old Hector

Non-fiction: Whisky and Scotland

THE SERPENT

by

NEIL M. GUNN

SOUVENIR PRESS

First published by Faber & Faber Ltd., 1943
Reprinted by Club Leabhar, Inverness 1969
This edition Copyright © 1978 by
Souvenir Press and John W. M. Gunn
and published 1978 by Souvenir Press
(Educational & Academic) Ltd.,
43 Great Russell Street, London WC1B 3PA
and simultaneously in Canada

*The publisher acknowledges the financial
assistance of The Scottish Arts Council
in the production of this volume*

ISBN 0 285 62327 3 casebound
ISBN 0 285 62328 1 paperback

Printed in Great Britain by
Fletcher & Son Ltd, Norwich

Chapter One

As the Philosopher paused on the upward slope to let out a stream of breath he felt the beating of his heart and heard its dark buzz in his ears. This for some reason gave him a momentary pleasure, as though he would applaud the organ, now as old as himself, yet still holding to it. His eyes were a milky blue and moved about him with the leisurely clairvoyance that rests lightly, yet so penetratingly, on what it loves. Almost they might consciously have been looking in farewell. But the Philosopher did not know he was going to his death within a few hours, a death so startling that deep in the mind of the country-side the old menacing images would stir and lift their dark heads.

The only image in his own mind was of the ground around his feet, and he saw it tumble in gentle frolic, in little green dips and braes, broom and juniper and whin and wild briar, and grey salleys huddled in clumps over the tiny burn, hushing and hiding it. He smiled. The wild roses had just come into bloom, pink roses and white, and the broom was yellow as meadowland butter with an eddy of scent now and then that choked the brain like a sickly sweet narcotic.

Glancing back the way he had come, his eyes were caught by the red petrol pump on the roadside, a dozen paces up from the wooden shop which he had built by the gable-end of the old croft house. It was a local holiday and every shop was closed except that one. Even as he looked, a car drew up at the pump and a dark figure moved towards it from the cream-coloured front of the wooden shop. Henry wouldn't miss any twopences that were going, holiday or no holiday!

His smile broadened in happy humour and he decided he might as well sit down. He had the whole day before him and it looked like being a good day, for though there were some large billowing clouds in the sky, they sailed, set a spinnaker, or hove to, against a vast blue ocean that was calm with summer.

As his heart-beats subsided, he felt airy within himself, withdrawn from the community he could see like a cork from a dark bottle.

And he could see a fair swatch of it. The village was little more than a straggling line of houses, at the near or western end of which stood the bright petrol pump. It lay in a broad valley basin, with hill lines against the horizon. Beyond it stood the solid grey gable-end of the church, with the hollow bell steeple about the size of a natural chimney. It shut out the manse from him though he could see an upper corner of the wall of the manse garden. Beyond that he caught a glimpse of the road which came from the country town of Muirton, seven miles to the east.

By church and village and petrol pump the road came, and continued up the wide fertile Glen (now shut off from the Philosopher by the shoulder of the hill he was climbing), topped ridges, wound by pine plantations and lochs, crossed an ultimate watershed, and then descended by birch tree and bracken and tumbling falls, to the western sea.

Here, towards the eastern seaboard, the fertile low ground of the glens had been cleaned of the folk and turned into great arable farms. Except for those left in the village, the folk had been swept up to the moors, to the Heights. Thus the farm which the Philosopher could still see before the hill-shoulder cut it off was called Taruv, and the croft houses far above it, the Heights of Taruv.

For a generation or two the folk who went to the Heights had retained a material relationship with the farms below. At harvest time they had descended to reap and to stook, at first with the one-handed hook or sickle at which the women were expert, and, later, with the two-handed scythe, the man's weapon, behind which the women had gathered and bound the sheaves. Great numbers of men and women were needed to harvest the large farms, and the Heights, while retaining the old life of the folk, were also a reservoir of labour for the new dispensation, a human dam whose sluice could be lifted.

Changes often appeared to be violent, and indeed were so frequently enough, but it was remarkable how, little by little, change was accepted in the lifetime of a man so fully, so fatally, that bitterness itself was forgotten. Children of the dispossessed, grown into men and women, reap, and sing as they reap, on the lands taken from their fathers. Many a story the Philosopher had heard of "the great times there would be in it" at the harvest-homes of the big farms. The eyes of bearded men from the Heights would glisten with memories that were pagan if not unholy.

Even in his own lifetime, consider the changes that had taken place in such a thing as a nickname. Tom the Atheist, he had been called; then Tom the Serpent; and finally, as the new young grew up and merely saw a quiet inoffensive little man, pottering about or sitting in the sun reading a book, the Philosopher. There was something derisive in the title, of course; the subtle off-taking derision that country folk like.

But the village had remained down below, in that wide basin of broken ground, perhaps because here were gathered together certain indispensable trades and craftsmen, the blacksmith, the joiner, the merchant, the schoolmaster, the postmaster, and, by inevitable complement, the widowed woman, the old maid, the young girl who went out to service, the young man who learned a trade or went gillieing or, from carrying a small bursary to the secondary school in town, flowered miraculously into a university student.

Yet it still was attached to the soil, a crofting hamlet, and as he looked the Philosopher saw figures singling their turnips in between the green cornfields on the narrow cultivated lands behind the houses. With their slightly bent heads they moved so slowly that it was easy to get the illusion of an inner meaning or design that never changed. And this somehow at the moment comforted the Philosopher.

The car roared and swung away. Some lads on bicycles. And here was the Fraser Arms bus from Muirton: a picnic going up the Glen. As it passed, Henry gave the driver a wave. A noisy cheer from the passengers rose above the whine of the mechanism. And there was another car swinging in—Doctor Manson, a tough old pagan if ever there was one.

He had been called in for his mother's death—how many years ago? The Philosopher tried to calculate, but got lost. Sometimes it seemed to him that there had been whole stretches in his life, as long as ten years at a time, when nothing had happened.

Yet whenever the image of his mother came to mind, at once life moved on its feet, working and suffering. And immediately other pictures were begot—of his father, the fields, the croft work, school days, sunny stretches of the countryside. A small stout dark woman, forever busy. He remembered little scraps of letters he had got from her when he was in Glasgow. She knew she could not write or spell very well and his father formally answered all letters, but these scraps, painfully and probably secretly written, had a curious suppressed warmth, though they attended entirely to physical needs. The ordinary phrase "see and be eating plenty" could make him laugh and feel awkward, and even, if he thought about it, slightly hot. It was almost as if she had come into the room and spoken to him with others there.

And that *would* have been awkward! Never any real idea had she had of the life he had moved amongst in Glasgow in the two crucial years between nineteen and twenty-one.

And it was as well! Bowed her head would have been then, and her back, like the women who turned away from Calvary as the darkness came upon the world. What agony there must have been at that scene, what incredible affright!

He was the only son. A second child had died at birth, following an accident with a washing tub, and conception had ceased in her after that. When a neighbour came with sad news, her eyebrows would go up, making arched creases immediately above, so that her eyes, now round and wide open and dark, seemed smaller than ever, while she sat with resigned palms on her broad knees. In a curious haunting sense, she was like an animal. She had never told him a story when he was a child, and if she did refer to bogles when he was obstreperous at bedtime, it was never more than a reference, as if he knew the creatures only too well himself. What a fearsome reality this often gave to them!

When society could produce beings like his mother, it could from that moment dispense with all force and coercion. He had realised as much more than once, and always in a moment of illumination. Was she in this respect in her simple way the embodiment of a once perfected mode of society?

Not at all so unusual a question as it might seem—in those days in Glasgow, away back in the late 'eighties or early 'nineties, when questions about society and socialism had an eagerness, almost a bloom, upon them which they have since lost, however a practical earnestness may have increased.

Huxley. Darwin. Robert Owen. Haeckel. Oh, the excitement in those days! Impossible for this late age ever to recapture that first fearful delight, that awful thrill, of Scepticism. The horizon lifted, the world extended itself like a Chinese lantern and glowed with strange beasts and designs.

He had taken to the Glasgow life, the life of the streets, almost at once and with a real avidity. For a boy out of the Highland country, this may have been unusual, but then he had always had a zest for life, and particularly the outsider's zest. He was not in himself a "character" so much as a "watcher"—something more than a spectator, ready if need be to mix in, and shout, and retreat, doubled up with laughter. Something of the gamin in him from the beginning, beyond doubt.

If his mother's mind had had to express evil in its two highest forms it would naturally have avoided definition and sought for images, and if Antichrist and the Scarlet Woman had been whispered to help her out, she would have gone silent in utter acknowledgment or, at the most, said "Yeth" on a slow intake of breath, solemn and sad, as though these two eternal figures, caparisoned in the scarlet and black of night and of nightmare, could hardly be on this earth.

Antichrist and the Scarlet Woman.

The little shop, before it sprouted a red petrol pump, had warred disastrously enough with the grey church.

In and around such war had come love, that red terrifying urge, and tragedy, that bitter defeat, and murder that had sat in his head through days and nights with so awful a clarity.

Antichrist. . . .

Coming into close contact with Dougal Robertson had been so simple. A customer, a stout noisy woman, had returned to the Glasgow shop, an ironmonger's, with a cheap clock she had bought the previous day, declaring the thing had stopped and would not go again. She had done nothing to it, she declared, and wanted a new one or her money back. The owner of the shop appeared and talked with the woman. Tom was called. He had sold her the clock? Yes. And it was all right then? It was, said Tom. While the woman repudiated his assertion angrily, Tom lifted the clock, shook it gently, and listened.

A faulty clock might be replaced, free of cost, by the makers, but not one damaged by accident. The owner was trying to explain something of this to his customer, whom he clearly did not trust, when Tom said, "I don't think there's much wrong with it." Quickly he left them and came back with pliers, tweezers, and a screwdriver.

His master, about to stop him, hesitated. The woman said loudly she did not want any mended clock; she wanted a new one or her money back. "Just a minute, ma'm," said Tom politely, "and we'll see what's the matter."

He knew he was taking little risk, because he had always been good with his hands, and never cared much for monotonous croft work. Indeed it was because of his intelligent fingers that his father's sister, who had married a widowed shopkeeper in Stirling, had got him this "beginning" in a city business.

Tom pulled the brass works clear of the wooden frame. Then he drew his master's attention to the pallet which had got jammed against the escape wheel. "When I sold the clock it was going. It could not have been going if it was like that. Someone must have given the clock a dunt." Thus he justified both himself and his master.

While the woman denied the allegation vociferously, his master watched Tom ease the pallet with a slow delicate pressure. As he removed his hand there was a whir of racing wheels. Soon he had the works screwed into the wooden frame, the little pendulum attached, and the clock ticking away normally.

"Well, if it was Lizzie did it and told me a lie, I'll tak' the skin off her, the limmer!" said the woman, her face blown red and apparently angrier than ever. Tom tied up the pendulum.

After watching her stalk away with the clock under her arm, his master, a dry humour in his face, turned to his young assistant. "Where did you learn about clocks?"

"I used to do little jobs like that for folk at home," replied Tom as indifferently as he could, but now feeling embarrassed.

"Did you?" There was a pause. "They are short-handed in the workshop. Dougal's assistant is in the infirmary, his head broken—they say with a bottle. Would you care to give him a hand for a day or two?"

"Yes, I would," answered Tom, with every appearance of calm.

"Follow me," said his master.

Some of the happiest days of his youth were spent in that repair shop. It was not a very big place and had the appearance of being extraordinarily overcrowded with tools in racks, laden shelves, a wall-face of small chocolate-coloured wooden drawers with wire and whatnot hanging even from their knobs, a smith's fire, two anvils, a turning lathe, heaps of metal and junk, weird assortments of household articles, an uneven clay floor, long wooden benches with vices of varying size, adzes, planes, chisels, and an outlet to a backyard stale with the smell of horse dung.

What a thrill—the first time he lit and pumped and handled the new-fashioned blowlamp!

Good days! Dougal, his boss, had slowly thawed. Not that he had been anything less than just from the beginning, but clearly a young counterjumper as a temporary mechanic had been a bit too much at first for an irony that could take filings off such a situation with the metallic precision of the turning lathe.

One day, nearly a fortnight later, the master came back. There had been an earlier interview between the master and Dougal, though Tom did not know that then. They had both, with a sense of fairness, decided to leave it to the lad himself.

"Well, you'll be longing to get back to your old job?"

"I wouldn't say that," answered Tom, in a quiet enough voice, but hardly knowing where to look.

His north-country expressions often made fellows laugh. His master smiled now and asked, "Do you mean you would like to stay on here and learn to be a mechanic?"

Tom's eyes lifted to a bench, to his master's face, and suddenly and quite clearly, he said, "I would."

The master looked at him in a concentrated considering way and then asked, as though it was not what was really in his mind, "What will your uncle say?"

Tom looked away. "I think it would be all the same to him," he answered reasonably.

"Think over it for a day, and then come and tell me."

A little later Tom said to Dougal, who was busily silent, "I'd like to stay if it's all the same to you."

"Suit yourself, my boy. If you'd care to stay, I'd like to have you."

Tom felt a swelling in his breast. The following night Dougal asked him out, and so it began.

Dougal was over forty, tall, with a slight stoop, dark, and spare. His forearm was hard as a board, his fingers persuasive but unyielding. He was a first-class craftsman and conscientious in so austere a way that it struck Tom at first as being almost religious. Perhaps of all he heard and saw in Glasgow, this alone he thoroughly understood and brought back with him, this (as it became) need of his nature to finish a job well. Outside human relations, it was surely the finest thing life had had to offer. The fingers loved it, and in the doing the mind was at peace.

There was pride in it, no doubt; even the religion of the individual, for it was the circle that Dougal put about himself against creeds and the existing economic system in which he did not believe. It took Tom a fair time to comprehend this fully.

Dougal had three of a family and a wife buxom and quick on her feet, good-looking with untidy dark hair, rather erratic and noisy, perhaps because she could never quite understand her husband. She had the quick warmth and intelligence of the Glasgow working woman, and once Tom caught her eyes in a swift sidelong look at Dougal as he crossed the kitchen. It was so secret and naked a glance, as if she would divine the ultimate propulsive mood in him at the moment, that Tom, feeling he was prying, removed his eyes.

So this was his new mate! She took in Tom in a bright look, laughed her welcome in a laugh that her quick tongue mixed up with bottles. She had the whole story of his predecessor and the latest information of how he was getting on. Dougal remained silent and she went into detail in an expansive admonitory way. Tom laughed and said that he was afraid he never touched bottles —at least not so far. He suddenly liked her, and liked, too, that something he could not define in her attitude to her husband. There may have been a woman's fear in it, a woman's uncertainty, but it sprang from something much deeper.

A girl of ten, with big dark eyes and black lashes, regarded Tom with a long solemn stare. A boy of six and another of three.

With the two little boys bedded at last, the woman bustled about, wrapped her head in a dark shawl, and said, "I ken fine ye'll be glad to see ma back!" She turned with a simple direct look at her husband. "I'm off ower to see Bella Power. I winna be long." Then her eyes swept Tom with a smile. "I'll be seein' ye." His hand began to go up in a country wave.

So it was talk then, quietly at first, about topics of the day, Keir Hardie, Trade Unionism, the political gossip of the yards and shops. Tom realised very quickly that he knew little or nothing about what was going on in this world.

Not that Dougal appeared to notice. He went from one topic to another casually, with the quiet ease that might not mean much. Presently Tom was describing his home country and Dougal asking a question now and then to keep him going. But no, Tom did not know how it came about that there were big farms in the valleys and crofts up on the moor. Yes, he had heard about the evictions, but he couldn't say exactly . . . they could hardly apply . . . he wasn't sure. With mounting discomfort he realised his complete ignorance of what had happened round his own doorstep at home.

Dark-eyed Jeanie came nearer and at last stood between her father's knees, facing Tom. When he looked at her and smiled, she held his eyes in a solemn stare before glancing down at her father's knee and picking it slowly.

Dougal told him of Tiree and of how his paternal grandfather had been carried out from the ancestral home, set on fire by the factor's men, and placed under an upturned boat where he died. He spoke not with anger but with a curious detachment, a remote wistfulness almost, that brought to Tom a silence in which he felt his neck grow stiff.

For Dougal did not blame anyone. Given on the material side the economic constitution of the clan, with the chief as its master, and on the spiritual side the constitution of the church, with the minister as its master, given these two idols of the tribe, the rest followed.

"You never heard the phrase 'Idols of the Tribe'? It's from Huxley. Come and I'll show you a few books I have." He put Jeanie from between his knees, half lifting her gently, and led Tom into a small room off the kitchen, little more than a closet, nearly filled by a bed. Here on a shelf screwed into the wall were about a score of books and a bunch of pamphlets.

Dougal pulled out a volume and as he turned its pages Tom glanced at titles and names. Apart from the *Origin of Species*, all were strange to him. Dougal began reading.

Tom was later to come across the expression "Idols of the Tribe" in works as far back as the *Novum Organum* of Francis Bacon, who divided the classes of Idols into four. In the mass they represented the observances, superstitions and customs "at the mercy of which" man is brought up; but now when Tom heard Dougal's voice advising the seeker after truth to beware of the Idols of the Tribe, they took on in his mind a curious darkness and power, as if ancient taboos were embodying themselves in menacing idol shape behind his inward eyes. He tried to shake this feeling from him as Dougal closed the book and put it back in its place. But he found it difficult to speak, smiled awkwardly, said he had not seen books like that before, had heard of Darwin, but—but——

"But what?"

"That we all come from monkeys," said Tom.

Dougal's eyes lit up. "And Darwin the Devil himself?"

"Complete with tail," said Tom. "Once from the pulpit the minister thundered at him."

"Did he?" said Dougal, looking at Tom now with close but smiling interest. His shadowed eyes glowed. "And what did the folk think?"

"Oh, I don't know," said Tom. "No-one believed we came from monkeys. Some thought it a good joke. But even then, you had to go canny with the joke."

"Something sinful about it—like blasphemy?"

"Exactly," said Tom, nodding.

"They have the supernatural world behind them as well. It gives them tremendous power," said Dougal thoughtfully. "Have you ever thought of that—the power it gives them? And it's cunning, too. You see, they have the earthly power. And when that power is questioned, they refer back to the supernatural power. The minister gets his power not from himself but from God. He remains the master of your thought—as the servant of God. Render unto the Chief the things that are the Chief's, and unto me the things that are God's. So we're back at the idols of the tribe, only now we're on the supernatural plane, a plane of superstitious belief, not reality, a place created by the first witch-doctors. In this supernatural world of the tribe, *the Devil is one idol. God is the other.*"

So clearly Dougal said these last words, with such quiet precision, that Tom's mind, completely emptied of thought, acquired an extraordinary awareness. Had God and the Devil come into the room his mind could hardly have been made more sensitive. It was something more personal than a vague rebellion by life, as he had known it, against blasphemy. It was as if Dougal were giving himself away, exposing himself personally. There was an intimacy somewhere that was too much, like a dark path opening up into Dougal's breast.

Yet at the same time there was a gleam, a gleam reflected off darkness, a frightening yet attractive gleam. It was beyond him—he wasn't touching it—like evil. Jeanie was standing by her father, looking up at him, her eyes dark as night.

When Dougal's wife returned some two hours later it was quite dark and they were still in the closet. Whether Jeanie had heard her come up the outside stairs, Tom did not know. Once or twice the child had left them, and come back again, and once she had asked her father if they wanted a light. But he was talking at the time, and beyond putting out a blind hand and stroking her head he did not answer. Now just as the outside door swung inward Jeanie appeared before them with a candle lighting up her fragile face.

"What a house of darkness!" called the woman, in a controlled voice, lest she waken the sleeping children.

That was the beginning of the awakening of his mind. The books he borrowed from Dougal were brighter and more exciting than any chance toy or "bonnie thing" he had ever got as a child. Their arguments were so clear, so obviously incontrovertible, that they had about them the quality of laughter. Often indeed he did laugh, laugh outright, and tilt up a face in which the eyes danced with merriment, keen in their cunning delight as they waited for Bob's counter.

Bob Barbour was a strange mixture, difficult to explain, though he felt he understood him to the bone. Bob and Dannie were his fellow lodgers in that first high tenement. Dannie was an apprentice in his own shop, but Bob worked in a large grocer's emporium, was a year older than both, bigger in bone and flesh, with thick brown hair, and followed his good nature into all sorts of swaggering exploits. Dannie was a dark Glasgow orphan, but Bob came from the Galloway country where his father had a village store. When Bob was bent on adventure, Dannie led. By the time Tom joined them Dannie was already in the habit of handling Bob's wages to the extent of ensuring that the landlady would be paid.

Earnings! Five bob a week for bed, breakfast, and supper. On the remaining half-crown they lunched throughout the week and comported themselves as young men of the world. When Bob got money from home he spent it royally.

What an entanglement and variety of life, what a breaking through of taboos, had there been in that early period in Glasgow!

Even the long shop hours—he had no grudge against them. They were there, like the streets and the purchasers. And that being so he accepted them and gave himself up to learn what he had to learn. Willingly he did his best to please. There was curiously little feeling or desire in him to learn his job in order to get on in the world. And actually he found very little of this desire in most other young men. They lived for the day, with its problems and stories and reprimands and rows, with its little conclaves and whisperings, its suppressed titters and swift scatterings.

Bob must have been brought up fairly strictly. Anyway, he could not get enough of street adventures, of seeing fights and women and bloody mix-ups. And through it all he sailed, not only untouched but with a deepening of his natural aptitude for romantic poetry. There was a laughing rush of life in him, and it almost seemed as if Tennyson had no more than prepared him for the appreciation of the full drama of a Saturday night in what he regarded as the more juicy parts of the slums.

The slums and Galloway moss-hags and the graves of the martyrs. Whaup-wings through the night of the ancestral mind. Anything for Bob was human and moving and full of laughter, anything— except this freethought which Tom brought back with him from Dougal Robertson and so assiduously hunted out of his books.

Bob struggled manfully, outrageously, blasphemously, but, like one caught in a maddening thicket, he could not clear himself because the arguments of the books were so lucid, with a lucidity bright and inexorable and deadly.

And Tom watched him like a ferret, waiting for the definite statement which he could destroy with logic, this instrument of the freethinker that was more precise and exquisite in its work than any turning lathe.

Then into their arguments crept a personal heat, a certain antagonism, that slowly but surely invaded and began to destroy their personal relations. It came to a head one Sunday morning.

> *Airy, fairy Lilian,*
> *Flitting, fairy Lilian,*
> *When I ask her if she love me,*
> *Claps her tiny hands above me,*
> *Laughing all she can;*
> *She'll not tell me if she loves me,*
> *Cruel little Lilian.*

Bob read the verse aloud, in a rich and tender bravado, then looking down his body—for he lay on his back above the bed-clothes—at Tom who was sitting on the single bed, reading the *Origin of Species*, demanded, "What do your wizened old potatoes think of that?"

"Just sex," answered Tom.

There was a pause. Then, "O Christ!" cried Bob, "you make me spew." As he spoke he flung the poetry book at Tom. There was a wild rustling of leaves in the air, a thud against Tom's body, and the much-handled volume fell to the floor like a shot bird, scattering poem-feathers as it fell.

Chapter Two

The Philosopher got up and saw the world around him with slow delight and his nostrils caught the delicate scent of briar. He remembered how, on coming back to it after his first long absence from home, he had thought it like the sun-bleached and newly-laundered scent of a countrywoman's linen. Or like the fresh pinafores of little girls at school when he was a boy. That clean freshness and living purity.

One high rose, wide open, was almost apart from the body of the bush below, as a girl's face in rapt wonder remains memorable in itself. It was a vivid scarlet.

Scarlet . . .

There was no scarlet about that first woman of the streets. There was darkness and there was night; the stillness of quiet dark streets and his own rushing feet.

"Of the streets." How profoundly apt!

They had been round, two other young mechanics and himself, at Sammy Dose's place. Sammy, in his late thirties, had a big bed-sitting-room all to himself. Some said that Dose was a contraction of his surname Douglas, and others lightheartedly suggested that Sammy had got "a dose". He had a powerful singing voice and sometimes, quite suddenly, would let it out in an opera song that lent itself to shattering the roof and putting this gimcrack world on its back for a fair distance round. The skin under his jaw would inflate and quiver like a taut dewlap as his mouth opened to its

17

utmost capacity. As unexpectedly as he began, he stopped. Then he would thump his chest, "Ha, that's better!" and proceed to tell the lads what he thought would do the world and them a power of good. He was ribald at times to an extreme degree, but for the most part with a rough core of sense, and nearly always with an elbowing earnestness that could not be bothered with ideal and nonsensical argument. He thought the constitution of society so amazing a piece of hypocrisy, that, so help his god, it was worth enduring as a sheer piece of wonder, a fantastic circus-spectacle.

To-night his parting oracle had been, "Free love, free beer, keep your mind and your bowels open, and no socialism." As the three lads, after leaving his place, stood at the corner of the street before parting, it was perhaps symptomatic of the state of their mind at this time that what struck them as particularly rich and ironic in the oracle, what they repeated as they laughed, were the words, "and no socialism".

As young Tom was going homeward alone, his fresh country mind was so amused by the experience of the evening—for it had the wonder of being entirely outside of him—that he quite forgot where he was, and when a woman spoke to him, he stopped, as he would have done on the Glen road at home, and said, "What's that?" instantly anxious to help.

She was dressed in dark clothes, the long skirt of the period reaching to the pavement, and took a slow step towards him, with two words of greeting in a quiet, low, but incredibly clear voice.

He could not answer and for a moment could not move. Then he gave a sort of stiff smile, looked away, and walked on.

Presently, glancing over his shoulder, he saw that she was following him. When a fellow did not want to be seen walking with a whore, this was the way to set about it. He had given her the tip.

From the increased beating of his heart, a tremulous weakening went up into his throat. His desire for escape made his feet feel so light that they might have had beating wings. But somehow he dare not run yet. He dare not. He could not run.

He quickened his speed by lengthening his pace lightly and stealthily, but when he half-glanced over his shoulder she was still coming on. They were off the main thoroughfare and it was fairly dark, with no-one about. She was still coming, dark, upright, without any visible motion of legs, without any sound.

Terror touched him out of that advancing figure and the lateness of the night, terror, thickened by the tremulousness in his throat, by a formless pulsing emotion that had knowledge of the body in it, and of its needs. But first he had to escape—to think.

He turned, right, up a side street, quickening his pace at once. He gained on her, and when he came to the next opening, he entered and ran swiftly along it on his toes. It was a short lane and soon he was in a somewhat narrow street but with lamp-posts here and there. Suddenly he stopped running, caught by a swift fear on seeing a figure almost beside him, upright and black, close by the lamp-post in the central shadow of the pool of light. The face turned, a man's face, pale, watchful, and, as it seemed to Tom, coldly inimical.

But it was not a policeman, and the man neither moved nor spoke.

Tom went on walking so quickly that his legs broke into a run of their own accord, and as he ran his mind told him with a fantastic humour, a wild careless humour, an urgent beating humour, that he had a shilling in his pocket, and that it was enough.

It was as though he had escaped from the woman and also some-how from the sinister man, and now in the half-won freedom already what he had missed was rearing its serpent's head.

He told it to himself and to the street up which he fled, a dark street of tall silent houses, a gloomy cavern with sickly lamp moons receding under a long slice of night-sky that it is doubtful if he saw at the time, but that he could swear ever afterwards he saw, and saw more clearly as the years went by.

For that particular impression of a city at night he never forgot. It remained as an impression secret to himself, holding in a heedless yet menacing way, in its stone walls and stark roof-ridges, in its blind face that yet could see, a terrifying immanence and power.

Through it he fled, with the turmoil in his breast and the hot shilling in his pocket. Would he stop or would he not? Would he—would he take a chance? As he rounded the corner within a few doors of his lodging, he paused and listened, but could not hear light footsteps because of the beating blood in his ears. Then he thought he heard them, the soft footfalls of a woman's shoes, small shoes and a woman's feet. He retreated to the dark entry leading to his tenement stair. There he took his stand, shielded by the pitch darkness behind. If she came—that would settle it. Would it? Or—would it?

Again he could not hear very well because of the surgings the blood made in his virgin body. Keeping his mouth open in order to hear better made it very dry, and his throat dry. When membranes met they stuck like damp gum.

Would it be safe, would he be safe, was it safe here?

Could he not talk to her anyway? But then—but then—if he did no more than talk, would she denounce him, denounce him in a loud voice to the street, say she had been assaulted? Had he not heard of it, over and over, as a well-known trick that she resorted to at the defeated moment? Dannie and Bob in company could bait a whore, using the most vile language to her, but then that was a game of the pack, the time and the place being chosen.

But now—here . . . his body held itself so taut, listening, that it began to tremble in its own fever. Would the footsteps never come? Were they coming? All at once in a moment of acute listening, so acute that his hearing penetrated to a distance in which everything was supremely still, in which his hearing became a second sight, he realised that the footsteps were not coming, that somewhere they had turned off, that they had ceased and were now lost beyond finding in streets receding into the night.

He stepped out on the pavement, and stood staring towards the corner in a fascination he could not break. His body emptied in a dark, defeated, spiteful way. He was restless and did not know what to do. He was dead tired, yet not tired. Then quite distinctly there were footsteps coming round the corner and at once his body stepped back into the entry. As the footsteps advanced his mouth opened and he thought of nothing. Quietly came the footsteps, but in paces too deliberate and slow, too long, for the small feet of a woman. He flattened himself against the black wall. The figure walked past and instantly, from a murderous evil in the air, he was certain beyond all doubt that it was the sinister figure he had seen under the lamp-post. In ways unknown to the instincts of beasts of prey, that man was on the prowl.

His body went slack and he turned for the stone stairs. A pervasive, unaired, sour smell, that he had got used to and hardly noticed, now came upon him with the pungency of his first visit. He groped for the wall. It was damp with cold sweat. He coughed, clearing his throat, giving the invisible a chance to declare itself. He pushed up against impalpable presence, body or bodies, and came to the first landing, groped around it, found the inner wall and mounted again. On the third landing, he stopped, breathing heavily, and waited until his sight, which could see nothing, cleared. When he found the door unlocked, relief ran over his body in a soft ease. Noiselessly he closed the door and slid the lock home; listened to make sure the old woman had not heard. Her bed creaked and she gave her rheumy cough. Blast it! he said silently, in a taut silent laugh, his mouth open, hearkening. She had warned them more than once against stealing out and unlocking the door secretly for a late comer. He faced right and his fingers ran over wood until they found the knob. He held to the knob until he had closed the door behind him, then listened for his two companions. Heavy regular breathing proclaimed deep sleep. Lifting his right foot to step carefully, he set it down in the middle of an earthenware vessel which, tilting, plunged him forward heavily in a wild stagger that fetched up with a crashing sound across the rail of his bed. The single loose brass knob fell with a tinkling clatter on the floor. The deep sleep of his companions turned into convulsions of choked mirth.

He hissed curses at them, as he gathered himself off the bed and listened. He had always been sensitive to the poor old woman's feelings, so miserable she looked, with her thin face and bent shoulders and mittened hands that cut another slice off the loaf only when she could no longer ignore their waiting eyes. Bob could look at the loaf until she squirmed, coughed, drew the back of a mitten across her watery nose, and cut. He prided himself upon this power. Now his thick laughter told of the bolster against his mouth.

The first thing Tom saw when he struck the match was the parcel of laundry from home. His father's handwriting was on the brown paper, but inside, as always with the washing, would be a scrap of a note from his mother. This was her opportunity also for sending a small gift, invariably in money, if only a sixpence and two or three coppers, ostensibly to pay for the posting home of his next parcel of underclothes, but actually something secretly saved, a token from her to him, outside the father's knowledge.

As the candle flared up, he began opening the parcel, his back to the two scoffing figures in the double bed now asking after his night's adventure with goodhumoured exaggerated ribaldry.

Pinned on the breast of his shirt, as usual. He withdrew the pin and unrolled the paper. A single shilling slid onto his palm. He looked at it for a moment, then gripped it, hiding it from his own eyes and theirs.

"Ma Gode!" came Dannie's appalled voice from behind. "The han'le's broken aff the pot!"

Tom stared at the floor with their staring faces. The crescent handle lay apart from the upended vessel. After a moment, Bob turned over on his face the more readily to stifle an ungovernable mirth. The bed shook.

Tom turned back to the letter. "Take care of yerself now and see you and be eating all ye can . . ." But the writing began to waver, his body grew hot, and, throwing himself on the single bed—for this was his week of it—he gave way to a mirth that bit on the bed-clothes and hid him.

Chapter Three

One other aspect of the Glasgow period affected him permanently before he returned home.

For while he was adventuring in these vast hinter-lands of Dougal's books, where first the world was created, then life in its simple cells, then the slow evolution of fishes, reptiles, beasts, of man himself, of man learning to settle down in agricultural communities, with the dawning need to explain his importance to himself (whence religions, priesthoods, gods and devils), during all these surprising journeys, he was aware of a constant patter of socialism in the working world around him. "Why the hell should *he* have all that?" Why, indeed! "Did *he* create the land—or did God?" "Well, *he* didn't anyway," agreed Tom. And so the hectic argument would begin.

Does youth always indulge in these orgies of talk and argument—or do they represent evolutionary phases in society? Bob's head-master down in Galloway had been daft, for example, on poetry. The Victorian era in its full still flower. A backwater that had not yet been touched by the new ferment.

Then one night Dougal asked Tom to come with him to a meeting.

Just as the talk in the closet bedroom had been for Tom of the nature of revelation, affecting his whole life from that hour, so did his attendance at this meeting provide a mental experience again of the nature of revelation. There is man, there is society, and the two make a rounded whole.

Right away, at the meeting, Tom had a feeling in the faces about him of restraint and power. At a gathering on the Glasgow Green one waited hopefully for the interruptions, the inevitable drunks, the banded opponents, the shouting, the police, the general fun. Often the stuff was good, and the talk fluent and whole-heartedly provocative. Often, too, the speaker was witty and scored over a heckler in a way that made the audience roar its delight. First-class entertainment that cost nothing.

Here in the rather dingy hall everything was formal. The cheap deal table, the chairman behind it, the speaker of the evening by his side fingering his manuscript. Men of all ages present, including youths no older than Tom himself. No women. Unobtrusively Dougal, amid the general hum of talk, indicated to Tom two or three well-known figures in the political world of Labour. Tom felt anything but laughter in him then; more like a feeling of being at some dark-figured conventicle. The smiling or earnest faces showed up ghastly and glittering in the naked gas light. Faces and eyes. They had an assurance, a concentration of purpose, that made him feel shy, almost afraid, of them. He could hardly take his eyes off Keir Hardie.

In the country they would have called the speaker's face brosy. But while he was still straightening out his manuscript he began: "Our chairman mentioned socialism as the goal towards which we all strive. Robert Owen, who died some thirty years ago, was the first to use the word socialism, certainly the first to put it in the title of a book, the book called *What is Socialism?* published in 1841. Thus if he is not the father of the idea he is at least the father of the word. The idea was in the beginning, but the word was with Robert Owen."

Over all the faces in that ghastly light a creased smile ran. The speaker maintained a grave stare, inflated his cheeks, pursed his lips, and glanced swiftly from side to side. In a moment Tom felt his intellectual power, his searching gift of humour.

"When what he made broke in his hands, he was not defeated. Our common human nature might fail him, did fail him, but it could not even turn him sour, much less defeat him. Nothing could defeat him except death, and it took death eighty-seven long years to accomplish its somewhat enigmatic purpose. Whatever some of us may think of certain of his ideas now, we can—and perhaps it is our small victory over death—salute in Robert Owen the undying pioneer. . . .

"Of Welsh artisan stock, he began life. as an apprentice in a cotton mill. Then he borrowed a hundred pounds and set up as a master spinner. He went ahead swiftly and by the age of thirty was a director and co-proprietor of the New Lanark Mills, getting a name for himself by his introduction of technical improvements, model workshops, model dwellings for the workers. Indeed his experiments there served as a model for the factory legislation of the next half century. He tried to interest his fellow employers, and when they failed him, he turned to foreign Governments, and when they all failed him—he went ahead on his own. He reduced his workers' working day from seventeen hours to ten. He abolished the curse and tyranny of workshop fines. He refused to employ any child under ten years of age, and supplied them with free education in schools specially built for the purpose. . . ."

Tom became aware of an intermingling of strong clear minds. And when the speaker chanced to complete a sentence with the words: "for the survival of the fittest may evolve from an unconscious to a conscious purpose, just as man has evolved to the self-consciousness that distinguishes him from the animal," Tom's own mind had a sudden influx of light.

So keen, indeed, became his mind that when the speaker entered upon the discussion of Association, which had "naturally developed" into Co-operation as we now knew it, Tom sensed in the audience a subtle awakening of the critical spirit. Co-operation, for the speaker, was the solution that not only by its nature and, therefore, organisation excluded profit, but was also the solution that made allowance for those irrational human factors which theorists of the reading-room were inclined to overlook when perfecting their mathematical or scientific systems. For let us consider for a moment the nature of this thing called property. What is property?

And from the audience a voice: "Property is theft."

Gravely but swiftly flashed the speaker's response: "Prudhon *also* said: 'Communism is the religion of misery'."

There was a burst of laughter and though the interrupter cried that he meant private property, the "abolition of private property", the audience was not going to be done out of its pleasure over the swift thrust, and the chairman called "Order! Order!"

Two known personalities, two variations of political faith, had evidently touched in a revealing flash, but the real nature of this flash, that amused the audience as if they were school children, was lost on Tom and he knew it.

Then in another moment Tom felt the faces and eyes of the whole hall flash on himself, while a laugh went up that he failed utterly to understand. The speaker had touched on "what is called progress, the progress of the machine age, of capital, of world-wide expansion. When we come down to human essentials, what does this progress amount to?"

"Progress and poverty," responded Dougal in his clear quiet voice.

Later Tom was to understand Dougal's leaning towards Henry George and his system of the single tax, the land tax, as formulated in his book called *Progress and Poverty*. He was even to understand how the fierce land speculation in America had affected Henry George and how a chord of sympathy had been struck in Dougal whose grandfather had been burned out of his home in Tiree; but at that moment, he was aware only of the faces, the white laughing faces, turned towards him where he sat uncomfortably by Dougal's side.

Question time was a very lively period, and when at last the meeting was over Tom rose stiffly and felt lost in the mingling crowd. He saw the man who had cried "Property is theft" go up to the speaker and say, "Ye fairly got me on the hop that time, Duncan!" "It's not often ye give me the chance," replied Duncan, and they chuckled together. Then Dougal got hold of Tom and introduced him to two or three young men. One was an Irish lad, Tim Mahoney, with a dark sleepy face in which satire stirred like an habitual element. Something in this face attracted him but at the same time made him wary and shy. Another, Dave Black, was Glasgow-born, with an oval face and eyes set so far apart that his expression seemed extremely wide awake and bright and full of energy. Two or three more came up to chuckle over special "points" in the meeting.

Six weeks thereafter Tom shifted his lodgings and went in with two artisan apprentices.

It had not been easy to do, because for Dannie he had a natural liking—they had both something of the same light-hearted gamin quality in them—and for Bob . . . what was it in Bob that drew him? After the disrupted-Tennyson episode, he forbore from saying anything provocative. But now it was Bob, shutting himself away behind a scoffing voice, who could not leave him alone.

But their working hours no longer coincided. More and more Bob and Dannie went off on ploys of their own at night, and Tom had meetings to go to, books to read, and was often fast asleep by the time they returned.

Two sets of lodgings, that represented two ways of life, almost two different worlds.

Toil and sleep still took up some twenty hours out of the twenty-four. There was no change in the streets, in the hurrying streams of folk, the night lamps, girls loitering about the mouths of closes. The city was one and the same city.

The division was inside himself, and this was brought home to him one night in a way all the more profound for being completely undramatic. Perhaps it was, after all, one of the most revealing experiences he had in Glasgow.

His conscience had been troubling him about paying a visit to Bob and Dannie. Several times in the last two months he had set an evening apart for this purpose, but always some of the new lads had interfered to divert his attention. But at last he got to his first lodging, climbed the stairs, gave the secret knock, his heart beating with the feeling of surprise, some of the old boisterous pleasure, waiting for Bob's face or Dannie's to look astonished and shout. The door opened slowly and the landlady, thinner and older than ever, looked up from her stoop. He greeted her heartily. She peered at him. "Oh, it's you," she said.

"Yes. Are the boys in?"

"I think so." She did not seem certain and a cheerful inquiry after her health died on his lips. "Are you in?" she called in her screechy voice. There was sudden movement and the door was pulled open by Dannie.

"If it isna' Tom himsel'! Wonders'll never stop!" cried that lad in a welcoming bantering voice.

Bob got off the big bed. "So you've found your way back," he cried, "at last?"

26

"Find my way is it?" cried Tom. "The miracle is finding you in. Do you think I have shoe leather for nothing else?"

When the banter had gone on for a little time, and Tom at last admitted that he had not called and began to explain why, something settled down upon the room that was quite indescribable but that could be felt. They all honestly tried to defeat this, and Bob was full of large gesture, but somehow it was a gesture that supported his way of life, that now was like a boastful defence of it. Not consciously meant to be that, perhaps, but something of that in it. It was somehow their old life against his new one, and though Bob could not know anything about this new life, yet it was as if he divined it and had to counter it instinctively.

Tom played up, asked after old acquaintances, probed new ploys, laughed with his old friends. He got Bob talking. Bob suddenly stopped talking and began to probe Tom with questions. Tom did his best, frankly telling of his new companions, the kind of lads they were, chuckled over their keen interest in socialism. "I thought I knew something about it—but, lord, I soon found out I knew nothing—not a thing. It was an eye-opener to me!"

"Swotting it up?" asked Bob, the laughing gleam held assessingly in his eyes.

"A bit," nodded Tom. "But it's in the arguments that go on that you learn most—or learn how much you don't know!" He shook his head as he smiled. "Very funny sometimes."

"I've heard them at it," said Dannie. "A lot of it, if ye ask me, is just fudge and bloody show-off." He said this with an abrupt good nature. "I ken some o' them. They dinna use the word socialism much, it's economics. Political economics!"

Bob shouted his laughter. Tom joined in. You could never be offended with Dannie, and as he opened out on a couple of "economic bastards" he knew, he nearly cleared the air.

But here was Bob helpfully suggesting, "Your atheism would be of some use to you? They'll all be atheists, of course?"

"Not all, but mostly, I should say."

It was no use. He could not get back to them, and when at last he was able decently to go, he did so with a sense of relief.

Once outside, however, he was overcome by a feeling of sadness, of regret, of real sorrow. The streets seemed darker than he had known them, more canyon-like, hidden more deeply from the sky.

Bob and Dannie were in a world left far behind. Their jokes were no longer real jokes, their ploys held no moving interest, their ways of life, their thoughts, everything about them, belonged to that distant world. It was a world complete in itself, an old-fashioned world. Airy fairy Lilian had an uncomfortable simplicity. She was terrible, guilelessly terrible, with little mannerisms. A wax doll, fixed in eternal hand-clapping, pretty. Prostitutes moving through their dark streets in an old-fashioned myth. Old-fashioned, distant, gone from him, that world.

As he walked along the quiet streets, he was overcome by a feeling of loss and sorrow. It's a pity, he said to himself. I'm sorry about it.

Why was he sorry? What was the something, particularly in Bob, that he was losing and that he was regretting?

For Bob knew, too. Bob was privy to this uncomfortable severing. The incommunicable was known to him; the gulf between the two worlds.

Like a countryman gone back home to the companions and scenes of his youth, to find he can no longer stay there, the bands of ancient custom irking him in a place gone small and grey.

Like one converted to a new religion who sees no more his friends as they have been, nor the streets, nor the habitual things that men do, nor all the ways of life.

An intuition of this difference, of this change, came powerfully upon him as he walked through the dim streets, and once he paused to look up and was strangely surprised to find stars in a black sky. And in a moment even the stars, the old familiar stars of a blue heaven, were flaming universes set apart in immeasurable space.

The intuition was swift and sure, so clear that for a little way his footsteps lagged, and by some curious inversion of the mind the place to which he was returning seemed enclosed and hard and without its attraction. An urge came over him to go for a long country walk, to go by himself, to be by himself.

Then as the intuition faded—and this was the second memorable thing—into its place there came a growing feeling of freedom. It seemed against all reason, but the hidden native humour rose to the surface, and the humans that passed were no figures of destiny. Being freed from Bob's world was suddenly an exquisite relief.

Even the difference in the attitude to girls of the two groups, or worlds, was typical, if difficult to explain. Dave Black's group was knowledgeable, could assess girls in a certain way, and knew what it was all about. Exactly the same might be said about Bob's group. Hunting is hunting. But there is a difference between hunting over a charted terrain and hunting in the primeval jungle.

The new group with a new social religion against the old group of the antique world. Perhaps it boiled down to something like that.

For nearly a year he lived with the new group. At first he was very much the outsider, sitting quietly at the apprentices' meetings, conducted so competently by Dave Black. The others could talk of socialism in a jargon he could not quite follow, but after he had had a hectic argument with Tim Mahoney, they began to turn to him naturally when Darwin or religion was mentioned. He was given a certain unique place, and a keen interest, not free from pride, spurred him to keep it.

Yet the two beings who attracted him, who remained most deeply in his mind, came one from each world, Bob Barbour and Tim Mahoney.

Though what it was in Tim Mahoney, with his sleepy face and his capacity for searing metaphysical argument—there was something bitter about him—any more than what it was deep in Bob's nature that attracted him, he found it very difficult to explain.

What might have happened had he stayed longer in Glasgow was quite another story. Winnie Johnston was in her first year at the university and that fact had been a thrill in itself. Dave had taken him to a social gathering for "raising funds", had introduced him to Winnie, and then had privately asked him to see her home. He certainly would never have risked the offer on his own! She was a fair-haired wisp of a girl carrying her head in the air. Afterwards he found out that she was really more shy than snobbish, with an ardent affectionate nature, very possessive. This possessive quality moved him strongly. It had sudden childlike attributes. It went completely to his head for a time. He would wait at street corners in the dark. Sometimes she would come rushing to see him for a moment, escaping from her home as from a powerful stronghold; sometimes she wouldn't come at all. She had the dramatic manner that could make small things all alive, she had hands that could clutch him in fear and possession, while yet she was elusive and virginal, as if hunted somewhere in her mind by something or someone else. He felt very tender towards her, and would not have hinted at an offensive word or act for the world. She was extremely conscientious about her studies and had very good passes.

Then one night she asked him if he loved her. It was not so that they might indulge their love if declared—neither place nor time was propitious—but out of some obscure need of the moment in her to have this assurance from him. He smiled, he tried to laugh, to pass it off. He did not feel it was the right moment. He found he could not make the declaration lightly, could not say it. It was as if by doing so he would make himself forever vulnerable. The reluctance that came upon him was amazingly strong. Something inside him that would not give way or be given away. So he tried to chaff her out of her mood, not lightly so much as affectionately, as if (the old country cunning) words were not needed.

"But I want to hear you say it."

"Not here."

"Please! Quick! Please—before I go!"

"Listen——"

"Please! I must go! Now! Now!"

Tom remained silent, smiling in an awkward remote way.

She tugged and shook the lapels of his coat, her face uplifted in burning impatience. Footsteps came along the darkened street behind them. She dropped her hands. When the figures passed, she did not lift her hands again. She waited, looking at him with a white straining face. He could not speak. Suddenly she turned and walked away.

He strode quickly after her and walked by her side. "Don't go in yet," he said. "Wait a bit."

But she was not waiting, and she went in without opening her mouth.

On the way home, he felt almost sick with excitement. He found he could not go inside, and kept walking about lonely side streets for what must have been hours. It seemed to him that life had suddenly come to a point of momentous, almost monstrous, decision; nothing like it could ever conceivably face him again. It was now and here.

It is impossible to exaggerate his extraordinary state of unrest. His mouth was dry. His legs shaky. Something irrevocable had happened, was about to happen. Winnie's face, life, time, fate—the night was charged with vast and irresistible circumstance, so that he could not think clearly, could reach to a decision only to slide down from it into despair.

He came to his lodging at last in a tired, weakened condition. His two room-mates were asleep. As he lit the candle, he saw the parcel of laundry from home. Memory of the scarlet night when he had returned to Bob and Dannie in a queer enough state of mind touched him but without even a flick of a smile. He was too weary to notice that the handwriting on the outside of the parcel was not his father's. He drew the pin out of his mother's scrap of letter and found inside it a pound note.

Dear Tom,
    Your father had a heart attack the day afore yesterday he is in his bed and will be for a while. The doctor was in at him yesterday he says he must not get up and he must not work for a long time. Theres no need to be alarumd for the meantime though one never knows. Its the harvest thats the worst. The doctor was saying that you might come home for a little but I don know what to say myself if it made any difference at yer work I wouldnt like that unless they could let you of for a little seeing its your father. Youll know best yerself and Ill always manage fine. Be looking after yerself whatever else and let me know.
                                        your mother.

So his father was ill. He stared before him, bereft at last of thought and feeling. The pound note was in his hand. He must put it away with the pound that he never broke on. She wanted him home. It was quite clear she wanted him home. He became worried, wondering whether the boss would let him go. He had never asked for anything. He would hate asking. And his job? They did not keep a job like his open. Dougal would have to get someone else. He would speak to Dougal first. That's it. He would speak to Dougal first thing.

Feeling relieved, he turned his head and stared at the blinded window. The turmoil of the night was outside, and Winnie's face.

Now there was his father's face on the pillow. He turned away from that. He was very tired. I'm dog tired, he said, and down upon him came a strange fatal quietude. This quietude went into bed with him and in its far wastes he wandered, seeing that which did not move, hearkening for the sound that never came in its great stillness.

31

Chapter Four

The Philosopher rested again, for though he had been climbing slowly, even a quickened thought could increase his heart-beat, and, anyway, there was no hurry. Besides, this deliberate seeing of his past had a certain detached interest, giving to the flight of a chaffinch, to its short airy waves of flight, an indescribable pleasure. How clean and bright were the feathers this sunny day, how vivid and immediate the song and the movement! The dip of the branch, the swaying of the green leaf. The green grass and the warm scents and the wind that found its pleasure not in far wandering but in immediate eddies of fun among the small bushes.

He could still see the red pump. Henry was walking back from it to the shop. Below the cream-coloured shop, stretched the old croft house, tarred felt, black where formerly had been straw thatch. Very quiet about the house, for no-one moved around it but himself. The straw had had perhaps a brighter air, but his idea had been to make the place permanently weather-tight for his mother.

He had been full of ideas in these distant days, full of projects. They engaged his mind, for his father lying on his bed was something not to be thought about too much. He had always been rather a solemn man, slow and quiet and big-boned, his ginger beard turning quite grey as he lay in bed, and his skin turning grey, too, in a clean, washed way. His father's spareness of build made him a tall man, his mother's stoutness made her a short dumpy woman; he himself was like something that had escaped from between them, slight in build and stature, fair in hair between the ginger and the black, and in mind very much like something that had escaped and secretly knew it.

For the first few weeks harvesting took his time and energy. As his father had been forbidden to do any work for months, Tom had reconciled himself to not going back to Glasgow, not anyway until next spring, and had written Dougal to that effect and asked him to explain to the master how he was placed. Any other decision was impossible, and though he could see his mother was sometimes a little mournful about it, yet he could also see she was glad to have him, particularly as he himself put as cheerful an air as he could on the business.

And some of the lads of the village, and even one or two of the young farm hands from the Glen, came in the evening to help. This was a neighbourly thing to do in the circumstances, but always, in the country, for young men to give a fellow a hand was not work, it was a sort of pleasure. One did not need to do it, so the doing held a light-hearted virtue. If there was any fun going, here was the time for it! An odd but undoubtedly true thing: that in such circumstances it actually gave greater pleasure to help one's neighbour than to help oneself. The same in peat-cutting and other half-communal tasks. Let a man look back into the crofting days of his youth, before the petrol pump came, and check his memories. The neighbourly outing for peat-cutting had all the preparations, the expectant atmosphere, of a picnic. That was, O Tim, a fact!

Natural enough, too, when one thought of the variety and interest, the meeting of friends in a common task, a common need, the flash and clash of personalities, and—no profits! Shades of Robert Owen!

And these lads who helped, how they pumped him about Glasgow! How eager they were to hear stories—especially about whores! Their eyes would glisten with wonder, their faces smile, half-embarrassed, as they looked away or studied the small hole a kicking heel made in the turf. Do you tell me that? A shake of the head from Andie, an older hand.

God bless me! Boys, we're fairly missing our time here. What! They all laughed. Sometimes they laughed until their sides ached, throwing suggestions at Andie, whose face worked in a wry humour. And us slaving here to get a few stooks in! Andie shook his head and looked from one to the other. It must be a terrible place, Glasgow. Yes, it was not a place he would like to be in on a dark night. Why, wouldn't you know what to do? I would have no idea whatever, answered Andie, his eyes gleaming.

It's sometimes not so easy as it looks, said Tom. And a fellow can get a bit of a shock many a time. He described his visit to Dose, as an example, and gave them Dose's parting oracle. They laughed at that until they could hardly stop. Hang it, it made a fellow weak laughing. So there Tom was going along the street, a dark-glooming street with no-one about, for it was fairly late, just as if he was going along the Glen road to Taruv, when a woman spoke to him. A young woman, slim and light on her feet, with a quiet clear voice. He stopped, of course—until he heard what she said and knew it was no woman on the Glen road to Taruv. What did she say? Oh, something like Hullo, dearie. He knew what it meant all right, so he turned and walked on. She thought this an invitation—and followed. So there he was and it was no joking matter. The dark lane—and he took to his heels. To your heels? said Andie, his eyes glinting and searching into Tom's. Yes, said Tom, to my heels. To your heels? repeated Andie and he looked at Tom's heels and shook his head in wonder at the strange uses to which heels could be put.

It was as good as a play and better, with the autumn air crisp about the stooks in the field and the darkness falling. It had been exceptionally good harvest weather and on the whole he had enjoyed the work. After the first week, when his body had got all muscle-bound, he experienced, for the first time in his life consciously, a rare sense of physical well-being. The morning air had a tingling fragrance and sweetness that came into mouth and nostrils like a cool invisible drink. The involuntary shiver in the frosted air made the body itself feel light and cool against its clothes. The eyes travelled over hill and glen and sky, saw it was going to be a good day again, and came back to the standing corn waiting to be cut. It wasn't a bad thing to be astir at that hour, preparing to cut your own corn. Necessity did make a difference. Assisting your father at work you didn't like was a slow silent rebellious business. But here, in the morning, all by yourself, before your mother milked, and fed the hens, and tidied the house, and fed and cleaned your father, and came at last to bind the corn you had cut, here in the fresh of the dry morning with responsibility and mastery in the order of your going, with a done father stretched on his bed and a dependent mother, here with a scythe that you knew how to keep an edge on—keep an edge on your scythe and you're laughing, said Andie—here in the cool morning it wasn't too bad, taking one thing with another. Your body was too light to keep going long at a time, but at each pause you wandered back and picked up the whetstone, and wiped the blade with a wisp, and rhythmically stroked the blade, until the ball of your thumb with a careful touch made you nod. That intimate feel of the perfect edge was, amid the broad heavy work, a moment's delicate pleasure.

Young fellows have to meet somewhere at night, and Tom's croft, situated both at the end of the village and the beginning of the Glen, could not have been more conveniently placed. They were not overlooked here nor overheard. And it was remarkable how the young men got to know about Tom. His stories circulated among them, with much embellishment. They were stories to them of marvel, of forbidden places, of sins that made them smile in a constrained way. They were eager to hear more and came— casually, with their reticent country faces, slow responsible youths, holding their own, not blatantly butting in, asking after his father, discussing the weather, waiting with no sense of time, until some- one like Andie came along and talk opened of itself and their bodies warmed.

Some of them were loud-mouthed, some merry, some quiet and watchful, but in all of them was a sense of the marvellous, of a pagan forbidden country, of divination and second sight and ghosts, of a door behind them that might open. They kept that door shut. In company they laughed at what might be behind it, referring to this weird story or that as "just a yarn". They loved laughter more than anything. For a good laugh they would go far enough. Laughter was the one thing they could let through the door, however solemn and earnest the holy might be. To come amongst themselves, to open the door and let laughter out, laughter at such things as Tom told them, and not be overheard, that was something to remember in the solemn dry hours. It was indeed. The secret thought of it made you laugh, inwardly.

The grain was stacked. The nights darkened. His father began to get up for an hour or two in the afternoon. The minister visited the house occasionally and talked and prayed. When Tom saw his tall dark figure and grey beard coming, he was careful to dodge out of sight. The possible visit by the minister exercised his mother strongly. By the afternoon, she had the kitchen very tidy, ashes removed, the black-leaded iron of the fireplace shining, the bed smooth and without crease, in clean pillow slip and bright quilted counterpane. A hush came into her voice when she spoke of the minister.

Other visitors came of an afternoon, mostly neighbour women; but sometimes a man from the Heights, visiting the village or perhaps even the distant town, would drop in to see how Adam Mathieson, now that his trouble had come upon him, was bearing up. Many knew Adam and referred to him sometimes as "the carter", for at one time he had done a regular business as a carter between the town and the village, and, right up until his illness, had frequently been on the road, carting coal or other heavy goods to a given order. Never without a good draught horse, he would plough a widow's land and help put down her crop at a rate of payment that was always reasonable and now and then amounted to no more than a dismissive wave of the hand: "It's all right, mistress. We'll say nothing about it this time." Many old creatures blessed him, and when one of them came into the kitchen and sat with his wife, Maria, she would recall the good deed done to her, and shake her head with mournful gladness, and together they would talk of Adam as of one in a former age, of one long dead. And then the visitor would say, "Isn't it fine that you are going to have him spared to you, with God's will, for many a long day yet?" And they would smile pleasantly together and with little courtesies of manner, for they were dressed for such an occasion and let nothing amiss touch its decencies.

When Maria saw her visitor off, she would come down towards the byre looking for Adam. But she need not have feared that she would find him working. He would be sitting on the boulder that though built into also projected from the lower gable wall, looking across at the shoulder of the hill with its bushes and sheep and occasional passing of the shepherd.

"Haven't I told you that stone's too cold for you? You should have something under you."

Adam did not remove his eyes from the hill as he answered calmly, "It doesn't matter, woman."

He had never been a talkative man, but in former days his silence had been quite natural and was often enough encountered among crofting men who had to do much of their work alone. Speech when it came out of such silence could be gracious, have something friendly or informative in it, and when directed towards the past could bring into the present a certain meaning and warmth. Often Tom had heard him talk loudly enough with other men, and laugh, for he could take a dram when it was going and had his own humour.

Now his silence had a new element in it, withdrawn from ordinary working life. For long spells he would sit quite still with his eyes staring so fixedly at something near or far that obviously they were not seeing it.

Maria soon got used to this, though sometimes Tom caught

her looking at her husband with a stare of her own. A woman could at times look at a man in a searching, hidden, but utterly objective way as if the man were a stranger, a kind of unique stranger whom she apprehended in this suspension of thought, this involuntary concentration of an inner faculty. Maria would turn away and leave him taking his rest.

Could she have so looked and turned away had it been death that was sitting with him? Yes. But it was not death, and this she divined, as Tom knew.

The figure that sat in his breast was not death but death's neighbour. And it said to him, You cannot do this, you cannot do that, because if you do it's death. Thus the desire itself to do anything was taken out of him. He moved slowly, carefully, went in to look at the horse if Tom was not working him, stood and looked at Tom from the gable-end if he was, looked at the two cows and the stirks, saw how things were here and there, sat down, and fell into his staring reverie, that may have had some thought or movement in it, or more likely had not.

Then he caught a chill and his wife blamed the cold boulder at the gable-end and made him stay in bed.

On the Sunday his wife said she would not go to church but would stay with him and Tom could go alone.

"You will go to church," he said. "There is no need to stay with me."

His voice was so level, austere, that it turned all possible objection into silence.

Tom did not mind much going to church with his mother. He would not have cared to go alone, but escorting his mother was a natural thing to do.

That was one blessed faculty that life had given him. Many a fellow in his position would have felt that he should have stood up for his new convictions and not have gone to church. Tom never felt like that, nor was he made in any way miserable by the thought of his own weakness. The thought of weakness or self-betrayal could not quite touch him. He was too evasive for it. When it tried, he could smile at it, avoid its solemn touch. Always there had been an untouchable core in him in such matters. Truly something to be thankful for, as for the invisible wind that played among the bushes, carrying a scent here, a bee there, in this strange life-business.

Not but that he had his own secret taboos and practices. When it came to the singing of a psalm he did not join in. That would be to take part—so he hadn't much of a singing voice!

Thus he could listen to the singing and be moved by its slow surges. It rose like a wave gathering way, many of the voices dragging a little behind the crest high-flung by the precentor. But these voices needed time for the swell, for the fall, and particularly, with a long breath spent, for the dead period in which the waters of song gather again.

His mother's voice had a curious effect upon him. He could hear it beside him, close upon his right ear, isolated from, while merging into, the great surge. Sometimes it gave him a twinge of discomfort, so queer the sound she made, a drawn-out *hee* sound behind her nostrils, pushing upward against the limit of utterance, almost an animal sound that was yet a tribal sound, going back into primeval time, before song as an individual, cultivated art emerged. It would have been ludicrous, but for a strange ultimate power in it; and even while outwardly it repelled him, so that he would not have liked anyone, listening, to have heard her, yet here, where her voice was lost, except to his ear, in the community of singing, it discovered in him, beneath his superficial reactions, a deeper movement of intimacy, of fondness, towards her, and discovered at the same time within him a sensation of far-reaching tolerance that had an element of lightness in it, of personal freedom, pleasant as a bright memory in an outside world, in a distant place.

The minister was a tall, straight man, with a natural grace of movement, strong yet finely cut features and a grey spade-beard, an aristocratic-looking man who, at sixty, seemed to have come into his full vigour, his final assurance. There was no longer any need for him to prepare his sermon with care. He could repeat what he had just said, with inflections, with variations, leaning back from the great open Bible; he could repeat it again as he came forward, his eyes glowing, and, gathering God's judgement upon the biblical man who was a fool, thump the pulpit, nailing the fool and his folly there for all to see. And even then he could lean back and begin again lightly, Yes, the man was a fool; oh yes, the man was a fool, a very great fool . . .

His sermon lasted for an hour and a half, so there was no hurry. And though he started from a given text and proceeded from a firstly to a sixthly, there was no compelling evidence of logical cohesion in the whole, not for the wearied bodies listening to him, but there was—what was far more compelling for them—an air of authority in the man himself. He was not the mere spiritual pastor, he was the patriarchal leader, the man who went before them, through the land of desert and plague, through tribulation and sorrow, toward the promised land.

In a sudden revealing moment Tom realized that here was, in very truth, the living idol of the tribe. Had any suspicion of his own backsliding ever touched him, this revelation freed him from it. In the minister's favourite phrase, it "encompassed him about".

In the manse pew sat the minister's housekeeper and his only son, a very good-looking youth, a year younger than Tom. Tom remembered him quite well at school, a clever boy, but mischievous, as if his freedom from the strict confines of the manse drove him beyond the normal boy's bounds. He seemed to have no conscience about harrying a bird's nest or doing cruel things to frogs and bees. Yet he could do it and laugh, not in a cruel so much as an interested and absorbed fashion. And occasionally he could be cheeky, flashing his brown eyes at an older boy in a mocking way. He had the gift of saying a piercing thing even then. His mother had died when he was three, and over the housekeeper he had developed an early and varied tyranny. She was now sixty-five, with one or two tufts of brown-gleaming hair on moles on her withered face, but still with the old-fashioned grace of manner that distinguished the lady of social position.

Now as he sat there in the manse pew, Donald Munro, who had spent a year at college, where he was studying for the Church, seemed far removed, with his young man's distinguished bearing and good looks, from the cheeky eye-flashing schoolboy, as he seemed far removed from Tom himself and the other youths of the congregation. Certainly Tom could have had no faintest premonition, in those early days of his return home, of the emotions that were yet to move him to the cold, deliberately conceived plan of destroying Donald. As near pure evil it had been, evil from which the last emotion is abstracted, as, surely, it is possible for man to reach on earth.

With the nights drawing in and the weather variable and often stormy, Tom had to spend more and more his evenings at home. He had taken some books back with him from Glasgow, but in the quiet of the lamplight, with his father in bed and his mother's knitting needles clicking away to themselves, he could not produce them, for his father would ask what they were, ask to see them; not even his books on socialism, for the word socialism was then a synonym for atheism.

For the most part his father lay quietly in his bed, his arms over the coverlet, staring before him; and though Tom, reading in some old weekly periodical, or mending a domestic vessel or implement, or glueing together a simple picture frame for a merchant's flamboyant calendar, could forget about him, yet he could not forget where he was, any more than he could forget where he was when in church. Sometimes this quietude had a curious seductive influence, and when at bedtime he got up and went through into the parlour where his own bed was, he was already like one in a state of dream, like one who had taken a mild narcotic and heard the outside world of wind and rain beat upon the walls and pass away, pass away, its own sounds whimpering softly as they left.

If his father read at all now in the late evening, it was out of the Bible. And one night, just before bedtime, he said, "I will read you a chapter. It is in the Gospel according to St. Matthew."

His father always "took the books" on a Sabbath night, but not on a weekday night, though many held this family service every night. When he had finished reading the chapter, he turned over the leaves of the big Bible and read three verses of a psalm. Then he looked at his wife.

She led the singing, and Tom muttered the words in his throat, muffling and muting them, singing like one who could not sing, rebellion stirring vaguely in his heart at being thus pushed too far. On his bed in the parlour, he sat like one who had taken part in a final and fatal rite, and the night outside passed away, passed away to the hills, in a sadness, seductive and without end.

From Glasgow, in addition to a few books—two of them presents from Dougal—he had brought home with him his own tools, and one of the new blowlamps. After his talk with Dougal, he had realised that he might have to stay at home a long time, and out of the workshop Dougal had given him lots of odds and ends. "They may come in handy," said Dougal. "At the last Fair holiday, I called on an old friend of mine in the country. He's the sort of man that can put his hand to anything and he was making quite a good living out of a little repair shop. He sold things, too; ironmongery stuff. And that year he had taken on the safety bicycle. He had two second-hand ones for learners. Threepence the half-hour he was charging. He was doing well."

Something in his tone had struck Tom and he had asked, "Would you like to go to the country yourself?"

Dougal had not spoken for a moment, then a characteristic dark glow had come into his eyes, and, turning away, he had said, "No. I would not care to live in the country myself."

Something enigmatic in Dougal's attitude at that moment now seemed clear to Tom. He knew why Dougal would not care to live in a country place; he knew it suddenly and certainly.

But Tom had his tools, though so far he had not had the heart to do much with them.

One night he returned late. His parents were in bed and the door on the latch. In the morning his mother asked him where he had been, and he answered that he had been to a certain house on the Heights as he had promised to oil a clock there.

And now the curious thing was that though he had borne the evenings at home with a certain kind of pleasure, yet when he was outside and on the point of returning, he found himself in the grip of an overwhelming reluctance to enter the house until his parents had retired. More than once he leaned against a sheltering wall, looking into the hurrying dark night, danced softly on his toes to keep himself warm, waiting for the light to go out. When he heard his mother's voice, its queer compressed nasal sound, singing far away in a still cavern of the night, he would hearken, the smile fixed on his face, and look around upon the night, in a momentary cunning glee, and feel himself withdrawn and invulnerable, friend of the eddies that whirled invisibly by, and of the darkness up in the mountains.

One sleety cold day, while in the barn by himself, reluctant to go in to the warm fire and his father's pale bearded face against the pillow, he suddenly had the idea that he would rig himself up a wooden bench, with racks pinned to the wall behind for his tools. There was no slightest chance of his getting away now before the crops were put down in the spring, and unless he were going to give in to the kitchen life altogether, he had better get something to do inside four walls. There was not much room in the barn, but by erecting a couple of rough wooden partitions, which would permit of animal feed being piled up, he would manage.

When his mother came out to see what was keeping him in the cold, he explained his plan. "Why should we go to the joiner to get a new door in the cart if I could do it myself? Or to the blacksmith for many a thing, like sharpening a coulter, when I could do it just as well. It would be a pity if I forgot my trade altogether."

He spoke indifferently, not looking at her, and was surprised at the readiness with which she fell in with his plan. He would need a little money to buy wood and nails and a few bits of metal, he said, but he could buy them cheaply in the town when he went to cart the coal to the schoolhouse.

She nodded thoughtfully. "You could surely have all the carting money for that, at least. And it would be something for you to do, in the winter days."

"Yes, I would like to have something to do."

As if a hidden sadness had come from his voice, she asked, "You're not taking long for Glasgow, are you?"

"No, not particularly. Only I would like to have something to do."

She stood quite silent, further personal words beyond her. "I'll go and see him this minute." And she set off, the concentration of purpose in her whole body.

That had been another rare period in his life, perhaps because it had been one of sheer creation, of making something to his own design to fulfil a purpose that was part of his being. Perhaps, too, the absence of all outside compulsion, particularly the compulsion of time, helped to give the undertaking an air of freedom, of choice, and this freedom may again have been enhanced by contrast with the cold miry fields and that warm dazing quietude of the kitchen. He had escaped into his own place, into himself, and in no time life came all alive in his hands. And alive in his lips that whistled a few soft hissing notes of no particular tune as he turned a shaft of timber this way and that, and eyed its possibilities, and saw the completed article before it was fashioned. The journey to the town was no drudgery, it was an adventure. He saw things on the way, observed them with the humour of the watcher's eye, and when it came to bargaining for timber and nails and iron in the backyards of contractors' premises, he was the working craftsman himself, the son who had come back from Glasgow to help his father, a happy, easy-going lad able to talk of Glasgow prices among other things, one of the workers themselves who could fairly ask for wholesale rates, and when it came to some piece of all but discarded junk—"och, shove that on your cart".

For the first time since returning from Glasgow he knew a genuine happiness, and when his thoughts now wandered freely back to his life in that great city he could recall individuals like Dougal and Bob and Tim with a certain air of amused surmise. What was happening to them now? Was Dougal introducing some raw youth to Huxley? He took a couple of books from the tin trunk under his bed and slipped them into his tool box.

Apart from feeding and cleaning animals, and an occasional day or two on the hand threshing-mill, there is not much to do on a croft in the winter season. Hanging about a small house in dirty weather is a tiresome business for a young man, and when it got known—as it quickly did—that Tom had a workshop, where one could talk and laugh while the rain pelted or the snow whirled, any or no excuse was good enough for those who had helped him with the harvest to slip away from home to visit Tom at his work.

A visit to the joiner's shop or the blacksmith's was not the same at all, for there real work went on under the eye of a master. But here at Tom's work was like play. One could handle a tool, test a fine edge, hold a board for Tom, become absorbed in punching a hole neatly, or even pump the hissing blowlamp. By the time a fellow took it upon himself to pump the blowlamp, he was getting on! Tom's assistants were of the kind who were secretly proud to be asked to do anything.

Then one of the lads from the Heights, Jimmy Macdonald, a pleasant brown-faced youth of about Tom's age, told a story of how his father, chasing a rat, had kicked a leg from under the dresser and torn away the whole of one side. His mother was in an awful state, but his father, who had missed the rat, said the wood was rotten. "And was it?" asked Tom, looking at Jimmy. And Jimmy replied, glancing away, "It was, a bit. But I don't know." "I must have a look at it sometime." "Well, if—if you were up that way . . ."

Tom spent two whole afternoons and evenings at the job, for much of the wood was worm-eaten. The second evening a few neighbours came in, including one or two girls, and there was considerable merriment and a song or two. Jimmy's mother took Tom, when the job was finished, into the ben-end or parlour. Tom felt reluctant to charge anything, but at last said he would take the cost of the wood, which was two shillings. She insisted on his taking four. A new dresser would have cost her nearly as many pounds, she said, and she was ashamed giving so little.

It was the first of small commissions of every kind among the poor crofting folk, who knew the price of things very well, and when they had saved a shilling or two by Tom's labour the money thus saved was more precious than a gift, and all the more because they knew Tom was satisfied. With his blowlamp and soldering bolt he went amongst them like a wizard. He straightened rods of iron with a nicety that brought a gleam of wonder into the eyes of old men who had never seen the hissing blue flame of a blow-lamp and kept well clear of it in case it burst.

In this way his absences from the evening service of praise increased. His father never said anything to him directly, but his manner seemed to grow more distant, more enigmatic in a grave way. Tom knew that his mother made excuses for him and perhaps exaggerated the number of shillings he gave her once or twice. Possibly she overdid this and touched in her husband not exactly a note of jealousy but some queer mood that got mixed up with his own physical weakness and those staring periods of meditation or vacancy. Sometimes a ghostliness of silence walked with him, or stood in his body and face like a presence.

One afternoon he came into the barn, and though it is the way of country folk, even of the young, to refer to an invalid's health, yet none of the lads expressed the hope that he was keeping well. He spoke to one or two of them and inquired after their parents, and they answered him with the constrained politeness they would have shown to the minister. There was a difficult silence and the old man went slowly out.

Then one dull cold evening Andie brought an old brazier he had picked up somewhere; thereafter darkness came into the barn to find their country faces brown and glistening in the glow of the fire.

The barn cut them off even from their own home world. Here they were completely freed; their bodies uncoiled, warmed and full of expectant pleasure, amid the smell of the straw and the wood, the shavings and the shadows. Their minds grew light and quick as ferrets, quick as their own glancing eyes. A ribald country story by Andie had the very smell about it of the natural functions. Laughter was a sheer joy. Nothing was ugly when you understood it. It just made you laugh, often helplessly, for once the mood of happiness was induced, it was extraordinary how even a facial

44

expression, a monosyllable, was enough to set you off. You knew what was coming!

In this atmosphere the slowest country mind grew unusually alert, and when discussion started on the beginnings of the world, on evolution, on God and Devil, every phrase used, every new thought produced by Tom, scored an impression with the sharp definition of a graving tool.

One day, in the dead of winter, his father looked at him with his grave stare, and in that moment, before his father opened his mouth, Tom knew that gossip about atheism had at last reached his father's ears. He felt the blood drain away from his heart.

Chapter Five

The Philosopher got up and went slowly on, for that look on his father's face, graver than death, could wither all things.

But only for the instant it took the eyes to focus on the sunny world. Then the face faded out, a ghost face conjured up in a daylight stare, and where it had been were the bushes, the soft grass, a warbler singing sleepily. Round the shoulder of the hill he heard the shepherd whistle his dog, heard the cry that had already sent the dog on a swift out-flanking race.

Life was a happy thought, wherever it came out of! And death's face intensified its beauty, its vivid loveliness.

What an amount of time he had wasted, so studiously, trying to find out the meaning of life!

He smiled like one who had found not a meaning but a secret. Thus to move slowly, under the sun of a temperate land, owing no allegiance, owning nothing now, was a great pleasure. One had to travel a long road, perhaps, before disinterestedness came so lightly about the feet, passing from the briars to the nostrils in an idle eddy of wind, from a warm throat to juniper bushes showing their green berries, bitter flavoured, like an essence of pine forests.

His wandering glance rested on a rabbit crouching in its shallow bed under the roots of a juniper. Its brown eyes looked back at him, hardly four paces away. The head was low, the ears flattened, the

after part of the body a gathered hump. Its stillness was an arrest-
ment of all motion. He could feel its living warmth. How clean
the fur, how full of light the dark brown eye! The fear in its body
gave it the tension of a compressed spring. Communication passed
between them, an alert subtle intermingling at the core of the
heart's beat. It could not be held long, and quietly he stepped away,
so that there need be no hurry and scurry in this world, and came,
before he knew it, into a narrow alleyway of close-cropped grass
winding between juniper bushes whose lower limbs were grey
with lichen. At once, as though he had been climbing strongly,
his breath quickened and a dizzying shadow passed before his eyes.
His mind quickened, and the orgy of sex and of the earth that had
overwhelmed him here long ago touched his body so that it
momentarily weakened into the living effluence from that past
scene. Then, looking up, he saw the goat.

The long, narrow, dark pupils in the pale yellow eyes, the air
of indifference that was yet watchful, the slanting, measuring look
of the antique world . . .

Inevitably the lads had thought of the goat and of no other
beast on that desperate ploy. They had hidden while the girls
had gone secretly by ones and twos to the thatched cottage by the
pine wood at the far-out end of the crofts on the Heights of Taruv.

It was Halloween, when the rein is withdrawn from the hallowed
and licence takes the bit in its teeth. Horses were removed from
stables, carts run down hills, turnips heaved down chimneys,
wheels sent hurtling, the painfully gathered gear of civilisation
broken up and cast away in the night by youth reverting in wild
glee to primeval freedom.

But the girls did not break up civilisation. While the old stored
and locked what they could, the girls secretly gathered at the house
of Margad, whom some called a spae-wife and others a witch, in
order to have their fortunes told. Each carried two fresh eggs.
One of these Margad broke and from the convolutions of the white
in a glass she read the girl's future. The second egg was a gift, and
as Margad retained the broken egg as well, she had payment for her
labours in kind. But this was the ancient custom, and the girls
had their own excitement.

That it was an extreme excitement there could be no doubt, for
Margad had her mysterious procedures, knowing well out of the

experience of her grey-haired years and out of the vast and cunning lore of tradition what sat nearest the heart of a girl on Halloween. The window was blinded, the peats heaped on the hearth until their slow yellow flames sent heads and arms to fantastic dancing on the walls. That the gathering, in the eyes of the church and its elders, was unlawful and unholy came at the very core of the girls' excitement, for though they would not disrupt material possessions on which the home was founded, they were ready enough to disrupt all schemes of damnation reared by male elders who fulminated against the evils of the body that conceived in sin.

The two ways of looking at things! And there was never any doubt about the difference between man and woman in that old world.

Margad made them give promises that never would they divulge what they learned from her. The promise took the form of a rite, and by the time the first egg was broken, the girls were all vivid expectancy, brimming with the spirit of wild merriment.

It was then that the lads of the Heights, who had seen one or two of the girls stealing towards Margad's, got together and decided that instead of removing old Donald Davie's harrows, as they were on the point of doing, and setting them teeth inwards against Duncan Donald's door (a crabbit old devil), they would invade Margad's and, by breaking up the unlawful gathering, join orgy to orgy in one wild splore.

Heaven knows who was the originator of the thought, but Jimmy Macdonald and Donnie Mackenzie were the leaders and Tom was in Jimmy's company for the night's fun.

So off they set. They approached the door warily, with many whispered consultations and the mounting wildness that only the thought of girls could give. But when finally they rushed the door they found Margad one too many for them: the door was solidly barred.

Foiled now, they started taunting those inside. But not in their own voices. They disguised their voices, and produced accents and weird sounds that rolled them off the wall, doubled up like animals. As their madness mounted they swore that they would not be foiled. Nothing would foil them. If the door wasn't opened at once, they would break it down. "Open the door, ye old witch, or we'll smash it in!"

They thundered at the door. They threatened to push in the window. Then a voice, rumbling and raucous: "T'hell, let us smoke them out!"

47

Broad divots they tore off Margad's potato-pit, and soon a lad was climbing over shoulders and up the gable-end. It was a wide chimney, a great hole in the roof, through which folk inside could see the moon of a night when they wanted to get some idea of the time. With the help of a wooden batten, the divots were supported, and the chimney choked.

Then it was that Kraak, the cripple, had his moment of inspiration.

No-one questioned it. It was too utterly apt to be questioned. Three of them would go to Taruv farm, bring back the goat, and drop it down the chimney. With soot and a rumbling sound it would appear before them in the flames of the fire; it would appear before them as the very Devil they worshipped!

The lads set off.

They kept a goat on Taruv then, as they kept a goat to-day, in order to ensure fertility and successful birth among the farm stock. No-one knew how ancient the tradition was; and to-day— well, the goat just happened to be among the sheep, standing between juniper bushes, with the long narrow pupils in the pale yellow eyes and that air of indifference which seemed privy to much hidden not so very deep in the human mind.

Back the three lads brought the goat, and now began that weird abracadabra of preparing the minds inside to receive their Satanic master. Only afterwards did the lads learn of the steady heightening of tension and of the awful scene that presently took place in the blue infernal smoke-gloom of Margad's den.

For the lads were at last riding the whirlwind of their mad spirits. The fight on the roof with the goat, its devilish yell, the scrabbling and scrambling and choked voices.

Heavens, it was an infernal thing to do!

Down through the hole came the goat and landed four-footed in the fire. Its hair went up in a singeing lowe and with a leap the demented brute was among the women.

The girls lost all reason. Two of them fainted. Their screams had a high horror beyond anything that could be imagined. Scream upon scream, abject and sickening, so that the knees of the lads went weak and their stomachs flat.

It was the moment for escape in the anonymous secrecy that was Halloween's rite. But the lads stood rooted, until Jimmy cried "My God!" and made for the door. He heaved his full weight at it, yelling at the same time to be let in. When the door suddenly opened, he went headlong into Margad's bosom.

The girls burst out, screaming still, and started running, like demented deer, and from amongst them, with an acrid singeing smell, the springing goat, like a four-footed devil.

The lads made after the girls, and here and there a lad knew a girl's voice, and here and there by ditchside and dike, he held on to her, crying his own name.

The same instinct moved all the lads, as the instinct of escape moved all the girls. Tom made after a girl who had turned for the down slope of the hill and the village. She went like a hind, her head up, screaming as she went. There was more than half a moon in a sky of broken cloud and the sight of her there in front of him, fleeing the horror behind, brought his manhood full upon him. He made up on her swiftly, but the beat of his feet and his crying voice only increased her terror, and, as he was stretching out a hand to grip her, she stumbled and fell, with a wild screech, whereupon, unable to check himself, he kicked into her back and went headlong over her body.

He was on his feet again in a moment, but already she was scrambling to her knees. "It's all all right! It's me—Tom Mathieson from the village!" he cried, and laid his hands on her shoulders. She fought him off like a wild cat. She was full-bodied and strong. He saw she did not know what she was doing and he came to grips with her. Her strength surprised him. Her hands broke free and bashed his face. He kept telling who he was, saying it was all right, it was all right. She nearly got to her feet, but he held her, crying now in a hushed intimate voice into her face, her ear, who he was, exerting at the same time his strength against her, until all in a moment she went slack, and lay down, and turned over, and began to vomit.

He felt sorry, he felt contrite, then. But he did not feel awkward. There came over him indeed an extraordinary competence. Normally he was shy of girls. But not at all now. Now he felt tender and contrite, and, on his knees by her side, put his right hand under her forehead, to support it, and help her with her sickness, continuing to whisper urgently at the same time that it was all right, that she would soon be all right. "Don't worry any more. It's all right. I'll see you home."

She tried to move her forehead from his hand in a repelling motion. But the action was not strong. At last she was too weak to

49

bother with him, and, turning away from where she had been sick, she lay with her face buried in the grass.

As he sat beside her, looking down on her back, he saw short spasmodic movements and wondered if she was crying. But he decided not to say any more, not to touch her, divining that what she needed was a few moments' utter rest.

He knew who she was now quite well. Janet Morrison was her name. In the class below him at school, she had been noticeable for her large dark eyes and a certain—not exactly wondering expression but something like that. For a time, at any rate, she had borne the nickname "Picture", because once a grown woman had been foolish enough to say, in the hearing of Janet's classmates, "Why, you're just like a picture!" He had heard the nickname used by one of her friends recently, however, quite naturally, and in truth fondly.

He had noticed her since coming home. No-one could help noticing her. For at twenty she was tall and good-looking. A dark country beauty, with a ready lash of colour in the cheeks. But there was something more than that, some subtle indescribable life about the eyes, in the glance, a distinction about the eyelids. The eyes could melt in shyness and yet crinkle at the same time curiously, almost assessingly, so that when the smile followed, it could be extremely attractive. She laughed abruptly, somewhere between the roof of her mouth and the back of her throat, as if she were trying to laugh awkwardly. But she could not laugh any other way, and the sound of her own laughter often amused herself. She would stop it suddenly, glance around, and laugh again. Already there was some deep consciousness in her of her power as an attractive woman. But what made this attraction more powerful was some simple lingering element of the child mind. Very difficult to define, this, and, perhaps conscious of it, she could, in her cleverness, use it. But though it thus might be a weapon, it was not an affectation, any more than her laugh was an affectation.

So that, altogether, on any other occasion, she might have intimidated Tom. But now her very qualities deepened his solicitude. For to-night she had been brought too low for anything but the utmost care. Towards any other girl in such circumstances on such a night, he would have experienced the same desire to help, the same emotion.

Halloween, with the humped moon moving in and out dark clouds. Behind them the unlawful experience of Margad's cottage.

The intense quickening of the mind, the primal fear, the shattering of the body, its awful cleansing in vomit.

Janet sat slowly up.

"Feeling a bit better now?" Tom asked gently.

Janet looked around her and then gave a sudden shudder. "I'm cold," she murmured. Her face looked death cold, her eyes pitch-black holes.

Tom, murmuring, put his arms round her, to crush warmth back into her body.

She protested.

He caught her hands. "You *are* cold. It was an awful thing to do. Heaven knows why we did a thing like yon. But you're all right now. I'll see you home."

Her hands lay passive, while he crushed and fondled them. Then she withdrew her hands.

He spoke to her in an eager encouraging voice as he might speak to a child, or to a companion who had come round after being knocked out. His words seemed to have no effect on her. Her face was dead white, and all at once he saw that she was extraordinarily beautiful, not only with a beauty of the face but also with something of the moon in the blue pool of the sky, with a fey fragile quality, the weird quality that inhabits the country beyond Halloween.

And this again did not embarrass him, but only increased his tenderness, so that the tenderness came into his own throat, and he was greatly moved to help her.

It was doubtful if she heard him, for a desperate weakness was upon her. She wanted to be left alone. But she could not be left alone. They both knew that. She never spoke. Then her unnatural control could not be borne any longer and her body, of its own accord, began taking great gulping breaths, as if it were being choked. Her hands stirred restlessly, aimlessly, and her body turned to this side and that in a futile effort at flight. Her face now shone tragic and wild. It could not be borne. As the cry came up into her throat, she made to get to her feet, but he held her, telling her not to hurry, to wait a minute. "Take your time, Janet. It's all right. I'll stick by you." The words were practical and friendly, yet they broke in his throat.

As her cry came through, some of her strength came back. But he held her firmly, and her strength broke, and she collapsed against him, her mouth in his shoulder. Her whole body was swept by convulsive sobs, and as though ashamed of them in some final deep of her mind, she clung to him and gripped him tight and pressed her face hard against his shoulder. He felt her brow clammy and cold against his neck.

He spoke to her now with a final tenderness, encouraging little words, soothing words. "Hush, Janet. Hsh, it's all right." His right hand patted her on the back, pressed into her back, pressed her against him. Never had he known such tenderness as this. It swept him in a warm living fire. There was nothing on earth or beyond earth, he would not have done for her, in the dim light on the lonely slope of the Glen. Never had his being known wholeness like this.

It not only felt competent, but full of an uncanny knowledge, of the night, of himself, but especially of the girl beside him. And his tenderness was directed in delicate instinctive ways towards giving her back her confidence, so that once more she would be herself, whole and of a living piece, herself coming alive and whole, her lovely natural self coming back to life.

This had to be made easy for her.

And her hair was against his mouth, and the smell of it in his nostrils.

Her sobs subsided and she lay without stirring, so inert that her body would have fallen from him had he not continued to hold her.

She lay so still that she might have fallen asleep or died. Like this he held her for a long time, until, half in fear, half in a searching urgency, he whispered her name. "Janet? Janet, are you all right?" He brought his face down to a level with hers, slowly, searchingly. The sweet madness of his quest for her lost spirit came upon him. "Janet?" The living fire bathed him. Her cheek came against his mouth. "Janet?" There was no life in her at all. A wild fear touched him, a hot urgency. He brought his mouth against hers. She gave a small shudder, her mouth drew back, and then, as if for the groping comfort of his mouth, it gave way to him.

There was no life in her mouth, but little by little life came back before the warmth of his life, and when her lips were warm they smothered away from his mouth, not hurriedly, and he had her still in his arms.

He spoke to her now only by the firm but gentle way he held her, not any more in words.

They lay like that for a long time, in the trance of youth, to which there seems no beginning and no end.

Then the strange nameless fear of this suspension touched him afresh, and he brought his mouth whisperingly against her cheek, and searched for her mouth against her reluctance, and found it.

When this had happened for the third time, he felt suddenly and for the first time the pressure of her lips, the living acknowledgement of her spirit and her body, a swift sweet gratitude, and now in an instant she was gone from him, and before he could do anything she was sitting up.

She did not speak, but lifted her hands to her hair. It had become disordered and he sat watching her pinning it up. But it was beyond pinning up, and with a shake of her head, all her dark hair was released and fell over her shoulders.

This action had something in it purely feminine and necromantic, there on the hillside. He could not intrude, but his hand went up and into her hair. She held her head back, her face tilted to the sky waiting for him to take away his hand. But his hand went through her hair and, pressing against her cheek, drew her face towards him. Her face resisted but came, and as he kissed her, her long hair fell about his face.

For one wild moment he lost himself then, but she pressed him away with her hand on his breast, gently but firmly. "No!" she said, as if she had shaken her head at him, in understanding.

The sound of her voice and the firm quiet action of her body were an entrancement he had no desire to break down.

Her hair was thick and long and before she had got it all up, her arms grew so wearied that they fell limp on her lap, and she sighed, and blew out her breath, "Oh dear." But as he stirred, her hands went up again.

In this display of her body, her uplifted hands and breasts and face against the sky, there was an intimacy that grew upon him. It was something that could not be avoided, and because of that he felt in her very attitude, in each quiet motion, a shyness that held a gentle humour and common sense, holding him away, because she had to hold him away, but doing all this before him because they were there together by the strange circumstances of the night.

At last her hands fell heavily and she sighed in relief, and her face turned towards him with a smile.

He did not know what to say or do, all direction in his mind dissipated by the enchantment of that smile as it hovered on the momentary verge of a laughter that he knew would not come. In that instant, she was the living embodiment of all grace.

"I wonder where Tina is?" she said, and her face tilted to listen.

"Oh, she'll be all right," he answered at once, repelling the very thought of intrusion.

"I must find her; we came up together."

"She'll probably be home by this time. There's no earthly use trying to look for her now."

"But I must. Perhaps she's looking for me."

They argued for a little, until at last she agreed with him, and said she must go home.

As they went down the hillside, he took her arm.

"I feel quite weak," she said once, as her weight came heavily upon him. "And oh so cold."

She did not seem to see very well.

"Look here, let us sit down. There's no hurry."

"No. Please. I must get home. If I sat down I might never get up again."

He caught her hands. They were very cold. Her teeth suddenly chittered.

He wished, he said, he could do something to warm her, and as this kept running in his head, he took the first opportunity of a stumble to hold her hard in his arms.

"Please, Tom," she murmured, "I am so tired." But she did not break away from him and her mouth was kind.

"You have been very good to me," she said, and for the first time it was as if there was no smile in her voice.

This made him feel not only tender again but very chivalrous towards her. The tall night felt keen and sweet on his face.

When they came by the turf wall, she sat on it, with an outward explosion of breath like a humorous comment. He sat beside her, and talked at once in a friendly pleasant way, as if only now and suddenly he realised what she had been through. Since she had come to herself after the sickening horror, she had never let up again, she had kept control, with a feminine grace he had never previously encountered, something beyond courage.

He could not help putting his arm round her, for she was bound to feel how genuinely he was moved to assist her, and now, as if indeed she knew and could utterly trust his protectiveness, she leaned against him and her head rested for a little on his shoulder.

He sat like one in a divine trance until strength could not be kept from his arms. As the surge went through his body, her head stirred, but before it withdrew he felt her chin in his neck, then a cool quick kiss below his ear, and she jumped down.

Much he learned about woman that night, that unforgettable night, every slightest incident of which remained clear, with the clarity of incidents in an unusual dream. And not the incidents only, for the incidents were little more than embodied states of mind, states of grace, utterly incommunicable apprehensions of being.

More friendly they grew and companionable, until they drew near the village. Carefully, now, their ears open, her hand gripped in his.

"I'll run," she whispered at last.

He gripped her hand hard. He could not let her go. When she broke from him, she walked away, and his heart went with the discreet motion of her body until, little by little, and then suddenly, she disappeared.

The night was empty now and cool. A divine moonlit night full of silence and a wandering wind. He turned for his own home but could not go in. Nor could he go up the Glen road lest he meet someone who would rob him of Janet. So he took the path from his home towards the mountains.

Chapter Six

As the Philosopher advanced a pace or two, the goat looked away indifferently, looked back, and then, reluctantly making up his mind about it, walked on his delicate nimble hoofs in between two junipers and on and in among yellow-flowered broom. But he was not done with the Philosopher yet for his head, rising above the fragrant broom, turned, so that there was the head alone looking at the Philosopher out of the long narrow pupils.

It had the stillness of stone, symmetric horns curving backward, outcurled beard, the carven head of an antique world.

The Philosopher's own face grew still as it held the stare of the agate eyes that saw him detachedly, without interest, yet saw him and was privy to him, in an expressionless prehistoric stillness which man could only flatter himself was derision.

The Philosopher moved on a couple of paces. The goat turned his head over his submerged shoulder and stared at the Philosopher across the yellow blossom.

The Philosopher removed his eyes and saw this withdrawn place of memory vivid with sunlight. Green leaves were translucent or glittered. The fragrance itself was colour. A small intimate world of close-cropped grass and winding alleyways, the yellow flowers, clustering like bees, glowing coolly in the sun's fire, a beauty that might have been too much, hanging still, now made light and playful in wandering eddies of wind.

Then it had been without sunlight, a darkening of the green in a small rain. He had lain down to rest, to shelter, and there had come upon his love thoughts the cool luxury of the damp grass, of the mist-soft rain, until . . .

But the thought could scarcely be borne, as the nostrils can bear only for a moment the scent of a rose, the dark fume from the core of a dark-red rose.

How Janet had affected him! The experience had been altogether beyond anything that he had believed possible could happen to a man. Even though he was only twenty-one, that made no difference. Indeed he could clearly say, thinking out of his own experience, that at that young age he had had far more of a hard sceptical attitude towards life in general than he had now. Which, after all, was understandable enough, because then he had had the assurance that he knew the meaning of life, in the sense that nothing happened but one was ready with a reason for it. Tim Mahoney, Dave Black, any of the lads could have explained any social manifestation, have given the motive of any individual act.

"Sex" explained that amusing manifestation which the romantics called "love". Sex was necessary, of course, to keep humanity going. Quite. But the trick of wrapping it up in love was a dangerous trick because it was part of the romantic structure which tended to uphold the existing order of society. One felt the power of sex, naturally. But all the "mystery" about it was man-made, as was all the "mystery" about religion. And once you understood this thoroughly you were freed from the more sickly toils. It did not make you cynical about "love". Anyone who became cynical was merely a romantic who had not freed himself properly. He still hankered after the romanticism he could no longer believe in. Poor fellow!

On that Halloween, his intellectual assurance had been dealt one of those invisible blows that scatter elements in a bewildering fashion. Dealt not by the known gods, whom anthropologists and the religious analyse with so omniscient or reverent a care, but by some dark fellow who simply lets out a wallop! As a boy gets a sudden wallop on the side of his head from his father and sits down among the ruins of his pride, yelling blue murder!

Not that he had noticed it as a wallop to begin with. He had been quite prepared to call it sex or anything else. Nothing mattered at all, except the thought of Janet. She was in his head like a new tune. She was all through him like an obsession. And he remembered her so vividly, even more vividly than he had actually seen her in certain movements and graces, as though only now had he time to dwell upon these and appreciate them properly.

And the more he dwelt upon them the more unique they became, the more utterly part of Janet's unique self.

There was a gaiety in the thought of her, a curious burning gaiety. He kept by himself as far as he could, so that no-one would waste the time he could spend with his own thoughts, and, in particular, so that no-one would surprise him smiling. For a minute on end he would lean on his plane, staring out of the little window in the back wall of the barn. This window had been a hole in the old days through which the wind came to winnow the chaff from the grain. Winnowing of a kind still went on!

He could hardly believe it all on the day after Halloween.

With the dusk, some of the lads dropped in. They caught him just as he was about to get away by himself on the off chance that he might run into Janet on the other side of the village. He had wanted the darkness for that. Now he had no excuse for going that would not bring one or two of them with him.

He had little time for secret regret, however, because he was challenged by Andie straight away.

"Me?" he replied. "You all left me quickly enough! So I cleared off home on my own."

"Took to your heels again!" cried Andie. "Well, you missed yourself. That's all I can say."

"How?"

"Mark the date," said Andie. "That's all I'll say. Just mark the date."

"What for?"

"Eh?" Andie eyed him. "My God, you're innocent," and he shook his head. "You may have seen strange ongoings in Glasgow, but och! och!"

"Surely it wasn't as bad as that?"

"I'm saying nothing," said Andie with a sober waggish air. "I'm an innocent fellow, too. But ditch and ley could tell a story or two. It was a wild Halloween."

Andie lit the brazier, his weathered face and hands and the twisting strings of his neck glowing in the blaze, a cattleman turned satyr.

Much of what he heard, Tom decided, was just talk. Whatever happened in the bothies of big farms, he knew that illegitimacy was a very rare occurrence in the crofting world, even in the days of the shielings, when girls were away from the paternal roof for weeks on end and the lads went courting them.

What happened then?

What happened with himself and Janet?

Girls and fellows in that pastoral world of immemorial custom knew whom they liked, and when fondness grew too strong they married.

Ditch and ley could tell a story all right! Many a story they could tell, thought Tom, with inward memory of Janet. Jimmy and Donnie did not tell what had happened to them, though their secrecy told more to Tom than it did to Andie.

And out of this secrecy they egged Andie on, or choked him off when he encroached too far. For when a lad has come near the tenderness of a girl he shies off the bawdy. The new wonder he will protect, in the girl and in himself.

What wisdom Tom had gathered in a night! Such new insight into the minds of those about him!

He accompanied Jimmy and Donnie up the glen until they came on the side road to the Heights. They decided that Halloween had been a devil of a night. The escapade with the goat, beyond redemption. Andie had said that the farmer of Taruv was going to the police. They shook softly with laughter. None of the girls would tell—unless for the two who had gone home alone. And what had they to tell? They laughed again, and cried good-night out of a happy companionship.

Quietly then through the dim darkness of the village, with some sort of excuse ready, for through the darkness a passing voice would call good-night out of friendliness and curiosity. Not to answer would raise doubt and mystery. Footsteps would stop. Who could that be? The silent one was up to no good, or up to some game that might be worth finding out! But if the answer proclaimed the voice of one going home, then friendliness was in the night and the sound of footsteps dying away.

Subtle communal feelers in the dark!

The voice called from the corner of Dan Morrison's shop. "Hullo!" answered Tom at once and strolled over to the small group. All men, of course, for no woman would be abroad at this hour. Tom said he was out for a last breath of air and wondered if the whole village was deserted! He sounded happy to be among them, and the talk that had been going on about Halloween got a new impetus. Tom did not deny he had been at Margad's, nor on the other hand would he affirm it, and thus for the amusement of the moment he kept them on a string. They tried to get at him in all ways, but he was too clever for them.

Then one said: "I do believe it was Tom who engineered the whole thing!"

"By George, I believe you're right!" said another.

This approach was meant to tease and draw him, yet somewhere in their voices, all in a moment, was the beginning of belief. It was the sort of thing an atheist out of Glasgow might do!

But Tom laughed.

Presently, when they broke up, with a certain grudge against him for his silence, Tom accompanied two of them along the road as far as the church. Then he merrily bade them good-night and turned back.

All in order to pass Janet's home! The night was full of secrecy and merriment.

The house still had a light in the living-room. She would be sitting with her mother, perhaps taking down her hair and combing it, before going to bed.

His whole body grew extremely sensitive to sounds lest they discover him, standing there. His mouth grew dry, listening.

Her mother was the widow of a merchant who had gone bankrupt in the village. The business was still called Dan Morrison's, though now run by Andrew Fraser. The bankruptcy had taken place while Tom was in Glasgow, so he had missed the whole hubbub and sensation. Dan had been a good-hearted, careless man, fond of a dram. All the children, with their odd pennies, had gone to him for their sweets and nuts.

There was no public-house in the village, and rumours about Dan's backshop had been rife for so many years that folk had latterly got used to them and paid little attention.

Besides, when a person suddenly got tied up with colic or other internal ill, Dan could be relied on not to fail a trusted messenger anxious for the only specific that would defeat the pains. Moreover, when folk were in temporary hardship—and who wasn't at times before money came from the cattle market, or when illness and death stretched a heavy and expensive hand?—Dan would allow them to run up book accounts. Many took advantage of Dan's softness. There were selfish, poor-mouthed people everywhere. But the unfortunate thing was that when the crash came and Dan's books were seized by the creditors, honest folk received statements of accounts which they had settled years ago. They were indignant, and no wonder, for they remembered so clearly the sacrifices that payment had entailed. Very well, replied the lawyers in the town, please produce your receipts.

In most cases they hadn't any receipts, and Dan could do nothing now. He had meant to write off their accounts, no doubt, but then the payment of a considerable debt would be so important an affair that Dan would have taken the man into the backshop. There they would have had one or two drinks in decency and congratulation. By the time they came out customers would be in the shop. Many a debtor could go over the whole circumstances in exact detail. But he had mislaid the receipt if he had ever got one, just as Dan had forgotten to write off the debt in his books. Dan's father had been a crofter, and Dan, being a bright boy, had got a grocer's training from his uncle in Dundee. But he had never been cut out for a moneymaker.

The sensation was tremendous, and this calling to account of decent folk, who were not in his debt, must have preyed on Dan's mind. He was a big man, quick on his feet, full of life, yet more than once, in that last week, tears were in his eyes. Some said they were whisky tears. But he went all soft, collapsed after a heavy whisky bout, and died in two days.

His funeral was the biggest from the village in many years. Even those who had reason to be bitter remembered his kindnesses. In their hearts they knew the carelessness that had ridden him, as, in all writing matters, it rode themselves. They would not let a man's faults follow him to the grave. Dan Morrison had always had the kind heart. It was his undoing.

The women of the village were kind to his widow that day. And some of the older men, returning from the funeral, cast a humoured eye at the shuttered windows of the shop. They had their own memories, and in Dan's company they had stolen many a happy hour from the solemn faces that rode life. The censorious could say what they liked, but at the end of the day Dan had made no money out of anyone. There were more than a few, if the truth were known, who had got money's value out of Dan for nothing. And the names of some of them would astonish you.

Dan had taken his wife from the town. Her father had been a lawyer's clerk and so, to the countrywomen she came amongst, she was a woman of some position. But she had been a quick-witted bright girl, very nervous over the birth of her first child, which had appeared some little time before it might reasonably be considered due. Older women said that if she was highly strung she would get over it in time. She was dark, like her husband, but slim, and now at fifty was thin, with a fire in her eyes.

She had had three children. Janet was the youngest, the other two being boys, one of whom had died from "inflammation of the bowels" at the age of fourteen. This death had affected Dan very deeply for he had been greatly taken up with the lad. The eldest son was in a business in Dundee, came home for the funeral, said he would do what little he could to help his mother, though he couldn't do much, and then had gone back to Dundee.

Meantime Janet had been for a year at the High School in town, staying with a grand-aunt, and coming home by bus for the week-ends. She postponed her return to school after her father's death, because her mother needed looking after. She would miss the rest of the session. The new session started. She did not go back. Some day, when her mother grew stronger, she would go in for nursing, she said.

That was Janet, with some air of the High School still about her. A movement of the head, a grace of the neck, dark hair and a white neck, and that sort of dawning humoured recognition of a fellow's face or speech that was so disturbing. The slow rich flow of her body, that did not bear thinking about. Heavy against his arm, unexpectedly strong and fluent, and then——

He walked on, glancing quickly about him, glancing up at the sky. The moon was there, for he could see the white edging to a long dark tongue of cloud. In a moment, the blue of the sky on

61

either side of the cloud was upon him in wonder. It was a newly washed, deep, living blue, beyond the blue of a queen's robe in a story book. Never had he seen that particular richness of blue before.

He glanced about him, then looked up at the moon again, while his feet went along the village street. He was conscious of the noise of his steps, of the human beings cooped within the houses, solemnly sitting behind blinded windows or already stretched out, imprisoned there, while the moon traversed the black spit of cloud towards the headland which it presently diffused in a white fiery light. All, while he walked down the village street!

Hush! he said to himself.

As the moon sailed out, the blue paled. Which was a thing he had never noticed before either!

The secret loveliness and laughter in things. The night should only be beginning. What would he do with himself through the rest of the long night?

By the peat-stack near his home, he paused on the sheltered side.

His father and mother would have read a chapter, and sung, and would now be asleep. Or did his father sleep?

It was difficult somehow to believe. The pale face would be staring into the darkness, hearkening for heaven knew what inaudible sounds, in that awful stillness.

All through the summer he had moved about with quietude upon him. Little tasks he had done, like twisting straw ropes or herding. He was very careful about giving the beasts a good bite where it might be missed and grow rank. When Tom found himself thinking his father did this not out of kindliness to the animals but out of a parsimony of spirit, a niggardliness that must turn a mouthful of grass to the best profit, as if the man were going to live for ever, he was ashamed yet half stuck to his thought in a sort of spite. In his father's attitude to him, he sensed a continuous criticism. Nothing directly was said now, or nothing that Tom could answer back in his own defence, but the encroachment upon him was there.

Once when his father looked up as Tom passed home from the field where he had been hoeing turnips, the expression on the grave face had not altered, but as the eyes resumed their distant look it seemed to Tom that the long hairs in the eyebrows had stood out in anger.

That was probably pure fancy, but then it was the sort of fancy that happened.

Ever since his father had dared to tackle him about his beliefs, he could not subdue his own mistrust and, in a surging instant, a sheer malevolence. The very way his father had on that occasion said, quietly, looking at him, "What's this I'm hearing?" had been too much from the first word.

"Hearing what?"

"About the opinions you have brought back from Glasgow."

"What opinions?"

"They say that you have brought back opinions which are corrupting the young."

"Who says?"

"Never mind who says it. That does not matter. What matters is—if it's true."

Tom could not speak. There was a power coming out from the father that choked him. His thoughts and feelings got all jumbled, and he began to tremble from anger. The father had never raised his slow voice.

"You can listen to gossip if you like. I don't care." Tom picked up a piece of wood and ran his eye fiercely along it. The wood shook in his hand.

"I want to know if it's true."

"I can have my own opinions."

"You cannot have godless opinions and live in my house."

"Then I can leave your house." Tom slammed down the board and walked past the old man, and out and up the hillside. His rage blinded him. As he lay down behind a bush he had a convulsion of anger and tore the grass with his claws. That settled it! He would go back to Glasgow. He was free now.

But when he returned, his mother was waiting for him at the end of the byre. He made to avoid her, but she ran out a step or two, a waddling creature with an anxious face, near on tears, and a thick husky voice going thin. "Tom, Tom, come here!" and against his new-found dignity and decision, she led him into the byre with an air of secrecy, of hiding, that made him speak out loud in his own clear natural voice, indifferent to whomsoever heard him.

She was all appeal. Any sudden excitement might kill him. "Oh, Tom, bear with him, bear with me."

"Well, but what right has he——"

"He's your own father, Tom, and a done man. You're young. Don't forget that. Oh, my boy, that anything should come between you and your father would break my heart. It would kill me." She wept, and the sounds she made were ugly and terrible. He felt their power in his bowels and his knees. Stark and terrible and naked, while she lifted her apron and choked her mouth with it and wiped her eyes. Sheer animal sounds, beyond everything, in the place where the heart bursts. She came round, and looked at him with her small wet eyes, and the longing stood in her face, beyond words.

"Well," said Tom, "he shouldn't say anything to me." And all at once, heaven knew why or whence, his mouth trembled and tears came into his own eyes. It was a weakness that he had not known since he was a little boy and its onset so astonished him, in shame and anger, that he turned away from his mother and picked up the hoe and began scraping the bedding down on the nearest stall, while his teeth ground and the tears broke wet on his lips.

Ah, you can do nothing against a mother when you see her like that. You can hold any opinions about her mind or person you like, but in the ultimate moment it makes no difference. And she was coming after him, coming at him. In a surge of unbearable impatience, he cried inwardly for her to go.

But when she spoke her voice was simple and confiding, like the voice of a girl, remembering still the trouble beyond them but now with his understanding taken for granted, in conspiracy, while yet her voice broke a little and her breath wheezed.

"It was William Bulbreac. He was in one day and I overheard him talking to your father. I didn't hear it all, but he was saying things, awful things about what happens in a place like Glasgow. He was saying you knew and—and—you were telling—I don't know what it was—but he was holding you to blame. I thought he had little to do to come talking like that to your father. And your father shouldn't have paid any attention to him but you know how he is now."

"Awful things . . . ye knew. . . ." The tones of her voice were charged with Antichrist and the Scarlet Woman. They stood, unlooked at, in her mind, while she shielded him away from unthinkable traffic with them.

There could be no arguing with her. Denial would have comforted her, but denial or affirmation was beyond him, as explanation would have been beyond her understanding. Words and words would convey nothing.

It irritated him acutely that at that moment her sheer ignorance had a simplicity and force in it beyond argument, deeper than knowledge itself. That it should usurp such power, that he should be aware of guilt—where demonstrably there was no guilt—in his silence, was maddening.

"William Bulbreac can say what he likes. That's nothing to do with me. Am I going to keep my mouth shut because William Bulbreac goes sneaking behind a fellow's back?"

"Hush, Tom! Your father will hear us."

"Let him hear us."

He was shouting. She looked out of the door, in dread or terror as if his father were not her husband, but some power that had to be watched and propitiated.

He found himself, even while he scraped the cobbles of the stall, listening for footfalls.

Let them come! Only the presence of his mother kept him from flinging the hoe down and walking away.

But he did not walk away.

And his mother talked to him, unburdening her mind, as to an equal, to one who could understand, so that he could feel the good that talk was doing her. And she did not blame her husband. She looked upon him as one afflicted. Her compassion was aroused by the mystery of his affliction. And this compassion, by telling it aloud, she conveyed to her son. "He was never the same after it. . . ." Simple words, but curling round him like strands of wire.

Chapter Seven

What was that extraordinary power in his mother, which he felt and must ever acknowledge? Often, in these latter years, he had tried to think out the problem. He had found it was just no good dismissing her as "a primitive creature". That was mere mental superiority or laziness, a slick intellectual trick. For often she would enter his mind, quite involuntarily, at a moment when a philosophical speculation or piece of reasoning was so intricate that he had all he could do to grasp it and give or withhold his assent. Take Hume, who was the first to lead him to tidy up his mind and see how it worked. Take his— *Were abstract ideas general or particular in the mind's conception of them*? Hume proceeds at once to agree with Berkeley that all "general ideas are nothing but particular ones, annexed to a certain term, which gives them a more extensive signification, and makes them recall upon occasion other individuals which are similar to them". The various particular ideas are not present in the mind when the general or abstract term for them all is used. Or as Hume puts it, "They are not really and in fact present to the mind, but only in power. . . ."

Well, he had to pause to think that out, for one of the most interesting things he had found in philosophy was the need for constant reference to the workings of his own mind in order to check the propositions of the philosopher.

Now his mother could use abstract terms in a profound manner. In fact she did not always use the terms, but as it were a reflection or thought of the terms, and even this thought did little more than inform a simple language which, in the very moment of its usage, had a curious indirect mythological power. But how could he know this? By experience, of course, but also by a certain if inexplicable intuition of what went on in her mind.

In learning or knowledge the use of the general or abstract term is a vast convenience. Like an x or y in algebra, as he had himself decided.

But, with his mother, it was not learning. It was power. Her algebraic symbols were not lifeless. They came out of some deep of the mind—like Antichrist or the Scarlet Woman.

And to something in this attitude he had to hold on, or the philosophers would altogether forget the particular in the general. She was a test that had to be met. And often indeed he felt that both Hume and himself were cutting pretty figures on the surface.

Or was he looking back on all this now with the eye of age, wherein his mother was the symbol of creation, his father of God, and Janet the symbol of love?

Add to that what little he knew of modern psychology, the analysis of the psyche, and where was he?

He was here amongst the juniper bushes and he was smiling.

You have got to watch those fellows! came his thought. You have got to watch them like a hawk.

You have got to watch them or they'll get you, each one of them: atheist, socialist, psychologist, philosopher, religious. Each is ready to take you "the only way".

How could there be so many philosophies, so many "perfect systems", each contradicting the other on the vital issues, if each were not a manifestation of a purely personal bias or need, an emotional fulfilment, of the individual philosopher?

That's what it came down to in the end. In the process many things were accomplished, of course, from efforts at social integration to personal "immortality". Quite. And excellent. And cheers all round. But watch them, or they'll have you in a cell or a beehive like so many willing exhibits, while the broom blows and the goat finds it unnecessary to smile.

Janet as a symbol!

High heaven save us from the symbolists, from the abstracters! Give us back the earth and the flesh and the lovely currents that flow in and between them!

The Philosopher smiled at the waywardness of his thought. Looking around, he found the goat had vanished.

He was climbing. He was getting up. There was a hidden inexplicable mirth in the earth so that at moments one's simplest thought—climbing, getting up—had a secondary meaning, an elusive humour.

Never mind. She had been lovely those days. She had in very truth been with him at the rising of the sun and in the dew of the evening. She was never far away from him. Like the swirl he made in the air, or like the stillness in the barn when he stood looking out of the little window, she was with him. Sometimes, alone in the barn, he turned round.

He had much plotting to do, in order to avoid or get rid of the lads, to deceive the village, to do anything and everything that would secretly bring Janet and himself together in the dark night. Why this secrecy? Heaven knew, but it had been part of the fun, the delicious essence of their escape into freedom.

One night, he had been fairly caught by the lads. And by way of excuse he said that he was going to spend the evening with the old folk. The implication was that he had better take part, once in a while, in their religious service. Remarkable how dutiful he had felt when he had permitted the implication, with how solemn an off-hand air he spoke!

They understood. A son had to do many a thing when his father was in a low condition. They held it to his credit and he accompanied them up to the main road and bade them good-night.

Then back solemnly to the house, and round it, and up the hillside. No main roads for Janet and him! Circling round the hillside and down by the crofting ground to within a stone's throw of Janet's back door.

And there at last she came, a tall darkness in the darkness. She was as tall as himself, or very nearly. He liked in those days to think that if anything he had it by half an inch.

"Janet!" And he caught her hand beyond the whisper. Not a word. This way, carefully. Take your time. When your eyes get used to it it's not so dark. Isn't it a fine night? Isn't it a marvellous night? Yes, it's lovely.

He was surefooted as any goat then. He could stand on the edge of nothing and pick up his balance with the greatest ease. She was not good in the dark, and sometimes hung against his hand, putting out her foot, trying for the ground, in a curious awkward fear, her whole body awkward, almost ungainly, as if about to step into a crevasse.

I'm no good in the dark.

You're doing grand. He loved her for being no good in the dark. He himself could have run full pelt along the dark hillside. But to find someone who moved with genuine difficulty, as Janet did, that was an amusing pleasure about which he was most earnest. This way now. We'll soon be there.

And then they were there, in their own place.

It was not that he was shy of her, not altogether, in the first moments of their arrival. He could not really, solemnly, draw her up to him and kiss her and stand there in straining silence, not straight away. He felt anything but the heavy romantic. All lightness and airy spirits, full of interrupted laughter and talk, introducing her to the place, making her comfortable. It was so extraordinary for them to be there alone. Keep everything else off.

Then she would sit, and look around her at the dark hillside, and up into the sky where the stars were. It was much lighter when you were out a while. She sat with her knees up and her arms round them, an intimacy with herself that was ravishing to see, and she would turn her head sideways and look at him, and laugh, and suddenly clap her hand over her mouth to stop the abrupt sounds. And then let the laugh out, controlled in a droll way.

She talked as readily as he did himself—or very nearly. For a long time after she came the disturbing element in her presence kept the excitement light and fine. Not that he ever got used to that element, that disturbing grace like a light in her flesh, a seduction in her simplest movement, issuing in a readiness to be amused, in play—a not altogether unconscious play, perhaps, but none the less disturbing on that account.

How cold some of those nights must have been! Frost in the air, a sheet of snow on the mountains. But the cold—ah, that was the final excuse. The involuntary shudder, the click of her white teeth, with two or three in front, above, rather large, giving her mouth at certain moments a rich fullness.

Come into the heart of life away from the cold. Come close in and keep the cold out, keep it at bay in a circle round.

That trance, with its tenderness. Was she as natural and simple as he was? Was it that they were coming into the heart of life, slowly, like entranced youth, wanderers approaching with the delicate wonder upon them?

For just here his Glasgow experiences were completely wiped out, as if they had never been. Unless indeed they intensified, in ways too profound to follow, the naturalness of the moment, moment simply following moment in an intensity of living, as if Hume were right!

Having seen and experienced so much—here at last was the thing-in-itself, and so he could not only experience it but know it.

As he had not known what to do with Winnie Johnston. What a fright he had got there! His mind dodging, instinctively trying to escape, but seeing it might be held. What a sweat he had been in! On his way home that night, life had seemed an inexorable affair, a vast gloomy prison governed by Fate, predestined. Invisible ribs to the prison, like the ribs that contained his beating heart. Wander as he would, he would nevermore wander out of it.

A terrifying fantasy it had been. Only youth knows of that fantasy, and only now and then in the odd moment that comes with an appalling separateness—who knows from what waiting or watching region? The uttermost experience makes little difference then—unless indeed to sharpen the awareness. Why else do people who have gone too far in experience commit suicide or murder? Or, if neither, get beaten down into "disillusion"?

But deeper than that. Much deeper it ran than that, and simpler, perhaps.

For here he was now back in his own environment, in his native place, where all the customs of his people, their immemorial mode of social life, held sway over even his most intimate emotions.

Was this possible? Yes, it was not only possible, but much more profound than any mere quantitative analysis of possibility because it concerned the quality of emotion itself. His emotion was enriched and directed in its expression because of the way his own folk had lived in the past.

Was the new analysis, then, that thought and emotion took shape as a superstructure from the basic economic life essentially true?

Yes, but the trouble here seemed to be that many thought the analysis thus "explained" emotion. Nothing could explain emotion. It was an absolute. But the analysis did account for the mode of the emotion, its general tendency in expression.

And that was a happy and a clarifying thought!

A lovely thought besides—that two persons can come into communion, gathering this extra treasure of assurance as a gift, this wordless understanding of emotion's method and mood.

For she could understand his tenderness. Of that there could be no doubt. It freed her. It left her without any feeling of fear. That had been certain. She could come away from the rapt moment, like a rabbit coming out of its burrow to look around.

Look around at the hillside and up at the stars, and sometimes she would utter a low drawn-out vowel sound, like the moan of the wind, and shake her head in a shudder, half of cold, and it was a heart-catching comment on the world of night around them, its inanimate mystery, its distance and nearness. And then she would turn her head over her shoulder and look at him, and he knew she was smiling.

Sometimes he would feel overcome, not by love but by an access of sheer friendliness. He just did not know what to do with himself, his energy and gaiety bubbled up so strongly, and if he attacked her she cried out, but, driven to it, would resist him and with such force and threatening sounds that he collapsed and cried for mercy.

For he had learned that though she was strong her flesh was soft, and a too firm grip left its dark mark. He remembered the first time she had pulled up her sleeve and shown him the discoloured skin.

"But I didn't do that?"

"You did."

"Let me see it."

The sight of it, the silken touch of the white skin, remained in his mind for days.

Small things like these—they were the intricate windings and paths in life's whole field and barn and hillside; they were the earth and the hoe and the tools; the juniper, the broom, and the blossom.

"It's time I was home."

"No."

"But yes," she said.

"What do you want to go home for?"

"Because I must."

"Do you want to go?"

"Yes, of course. Why do you think I came?"

"You're asking for it again!"

"I never asked for anything."

"Don't go."

"Really I must. Mother will be wondering."

"Where did you say you were?"

"With you, of course!"

"You didn't?"

She brought her chin to her knees. "I must go," she said, drawing out the words in a monotone. "See the dark bushes there, watching us."

"Do you like them?"

"I don't know. Do you?"

"Have you ever seen them in daylight?"

"I suppose I must have. But I don't remember them."

"You have never come up here in daylight?"

"Not—for a long time."

"But why not—seeing your mother knows?"

She laughed through her smothered mouth. "Do you come here in daylight?"

"Sometimes."

"Don't you think that's mean?"

"That's not what troubles me when I come."

"That's one thing I like about you."

"What?"

"You can talk."

"I like the sound of your voice. You have a rich clear voice."

"You think so?"

71

"You have the voice of an actress. Only far richer than anything I ever heard on the stage."

"I don't believe that."

"Yes, you do. You know it."

"Do you think I am conceited, then?"

"No."

It was easy to make her forget about going home, and when thought of it returned she would jump to her feet with a start.

Along the slope behind the crofts then, and down to the corner of the field where he left her.

"When will you come again?"

"I don't know. It's really difficult for me. Mother is—difficult—sometimes."

"Could you come—Friday?"

"I don't know. I'll try."

"All right. I'll wait. If you can't come, I'll understand."

She responded to generosity impulsively, and when she did so respond he hardly knew for a little while whether he was on his head or his heels.

Suddenly he ran down after her.

"Janet," he whispered. "Why not come in the afternoon? Any afternoon. You could go up this way as if you were making over for Altdhu, then circle round away behind. There's no-one ever up there but the shepherd. And I can always tell where he is."

He was panting from running and eagerness, like one who had brought an urgent marvellous message.

She stood quite still.

"Why not? No-one would ever see us. It's fine up there."

"I would like to come," she whispered at last.

"When? Could you come to-morrow?"

"No. I'll see. Leave it just now." She spoke slowly, as if turning over ways and means in her thought. "Good night," she whispered quickly, and walked away.

He waited to make sure that no ominous sound had disturbed her, then turned back up the field, on fire with this new vision of her coming in the daylight into the hills.

It was then no doubt, imperceptibly, little by little, that there was born in him a first real intimacy with the earth, the earth of his own land.

72

Imperceptibly, because at first it was not the earth but Janet. The earth was merely his fellow conspirator. He could call it to witness silently, when he came into the hollow where Janet and himself had met in the dark. He could look at a near bush and smile in that secretive way that would often come over him when he was alone. He hardly saw the bush and the bush was more placid than a sheep, but then in a moment it was still and tough, with tough roots, a bitter invigorating tang in its bark (not that he tasted it, unless absently), and ah, so quiet and innocent a look. But it was rooted there, and the boulders were rooted, with a warm covering of grey or bluey-grey lichen. The lichen gave the boulders and rocky outcrops fantastic features, like the pictures of grotesque faces some folk say they can see in a fire. Out of sheer idleness, he would search for those faces to keep pictures of Janet out of his mind—and no more. On the verge of his mind, slipping in and, by a need for sudden action, pushed away by him.

And action would take him up to the heights, if only for a look at the mountains. And for a full half circle the peaks and broad shoulders of several mountain ranges stood against the distant sky. In winter they were mostly snow clad, even and white and smooth, with light taking them and their hollows of shadow into vast perspectives. A shiver and a solemnity of beauty, then. Yet in a moment they were invigorating, like the sound of a sledge in boyhood, faraway cries in a white world. Standing against the remote blue-green sky of evening, frost in the air, and the blood itself a stilled cry.

That oncoming of frost from the sunken sun, with the horizon losing its outline, slowly, in pearl and then in rose, in a haze of rose more chill than the snow, foretelling a morrow of blue sky and sunlight and icicles in the shade.

Who created this world for him? Not God, but Janet. A demonstration would have presented little difficulty even to Hume, let alone the present-day psychologist!

Without Janet, would he have found it?

Janet. Janet. It was a lovely name. There was colour in it, somewhere between the yellow of peat flame and the red of a wild rose. The warmth of hands stretched to a fire; a yellow crocus in the snow. A Scots name. Janet. The syllables quick with life, moving over green grass to a little house on their own two feet.

He did not begin to think about that house, but that winter he began to plan.

He could not see Janet in a tenement stair in Glasgow. He did not try, for in these early days thought of marriage did not directly trouble him. Just as no protestations of love came from him. How could they, the solemnity of them, be pulled into the living moment, like an asking for something? What could words add to the living moment? What did they want to do but pin it down, pin it down in security? Doubtless a time would come in its own fullness for a profusion of protestations. Do you love me, ah, do you love me? But not yet, not now.

Some two months after Halloween, Jimmy Macdonald suddenly decided to get married. When Andie heard the news there came a certain look into his eye that made Tom turn away with a laugh and then reply, "Whatever happened, I don't believe you."

"Why so all of a sudden between them?"

"Well, isn't that the best way? Why should a fellow tell till it's all settled?"

"Did you know he was going with her?"

"Yes."

"Oh, you did! If you think you can bamboozle me. . . ."

Now he had once said to Jimmy as a joke, on some occasion or other, that when he got married he would give him a clock, and someone else had said that was a good idea because Tom would be able to mend the clock when the bairns swung on the pendulum.

A clock! As many wheels began to turn in his head as in a clock itself. The whole business between making and retailing went revolving in his mind. Why should he, who had been in the business, pay more than cost or wholesale price? All that was necessary was for him to be accepted as a genuine retailer. And to accomplish that all he had to do was to have some notepaper or stationery with a printed business heading. But naturally he must also have some sort of shop. The barn was not good enough. Unless he had a real shop, the shopkeepers in the village and even in the town would jeer at him, would say that he was trying to get things on the cheap, and might—and quite rightly—report him to the wholesalers as one who was interfering with their legitimate business by getting goods for himself and his friends at cost price.

No, he would not care to do that, even if he could. Besides, if he had a real shop he would sell to make a profit. And he knew scores of little things, neat new things, inexpensive, that would attract country folk. Even take this rather expensive matter o f getting a clock, for example. In a country shop you could buy only what was for sale. Take it or leave it. But supposing he got the new catalogue from a clock-maker's which he had one day happened to see when a traveller had called at the Glasgow store? Take a country eye looking at the fascinating illustrations. No need to have clocks in stock . . .

Or take the country boys he knew and the fun on the Glen road of a summer evening with old Benjie's penny-farthing bicycle. Supposing he managed to buy a couple of second-hand bicycles, but of the latest type, the new safety bicycle—and hired them out at twopence or threepence a half-hour as Dougal had said? They could pay for themselves in a summer month. Beyond doubt. He would sell new ones to farmers' sons, gillies home with their wages and tips. The lads would never be away from the shop. He would become a Cycle Agent!

It would be a new kind of business, a business to interest the young and energetic, and, along with it, his blowlamp and his tools.

In the country everything is behindhand, old-fashioned, but nowhere more than in the country do folk like what is gay in the new-fashioned, especially if it is serviceable, if it is sound. The real go-ahead country lads and girls were always like that. So few new things came their way that when they did come they held the fascination of the marvellous.

Tom had only got to look into his own mind to know all about it.

For many days and nights his inner excitement, while he went about his home and talked to the lads normally, was so great that he mistrusted himself. Country caution was part of him, as of the roots that took a good grip of the soil before they permitted a green adventure in the upper air. He drafted dozens of business headings in many styles. He even wrote out his name in full—Thomas Mathieson. But no, Tom Mathieson it would be, Tom, one of the lads themselves.

Then he wrote Dougal Robertson, saying he wanted a certain mantelpiece clock at a certain price, and wondered whether he couldn't get it wholesale because he was half-thinking of starting a little business, his father being ill, and not likely now to recover—

and so on. No chance of a socialistic adventure here! It was a non-committal letter, which did, however, convey to Dougal a clear picture of his present position and condition of mind.

When he had posted it he felt a sense of relief, then a fear lest he had expressed his desire for the shop too strongly, followed by a doubt as to whether he had expressed it clearly enough. When eleven days passed and no word came from Dougal, his mounting impatience was invaded by a despair that relieved and quietened him like a smooth passing over his head of the hand of fate.

On the thirteenth day the clock arrived together with a long letter from Dougal, and excitement was upon him again, but now like spring weather, in sun and wind.

This mixture of starting a new business and of love for Janet did breed in him through the stormy opening weeks of that year an extraordinary gaiety of happiness. Every muscle, every bone, every cell in his body took part in it. Against the things that countered him, like his father's face or a task held up by the weather, he was whole and cunning in himself. Nothing could get at him. What he couldn't flow over he could flow round, and when he could do neither he remained contained in himself like a well, a well-spring of life. Had he been thrown into an icy well to the neck and left there to perish, it is almost certain that he wouldn't even have caught a cold. No fanciful exaggeration, that. Just the plumb truth.

It was really a remarkable time. No need ever thereafter to tell him of the effect of the mind on the body. Though that is really a silly, sententious way of putting it. Where the body-cells sing or race they become mind itself. Mind is everywhere, and all is shaped and unique and of a piece, while yet it is fluent and everywhere. Anyway, that was how it felt; but then who can ever understand until he *has* felt? Who can know the singing in the busy finger-tips? Who can know the busy-ness that is itself a state of song? The tune that sings out of the shaping wood?

Get away with you! he would have laughed at any questioning thought.

And behind all this, as the glow in the brazier, the white in the snow, the cry in the storm, wandering through landscapes inside him, the tune on his lips, the brightness in his sight—Janet.

There was only one thing for it—he would have to build, and the only place to build was against the upper gable-end of the house.

That would not only provide him with one solid wall, but would place his shop just the right distance from the road for business and privacy.

One winter's day in the barn he spoke to his mother. At first the idea of a real shop quite overcame her, awed her in fact. He found himself, however, talking to his mother more naturally than ever before. For the first time in his life he consciously treated her as an ally, though even then it was somehow impossible to be altogether friendly and natural. His manner of talk was still a little off-hand.

She was excited almost to the point of dumb stupidity. "I don't know what your father will say."

"I have got to think of myself. If I start this shop here, then I won't go back to Glasgow. It's got to be decided one way or the other."

"Yeth," she said, sucking in the word, "yeth." She was deeply moved. Plainly the thought of having him at home with her for good was overwhelming. He had known it would be. Though not using it as a threat, yet a threat it was. They could deal with it as they thought fit!

It was surprising to him how cunning his mother was, how absolutely she seemed to know his father's hidden mind and mood. "Don't say anything till we see." And the following day, she got him alone again in the barn, in conspiracy, in undertones, with an ear hearkening for footsteps outside, though she knew her husband was in bed. How could it be done without a lot of money? Where was the money to come from?

If he got ten or twelve pounds, he could start with a small shop, he answered. But if he got nothing at all, he had enough to buy the wood, and he could build the little place himself. After that, he would see how things went. He would take the risk of that.

His mother moved about the croft with a lot of energy, as if she could think better when working hard.

One morning when he went in to breakfast, he knew at once that the subject had been discussed between them the night before. Nothing was said to him. The curious dull tension in the room, however, was enough to explain everything. His father's face was paler and more graven than ever, with a patriarchal solemnity that added the awful power of the other world to the forbidding dignity of this.

Tom could not look at that face, and went out with a dumb anger in him. Presently his mother joined him in the barn. She spoke in undertones. But hope was in her face. She nodded. "I spoke to him last night. At first he was against it. But in the end he came round a little. If he won't help you, I don't think he'll stop you doing it. But we'll have to give him time. Don't do anything, and don't anger him, till we see. Just wait till we see. I'm hopeful it will be all right."

"Why was he against it?"

"If the croft and the carting kept us and a decent house over our heads he thinks it should be good enough for you. Then he got on again about—about the other thing."

Tom turned away.

"Don't you be upset. It'll come all right. Just wait a bit. We'll manage it." There was a curious hopefulness in her, an eager conspiracy, as if she were managing things against the fates. Her eyebrows arched into their two sets of concentric creases and her small dark eyes grew round and bright like a hen's after drinking. She bustled away from him, looked up towards the kitchen door, then came back for more talk. Her stout dumpy body was full of warmth and life. But she did not stay long, as though conscious that the face on the pillow would know she was there.

In the afternoon she was back again. "He's not up yet, but I was looking in the kist when I was doing your room just now. I can give you at least five pounds and maybe six. I don't know if he knows that I have the other pound. But I have been going over things. Maybe I'll manage more. Anyway you'll not be stuck. You can leave that to me. But just let us take our time meantime. It'll come all right, you'll see."

"Has he much money?" Tom asked.

"Yes, he has all of fifty pounds in the kist, and he has a receipt from the bank for seventy on a piece of paper. But never let on I told you that, never on your life! He was always particular about the money. And we must thole his ways, now that he's ill and not himself. You can see that yourself surely?"

"Yes," said Tom quietly.

"It's a lot of money and—and it's there, should anything happen to him—or to any of us."

Tom nodded.

Her knowledge of all this wealth warmed her and kept her near her son. She spoke confidentially to him, glad of his company, and told him one or two little incidents over money in the past. He might have been another woman, the way she talked to him. She forgot time in this intimacy, and Tom forgot it, too, knowing that his mother would do anything for him, anything, so long as it would not be found out by his father.

Then suddenly, as if translated noiselessly from the kitchen, the father was there in the doorway, and by the very look in his face they knew that he had overheard something. He did not speak. He just looked at them, coldly, objectively.

The mother gave a small cry and said, "You should have waited for me, you should have waited."

"So you conspire against me, my wife and my son?" His eyes had a hard glitter.

"We're not conspiring," answered Tom thickly, his flesh all in a moment jumpy and uncertain.

"You should have waited until I helped you," said the woman again hastily. "You should have waited."

"I can manage without your help, woman," answered the man, "and without yours," and he eyed his son.

"Don't speak like that," cried the woman, "oh, don't speak too soon!"

"Be silent!"

Tom's anger leapt up in him. "All right, if you want me to go, I'll go."

"Don't you dare answer me back like that!"

The power in his father entered Tom and scattered his wits so that he picked up a board and slammed it down again and turned his face away to the little window. He was quivering all over.

"Oh don't say anything more. Don't say it," cried the woman, gripping her hands. "Wait. We were just speaking about the shop. It was only what I was telling you."

While she went on talking like this, the man paid no attention to her but kept on staring at his son's back. Then his eyes dropped upon her. "Be quiet!" he said as to an unseemly and treacherous animal, and walked away.

79

Chapter Eight

What had possessed his father throughout that last year of his life? Before his illness, he had been a normal decent man, a bit quiet perhaps, and stern sometimes, but never really vindictive.

Though for that matter, what had possessed himself so that he had reacted to his father as he had done?

Why had he not gone to his father and explained the whole business and asked for his advice?

There was something more in it than the Father and Son relationship. More than the Idol of the Tribe conception. For the father there was defeat in it somewhere that affected the very strands of his being. So much he could see. The father was defeated before he should have been defeated, and his place in life was taken by the mother and son in conspiracy, and for company he had grey relentless death.

But that did not explain anything really. It left him without understanding, and when one day he made up his mind to start building, he would have been dour and stubborn with the excitement of antagonism had he not Janet behind him. The taking of Janet into his confidence had turned an evening in the hollow into a memory that could never be forgotten, not in this life nor any other. It was not what happened at the time. It was the power of the memory afterwards.

He had been reluctant to mention the matter to Janet, possibly because he had not wished anything to·interfere with that free relationship that was between them. And he certainly would not have hinted at his difficulty were it not that he had made up his mind to use the building as a test between his father and himself. He would start building. If his father stopped him—which he had a right to do, for it was his property—then he would tell his father that he was going to clear out. And he *would* clear out. He was to be allowed to put up his shop *or* he would clear out. The test was to be final.

There was something dour in himself that held him to this fatally. It got to the point beyond argument. He could not help himself.

So he said to Janet, when the first excitement of their meeting was over and their minds came out to talk, "I may be going back to Glasgow. Will you miss me?"

She turned her head quickly, for though his voice was light she detected a real note.

"You're not!"

"I don't know. I may be."

"You're not! You're just teasing me."

"Would you miss me?"

"What makes you say that? You're not going?"

"I may be. Listen, Janet. I didn't want to tell you. I hate dragging in any family affair. But this has been worrying me." He now felt extremely reluctant to go on.

"Surely you're not afraid to tell me?"

But not until he had gone well into his story, haltingly, smiling now and then, did the sweet assurance of companionship begin to flow within him. Never before in all his life had he eased his mind to anyone; not to Dougal nor any of the boys in Glasgow had he ever personally committed himself. He had committed himself to ideas, to freethinking, to socialism. He had been one of the workers and arguers. But only that.

Not even now, of course, did he let himself completely go with "I" and "me", but there was suddenly a freedom in talk, with Janet there, her skirts draping her knees, her arms round them, listening and looking at the dark bushes. Quietly, within the talk, they were together, and stress fell away, and a rare comprehension of the moment, of some ultimate companionship, turned the cold night air to an elixir that separated their bodies in friendliness and communion.

When he had finished, she did not speak, and quietly he asked her, "What do you think?"

"Your father is ill," she said.

"Yes, I know." Even if she was going to go against him, he would listen to her.

"I don't know if you should have more patience or not," she said all at once in a queer choking voice.

"Janet! What's wrong?"

Her head had fallen forward to her knees, then turned away. She was crying.

"Janet! Janet!" He took hold of her and she crept against him.

As she pushed herself away and began wiping her eyes in confusion, she said, "It's Mother. I—I have my own troubles with her. I want to go away—to be a nurse—but I can't go. I daren't leave her. She is all right for a spell and then—she has a terrible outbreak. She gets violent."

"You can tell me everything, Janet."

"It was after Father's death. I think before then it started. I think he used to give her drink to make her sleep. Then when she began to know he was going under, her nerves went wrong. Then—then he died. Oh I can't tell you!"

She began plucking at the ground, her head averted. Her forehead went down, her arms circled her knees, and he heard the choking of her breath and the swallowing in her throat.

The unexpectedness of her confession brought the night-world to a standstill. He had the sensation of its opening before him, as it might open in an earthquake to reveal an interior of which he could never have dreamed. He was appalled and silenced and gathered coolly and strangely into himself. He did not speak to her, staring past to the dark hillside. Then his eyes, with a feeling of extreme clarity, turned upon her and saw the curved dark body, the droop of the head beyond the smooth downsweep of the neck, and—this was Janet.

"Janet!" he whispered. But he did not touch her. The silence came about them again. When she grew quiet in a long moment he put his arm about her shoulders, sat close beside her, drew her slowly and firmly against him. "Janet!" He put both arms about her, firmly but gently, and whispered her name into her hair. "It's all right, Janet. I'm glad you told me."

After a little time, she lifted her head and wiped her eyes with her handkerchief, staring before her. Giving her time, he did not force sympathy or understanding upon her. But he was there, and she felt him there, and suddenly turned to him and gripped him, crying, "Oh, Tom!"

He soothed her then in small caresses that healed her broken spirit and in a little while she was herself, sitting beside him, talking at first uncertainly, but soon drawing pictures of what sometimes happened at home.

He listened, moved to the core, yet with an odd feeling of detachment in the chill night air. Her voice ravished him, and what she had endured she had endured and his heart bled for her, but this was Janet, this was Janet at last on the cold hillside beside him.

It was late that night before she returned home, and her teeth were chittering with the cold. Before they parted he held her strongly against him, as strongly as he could in order to drive the trembling out of her. And she exclaimed softly as if he had crushed her bones, and smiled to him, for now she was healed.

Back along the hillside he went with the vision of her as the immortal companion born in him finally that night.

Surely caution was needed now and all the cunning of the "watcher", which he believed so truly made up his character. Surely this was the time to think of Janet and of what might happen to her if he took a wrong step.

But no; on the following day he suddenly decided to start building, let come what might. He was full of force and assurance as never before. Let his father try to stop him!

He had his plan all ready and in the afternoon he started marking off the ground, hammering pegs into the spots where he was to sink his main beams. Then he passed the kitchen window with the pickaxe over his shoulder. He knew the critical moment would come with the thudding blows. If the sound of them were ignored, he had triumphed. But well he knew they wouldn't, and when presently he saw the grey-bearded grey face staring up at him along the wall of the house, he realised the moment had arrived.

The face began to advance. Behind it, the mother stood twisting her hands in her apron, then tentatively she, too, advanced.

With all his might he swung the pickaxe into the ground, levered it backward and jerked up the soil. An insane energy flowed into him. From a stone sparks flew and a smell of brimstone assailed his nostrils.

"What's this you're doing?"

The pickaxe swung. The earth sounded. Out jerked the soil.

"What's this you're doing?"

Tom looked at his father. "I'm making a hole for a beam," he answered in an indifferent way.

"What for?" His father's calm was deadly.

"I was going to build a shed," said Tom. "The barn is not very suitable for my work." He looked his father in the eyes, his face pale and drawn, then dropped his look to the loosened soil and gripped the pick.

"Who gave you the permission?"

"No-one," said Tom, glancing about the pegged ground like one interrupted in his business.

There was an intense silence, then he glanced again at his father. The old man's features had so extreme a pallor of concentration that they seemed to emit a deathly light. The eyes were glinting like green glass. The mouth opened and the lower lip showed dry as oatmeal above the beard. There was a sheer malevolence in the face that yet was caught back into patriarchal power. Tom's wits began to scatter. The evil anger behind his brow went down into his fists and tightened them on the smooth ash handle till the knuckles whitened.

"There's Sandy Maclean," said the woman drawing nigh.

Tom looked up towards the road. Sandy, with a wave, cried, "Glad to see you about, Adam!" As he came down, he rubbed his brown whiskers in a characteristic gesture and his eyes were bright and merry. "The wife and myself were talking about you no later than this morning and I said I would look in, for it's not often I'm down now. And how are you, man?"

As Adam turned to him, his expression lost its intensity in a bleakness. "Oh just that same way," he answered.

Sandy's merry eyes glanced at him sharply. "Man, you're not looking too bad. There's a lot of life in you yet, if you ask me!"

But as Adam shook hands, his bleak expression stared distantly over Sandy's shoulder.

"How are you all yourselves?" asked Maria coming forward with a warm eagerness.

"Oh fine, fine," replied Sandy. "We have a lot to be thankful for and we aye have our bit of meat. So what more do we want?"

"As long as you have the health," said Maria, "that's the main thing."

"True for you, mistress."

"You'll come away down and have a cup of tea. It's not often we see you. Come away," invited Maria.

But Sandy hesitated now. "Thank you indeed, mistress, but I have a few things to do. So you'll just have to excuse me to-day. Some other time. And what's the great work that's going on here? Eh?" And he turned to Tom, smiling awkwardly and shifting his stance.

"You'll at least come and have a glass of something," said Maria. "I won't have it said that you passed our door."

"Well, now, that's kind of you, mistress. What do you say, Adam? Do you think it would be safe?"

"Come down," said Adam calmly.

"So you're extending your business premises," cried Sandy to Tom. "Well, there was much need of you in the place. I'll say that."

But Adam had now turned towards the house, and as he took the first step away he gave a slight stagger. Sandy's eyebrows gathered sharply over his eyes and he caught Adam up. Maria went before them, waddling hurriedly.

Tom felt sick. He gripped the shaft, but his muscles were weak and trembling. A deep disgust assailed him, a loathing for the very ground about him. His hands slid on the smooth ash. He spat into a palm, gripped, swung the pickaxe, and its iron point thudded into the ground. The noise rose up around him and went down into the house. After he had swung the pick once more, he laid it aside, lifted the shovel, and began heaping the loosened earth to one side. Soon the ground was hard under the shovel and nothing more could be scooped up. He caught the ash handle and swung, once— twice—thrice, loosening the soil. And again, once—twice—thrice, more strongly. But the sounds dizzied and tortured him. He heard them going into the kitchen. If Sandy returned he could not speak to him. He might be coming any minute. Dropping the pick, Tom turned down to the barn, walking without haste, uprightly, past the kitchen window.

But in the barn he leaned against the bench and experienced weakness as of a long hunger. His palm found his forehead damp and cold. Damnation! cried anger in him, but weakly, in futility. He was giving in. He wanted to give in. He wanted to clear out, to clear out for good, away, never to come back.

His father's opposition was insensate, maddening. There was no point in it. It was just sheer spite. He was jealous of him getting on, of achieving something beyond the croft. Could anything be more small-minded, more contemptible? And to think that he had come back to help his father, had thrown up his job, his whole prospects in life, the job he liked, the free life in Glasgow. It was maddening. Really it was. By God, it was. It was too much. Too much altogether.

But behind this verbal rebellion was his father's face. And it was stronger than rebellion, stronger than argument. It stood still, portentous and meaningful out of immense time, and he broke against it, like something flung against a wall.

And even if he succeeded in defeating his father, breaking him down, what would follow from the victory but spite, a spite that would dog him and drain the essence of pleasure for ever?

He felt beaten and a dry bitterness invaded his mouth. Thought would no more concentrate and, wandering, found Janet. But he could not speak to her in his mind for the moment. He let her drift away.

Presently all he could do was hearken for sounds. What about lifting some of these battens and walking up with them to the pegged ground? Why give in? Why not, without any further thought, automatically, just carry on? The thing had to come to a head. It could not be left as it was.

Janet had her own trouble.

If he could not make a stand, what damned use was he?

At last there were noises. Sandy was going. Tom picked up a plane, made one sweep, and listened. Sandy's voice was loud but not too hearty. No sound of his father's voice; only his mother's. There was Sandy off. Silence now. He began working steadily, pulling the shaving away when it stuck, hissing through his teeth. After all, he had to have planks and battens ready. There was still a whole lot of work to do in that respect. And measurements. Though he could not get the exact measurements, of course, until he had sunk his main gable beams.

No-one came near him. In a little while, he heard his mother's footsteps. She passed the door, shook her head for silence, and indicated that he was to remain where he was. There was an anxiety in her face which she tried to infuse with some confidence, but her effort at pantomime was pathetic and when she had gone, a small bitter smile came to him.

He worked on in a dull timeless way.

His mother came out and hit the side of a tin basin with a spoon. Hens cackled and ran and fluttered. "You needn't be going away," she called aloud to him. "Supper will soon be ready." Then she came to the barn door and said in a low voice: "He had a bit of a turn but he's feeling better, you'll come in to your supper and say nothing."

"I don't think I will," he replied, indifferently.

"You will," she said. "Don't do any more digging just now.

86

Just wait." Her voice was harsh with concentration. She was plainly deeply disturbed. But there was something cunning, too, in her eye, and resourceful. "Don't you desert me," she added suddenly on a breath of distress. Then she listened—and withdrew.

He worked on automatically. There could be no satisfaction any longer in what he did. He wanted to drop things from his hands, push them away, and walk off. The mountains drew him, drew him powerfully. To go in and eat his supper was beyond his strength, beyond the power of his stomach to take the food. The vision was revolting. But up in the hollows, on the lonely sweep of the moor, he could wander, and lie down and be hidden, and gather that strength which could take him anywhere.

Presently he went to the door and looked out. The barn was small and stood by itself, opposite the byre but a little lower down. The house and byre had the one long roof and sloped gently downward from the main road. Just beyond the barn the ground flattened and then began slightly to slope upward for the length of the cultivated fields. Beyond the fields the green braes rose steeply.

He looked at the braes, saw where they angled into the hollow of the burn towards his right, with its bushes and its tumbling hillocks, with its sheep paths to the moor and the moor stream and the mountains that lay beyond the last visible crest.

It was a chilly evening and already there was a faint darkening in the air. The sodden ground was drying and ploughing was at hand. The world looked solid and drab. All at once he heard bird-singing. It was a sound he did not hear consciously very often, any more than he heard the lowing of cattle or the whinnying of the horse. And even now he hardly listened, as if the notes were trivial and meaningless. But suddenly something came out of the land, out of the air, some cool shiver of spring like an immemorial essence, an elusive scent, and it ran through his flesh and into his blood. It was enlivening, touched with hope and promise, and for a moment it set him whole within himself in an access of fine courage. But when he turned into the barn he was beset by a new and sad despair, and he stood staring out of the little back window, hardly hearkening for that fugitive beauty which had touched him from so far away, from so near.

When his mother's voice called, he went towards the house not nearly so much on edge as he had been before, in a dumb mood that could bear much, and he felt relieved at this and glanced about him and heard a thrush on the bourtree bush by the cabbage plot behind the house.

His father was in bed and his mother was dishing out a stew, the steam rising about her bent figure with a strong appetising smell of onions.

"Sit down," she said at once; "it's better for you hot in this weather."

The father said grace and they began eating. The mother got up, attended to a pot, and sat down. It was the usual sort of movement and little was spoken. But often a meal was partaken of in silence, except for a remark about the food itself.

His father to-night was more distant than ever, and now and then there was a sighing as of deep thought and a far weariness. Tom felt it like an unspoken condemnation. Never once did he look at his father's face. The presence of the father was strong in the house, so strong that had Tom not got this dumb quiet mood from somewhere, he might have been irked beyond endurance.

The father said grace after meat with an austere unction. It was a silent calling-to-witness of that which had come to pass under his roof.

Tom got up. His mother turned to him. "You haven't to go out to-night, have you?"

"Yes," answered Tom. "I have some things to do for Jimmy Macdonald's new house." He spoke quietly, indifferently.

"Well, see and be finished as soon as you can," she said.

Tom did not answer. He hesitated for one moment. Now was the time to say that he thought of putting up a wooden place—he needn't call it a shop—at the end of the house if it was all the same to them. But somehow he could not command himself, could not control the feeling that immediately started beating up. He glanced at his father's face. That settled it. He took his cap off the peg behind the door and walked slowly out.

Bitterness assailed him sharply as he faced the gloom of the night. His father had been deliberately using his illness to dominate the house and them. In a cunning austere way he had been play-acting. He hadn't been so bad as he silently made out. He had impressed Sandy. That stagger, as he had turned away . . .

Tom felt ashamed. Even he himself had been weak in the flesh then, his muscles jumpy, and he hadn't a bad heart. Too great an excitement, an over-concentrated moment of emotion, and his father would drop dead. That was certain. His father knew it.

Tom could not work in the barn and, dreading lest some of the lads appear, he left the barn and made for the hillside. The hollow where Janet and himself met he avoided on his left, climbing steadily for the moor.

Presently a scent touched his nostrils like that scent of spring under the singing birds. It had the same elusive character but now it seemed more real. As he came out on the moor he saw a long low wall of red flame in the distance, strange and beautiful against the darkness. Heather-burning. The gamekeepers of the Castle were burning the moor, on the slope beyond the stream towards the mountains. The fire must have got out of control, but now the wind, even up here, had fallen and he could see small dark figures like demons beating down the flames with their long birch switches.

It was a necromantic sight and he was held by it completely. The flames were a living red against the dark mountains. He could see them leap in tongues and tatters and vanish magically in the air. The crackling of their fierce joy was removed by distance, as his own boyhood was removed, leaving the wonder and the vivid glow, like a memory of times long past.

His boyhood called to him, and boyhood beyond boyhood, from far mornings, from still twilights, with their scent about him, this scent, keen on the air and in the nostrils.

He stood gazing towards the fire unable to tear himself away. He would have liked to join the men and the lads in the fierce tumult of their switching and their cries. He would have hit and hit the swerving beast as it chewed up the thin bones of the heather in a crackling roar, hit and directed it with man's cunning towards the drowning stream and the sweet tired darkness of the end.

But solitariness was upon him and, as his skin shivered after the warmth of the climb, he started back the way he had come. Every now and then, he turned his head over his shoulder, and at last on the brow of the moor he paused for a long time. The fire glowed now like a jewel on the throat of the night, beautiful to look at, holding his eyes in a mood that was beyond all understanding, joyous and yet strangely sad.

What curious quality was this, calling him back to the hollows and the streams, to the lonely moor and the mountains? And why "back"?

That night he had a disturbing dream. As he thudded with the pick he was aware of the effect the sounds had on his father, precisely as if he suffered them himself. He was in a moment somehow present with his father and mother in the kitchen as the thudding went on. And his father knew that the sounds meant the digging of his grave, and he heard them as a condemned man might hear the hammering that set up the gallows beyond his prison wall. No power now could stop the thudding. It went on remorselessly in soft deadly impacts. Nothing more could be done. They had to accept—and wait.

The dream was disconnected, for now his father was dead. His body was naked and the mother, sitting on a kitchen chair, held it in her extended arms, one arm under the knees and the other round the shoulders so that the head fell slightly back and the body slumped naturally to her lap. The naked body was white and smooth, and with the white beard on the ashen face, the eyebrows gaunt and jutting above the sunken closed eyes, the mouth slightly open in a remote solemnity, the whole figure looked like a Christ grown old.

The following day he left the pick and shovel lying by the hole which he had started to dig and busied himself with many things, for the spring season of ploughing and sowing was at hand. Whatever happened, he realised now that he would have to put down the crops. He could not leave the burden of finding ways and means on his mother. Besides, that evening he was taking the clock up to Flora's home—his wedding present to Jimmy and herself. Quite a few would be there and it should be a good evening. He had told Janet he was going and she had said Flora had specially invited her and she would certainly go if she could. She would go, of course, with Tina Sinclair.

As he took his supper before setting out, there was no sign of any satisfaction or hidden triumph in his father over the cessation of the digging. There was indeed about the old man an air of extreme weariness. Something genuine and as it were withered in this forsaken weariness touched Tom, but his own life was too near him to let it penetrate far.

Nor did his mother ask him where he was going, as though she sensed that any words of hers would not help but only irritate the father and perhaps stir him out of his weakness to say in a cold, rejecting voice: "Let him go."

All the same, outside, in the darkness, on the road, the gaiety of escape assailed him. His body felt light and full of energy, and the clock would astonish them.

There was a whole lot of girls in, with a fair number of fellows and more coming. Everyone was laughing, and now and then a girl let out a yelp. Flora met Tom at the door, for she rushed forward to greet each newcomer, and there she was taking him into "the room" where the presents were laid out. They heard her say "O Tom!" in the proper breathless way. But she did not add "That's too kind of you" or other phrase of the sort. So they went on talking in the kitchen, but in a moment came her quick feet and her flushed face, and she said, "Jimmy, this is Tom."

Out Jimmy went awkwardly as much as to say, What have I got to do with it? and the girls laughed. Jimmy and Tom were special friends and the present therefore would likely have some particular character on Jimmy's account.

Jimmy's brown face flushed with surprise and pleasure when he saw the clock. Tom, on his knees by the table, was fixing the pendulum and looked up at Jimmy with a quizzical smile. "I promised I would give you a clock," he said.

"This is too much, boy," said Jimmy slowly.

"Nothing could be too much for either of you," answered Tom lightly.

"O Tom, that's lovely of you," said Flora in a trembling happy voice.

Tom got up and shook hands with both of them. This somehow came also as a surprise. "I wish you the best of luck," said Tom, his face merry, "and may your good times never stop."

Flora was an impulsive girl, big-boned, dark, and kindness or generosity invaded her face in a spate. Now she gripped her own hands and swayed, smiling warmly, shyly overcome. She hardly knew what to do about it. No more did Jimmy. Tom laughed, bunching together the wrappings. "Where will I put this?" he asked.

"Oh anywhere," said Flora, taking it from him and crushing it still more.

"Well, let us go through," said Tom, "lest they come in."

But Flora could not help saying to her mother that Tom had brought a lovely clock. In no time everyone was having a look at it. It was over two feet in height and the glass front had a beautiful painting of a country scene. Not a Highland scene, more like a real English scene, with tall green reeds, not rushes but broad reeds that turned over at the top in a delicate refined way, and with the smooth water of a quiet river, if not a lake, held to a stillness that time would never change. And when you looked carefully there were other interesting features: two big ducks and four little ones, for example, and a tree, and a dark cavern. Hanging dead centre, over the water, and between the reeds was the round brass pendulum, with a brighter glitter than that of gold.

"Ay, ay," said slack-mouthed Dan, his droll humour now held in wonder. He was fifty and modest girls were always a trifle afraid of what he would say next. But now he was examining the clock with the keen eyes of a neat-handed man, nodding in tribute.

"It's a fine thing," he said, "to have a wealthy friend from the south."

"What was the good of being in the trade," said Tom, "unless a fellow could get a clock like that for nothing?"

There was a laugh and Tom, glancing round, saw Janet. A sheer living freshness about her struck him like a sudden light. She seemed to him at that moment to be apart from the others, reserved and distinguished, yet with her eyes crinkling with humour as if she were taking everything in and might all at once laugh outright. Usually she wore coloured homespun tweeds in soft greens or blues or browns like the other girls. Now her skirt was black and her blouse snow white. Her face was fresh as if it had been washed in spring water, its contours full and firm, with the top teeth showing in the smile that was about to break. Yet in an instant he saw nothing but her eyes, and they looked at him, and from them something came towards him, and stilled in a recognition that only he could see, and withdrew, and she turned her head away and laughed with the others.

"Does it go?" asked Dan.

"Yes," said Tom. "But I think we should leave it to Flora to start it up."

"There's no hurry," said Dan. "Do you see the little ducks? Now I wonder what the mannie who painted them meant when he put them in?" he asked in wondering innocence.

But that was enough of Dan and one or two of the girls pushed him aside. Dan saw a strained look on Jimmy's face and he winked to some of the lads. But this was no place for practical fun, so back they went into the kitchen.

There were songs and stories and Dan, who suddenly had an inspiration as to the meaning of the baby ducks, was physically set upon by three young women and shown no mercy. Dan had good sense and put up no fight. But the girls were in great form and soon nothing would reduce their energies but a set dance on the kitchen floor. Inside an hour the evening was made, unison was complete, and nothing that was said or done could go wrong.

Tom had an extraordinary liberation of spirit that night. Janet seemed to have been revealed to him in a new and thrilling way. Flora's mother spoke to him specially, and Flora's father, a large, ungainly, neighbourly man, had a few words for him about nothing in particular. He did not need to look at Janet. Her brightness was behind his eyes, was everywhere. He could feel that the folk liked him, were attracted by the seemingly careless but actually intense happiness that made him dance, and double up with laughter, and promise anything.

"I'll see you down the way," said George Macrae, a tall handsome young man, assistant to Fraser, the general merchant, and not unaware of his own importance among the crofting lads. The evening had come to an end at last and George had spoken as it were negligently to Janet. Tom's whole being stood still as if the living muscle of his heart had been gripped. An immense time seemed to pass before Tina said simply, "We're waiting for Tom."

"I'm here," said Tom cheerily, pulling on his cap as he bobbed up against them in the dark.

"Come on then," cried George, in his boisterous managing way, and he must have caught Janet by the arm for in no time he had swung her ahead.

But she turned round, "Are you coming?" and waited for Tom and Tina. She took Tina's arm. "I enjoyed to-night. Wasn't it good?" She laughed in her abrupt way, and stopped dramatically. She sounded very happy, inwardly excited.

All four kept together, chattering readily and at random. Tom was between the girls and George on the outside next Janet. Tom caught Janet's hand as their arms swung together. Her fingers spoke to him in secrecy and withdrew. Then their hands hit in passing and Janet was full of gaiety. Tina mocked and challenged George over something. George in his somewhat heavy large way said that if she wasn't careful he would throw her over the hedge. "I would like to see you try it!" challenged Tina, who had a game spirit in her small but sturdy body. "You talk a lot," she added. George's manhood felt it had to go to the attack and Tom, gripping Janet's arm, slipped ahead. Tina was obviously holding her own and fighting well, but Janet could not go quickly in the dark. She stumbled, as she did on the hillside behind her home, and Tom swept her against the blackthorn hedge. "Hsh! they won't see us here." He kissed her and she responded and for a moment the night shook its stars about them. He pressed her into the hedge, shielding the white of her face, and there in stillness they stood, while the other two went past arguing and bickering.

"Janet!" he said, as if he had found her at last.

"Tom!" she whispered.

After a little time they stepped onto the rough cart track, for this was a divine game and they could not let the others escape entirely.

"Janet, where are you?" called Tina.

"Hush!" whispered Tom.

But Janet called: "We're here!" And as they drew near: "How cool of you to walk past us!"

George was nettled and not in the best of humours, and when he felt that Tom and Janet were hanging just behind in order to enjoy this game, he walked on with Tina. They all kept together, however, and when the main road was reached, Janet took Tina's arm.

"I do hate coming down that road in the dark," Janet declared.

"You fairly showed it," George retorted.

They all laughed so heartily that George was mollified by this acceptance of his wit.

Tom got no further words with her alone, but that did not matter, for in the very way she said good-night was all the conspiracy of their next meeting.

As he hung about his home, reluctant to go in, late as it was, he somehow could not get over the sheer marvel of Janet and the relationship between them. It was like something that could not be true, that could not really have happened to a fellow like him in this life. That first glimpse of her up in Flora's . . .

His nostrils caught the warm interior paraffin-lamp smell, and as he noiselessly closed the door his father cleared his throat in a deliberate portentous cough. Tom's face puckered up and, treading softly, he entered his own room and lit a candle.

Then he sat on his bed, his eyes gleaming through the puckered expression on his face. That dry forbidding cough of communication! Ay, ay! The vision of the white body like the dead Christ came through his mind from his dream. But it could not touch him. Nothing could touch him. He would talk to his father tomorrow. Sitting there, he began to dream about Janet.

Chapter Nine

Next morning the wind was blowing on a bright day. Tom's heart was affected by it and all his body, as though spring were coming beyond the mountains and the wind had rushed on eddying everywhere to tell the news.

His happiness induced a generous and forgiving mood in him, and when his father appeared in the early afternoon Tom, working by the barn door, felt the moment for speech had arrived. Slowly his father advanced, upright, as usual without the aid of any stick. But he did not pass by the barn door and Tom could not go to meet him. Refusing to be put off by this indifference on his father's part, Tom presently created a natural opportunity, and with his shoulder to his father said in a quiet even voice, "The barn is getting a bit full up."

"Is it?" said his father. "It was big enough in my day."

"Yes," answered Tom, "but it's not big enough now with the jobs I have to do."

"What jobs?"

"You know the jobs," said Tom.

"You did not mention them to me," said his father in the same level tones, looking into the distance.

"I was wanting," said Tom, coming to the point before his father's voice would defeat him, "to put up a place at the end of the house."

"What sort of place?"

"A wooden place. I could have my tools and do my jobs there. That would leave the barn free."

"Oh, I see," said his father, but it was as if he saw some motive or design far beyond the obvious and noted the fact in a dry mockery. His voice, however, held no emphasis.

Tom could not look at him. He had stated his case. He would hold himself there at whatever cost and wait for a definite answer.

He heard the shuffle of his father's feet, the movement of his body. Tom turned his head. His father was walking away.

Tom went blindly into the barn and for a few moments struggled in the grip of a sheer physical paroxysm of anger. It was too much, too utterly unforgivable. He gripped a plank and sank his nails in the white wood. Anyone could see it was no good. No good giving in to this. It must be one way or the other. And now.

He allowed himself a few minutes to cool down and then walked up past the house to where the pick and shovel were lying. His mother came out at the kitchen door but he did not look at her, nor for that matter did she call him or give any visible sign. He did not know where his father was. He would no doubt find out soon enough!

Thud went the pickaxe and out shot the soil. His mind was working feverishly underneath the thudding sounds. If his father came up and said, "What's this?" he would look him straight in the face, right into his eyes, and say, "I told you." And if his father answered that he had not given his assent, then he, Tom, would widen his eyes and say, "But you said 'I see'. I thought you meant it was all right." And they would look at each other, behind surface words, and Tom would wait, would not budge, until his father used definite words, stopping the work. He would force him to use definite words and so be done with the whole accursed business. Then he would throw down his pick. That would be an end of that. What would follow would follow.

He was working on a hole in line with the front wall of the house when he saw his father come round the lower gable-end. He tossed out the shovel and started on the pick, glimpsing his father from under his eyebrows. The old man went over towards the barn and stopped and examined the plough that lay by the wall, its coulter sharpened and ready for work. He bent down over the plough, jerking at something, slowly straightened himself and went into the barn. Tom swung the pick with all his strength. What was his father wanting in the barn? The chest of tools was shut but not locked. If his father lifted the lid he would see the two books, Huxley and Haeckel, as well as the pamphlets on Rationalism which Dougal had enclosed as packing for the clock. Would he dare lift it? Tom knew he would. It was his barn.

Tom worked with fury. If his father appeared in a minute it might be all right. He did not appear. Tom had a wild urge to drop the pick and walk down to the barn.

In a little while his father came out of the barn and, going to the plough, began to hammer at it. Tom swung his pick now in a wild derision. His father went back into the barn and stayed there. Tom felt that all this was being done deliberately, to torture him. He apprehended it, not vaguely, but in a piercing intuition.

His father came out and stood at the barn entrance, then crossed over to the door into the conjoint byre and stable. Perhaps he was going to take out the horse to start ploughing the stubble. By God, it was just the sort of thing he would do at that moment! The final and devastating thing to do!

Now Tom caught the movement of his mother's shoulder in the kitchen door and knew in a flash that she had been standing there the whole time listening, peeping out unseen. With a tin dish in her hand she appeared and went down towards the byre. Gathering her eggs, by way of it! The henhouse was a black lean-to shed against the lower gable of the barn, but one of the hens laid away in the byre behind the grain barrel where the horse-feed was kept. So naturally she went to the byre, hesitating, however, in a listening moment at the door before going in.

Let them fight it out! thought Tom. Let them get on with it! The point of the pick sprang off a submerged boulder, just missed his shin bone in the narrow hole, and numbed the whole right foot in a glancing blow.

The numbness, the pain, took up his attention like an urgent companion, dissipating the weakness of excitement against his father and leaving him more formidable in himself. As he exploded at the pain, he turned down his sock and examined his ankle. It would probably swell, though the skin was not broken. He examined it carefully and for a long time. Let his father come on him now!

But though he lingered, thus engaged, his father did not come. His mother emerged from the byre door. One glance at her swithering body was enough to assure him that she had been overborne, had been turned out. He bent his head in the hole. When he looked up again, she had disappeared.

He went through the motion of spitting out of a dry mouth on his palm and gripped the shaft and swung it. Half an hour afterwards he saw his father coming up the wall of the house, walking slowly and deliberately like a man who has had a dram too many.

Tom bent to examine his ankle, needing the strength of an ally against this maddening mixture of weakness and fear which at once beset him and which he could not control. He pushed down his sock, but hardly saw his ankle, felt no pain.

There was a final white moment when his father looked up at him; then he went in at the kitchen door.

Tom worked on in a dogged, dumb endurance, keeping thought and feeling at bay. He had conquered, but the end was not yet. A certain calmness came over him, a tired fatal feeling of bitterness. He hung on to it, but when at last he stopped digging and went down towards the barn, his body dragged wearily as if it had been mauled.

He looked at the tool chest, lifted the lid. At least nothing had been purposely disordered. Tom tried to think this out but could make little of it. It might be against his father's dignity to let Tom see that he had been peeping into the tool chest's private property.

The father had the all-knowing power to gather information and hold it against the day of final judgement. His restraint held a cunning yet terrifying quality. It could break a fellow's spirit. But it would never break Tom's. Never! Not on this earth!

His mother darkened the door. "I told him," she said, "you were going to start ploughing to-morrow."

The whisper in her presence irritated him and he turned away to the bench, his eyes roving over it as though looking for something.

"Tom, will you start to-morrow?" she pleaded.

"If I can get Norman's horse," he answered indifferently.

"Oh that's good!" she muttered, like one given an unexpected present, and off she went.

The ploughing was a great relief, and as he looked down the gleaming furrows of black soil, straight enough for a ploughing match, fine pleasure sharpened his spirit, a loneliness that was a near friendliness of the earth, of the flighting and alighting gulls, a wake of gulls white as blown foam, with the inevitable one or two black rooks amongst them. The work would normally have been heavy drudgery, but now out here in the open field it had somehow a rare freedom. And more than once, on returning to work after a meal and finally as he paused to look over the black furrows that lapped the little grey dikes, he had been caught up by a feeling of great happiness, light and delicate, a stillness and a dancing. Where this came out of, or how or why it came, there was neither knowing nor desire to know. It was there, like that curious stilled laughter which he came to find in bushes or outcrops of grey rock or tumbling green hillocks or wild flowers nodding now and then. It was not in them, of course. They were inanimate. By an understandable illusion it was communicated by him to them. Naturally. Of course. These "explanations"—how amusing! How easy! Worth a laugh on their own account. What a solemnity of importance man had achieved!

"I finished the low ley," he said after supper. "Norman is coming for our horse to-morrow."

His father did not speak. It was a long-standing arrangement between Norman and himself, and while the dry weather held it was as well to have a shot at getting the heavy ground of both crofts ploughed. They had always suited each other's convenience and more or less kept evenly abreast of the work.

On the following afternoon, Tom resumed his digging at the end of the house and felt for the first time a confidence in what he was doing. His father could have no real reason for interfering now. But he remained uneasy until supper was over and nothing had been said. The next afternoon he worked with a will, and before Norman was temporarily finished with their horse, the uprights were in position and some planking on the roof. But he had not nearly enough wood. However, he left the work and started ploughing again. One afternoon he saw the minister call and at supper his mother said to him, "The minister wants you to take two ton of coal for him from the town."

"All right," said Tom quietly. "When does he want it?"

"As soon as you can go. He said he did not want to interfere with the ploughing if he could help it."

Tom was silent for a moment. At this season how could the minister help interfering with the ploughing? "I better go to-morrow then—in fairness to Norman."

His mother looked at the father, but the father said nothing.

Two loads a day were all he could manage. But he so arranged his loads that on the last one he carried the planking he needed. On bringing home the horse and cart in the evening, he stopped by the gable-end and quietly unloaded his wood behind the new erection, taking care that the boards did not slap together.

That evening he waited for Janet in the hollow, but she did not come. After an hour, he slipped along the hillside and stood gazing

99

towards the back of her house. All was dark and dead down there. Growing chilled, he returned to the hollow. But though he waited about the bleak hillside for a long time, there came no sign from her.

In the morning he went round to see Norman, who was a jobbing stone mason, over sixty years of age. As a young man he had become an apprentice mason to a firm of builders in the town. On the day he drew his first pay as a journeyman, his elder brother, Iain, got into trouble over a fight which the fond but cantankerous mother of the lad whom Iain had laid out insisted, against all local custom, should be investigated by the police. Iain disappeared and when next they heard of him he had joined the soldiers. Two years after that, the father had died, and Norman had come back to run the croft and look after his mother and two younger sisters.

Norman was a pleasant decent man, with a twinkling greeting in his eyes and the easy-going ways that made young fellows treat him as a companion. His face was thickset with a dark whisker.

"Man," he now answered Tom, "I must get some stone from the quarry for a little job they want done at Taruv. I have the stones ready and I'd need to cart them to-day and to-morrow. It's a pity, but I sort of promised."

"In that case I'll yoke Prince and come along with you."

"No, no, that would be too much——"

"It'll shorten the time you need your own horse and that's a good enough excuse for me!"

Tom went home and in the kitchen explained casually that he was going to give a day to Norman. It would mean he would have both horses for the ploughing all the sooner. His mother would clearly have liked to have told him it was a neighbourly thing to do, but she waited for her husband who said nothing.

Tom started off with the air of being on holiday and in the quarry Norman and himself worked away quietly, loading the carts. Norman asked him how the new building was getting on and Tom answered, "Slowly but steadily!" Norman glanced at him and paused to take a snuff. "You're doing fine," he said, nodding pleasantly. "Once a craftsman always a craftsman, and you need some building of the kind. How I could have got on myself without the extra bit that came in from the mason-work I sometimes wonder. But it's made life very comfortable for us. This work is a change, too, it takes you out of yourself."

Tom agreed and presently he found himself saying, "In fact I thought of turning it into a bit of a shop with the ironmongery and odds and ends you don't get readily here." He smiled, as though amused. "I mean, with the sort of stuff I could handle and mend and all that. I could get my material then at wholesale price. I'm not like you—with the stuff of your trade lying to your hand!"

"That's very true," answered Norman, "very true indeed." He looked thoughtfully at Tom. "Have you mentioned it to your father?"

"This is the first time I have mentioned it to anyone," answered Tom, looking at the stone he was about to lift.

Norman bent down and gripped the stone with him and together they put it on the cart.

When they had the carts loaded, Norman hitched Prince to the tail of his own cart, and then Tom and himself walked along together, leaving the horses to their own pace.

"Your father is a fine man," said Norman, "a fine conscientious man. I've known him all my life. In our young days there wasn't much schooling in it, but your father was one of a little group who was always keen on the learning. There was no Board of Education Act and High school in it then. Your father was always neat-handed, and he could make the finest goose quills for writing that ever you saw. I sometimes think he would have liked to have been a teacher. I don't know. I was never a great one at the writing myself, though I must say that when I had to sign my name in the town I was proud to be able to do it."

Norman went on talking in this discursive way, recalling old days, as if he had quite forgotten Tom's father. On the way back to the quarry which was no great distance from Taruv (it lay at the base of the shoulder of the hill to their left as they entered the Glen just after leaving the village) Norman said, "Man, I remember the curious effect that Iain's joining the soldiers had on my father and mother. They looked on it as a great disgrace, of course. My mother was very upset. You would think she was never going to get over it. She would greet to herself. She went clean throughither for a while. But my father went quiet. To tell the truth there was a while I didn't care for going home over the Sabbath. But when they heard from Iain, it was wonderful how my mother came round. But my father seemed to have lost all interest in him. There was something about it, about the whole thing, the fight and the soldiers, that somehow got the better of him, whatever it was. I can remember well the awful feeling of disgrace. You would almost imagine that the blood spilt in the fighting was red murder itself. A queer feeling of guilt. I never quite got to the bottom of it. And I won't go the length of saying it hastened my father's end. But he undoubtedly grew careless about himself, about getting wettings and that, and it was no good saying anything to him. He just paid no attention, as if he hadn't heard you, and talked about something else. Congestion of the lungs took him in the end, and he went away as quietly as he had lived over the last while."

Presently Norman said, "It's queer when a thing gets the better of you. That's one thing a fellow has to watch. When you're in health you can break yourself of it, but, man, when you're ill it's not so easy then. Your father is a sick man, Tom, boy, and you should take him carefully."

"It's not always easy," said Tom, flushing slightly, for they were both finding the subject difficult and embarrassing, "when he won't say a thing one way or the other."

"You can do little about that," answered Norman. "You go ahead quietly, keeping your eye open. And look here, my boy, if you need money, just ask me. But I would like that always to be between ourselves. I haven't a great deal, but I have plenty, and you'll be starting in a simple way."

Tom was deeply touched by these words. But more than the offer of money was the sense of comfort and companionship that came from their thus working together away from home. The day seemed large and long, and at the end of it he felt refreshed and pleasantly tired as if he had indeed been on a holiday.

He would have liked now to have stayed with his parents until they "took the books", but it was long agreed between Janet and himself that if she could not come on a set night, she would do her best to appear the following night. At first she had let it be understood that her difficulty was due to chance visitors or other social cause, but now he knew of her secret trouble with her mother and this not only made thought of her more tender but gave him a strengthening assurance of her dependence on him.

As he got up, his mother said, "Surely you are not going out to-night?" It was a hidden appeal not to endanger things that now were shaping well.

"I have got to go," was all he could say.

"I would have thought you had a heavy enough day as it was."

She spoke as if thinking only of him, but he heard the dismay in her voice.

He hesitated, not knowing what to answer, wondering indeed for a moment if he would stay.

"We want no-one here," came his father's voice, "who does not believe in worshipping God. If he believes, let him stay. If not, he can go."

The cold penetrating voice was a rod that pierced the room. Before these words, all other words fled from the air about Tom's mouth and he turned slowly for the door in a heavy awkwardness. Mindless he pushed on into the new darkness and was still numb as he came by the barn.

It had gone beyond anger now, beyond rage. His body was quiet, his hands a little unreal. He listened to all things, but heard nothing. He went into the barn, over to the bench, and stood there. Presently he was sitting in the darkness.

His father's logic penetrated, like a rod of grey metal. It was accurate and remorseless.

Believe in God. Had he ever believed in God? Tom saw that he had never had any interest in God, that he had always dodged Him, as a boy dodged his schoolmaster. Dodged all thought of Him, so that life be freed from that fear or terror. And in Glasgow, with Dougal—they had dodged the fear out of existence, so that ordinary life could be carried on and opened up and enjoyed.

As he sat there in the darkness Tom's thought worked in a curious way. This logic about God did not really touch his mind. His mind was in the place beyond argument where it apprehended in a stillness the forces that moved before words were born. And there he saw that what moved his father was not Tom's disbelief in God although that was the visible power his father used. What moved him was something more terrible and penetrating than that. Grey and ancient and destroying.

The clearness of his apprehension quietened him, and, crossing to the hay-stall, he stepped over the partition-boards and lay down. His head drooped towards his drawn-up knees and, curled there, with the clean hay-scent in his nostrils, he let his mind go in a tired craving for sleep. His mind roamed in a disembodied way, and if it lost consciousness it seemed to him that it did not, but was awake in many strange places, known to him but distant, yet near as clear places seen with the eye.

His eye went up the hillside behind the croft, seeing through the darkness as in a dim light. Janet was coming along the hillside, not stumbling, but walking upright and quickly, yet not to outward appearance in a hurry, because she was coming to him secretly.

When he arose and went to the hollow, however, she was not there. It was now so dark that it was like the dead of night. She would be afraid to come along the hillside alone; it was too dark for her feet. The full moon would rise late.

He waited, and wandered over the hillside, and presently came to the corner of the field where the footpath ran down towards her back door.

Stealthily he went along this path and, rounding the henhouses, saw the light in the small kitchen window. Other houses were at hand, and he listened for a long time before approaching the window on tiptoe.

At first there was complete silence, then he caught quick feet that could only be Janet's. From a little distance, he heard her mother's voice in a harsh, querulous, summoning cry. Janet went away and after a time came back. Just inside the back door, he heard water being poured from a jug into a kettle, the clank of the lid, and in a moment the kettle being hung over the fire. Janet went away and came back again. There was plainly none in the house except these two.

He felt he was intruding and exposing Janet, but he could not leave. You did not like anyone coming in on you at the wrong moment, least of all, perhaps, the one you loved. He had better go. He retreated to the corner of the henhouse, but stayed there. Clearly Janet's mother slept in "the room", Janet herself in the kitchen. In every cottage there was a boxed-in kitchen bed where the mother or parents slept, but now Janet's mother was in "the room". She would be safer there. Janet herself, sleeping in the kitchen bed, would be mistress of the house should anyone call.

It was the first time he had ever thought of Janet in the intimacy of her night arrangements. His mind did not think of her in any prying way, but responsibly. She went into bed, as he went himself, and took her trouble with her. But a deep tenderness came upon him. And perhaps because his mind had been working so strangely that night, it saw her going into bed in her long nightdress, and in a moment he had called her to the door and comforted her, and her body was soft and her hair fell about his face as it had done more than once.

104

He knew he could not leave now, and listened until his throat went dry. But despite this new excitement that came so intimately upon him, he stood there for a long time by the stone wall of the henhouse with the patience of a Red Indian. Then he went back to the window.

When at last he was satisfied that her mother had passed beyond troubling anyone, he waited until he heard Janet move. With his finger-tips he beat four soft notes on the window-pane. He knew she heard by the very nature of the silence, so he repeated the notes, and, under his breath, his mouth to the glass, called, "Janet".

The silence now so startled him that he looked swiftly around at the night. But at last there was movement, the quiet closing of a door, feet stirring in the little back porch, a slow, careful opening of the outside door. He stood before her. "Janet. It's me."

She groped outward a pace and drew the door behind her, but not so that it would make a sound. She could not see him. He touched her, caught her arm.

"Oh, Tom," she whispered, "go away, go away at once!" Her manner was agitated and intense.

But he put his arms round her and drew her to him, murmuring it was all right. She struggled against his arms like one caught in a trap. Her body was soft and strong and slithered in his grip. She had an overcoat on.

But he could not let her go, could not be defeated, could not walk away with the bitter feeling that his intrusion had been worse than futile. So he tried to soothe her, fighting her strength. She brought her right elbow against his chest and her forearm, extending upward, laid a firm repelling palm on his mouth. At the same time she seemed to stand still and listen. He listened with her. There was no movement. No sound.

"It's all right," he murmured calmly. "No need to be frightened." He brought down her arm firmly.

"Oh, Tom, go away," she whispered, and then she collapsed against him, her face in the hollow between his neck and shoulder.

He knew there was no desire for love-making in her now, only the need for protection, the need to let go and forget. And sweet it was to surround her with assurance, and caress her, holding her to him. Her hair had the smell of sleep, and this brought her very near to him, beyond all artifice, and he kissed her hair and breathed in her living human body. She had given way completely, like one fallen asleep, and standing there, utterly still, his senses wide awake and listening as it were a little beyond him, alert in a subtle triumph against the night and all life's circumstance, he had a man's deep tenderness for her in her trouble, held quietly in strength.

This strange suspension of her being, which had more than once irked him and touched him with a finger of panic, now did not disturb him, and he listened for her, aware as he listened that in her mother might be a cunning stealth. But he was equal to all chances of the night, and when she stirred and began to push away from him, he spoke in a soft friendly voice.

In a moment he saw that whereas she would have fled from ardency, from this smiling friendliness, this cool care of her, she could not go away.

"Don't be frightened of anything in the world, Janet. I'll always come to you. I'll always save you." His voice was gentle and eager.

But now that she was fully awake again, she began to be uneasy.

"You shouldn't have come," she breathed. "You must never come again."

"Aren't you glad I came?"

"Yes." But she was disturbed, and suddenly her body went rigid as if she had heard a sound. With extraordinary force she pushed down his arms, and together they listened.

"It's nothing," he whispered.

But she could not quite come back to him. All the same when she said quickly, "I must go now," she brought her mouth near his ear and it was the living Janet who spoke.

"Don't go yet for a little while," he pleaded.

"I must go." Her voice was nearer him than ever, and lingering. Her breath was on his cheek.

He let her arms pass through his hands. She withdrew herself slowly, looking at him, and though he could not see her face, he knew now there was a smile on it.

As she backed into the door, he started forward impulsively, meaning to ask her to stay yet a little, but as his out-thrust hand passed beyond her coat, which must have fallen open at the neck, it landed full against her soft breast and the nipple pressed against his palm through the thin soft stuff that covered it, and his half formed words died away.

She drew her coat over her breast as she got into the door, and in a long moment she seemed to lean out towards him, though she was standing upright. "Good-night," she whispered, and slowly the door closed.

He turned away at once, but half-way up the path he stopped, and then came back to the henhouse wall.

He stayed there until he saw her light go out.

This meeting with Janet and the words his father had used about worshipping God had a decisive effect upon him in the days that followed. Hitherto he had always been dogged by uneasiness when he missed evening worship too often and too obviously. Now he said to himself: "That's finished." It was a relief to have the situation made thus definite. His nature firmed up and grew hard and objective. Immediately the ploughing was over and there was nothing for a time to be done about the croft, he started building. Dovetailing the planks and nailing them to the cross-beams and uprights was a simple job, and soon his shop was completely enclosed except for the door and a long front window. He moved all his gear from the barn and established himself in the new building.

Now his light at night and the cheerful hammering could be seen and heard from the road, and he had more callers than ever before. There was a brightness about the new white wood which reflected the light and quickened the spirit. No need for him to repel unfriendly or stupid lads. The others saw to that. "No room for any more," and Andie would shut the door and lock it. Tom would not have liked anyone to think he was inhospitable. The others knew this, and were delighted to take the blame. The new shop, with a blind on the window, became like a club, and soon the old arguments were in full swing.

There was one dark lad, Alec Wilson, about Tom's own age, who preferred a good-going argument even to a dance. There was more fun in it, he affirmed. In starting an argument, he was full of sly resource, would wink and smile secretly to those near him when about to set two combatants going. But as often as not he got caught up into the argument himself, unable to resist it, and then his voice was as high and heated as any. He would go miles to get two men arguing at each other. More excitement than in a fight, he said. In playing reels and strathspeys on the fiddle, his bowing was lively, his notes crisp, for he had the flashing spirit of the music in him. Normally he was sensible and good-natured, and willing to do anyone a good turn.

But Tom developed a tactic even against Alec. It was in its method the tactic Tim had employed against himself, but whereas in Glasgow they had all got used in some measure to metaphysical argument, here in the Glen the terms of the argument could not yet be accepted as intellectual counters, could not yet be readily separated from the forces they represented. God was more than a word: God was still God, and all the more so because vaguely apprehended.

The Bible was the happy hunting ground. "Name one single case where the Bible is wrong. Name it!"

"I don't know what you mean by wrong," answered Tom, drawing his pencil across a board against his folded three-foot-rule. "Let us say it's obscure or not clear."

"Ah, that's just because you don't understand it. There're many things in the Bible difficult to understand. Everyone knows that. That's different."

"Perhaps you can help us to understand?" said Tom with a friendly glint.

"I might," answered Alec. "You never know! Name your case first."

Tom took up the saw. "God created Adam and Eve. Then Adam and Eve had two sons, Cain and Abel. These were all the people on the earth at that time, according to the account in Genesis, weren't they?"

"Yes."

"Then Cain killed Abel. And the Bible says Cain went into the land of Nod and took unto himself a wife. Where did she come from?"

This simple difficulty they had never pictured, and it now struck them with much astonishment. There was something so neat about the difficulty that their eyes shone. It was like a statement of some wild unholy humour, yet, by the devil, there it was!

"I don't remember—exactly—what it says," began Alec.

"You go home and read your Bible," said Tom, and they all smiled, but with the restless gleam in their eyes.

Discussions like these stuck in their minds and travelled with them. On Sunday in church Alec cunningly read the account of the creation in Genesis during the sermon. To a couple of friends on the way home he admitted that Tom was right. It was really like an unholy joke, and they glanced to right and left so that no-one would see them smiling.

Some of these biblical difficulties Alec kept in his sleeve as ammunition, and when he had an opportunity with older men, who were not religiously solemn, he would "have them on". Often he was surprised how a man with a tongue as ribald as Andie's would turn on him angrily. Then Alec delighted in using Tom's manner. "I'm only wanting to know. If you can't tell me, it's all right."

Eyes would stray towards Tom while he was sitting in church.

But largely Tom was unaware then of what was happening, for the arguments were to him old ones and pretty simple or primitive. Moreover his own mind was taking on a firmer definition because of the relationship in which he stood to his father. In his private time, he could say what he thought. Than the truth there could be nothing more important, more final, in this life, either with God or man. That being so, let it stand. He would not go out of his way to hurt anyone with truth, but neither would he deny it.

A dour, almost sullen, spirit which occasionally came upon him while working about the croft, particularly when he saw his father walking slowly or standing staring at the fields, would get completely dissipated in the shop at night. It was a pleasure to his whole body to make things, drawers that slid out and in smoothly, shelves and racks, small wall-cupboards with locks. There was an exactitude in measurement that worked like magic. All his books were now securely locked away from prying eyes. An instinct warned him against showing them to his friends, though it had been difficult often to refrain from handing one to Alec and saying, "Take that home and read it."

Meantime Janet's trouble was also on his mind. And when next they met she seemed to him to look paler, with dark eyes large and tragic, though when she smiled her beauty touched him profoundly. That was a curious thing—the effect of responsibility she always had upon him. It produced in him a feeling of strength and tenderness, so that he would not have hurt her or forced himself upon her for the world, not even when all her body seemed compliant and lost in that small still trance.

She wondered, she said rather shyly, if he had been upset. She sat with her arms round her knees. "She's all right now."

"Does she often have these turns?"

"No. About once a month or so. But they terrify me. She says the most awful things. I couldn't tell you."

"You know you can tell me anything, Janet. But don't tell me yet—if you would rather not."

"It's about Father. She says the most awful things." Her voice choked abruptly. "I was fond of Father."

"Yes," he answered compassionately. "No wonder. He was, I think, the most generous man I ever knew."

"Oh, Tom," she called, and turned to him, and began weeping in harsh abrupt gulps. He soothed her as best he could, and spoke tenderly against the gulp in his own throat. That was the first time he ever used a real term of endearment to her. "Janet, Janet, my own love," he whispered, "don't you cry."

She began to tell him then of some of the real trouble she had with her mother, slowly at first, wiping her nose, sniffing back and swallowing. The small physical mannerisms of her distress curiously moved him, setting her apart from him in the still chill darkness of the night.

She knew when her mother was going on one of her bouts. She got restless and cross and wondered, she said, why she was living at all. She would be despondent and silent, yet the least thing would make her flare up. She would snap Janet's head off for nothing. Then without any warning to Janet, she would be gone from the house and away on the bus. At first she used to say she had to see her father in the town. But now she did not say anything. It was no good pleading with her mother. At first Janet had tried hard, had threatened to leave her, to tell the minister what she was doing, but that only made her mother worse. When she was opposed, she became violent. She would nag Janet into speaking against her, so that she could become violent. When she was roused, she was full of force and went about in her rage like a mad woman, saying the most terrible things, and doing things, too, that Janet would be ashamed to mention, and breaking things. She hated the whole place, she said, she hated her own family. They had all deceived her. "She said that—that Donald, my brother, was not born before his time, and that—that father——"

She could not go on. The shame of it was too much to remember. And Tom said nothing. He sat quietly beside her, staring before him, cooled in a bitter forlorn way by this revelation of the fruits of passion.

"Oh, she hates my father, she hates the memory of him," Janet said, with a sudden energy. "She hates all men. If she had found you that night at the door . . ." Her body shuddered.

She wiped her eyes. "I shouldn't be telling you all this. But I have no-one to tell. I'm sorry."

"Don't be sorry, Janet. You must never be sorry that you told me. Never. Do you hear? Do you understand, Janet my own one?"

"Yes."

He caressed her, but there was no response in her body. When she spoke again, however, her voice was more natural and calm. He asked her how long the turn lasted.

"At first it was one night, and then she kept to her bed in an awful condition next day, moaning as if she was ill and dying. But now she has a second night. Then she gets all right, and will go to the shop and speak to the neighbours and be all right. I sometimes wonder if anyone suspects. I don't know, but I don't think so."

"I certainly never heard a whisper about it. And you know how things can go round. You can take it it's absolutely dead certain no-one knows."

She went on talking as if she had hardly heard him. "Sometimes, too, I have been sorry for her. She's not always in the same rage. And one night—there's always a short time, in the beginning, when she can be in a fine mood, all alive and sweet like a girl— one night, when she was in that mood, she told me about her life when she was a girl. She loved her mother and hated her father. She said he was cruel and a bully and ill-treated her mother. She told me of the fine times her mother and herself would be having when they were by themselves. And she sang to me a little song that her mother used to sing, a fairy song about the mountains and the glens. Oh, I cannot tell you how much it affected me. It was like something in a world far away and lovely. I broke down and cried as if my heart would break."

She sat quite still for a little, then shivered so suddenly that she startled him. "It's cold," she said.

He tried to press warmth into her, using his arms and his hands. He took her hands and rubbed them.

"You're very good to me."

"Be quiet, Janet," he answered, rebuking her because there was so little he could do out of so much feeling for her.

She looked at him with her smile that was more intimate than spoken words, alive yet shy, and looked away. "I feel better now," she said in a practical, sensible way.

"That's good," he answered, forcing the words brightly.

She turned her head and looked at him, then dropped her eyes to her fingers plucking about the grass. "Don't worry about it. I would hate to think you did that. I am used to it now and know how to deal with her."

He did not answer.

"Promise!" she demanded and caught his knee and shook it, not looking up at him.

He caught her hands and drew her to him. She kissed him lightly with a cold mouth and drew back. "You're good to me," she said, and impulsively pressed his hands, and got to her feet. "I don't know what's made me so cold."

"There's frost in the air."

She paused as though he had said something arresting and looked about her. They stood quite still, side by side. The stars were sparkling in an almost black sky. There was no moon. She could see outlines of the hill against the sky. Each solid blackness was listening, not to them, but for something that no human ear would ever catch.

Before they parted at the corner of her croft, she was light and gay in manner, and tugged the lapels of his coat as though tugging the last remnant of a sad mood out of him. When she had gone a little way she turned and waved.

He returned slowly towards his home, stood at the peat-stack for a time, then very quietly unlocked the shop door and relocked it, drew the blind carefully, and lit the lamp.

With pen and ink he began drawing up a definite letter heading for his business. Tom Mathieson, Ironmonger. Cycle Agent. Repairer. The address. A line for the date. The printing firm would know exactly how to set it out. Not too showy. Quiet, for a country district, say in pale green lettering on white. Dougal himself would know the sort of thing.

For over an hour he sat writing Dougal.

Then, the sealed envelope in his hands, he looked about the bright wood of the shop, stared at the thoughts that turned over in his mind. Life was shaping, was being shaped by his hands, into an intimacy, a goodness, into days and years of communion and kindness, of work and real comfort, of interest, of eagerness. No human opposition could do him down, neither father nor mother. Nothing could beat him down or back. Just nothing.

Chapter Ten

The Philosopher sat on a half-buried boulder which was warm with the sun. He was well up now towards the ridge that gave on the moor and he commanded a fine wide sweep of country. The liberation of the hills was upon him, of the wide stretch of valley land that went away towards the town, of the sky that ran with the high horizons of the earth, a summer-blue sky alive yet half-dreamy with white clouds, distant horizons with the blue arch flattening beyond them into unimaginable remoteness.

The Highland hills. The mountains that stretched north and south and far to the west, and the glens that wandered with them. Little villages by seashores of the west, by narrow inlets, curving with sheltered bays far inland at the feet of mountains, crofting townships on windswept headlands, all to-day lying quietly in the sun, the straw of their thatch a pale-gold memory of old harvests, their roofs curved against tempests past and to come, patient as the backs of cows, smooth as rounded wings from which the living brood adventured, lying at peace under the sun of this friendly day.

A good land. Wide and high and far, yet it could be encompassed. A land that changed from bend to corner, from ridge to crest, yet had that in it from ancient time that did not change.

The plover fell there in the air as it had fallen at the sudden sight of man on this hillside thousands of years before Joseph went up to pay his taxes at Bethlehem, taking Mary with him. Thus it had always cried and beat the air and its young had heard.

A reluctance came on the Philosopher to pursue his past, as though it were enough to remember on this halcyon day that early reality of love which had beaten its wings in him. Yet the pattern was inexorable and pursue it he had to, from some inner need in himself, on this day that was to him, for some reason beyond apprehending but impulsive as a light-feathered mood, a day of days.

Away over from him on the left, the shepherd was now standing leaning on his long stick, its point grounded on the slope, his hands cupped over the crook beneath his chin.

Not so old a vision as the tumbling peewit, perhaps, yet in another and mythical sense so immensely old that it lived in legend, before reality was shaped out of legend.

From the shepherds on shaggy hillsides, on great plains, in straths and glens, by the green pastures of still-watered valleys, slowly, through the countless centuries, drawing to a focus, drawing nigh, One who is at last the living Shepherd, who moves in historic time, tending his sheep across the continents and islands of the world.

The Christian religion had the imagery! It focused man!

The Philosopher smiled lightly to himself as he always did when an image entered and crystallised a mood of thought or reverie. This was one of life's rarer possessions or capacities. And when the image formed and passed the mind was freed and uplifted.

So that he looked now at the shepherd and remembered him as a boy of, it must have been, about nine, when he was so desperately anxious to "learn the bicycle". A dark boy, with a fringe of hair over his brow and a shy manner. He was inclined to speak in a whisper and then look up at you. But because there was something taking in his face, you bent your head to listen, saying, "What's that, Norrie?" His father was the estate shepherd then, and their home stood back from the road that went across the moor to Altdhu. No other house was visible from it, and now Norrie lived there with his wife and three children. He was over forty, naturally intelligent, with the dark eyes in which there was still a certain wonder. He was the first man—and that only in recent years—who had given the Philosopher some new thoughts about the old bugbear, superstition.

Learning the bicycle! What a rage it became amongst the young fellows that first summer!

Threepence a half-hour and a waiting list for the two boneshakers in the long evenings. Solid tyres and a loud bell. You could hear the shouting voices up the quiet glen road where there was about half a mile of straight. That was the learning place. When three were lucky enough to raise a penny each, one would come for the bicycle and the other two wait up the road. Then it was turn about, with the distances jealously measured. On one side of the road was a ditch and on the other a thorn hedge, but the bicycles were tough and rarely bore any evidence of conflict beyond a surface scratch or two and an odd drop of blood.

When a lad had "learned" and in one way or another had amassed his fortune of threepence, he would look at the weather, button his jacket over his excitement, approach Tom's shop and ask calmly if he could hire a machine for half-an-hour.

"Thinking of tackling the village?"

"I thought I might have a shot at it."

"Watch Peter Grant's dog, then."

"I'll watch him all right."

Peter Grant had the little shop with the post office and his wife kept a wire-haired terrier for no reason that anyone could see, though Peter claimed exemption from licence for it because he had a cow on his bit of ground. The dog was a born yapper, but if you rang the bell at him he went clean mad and followed you far enough, and you couldn't put on a spurt because his favourite tackle was the front wheel. When he went yelping mad like that, all the other accursed brutes in the place would join in the chase. With every available inhabitant of the village enjoying the fun (excepting, perhaps, Mrs. Grant) and a few young men shouting sarcastic encouragement, it was beyond your dignity to dismount by the back step, even had you been able to do so with the assurance of custom, which you weren't. Moreover, you had also to guard against the perversity of the machine itself which could develop an ungovernable tendency to run into that which you wished it to avoid.

Life had certainly been crammed with interest that summer. After the crops were down, the stuff for the shop began to arrive in small quantities. Tom did not put up a sign, nor at first, in fact, lay out the new erection as a shop. No advertisement was needed, and small shops never had a sign in any case. His friends soon had the news round the countryside, and with the news went the intelligence that Tom could get the very latest things. Not a shop for women, no display, not even the goods on the premises— beyond a limited supply of tools and odd material that men with ready hands wanted—but Tom could get knives and forks and spoons, every kind of household gear, in beautiful cases and without cases. And, my word, if you saw the catalogues of the better-class stuff!

In Fraser's shop in the village the womenfolk bought all the cheap household goods they needed, unless it was a matter of cups and saucers and bowls, when they bought them from Stewart tinkers, trading-in rabbit skins at a halfpenny each or even a penny if it was a good one, had been skinned well, and the bargainer was firm. Tom never expected—or desired very much—to have anything to do with that type of small business. But outside it there was a whole range of stuff which could be got "on order". Not much of this might be wanted, but profit from it would be considerable, and the very knowledge that he could supply it should give his repair work a real foundation and body. His expectations were altogether exceeded. It started with the clocks—a backwash from the social gossip over Jimmy Macdonald's wedding present. The farmer of Taruv asked leave to take the catalogue home with him. "It's the mistress," he explained. Two days afterwards he came back with the catalogue a little the worse of wear. "That's the one she's set her mind on, but it's damn dear." "She has good taste," said Tom, with a smile. It was a black marble French clock marked at £4 5s. "It's easy having good taste," said Taruv, showing a yellow tooth or two in the left corner of his mouth in a characteristic grin. "It's dear enough," said Tom, "but it's good value. It'll go forever." "That'll help me a lot!"

A fortnight later Taruv pulled up his gig at the shop door. Tom went out. The farmer leaned over, his face reddened with weather and a few drinks, for he was on his way home from a cattle sale. "That clock," he said. "Braelone's wife was in last night and didn't the mistress show it to her. Women are like that." He nodded.

Tom smiled, waiting. He had done several small jobs for Taruv and knew him well.

"Braelone—you know Braelone?"

"Yes," said Tom under these watchful eyes. Braelone was inclined as a big farmer to act the little laird and his wife gave him a lead.

"She'll be wanting the same clock now or I'm a Dutchman and, damn it, didn't the mistress tell her you took five shillings off. I thought I'd mention it to you." Taruv nodded and pulled on the reins.

"Thanks for telling me," said Tom, suddenly touched by this delicacy on Taruv's part.

"All right," nodded Taruv, with a rough manner, at once relieved and irritated, and drove off.

Braelone's wife ordered a clock marked £5 5s.

In that first month of June Tom's clear profit was nearly £8 from these and other orders.

It could hardly go on like this, but it was exciting. He had to be prepared, too, for bad debts. Between the order and the getting of the money was a somewhat anxious time. But when he was in real doubt—the Gilchrists of Ardbeg, for example, were known to be in a bad way—he resorted to a certain measure of cunning. "That's the price. But I could knock six shillings off it, if I got the money with the order. They want cash down from me as a beginner. If it's all the same to you, it would help me, and I could give you that off." Then he would add quietly, "You needn't say anything about it."

He had taken six pounds from his mother—all she had, apparently, except for a few shillings which he refused. How she had gathered this money, he did not try to think. Perhaps she had started gathering it from the day he was weaned, putting a penny by now and then from an odd dozen of eggs which she would claim as her own. She had the saving nature in her, a little of that mistrust which moved the hen to lay away. Yet for her son—as for her husband, indeed, if in another way—she was completely unsaving of herself.

He did not want to take the money, but the whole circumstances of its presentation were too much for him. She caught him in the byre in the morning, while his father was still in bed. She breathed secrecy, and, turning slightly from him, fumbled about her person and produced a knotted handkerchief. She had tied the knots so tightly that she had to use her small teeth. Six golden sovereigns were displayed and some silver coins. "Here, take them!"

"No, Mother. I'll manage——"

"Hsh! Be quiet." She picked out the six sovereigns first and thrust them at him. "That's six."

"No, no."

"Hurry up. Quick now."

He turned away, but she followed him. And there in the byre her urgency was warm in its own understanding of his reluctance, thrusting the money at him, breaking through the embarrassment of the moment with impatience as if it were just nonsense. "Here, take it. It's nothing. I only wish it was more." And now she had gripped his hand.

A couple of minutes later he heard her outside tapping the tin dish with a spoon and even calling "Took! took! took!" in a relieved voice.

Then she developed entirely on her own a method of watching for a customer and signalling to him. If the father, for example, was sitting on the boulder at the lower gable-end, she would appear at the back of the house and, lifting her right arm, swing it round and round over her head. If he hesitated to drop what he was doing in the field, she signalled him again, more urgently. Then he knew that she had assured herself of the value of the customer. Of a boy or youth, she would ask, "What are you wanting?" and guide herself by the answer. "All right, you come back at two o'clock. He'll be in then." Or, if the boy was a messenger, "Well, I'll try and get him for you. Wait here."

In this way, Tom was able to attend to the croft sufficiently well to forestall any reasonable criticism by his father. And actually there was little to do in the fields during the growing months, and more and more his mother took complete control of all the beasts except the horse. When it came to singling the turnips, she worked with untiring persistence and a tidy skill. In a glance from a distance she was a stout dark body forever rooted in that field, but a closer view disclosed a hoe-blade ceaselessly working like a swift iron hand.

It is not impossible that a certain happiness, a newness of life, came upon her at this time. The illness of the father was accepted as inevitable, the sort of fate which life brings, and she had to make the best of it. So long as there was work to do, she was for ever adaptable; the deeper the wound in life the greater the need, not for protest, not for opposition, but for the endless resource that knew how to hide and yield—without giving in.

If she got Tom alone after the customer had gone, she would ask, "What was he wanting?"

Tom would tell her. If it happened to be a catalogue for a wedding present, she would nod and her eyes would speculate: "He has the money to buy a good one, but I don't know about herself." Sometimes she would give him a surprising amount of information concerning folk. "Have you seen her?" she would ask about the prospective bride. "Yes, I saw her one day in the village." "What's she like?" "Oh, quite a nice-looking woman." "She'll be dark and well set up, is she?" "Well, she is, yes." "I knew her mother: a fine girl, but proud a little. All the Macleans were proud. But they were a good family." She said it in a solemn memoried way. She clearly liked talk of the kind. It gave her snatches of life from the past and, because of a continuity in human relationship which she understood in her own way and from her own experience, snatches of life in the future. After the quiet talk, she would go away refreshed, full of her thoughts. That Tom, through his business deal, had a certain contact with the world of which they had spoken probably gave her also some real satisfaction. She nodded, anyway, as she went.

Did she ever venture on such talk with her husband? Probably she did, but in a different way, keeping Tom out of it, until perhaps at the very end when she might introduce in an off-hand manner the approach to Tom over the wedding present, to see how he would take it, covering any lack of response by getting to her feet and doing something. That they talked together, Tom knew, but the talk grew less and less, and certainly before the summer was at its height, it dwindled into little more than occasional fleshless words.

The processes by which the father withdrew into himself were slow but cumulative. It was remarkable how Tom and his mother got used to this. Sometimes they would talk to each other, not only about their own crofting work but about a neighbour's, as if he were not present. Yet even such talk was meant in some measure for him, so that he could listen to it and know what was going on without being directly involved. When it came to selling a calf, the same method was employed. "If we're going to sell the calf at all," said Tom, "we should send him to the sale on Thursday." "We'll *have* to sell the calf," replied his mother. Then they waited. The meal continued. "Is Norman putting his to the sale?" his mother asked at last. "Yes, they're all going," Tom answered. The father remained silent. Nothing more to be said.

The father's silence could sit in your stomach like an undigested ball. It even affected your attitude to the calf. You were less kindly to the brute, less inclined to curb its antics with good nature. After all, it had been produced to make money, you thought. But a bad taste was left in your mouth, and if the price was better than had been expected, the old pleasure, the pleasure of the countryman in a good sale, was not as it had been.

However, all that one could get used to. One could even get used to the feeling which assailed one now and then, horribly, that the father was conscious of the effect his silence made on their hearts and used this silence in a deliberate way. At times Tom had his piercing intuition of his father's mood towards them, an extraordinary feeling of certainty, particularly when he looked up in an expressionless way and stared at the window, or cleared his throat, or—most expressive of all—simply sighed, not to them, as it were, but to himself. The sigh was not all soft breath, there was a sad firmness in it as if the throat were pliant bone.

Yet this did not destroy all respect for his father and so help to free him. These were still mannerisms, outward manifestations, a remaining jealousy, a worldly ruthlessness—behind which was a power Tom felt rather than comprehended, a mystery of austere unfathomable power. He could feel his father's presence when it was not there.

Neighbours, men of his own age, had practically ceased now to call on him. He no longer smiled to them. He had little to say and his words held no human or worldly warmth.

"To tell the truth, boy," said honest Sandy to Tom, "I don't know whether he would like to see me or not."

It was very difficult for Tom. "Sometimes, when he's a bit down—he's like that," was all he could answer.

From a sharp look at Tom, Sandy glanced away. "It's a sore trouble and takes the heart out of a man. I'm in a bit of a hurry to-day, as it happens, so perhaps you'll tell him I was asking for him?"

"You could take a walk down and see him."

"Not to-day. I haven't the time, truly . . ."

But every other week William from Bulbreac called and stayed with him for two hours. Both the mother and Tom took care to be out of the house then, and Tom deliberately dodged William afterwards. If the afternoon was very quiet you could hear William reading or praying almost from the shop door.

Once the minister, holding his hat on in a high wind, came suddenly upon Tom at the corner of the shop. "Yes, you have a fine place here, oh a fine place. Yes. And I hear you are doing well?" He shook hands.

"Yes, quite well, thank you," answered Tom, making no effort, however, to show the minister into the shop. His modest expression implied that the minister could have no interest in it.

"And how is your father?"

"Just about the same."

"Ah. Poor man. He has had a hard time and bears his trouble well. I hope he is an example to you?"

Tom smiled modestly.

The wind was troublesome and though the minister's strong eyes were on Tom, he was blown backward a yard, holding to his hat. Tom did not follow him into the shelter of the wall, but stood where he was politely, and as it was not the ideal moment for further cross-examination, the minister, saying he hoped he would see Tom presently, went down to the house.

It was no doubt an invitation to Tom to appear and join in family worship, but Tom could elect to look upon the occasion as a visit to the sick. He went to church on Sunday. That was enough for them. When at last the minister reappeared the shop was locked and Tom was gone.

"There was no need to wait for me," Tom answered his mother later. "You could have told the minister I had business to do."

"That's what I told him," said his mother a little sadly.

But, over all, Tom had the measure of the situation, because he worked the croft and now openly had his shop and little business. His father never came near the shop. There was no interference. His father's indifference was such that the shop might not have existed. That suited Tom very well. He wished for no more.

And he was working hard and slept for six or seven hours like a boulder. He had no desire to linger in bed when he awoke. He leapt at once. His mother did not waken him. She would have let him lie. On Sunday he lay in bed until he thought his mother was never going to move, until he could hardly bear the bed-clothes any longer.

But there was real keenness, a triumphing quality, in his work. By the beginning of July the two second-hand safety bicycles had arrived from Glasgow, and in the evenings the space between his shop and the road was besieged by boys and young men. Once he did say to a group of boys, "Look here, don't be making such a row. My father is not very well." It quietened them, but only for a short time.

In the long bright nights, it was impossible to have a meeting with Janet in the hollow or anywhere in the open, without risk of being seen. His shop was open, too, until ten o'clock. Yet though he could not have her alone, she was with him, not only in what he did, not only in the present moment, but, far more vividly, in the future. The time ahead was bright with her. They were together in that near future, which he was building for them both. They had endless time inside its walls, the walls of its house, where the face was Janet's face and the eyes Janet's eyes, and the strong, soft, swaying body Janet's body. Sometimes he saw her face quite vividly in a room that was not full of daylight but dimmed a little as in a dream. The room was a cottage kitchen and her face was dimmed a trifle, too, but in such a way that its living colour was heightened. It was full of life and turned away or flashed away from him in a gay humour.

Once or twice he met her in the village and spoke to her for a few moments. In these moments their lives were brought over the dead days into the living present. "No chance of seeing you?" "Tina and myself are going out on Thursday night——" "I'll wait for you at the back. Don't go in the front door." "But I mightn't——" "Never mind. I'll be there." Their faces had not lost the innocuous neighbourly smile and they parted at once in a neighbourly way. If Tom's heart was beating too thickly he tended to hiss vaguely to himself in unconcern. For a few minutes he had to be careful lest a quiver in his voice betray him to anyone who had seen them talking together.

These snatched moments had an intensity of their own, all the greater because in the summer nights someone might be moving about at any hour and it never got black dark. After one of these short meetings by the henhouse wall near her back door, where they could hardly even whisper, he stole away up into the hills, his whole body full of suppressed singing and an invigorating mirth. There was defiance in it and a secret glory. This mood was rather rare at that time, because the whole circumstances of his life tended to breed a sense of responsibility and youthful purpose, a humourless solemnity. He was no longer the "watcher": he was the doer, the builder, in the teeth of difficulties that should never have beset him.

But when moments had to be stolen from rushing time, when they dare hardly whisper lest prowling feet discover them, when, beset by this imminence of danger, Janet in the wild snatched moment let herself go in a quiescent rapture, so that they stood lost, or overbalanced to lean against the wall and draw their rapture still more closely to them—when that happened—after that happened—the hills were friendly to his silent singing.

And then it came.

It was an evening in the beginning of August. The nights were already closing in and before ten o'clock it was quite dark in their hollow. He had not spoken to her, had not even seen her, for over a fortnight, until the previous afternoon. In a careless but swift moment she had made the appointment herself. Probably she had some special news about her mother. Yet there had been something pleasant and exciting in her manner and the fact that she so naturally needed to see him pleased him more than he might admit to himself. The trouble she had with her mother had never impressed him very much. As a danger or difficulty from which he could deliver Janet, it might be deplored but not without a certain underlying pleasure for the deliverer. In the degree to which it brought out her dependence on him, it strengthened his assurance of her. He certainly had never consciously wasted a moment's sympathy on her mother.

When he had gone back to the shop that previous afternoon, Donald Munro, the minister's son, was there, home from college for the summer vacation. Donald was obviously pleased to see Tom and called to him in the friendliest way as Tom approached. "By Jove," he called, "you've been fairly doing it!"

They shook hands and Tom was warmed and delighted with the meeting. Donald was taller than Tom, dark, with an athletic grace in the easy sway of the slim body as he laughed. There was nothing of the clerical or ministerial about this young man, bubbling over with good spirits. His eyes were brown, with tiny black flecks, and had the strong penetrating quality of his father's. His eyebrows were dark and defined in a noticeable, attractive way. When he liked, he saw what he looked at, making sure of it. And when he smiled slowly he was really very good-looking.

Though he was friendly as the boy Tom had gone to school with, capable at any moment of remembering an old ploy, the college air was still about him, about his clothes and his collar, the air and the manner of the college student, with its elusive distinction.

Coming from his short encounter with Janet, Tom was slightly elevated by this meeting, even in some way flattered. Donald looked at the bicycle critically, got onto the saddle with Tom's help, gripped the handlebars, and, pressing down a pedal as his muscles tensed, nearly knocked Tom over. There was a shouting scramble and Donald in a moment became thoughtful.

"Here," he said suddenly, "I'm going to learn this thing. I could then ride into the town and back?"

"Yes," said Tom, smiling. "Threepence the half-hour."

"But I might want it for two or three hours. I have some—some college friends in the town. I should like to see them." His face slightly darkened.

"Well—they're for hire," said Tom frankly, with a laugh. "The other one is out on hire just now."

"But, dash it, I haven't a sou," said Donald. "Couldn't we—but, here, let's have a shot at it." Full of energy and eagerness he led the way to the road. Tom ran beside him, holding the saddle. "Let the thing go!" shouted Donald recklessly. But Tom held to the saddle, knowing that however long Donald might keep going he would have to come off in the ditch or the hedge.

"I'll raise the wind somehow," said Donald as he departed. And Tom knew that, somehow, he would.

Tom was in a happy mood and all expectation when he met Janet. She had the carefree managing manner which gave in to him and kept him off, which enchanted by tantalising him, which reserved to her her own personality in a delightful playing or play-acting. It was a form of teasing him and yet being sensible that he could not exhaust, could not get enough of. They chattered and laughed, and remembered every now and then to subdue their voices.

Tom told her amusing stories about the clocks, about Taruv and how the Braelones went one up, about the lads who were learning to ride the bicycle. The feeling of responsibility and dogged purpose that had been enclosing him like a clamp was released and his spirits rose into freedom. "I'm making money, too, hand over fist!" It was really laughable—and a way of covering his pride and hope in the telling.

"You're not the only one," she said with a teasing sidelong look.

"How the only one?"

He glanced at her quickly, waiting.

"I've got a situation," she said.

"You haven't?"

At his undernote of dismay, she laughed, controlling her voice into a gurgle. "Yes, I've got a situation."

"Janet! You're not going away?"

She did not answer, regarding him in that distant quizzical way, with the smile about to break, which he could never get used to. "Would you be sorry if I went?"

But he could not play, could not pretend to think the matter over. He could not speak.

"No, I'm not going away," she said.

And now he could not even feel relieved.

"Where?" he asked.

"Well, I'll tell you," she said, giving way to his curious mood. "This morning the minister called at our house. Miss Williamina, the housekeeper, has taken ill. It appears she has had some sort of small shock and will have to stay in her bed and then take it easy for a long time. They have no-one to do anything for them, and he asked Mother if I could be spared for a month or so until they saw how things were going to go. And Mother said I could certainly, and the minister said he was delighted to hear that and it was a relief to him. Miss Williamina would be able to watch over everything from her bed and tell me what to do. If the illness was likely to be prolonged, proper arrangements could be made later. So there you are!"

Janet's tones were practical, slightly mimicking the minister's verbal manner, but with an undertone of excitement.

But for Tom it was exactly as if a finger of premonition had touched his heart; and from the touch a darkening, a dizzying, spread over his mind, obscuring everything but a nameless dismay that with immense effort rose to a point in him and then slowly sank.

"I must say you are full of congratulations!"

"Do you want to go?"

"Well, I don't mind. It will be something to do at least. And besides . . ."

"What?"

She did not answer.

"What?" he repeated in a light expressionless tone.

"Well," she said, "we must go on living. I'll have to earn something. It won't be much but it will be a little."

That touched his heart; their hidden domestic problem left him without a word.

"Why don't you want me to go?" she asked.

"It's not—I don't know—I'm not against you," he replied slowly. "I suppose I don't want things to change."

"But why should they change? I won't be staying at the manse. I'll be coming home at night."

"Oh, will you?" he said. "That's good!"

"You don't sound too cheerful yet!" she rallied him. She had been keeping the news about coming home at night as a surprise. She was not puzzled by his behaviour, though curious over some note of excess in it.

"Well, I'm glad, if you're glad," he said.

"You sound like a sermon!"

"Do I?" But the attempt at lightness was not convincing. "I'm sorry. I don't mean to."

She laughed, closing her throat to a low note. "Oh, you're funny!" she said. She hugged her knees, distant from him.

But he could not rise against the extraordinary feeling of inertia that had overcome him. This annoyed him, but he could not help it. All at once, however, a surge of emotion rose out of his dismay and he suddenly put his arms round her and muttered against her temples, "Ach, I'm sorry, Janet."

She put her arms round him then, as if he were a hurt boy, and murmured, "You're such a foolish one!"

Thereafter relations became more normal and he discussed the matter frankly, asking when she would be home at night, agreeing that it was difficult for her to be definite about anything until she saw how she was placed.

At the corner of her croft, he could not let her go. She was still inclined to laugh at him, to tease him. She had a way of raising her eyebrows, of drawing herself back, a little bit of acting, of grotesquerie, with pontifical words spoken deeply. She did this rarely and only when complete mistress of herself and the moment. An echo of the town, of her High School days. It never failed to flood him with mirth. "'To-morrow and to-morrow and to-morrow' . . . "

Five paces away she turned and threw him a kiss, and was gone.

Chapter Eleven

It is difficult to describe that feeling of impending disaster for which there seems to be no rational basis. Tom could argue against it as he liked, could face up to it frankly, mockingly, say inwardly, "You're jealous of Donald Munro, that's the whole thing!" He could even agree with himself, see that whatever might happen in the future at least nothing had happened to make him jealous so far, that everything was as it had been. Had he any reason to mistrust Janet? The question warmed him with shame. He remembered the handsome George and how Janet had dealt with him. All in a moment the feeling was dispersed, and he smiled in relief and forgot it.

Working away, happily intent on what he was doing, suddenly he was beset by the notion that he had forgotten something, that he should be somewhere else on a job. He dropped his tools and stood up to think, worried. And in upon his mind came that which he had forgotten, stronger than ever, with the beat of a pulse in it, a hunted pulse out of the wilds.

He became haunted, against all sense and reason, by his premonition. He could drive it from him no more than he could his shadow. For spells he forgot it, and then, without actually recognising it, he knew it was walking beside him.

Once his desire to see Janet grew hectic, worked him up into such a rage that if she had been at home he swore he would have gone to her door and asked for her. But she was not at home. She was at the manse, and he had not heard from her. He made himself realise that she had only been gone six days. After that bout of unreason—short but disturbingly intense—he realised that he had better keep himself in hand.

On the seventh day Donald appeared. He had raised the wind and was in great form, and Tom found himself delighted to see him, genuinely delighted, the shadow lifted, gone. There was no explaining this. It was early afternoon and no-one else about. "Out with the iron horse!" cried Donald, taking it for granted that Tom would come with him, though normally Tom did not waste his time teaching anyone to ride. Alec and himself had taught each other when the cycles had first arrived. The process was known and youths did not want Tom around when they were having their spills. "One of the spokes just broke," said a trembling, sweating boy of thirteen. "It was probably weak," answered Tom, "but don't you let it get weak again." "No," answered the boy.

Donald twisted the handlebars, tore a small hole in the left knee of his trousers, and gave his leg and shoulder such a crack that he rolled in pain. "And I was nearly off!" he moaned.

As he limped back to the shop, Tom agreed that another lesson was all he needed, for now he could mount and keep going without help. The handlebars were straightened. But the front wheel was slightly off the true. "That's going to be a job," said Tom cheerfully. Donald made himself more comfortable and watched Tom at work.

He stayed for two hours, chatting away, telling Tom how lucky he was to have such an interesting place of his own. He put his threepence casually on the bench, dusted his clothes, found the small hole in his trousers again, and smiled ruefully. "Williamina is getting a bit cranky," he said. His dark eyes, lifting to the door, paused and glimmered, as if taken by a new and amusing thought. "Well, I'm off. I'll be back the day after to-morrow. And oh, look here, if I went into town, next week or the week after, and stayed away the night, how would you? . . . I would be staying with a friend. I mean I wouldn't be riding all through the night!"

"Oh, we could fix that up, I think," answered Tom, smiling also.

"That's grand. Just to go there and come back in the morning—at the latest in the afternoon. We'll see."

"Right," said Tom.

Tom stood facing the window, but when he saw Donald's dark-clad slim figure going up to the road, he at once turned away, a wrench in his hand, and began looking about the shop as if he had mislaid something. Presently he was staring at the bicycle, upside down on its saddle and handlebars, and, going to the front wheel, he spun it. There was still the least suggestion of wobble. Trueing a wheel absolutely was a very delicate operation. He looked around for the wrench until he found it in his hand.

Two days later Donald appeared again. Tom went with him, and ran out beside the bicycle when Donald slowed down to dismount. After one or two awkward attempts, Donald succeeded in jumping off by the back step. "I have got it now!" he cried, delighted with himself. He mounted, rode for a short distance, and got off again. Tom began to walk home. Donald flew past him at a great speed, letting out a cheer and ringing the bell.

When he came back to the shop with the bicycle he was sweating but still exhilarated. Then he felt between his legs. "That seat is made of iron!"

"You'll be a bit sore to-morrow," agreed Tom.

"Never mind. No torn trousers this time!" And he glanced, laughing, at the neatly darned rent.

"Had Miss Williamina a few things to say?"

"She didn't get the chance," said Donald. Then he looked at Tom, his eyes glimmering with mirth, as if he might say something, but he didn't. Tom seemed duller a bit to-day.

"How's your father?" he asked.

"Much as usual," answered Tom, pleasantly but quietly. Then he looked at Donald with a smile. "I'm afraid I'll have to go. I have a job to do outside."

"Have you? Oh well . . . How long was I?"

"Let's call it half an hour," said Tom.

They went out together and Tom locked the door, acknowledged Donald's farewell, and went down to the barn. He had nothing to do in the barn. Through the door he saw his father walking slowly past the byre towards the lower gable-end. He looked like a figure in a dream of an ancient and relentless world, a patriarch who spoke to the invisible God in waste and arid regions.

A dream of pity that had died and was no more. The vengeance of the Lord God.

Feeling that his father might come upon him, Tom left the barn and went back to the shop. Already his mother had come to the door, but Tom walked by in his usual way. Then he suddenly stopped. "I've got to go up the Glen," he said to his mother absently. "I'll leave the key in the lock and if any of the lads come you could let them have the bicycles. It'll be all right."

He listened to her, and answered, and then went away.

It took him nearly two hours to climb and circle round the hills, but at last he got to the ridge at the back of the village from which he could see the manse. It was still a long way off and the outhouses obscured part of the back wall, but he could see and recognise anyone who left it for the village. Presently a young woman appeared going towards the manse. It was Janet. She was carrying a hand-basket and he lost sight of her just as she was entering at the back door.

Some time afterwards, Donald appeared round the gable of the house, passed the kitchen window and was lost in the outhouses. Half an hour later he reappeared, stood by the gable for a few minutes, and then went round to the front door.

It began to grow dark. She would have to prepare supper, wait until it was over, then wash up and leave things tidy for the night. When it was so dark that he could no longer be certain of any movement, he caught a figure against the pale gable-wall and knew it was Janet going home alone.

By the time he got back to the shop it was deserted. The key was not in the lock but he found it on the narrow ledge under the wooden eave. He locked the door behind him, but did not light the lamp. He was very tired now. After ten minutes he was on his way to the hollow. It was Friday night, a lucky night between them hitherto. He waited in the hollow for over an hour and then went along the hillside and carefully down to the henhouses. There was a light in the blinded kitchen window.

Presently voices arose at a back door twenty yards away. Tom crouched against the wall, his face hidden as a man went by with a dog. If the dog had discovered him and barked, the man, in the country fashion, would have investigated.

He stood looking at the lighted window. It had the blindness of his father's face.

A dull heavy spite came down upon him. He could not go to the window. All at once, without making any conscious decision, against his will, he turned away and, without looking back, went up to the hillside and back to the shop.

God knows what it was had got hold of him so strongly. But he could not shake it off. Common sense told him not to give himself away. "I won't give myself away," he answered. "You can trust me for that!" Common sense told him not to take it in that bitter mood either. But already he was not listening.

On Sunday he saw Janet's mother in church but not Janet herself. She would be busily cooking the Sunday dinner for the minister and for Donald, who was alone in the manse pew. Donald's black hair rose from the white parting and was brushed over, smooth and trim and glistening, with a simple natural wave over the left temple. He had his father's delicate straight nose. There was an underlash of colour in the skin, not the pallor of the student.

Janet's absence was in some strange way a relief. It drained the church of a living quality, turned the worshippers to mindless beings who let the minister's words pour over them as they stared in silence. Tom heard the words but their meaning was distant and the mindless hypnotic state caught him, so that he was lost for a time in a trance, then wandered beyond it into sad hill places he half knew where nothing moved and no-one came. Without change of mood, his mind came back and felt the worshippers about him, and he looked at the minister fixedly and his words had no meaning. The singing caught at a high supplicating terror, at sacrificial rites. From the wail of his mother's voice his mind closed upon itself, smooth as wet stone.

Three nights thereafter he met Janet in the hollow.

"I wondered if you would understand when I mentioned to-morrow night," she said gaily. She had cleverly introduced the words "to-morrow night" in a chance meeting the previous evening on the Glen road with Tina and a few others. "I was longing to see you."

"Were you?" His mind came out from its burrow to look upon the green earth.

"Yes. Were you waiting for me on Friday?"

"I was."

She was silent for a moment. "I couldn't come." Her voice was sombre, but quickly it came clear. "Never mind! Here we are. Let us forget about it." And then she added, "But you mustn't be disappointed if I cannot come. It's not always easy for me."

"I know. But I cannot help it. And, dash it, I did miss you, Janet. I did really." And he caught hold of her.

She gave in to him, indeed for a moment as if a deep passion moved her, a new need of her body. She clung to him—then broke away from her own ardency, but lingeringly, with a hand that stroked his face. "Poor boy!" she said.

He could not get enough of her, not nearly enough of her, and the dumb craving mood that was deep in him made him feel awkward and shy.

Her brightness, however, her spirit of gaiety was something he so loved that its presence renewed him. He could not destroy it out of any boorish craving to salve his own wounds and in no time she was telling him about her "situation". She mimicked Williamina so well that Tom shook with mirth. And what a wealth of detail she had, of trivial happenings and sayings! She was not naturally a quick talker, but now her voice could race. And then there was the minister himself, quite different from what he was in the pulpit, talking in a pleasant sort of sing-song voice. He was really very kind and thoughtful in his own house. "You could not believe how nice he is." It was Williamina who ran everything and looked after the pennies. "Of course I only see them at meal times—except for Williamina. They never come into the kitchen."

"And you like it?"

"Yes, it's new. It's a change from being at home. I like it fine," she said frankly, her voice already bubbling with some new memory.

And when, for the moment, she had exhausted her memories, she asked Tom about his own affairs.

Tom came to Donald's learning to ride the bicycle. "He tore a small hole in his trousers. He was wondering who he would get to mend it!"

She was silent. "I know about that," she said.

"Did you mend it?"

"Did he say I did?"

"Well, no—but I gathered as much." Keeping the amusement in his voice he had to ask again: "Did you?"

"It was like this," she replied in a confidential voice. "He beckoned me into the front passage. He whispered that Williamina would be angry with him if he showed her what he had done. He pressed me to do it. So I did it, but I was in terror lest Williamina would find out. What else could I do? And they're funny, too, in some ways. The minister himself is a bit frightened of Williamina about certain things. He raises his voice high as he comes near her door and cries, 'William-eena, may I come in?' The other night, just before I came away . . ."

She made no further reference to the mending and Tom was vaguely relieved, because he had felt mean, bringing it up. It had been the one thing his pride was not going to permit him to mention. But he was glad now he did, for Janet's attitude was so natural that he understood it.

Their talk, however, was altogether so natural, so set them apart, that when Janet exclaimed that oh, she must run because she had said she was only going round to see Tina for a few minutes, and got to her feet, Tom could not break through to a more intimate mood.

At the corner of the field they said good-night. She responded again with an unexpectedly swift and strong warmth—and was gone.

Her presence remained with him as he went back along the hillside. Everything was all right. She was excited about her new job and that was only natural. There had been, too, an extra entrancement about her to-night, something that was hers alone. He had wanted to invade it and break it down and take it to himself. Because he hadn't, he was feeling a little baffled. That was all. Selfishness.

He did not think of the hills and found himself presently in the shop, but he was too restless to settle down to anything.

She did not come on Friday.

He lived through the days in a curious poised state, his mind unable to think one way or the other, waiting, dumbly waiting.

Then one evening, as he locked the shop in the dusk and went up into the village with a few of the lads, he left them to inquire about some parcels he was expecting by the bus. When he had done this, he did not return to his companions, but walked on out of the village towards the manse. It was getting quite dark, but when he discerned two figures coming towards him, he at once swung off the road and through a field gate.

The figures stopped at a little distance, their voices low-pitched. "No, please!" rose Janet's voice with a pleading intensity, stopping her companion from doing something or coming farther. Donald laughed, restraining his voice.

Janet's footsteps now came alone and quickly along the road and passed Tom, crouched behind the low hedge.

Tom sat there for a long time.

The following Friday, Donald in the late afternoon rode away to the town on one of Tom's bicycles. That night Janet came to the hollow.

"I'm not going to wait long," she said. "I'm frightened for my mother to-night." She seemed nervous and uncertain, but was determined to be gay, too, with much of her managing, practical air sensibly in evidence.

Tom had made up his mind to take their old relationship for granted, never by sign or word to insinuate or reproach. But it was difficult work, for everything in his body and mind urged him to insinuate and reproach. Words and intonations moved in him like serpents.

Suddenly she broke down and began to cry.

At once he was overwhelmed, and all the horrid stuff like venom was swept from inside him, and he took her in his arms, but did not speak to her because he could not trust his own throat. He blinked the tears out of his eyes. "Janet! Janet!" And as he brought his face down he wiped his eyes against his sleeve so that she should not know how weak and moved he was. Janet, his own love.

"It's Mother," she said.

Yes, he knew. "It's hard on you. I know."

"It wears you down."

He comforted her tenderly and presently she was sitting wiping her eyes with her small handkerchief.

"I had thought that—that—by me going to the manse, she would—she would—stop."

Her design was a small revelation to him, so hopeful, so wise. She had always borne her burdens alone, with a brave, gay air. Anyone would think she was the most carefree girl in the whole district.

He knew that she was thinking now of nothing but her mother's trouble. It was with them and around them. Nothing but that.

It remained with them when she smiled and said she was sorry for making a fool of herself; and with them when they went along the hillside. It bound them together and he said good-bye to her gently and stroked her hair. She almost broke down again, and pressed her forehead hard against his chest. It was her way of saying, "You are good to me", as she had done before, but this time she did not say it. And she walked away soberly and quietly, like one overcome by the sadness in life which they both knew.

The following night, late, he came by the henhouse wall and listened at the window. He knew the mother's voice and after a long time, when all was quiet, his finger-tips moved over the pane. She came. She did not speak, but resigned herself, her face in the hollow of his neck, like one given completely, caring no more.

She stirred. "Oh, I wish," she murmured, "I wish you——"

"But I will, Janet; I will take you away," he murmured back, knowing he was completing the thought which had halted on her lips.

Slowly, sweetly, she rubbed her forehead on his shoulder and withdrew. And if somehow she withdrew, too, from her thought which he had spoken, it was with a smiling sadness in which there was strength and assurance for the future.

In that moment, in the dim light of a waning moon risen behind narrow bands of summer cloud, she stood there against the black opening of the door, his vision of love and beauty and all desire.

Quietly he went along the hillside, strangely chastened, in wonder, and to listen was to listen to the hillside, to know what the hillside said and to look at the moon.

She was waiting for him the following Friday, and her mood was now the old mood. This delighted him, because he had hatched a scheme in his mind. If driven to it, he might have told her about it, but not otherwise.

Old Widow Macrae was on her death-bed. Neighbour women went in to see her every day. She was ninety-two and had no-one of her own to look after her. At long intervals a son in Canada sent her money. The cottage had been badly neglected and there was practically no land attached to it, so it was certainly not the kind of place there would be competition for. Tom could easily outbid any likely offerer. What a joy it would be to turn that cottage into a model dwelling, with front porch, back porch, and all! His job would still be exactly the same—to run his shop and work his father's croft, and by the one stroke he would be freed from his father's eternal presence! Janet's mother was no distance away and Janet could look after her to her heart's content!

Such ideas of marriage as may hitherto have floated through his head had not been definite, had referred rather to a future, not a distant future, but still an uncertain future in which he would have established himself. The glory was to come. Now, breaking upon him like something seen with the eyes, it was here. Like a bird out of a legendary forest, out of a haunting dream, it was here in his workshop, flashing in magical colour, singing in the long moment when he was alone, his hands still.

What a fury of work was in his hands when the moment passed! And the plan was so simple, so complete and satisfying at every point, that it could not be countered. It had the perfect simplicity of the inevitable.

But he would not mention it to Janet. Girls were very superstitious about the simplest things, and to reveal a plan that hung on another person's death, even the death of an old woman, might carry an air of ill omen. And he would yet have to deal with his own father.

So that to find the old Janet in the hollow was just what he wanted. Even if she seemed a trifle withdrawn into herself, more given to pleasant talk and good common sense than to showing her personal feelings, surely that was understandable, a tribute to the independence that would make up for her recent weakness by the back door. She was asking nothing from him! So delicately she kept him at a slight distance! Their play was delightful and rarely had she been so continuously alive and various. When he kissed her she sank into a strange apathy, but even that he understood as a backwash from the mood of fear and hopelessness.

What if there was something hidden and strange about her, alive and yet reluctant, keeping him off now and then with a gaiety just a little forced? She would not want to break down again—and ah, now, he held the secret key! He was making no demands upon her, none, until the cottage was empty and his plan mature.

His plan obsessed him. It held a brightness that nothing could dim. Janet had asked him to take her away. She had gone to the manse for reasons that moved him. If he could read signs, Donald had a student girl in the town. And he, Tom, had his plan!

When next Friday passed, and the following week-end, without sign of Janet, he was pursued by a restless impatience rather than that first awful premonitory fear. His desire to see Janet alone began to burn in him, but the strength that came from his command of circumstance was greater. He was distracted, too, by thoughts of the cottage and Widow Macrae's death. He now made up his mind that immediately Widow Macrae died he would tell Janet his plan: a definite point that steadied his whole world.

Meantime he had money to make and work to do; he had to work for the future, and the more he was troubled by not seeing Janet the harder he worked.

From his next meeting with Janet, he came away uneasy. There had been much of the old liveliness, but now he saw that she was troubled about something, that she was keeping him at a distance,

136

as if she were weary of emotion. She denied it—or at least she said he would have to forgive her, because she was tired. No, there was nothing wrong, but if he could just be friendly it would help her.

His uneasiness in the following days was slowly eaten up by the old premonition, but not now a vague premonition descending in stillness. This premonition had a claw that caught at his physical heart. It could pounce upon him at the oddest moments, clutch him and stop his breathing.

She was overworked, had trouble at home, was tired. Anyone might get tired and despondent. Look how his own father had affected himself at times.

He worked like a slave, but now sleep would desert him for spells, awful desperate agony of midnight hours that saw new meaning, revelation in a gesture, a smile, an attitude, an intonation, the slightest movement of reluctance. Those awful eyes of the midnight hours that he cursed and blinded with Glasgow gutter-oaths.

Widow Macrae died in the second week of September.

Tom had not seen Janet for a long time. He now had to see her at all costs. Running into Tina in the village, he stopped to chat and asked her if she had seen Janet lately. "Yes," she answered lightly, "I saw her last night", and she gave him a curious glance. In a flash he realised that Tina must know of their meetings: Janet would have had to tell her, if only to prepare Tina for a possible question from Janet's mother.

"I would like to see her to-night. Would you tell her that?"

"Yes, I will," said Tina. "I don't think she has anything on."

"Good. How's George?"

"Who? That fellow!" said Tina.

Tom went off smiling.

And Janet came, making no excuse for her long absence, friendly and pleasant, in the night-light by the field corner wrapped coolly in herself, like a pillar. She had at times a lovely grace of slow movement.

He saw at once that she wished to keep him at a friendly distance, that she desired this friendliness above all else, that she deliberately set herself to achieve it, using her full powers.

Though more uneasy than ever, her manner bewitched him and he had the surprise and hope of his plan.

Then, after some time, leading up to it not without cunning, he told her of it.

To begin with, his words came haltingly. He had been thinking over their difficulties, he said. Something would have to be done for both their sakes. His own father—he was not actively against him now, but—it was like having something hanging over your head, it preyed on you, it got you down. It would be best for his father, for his mother, if he wasn't there at all. And Janet, having to work so hard all day, and then—at night—her mother. It was getting her down, too. If all this went on, it would tear them to bits. They must look at it sensibly. Life was only beginning for them. They must take it into their own hands.

A silence had come upon Janet. He felt her stillness.

Widow Macrae's cottage was not much to look at, he went on, keeping his excitement down. But it could be made a fine place. It could be added to. It could be made one of the neatest little houses in the whole district. And he could make it that. His excitement was difficult now to keep down. "If you and I were living there, Janet, you could look after your mother and I could look after my own folk. What do you say?"

She did not speak.

"I could get it ready for the November term." The quiver of his excitement got the better of him. "Janet?" He put his arms round her shoulders, "Janet," cried his quivering voice through a rush of eager feeling. "isn't that—wouldn't that—be lovely for us? It's the one way, Janet, Janet my own one. Janet!" He crushed her and shook her. "Janet!"

But she did not respond to his wild play. Naturally enough she was overcome. It was a big thing to have come upon her all at once.

She stirred like one in a heavy dream.

"I never thought—I couldn't——"

"I know, I know, Janet, but isn't it the perfect way? I have been thinking over it for weeks. Oh, I have everything worked out."

She was silent.

"Look at it this way," he began eagerly.

"My mother——"

"Yes, I know. But don't you see that this would settle everything? You would not only be able to look after your mother, but you would have me behind you."

"My mother—I couldn't. Not yet. Wait, Tom. Let us wait for a little."

"But what's the good of waiting? Things will not get any better. They'll only get worse. And the house is there. It's there now!"

"My mother—it would kill her."

"But if you're going to wait for your mother, you might wait all your life. For heaven's sake, Janet, let us be sensible."

"Give me time, Tom. Let me think it over." Her voice had the quiet desperation of one under a paralysing burden.

"Yes, but——"

"Please, Tom—don't—make me break down."

He was swiftly moved by that appeal. At the touch of his hands, she got up, turned away, and he heard her controlling the threatening gulps.

Sensitively he stood beside her, giving her time, but as he looked at the dark hillside, a strange withering came upon him like a shivering of cold, an immense, an immortal loneliness.

It made him feel bleak and bitter and yet in some aloof way tender. It passed, leaving him quietened, and as they went along the hillside his voice came back, helping her, for she seemed blinded now and altogether uncertain of her feet.

"Think it over," he said quietly at the corner of the field. "You'll have to let me know soon. Others may be after the house."

Her lip pressed down over her top teeth. "Give me time to——"
He heard her hold her breath. All at once she turned and walked away.

What was it? Could it possibly be her mother? Could it possibly be that it was just her mother?

If she had really desired to go to the cottage would not that at least have been clear? asked the eyes of the midnight hour.

But if she had been overcome by the plan, he reasoned, if she had been so overcome by her own desire to go to the cottage, to get away from her mother, that she couldn't—even—speak of it?

The eyes smiled.

But he refused to give up that immense hope, that fathomless possibility. Janet did keep things to herself, and there might be something in her home life far more desperate than he dreamed.

One day passed, two, three. He would have to see Janet. He must put in for the cottage; and at once or he would be too late. Already perhaps someone had spoken for it, had been to the estate office. His impatience grew fevered.

To go along the road and watch for Janet coming home in the dark was like prying. Normally it would have been a natural thing to do, but it wasn't so for him now. He had hated spying on her before and had sworn he would never do it again.

On the third night he waited by the dark shadow of the hedge beside the field gate. Donald and Janet came along. They stopped exactly opposite him as if at the direction of an invisible stage-manager.

"No, no farther," she said, not quite in her village voice, with the slight anglicising of the High School, a delicate excitement.

"You *are* frightened," said Donald, laughing, enamoured of her.

"Well—but——"

He took her in his arms. Their embrace was long.

"See you to-morrow," he said.

She did not speak. Her feet went quickly and then more firmly along the road. Donald stood for a moment, as if listening to her, then went back to the manse.

Chapter Twelve

The hours, the days, that followed had a bitterness, an inner cruelty that changed his nature, hardened and shaped it blade-sharp.

And the blade was turned on himself. Inwardly it cut and twisted, shearing off the soft adhesions of sentiment, of tender belief, whose existence he now regarded with an excruciating mockery.

Her mother! "My mother—I couldn't." O God!

The enormity of it was almost beyond belief. The sheer wantonness of it.

She was a wanton by nature. He saw it now, not in vague spite, but in the record of every gesture and thought and act. She was a book he had read but whose meaning was only now revealed. On each page, every character was inked in acid.

It was beyond all considerations of anger and hate. She moved beyond them still, the same body, the same grace, only now he understood what moved her, understood it in every twist of secret thought and desire, to the last fibre of her being. She was revealed and he saw her.

"Not yet. Wait, Tom. Let us wait for a little . . . My mother."

Genuinely moved, the break in her voice. Trying to think of her mother. Being moved, thinking of her mother. And behind it—the real fear, that she was not yet on with the new love, not yet certain of the new love, not yet sorry for the old love, clinging to the old love in a clutch of fear, lest the new love be too good to be true.

By God, behind the sentiments and play-acting, behind her nature, behind her very self—what a sheer ruthlessness!

She would have had him, for lack of anyone better. He would do, until the more attractive turned up.

And this is what he had known by an intuition whose implications he had never faced. This was what his premonition had meant. Donald was the test, the crisis, and he had realised it when she mentioned to him—that ironic stroke of fate—that she was going to work at the manse. Not that working at the manse was necessary. It merely created the opportunity which otherwise, by the customs of the tribe, would not normally have presented itself. Though it might—if Donald's girl in the town had disappointed him; and he had looked a bit travel-worn and dejected when trundling in the bicycle at midday!

Perhaps Donald's girl in town had another scheme on of her own! He would be needing sympathy. Well, he had come back to the right place for it!

And it wasn't as if Tom didn't know all about this. Great heaven, what had all his life in Glasgow meant, that life with Bob and Dannie and the girl-hunts, with Dave and Tim and the Winnie Johnstons? It was just the kind of stuff he did know. He had seen it in the open.

"The little bitch—she thinks he's more of a swell!" The lament of the disappointed swain. Everywhere, with an echo of bawdy laughter.

Had he expected something different in the country, with its ancient customs and decencies and loyalties? He had never really been part of the Glasgow scene. He had observed the scene with an extreme clarity, taken part in it as far as need be, but something in him had held back. Thus he had often enjoyed its fun to the highest degree, but with the watcher's enjoyment, with a queer liberating detachment that made the happiness at times almost pure.

This was his scene—*here*, at home. Not Glasgow, known and honest. *This.*

The slashing and cutting was not continuous. He worked with a hard pith, choosing jobs that needed brute energy rather than accuracy or finish. The spasms were intermittent, involuntary cleavages inside him, and his insight was sustained by a light that switched on of itself, coming from God knew where, but holding him remorselessly to the moments of revelation.

But beyond anger, beyond rage and bitter misery, there was this that was happening to his essential nature. He felt the change taking place, and held to the new edge of hard cruelty. Out of the bloody violence to the old simple kindly nature, the new nature was being fashioned. It might have to bide its time, but it would be quite merciless.

Janet made no effort to get in touch with him again. The house could go. The house went. One day he saw new planking by its front wall and Willie Ross, the joiner, coming out of the door, folding his yard-rule.

The first symptom of the new nature showed itself one afternoon when he suddenly found his mother looking at him. He had been standing gazing at a pile of timber for which now he had no immediate use. Or perhaps he hadn't been gazing at it. Anyway he had been standing quite still and, on becoming aware of a presence, glanced round and saw his mother's eyes, her expression. At once, such anger gripped him, so swift a hatred of her prying sympathy that he had to grit his teeth and turn away. She did not speak, and he went into the shop, hissing to himself, emptying his mind.

Work was the sure salvation. Work for the night cometh when no man can work. Tom edged his tools and worked far into the night, disproving that primitive conception of darkness. October came in and the days shortened; the lads drew the blind. The winter session of talk and discussion was on the way.

Tom welcomed them. "Come in and shut the door." He was as ruthless as the next now in keeping out those whom they did not want. His friends noticed the change in him, but found it exhilarating. In argument he was not only more incisive, but full of mockery.

Months before, Dougal had sent him some translations from the works of Voltaire. He had read them at the time, as he read all that Dougal sent him, for he felt that the best way to express his thanks was by showing his appreciation of the matter. And he had liked Voltaire, his seeming innocence in not understanding God's partiality towards some criminal individuals and tribal atrocities among the Jews, his suave irony. To tell the truth, much of what he had read in criticism of the Bible had secretly repelled him. He saw the force of what was written, but was repelled by the spirit of the writer, by what appeared a sheer destructiveness for its own sake. At least, it had often made him uncomfortable. They were like fire-eaters, destroyers, and in their presence whatever was amiable or amusingly irrational in human nature withered. They licked up the purely likeable in man in the best tradition of the avenging Jewish prophets.

But with Voltaire it was quite different. Just as the normal atheistical writer might be compared with the avenging prophet, so might Voltaire, it seemed to Tom, be compared in a certain way with Christ. Tolerance was his cry. No wonder the intolerant church of his day had hated this "lewd atheist". "Voltaire the Mocker", whose plea was "Justice, kindness, compassion, and tolerance".

And did he not make a mess and a battlefield of the Old Testament! Did he not lay about him, with a thoroughness that surpassed all others in the field, with a courtesy that was as subtle as the edge of his sword! There was a leader a man could follow, and feel he was doing something for his own human kind.

Tom could lay about him, too, and use tolerance as a weapon, for he had not a great deal of tolerance for his own kind now.

And he did, producing for the first time his book or pamphlet, reading from it to clinch an argument and leave his listeners in an amazed silence. Sometimes the silence would last for a minute. Even Andie began to feel uneasy, for on the dark Glen road home, heaven alone knew what gargantuan shapes might come at him for such mockery of the great figures of the past of God's world, like Abraham and David. The Psalms of David. By God, it was not canny.

But Alec stretched out an arm for the book. He read, standing by the lamp, others grouped round him.

Tom went on with his work, hearing their snorts, their suppressed gusts of half-frightened laughter. Alec did not read aloud. "Wait a minute," said a voice. "Let me see that," said another. None of them repeated aloud what he read. Not all of it they understood, and the learning which was beyond them served to add a mythical power and wonder, impressive as the Devil's sleight-of-hand, marvels on the edge of the unseen that took the breath with the nearness of an ominous presence.

Alec asked leave to take the book home with him, and enjoyed the sensation of his own courage. There was excitement and to spare. "By George, it's going to be a winter, this!" said Alec leading the way to the road.

Tom shut up shop and went to bed.

Alec would now have plenty of secret ammunition. He would spread the news to add to the turmoil and gaiety of life. Get people by the ears and have a good joke.

Well, why not? What the hell did it matter to Tom? The church and its servants, its idols, its students. It's young Donalds!

He would clear out. Why should he have had to bear what he had borne? Duty to his father? His father did not want him. His father hated him. That had long been clear.

But he would not give in to him any longer. He would stare him back in the eye. He would make him speak, make him say the irrevocable word.

Go back to Glasgow. Or start a business elsewhere. But no— not elsewhere in the country. The childish simplicity of his mind when he had asked Dougal if he would not like to go back to the country! Enough to make one grovel.

God, this sleeplessness!

Up in the morning. Breakfast, and there was his father in the bed with his graven face. That face that looked at him and lifted. That pursuing face. That expressionless, blinded face, with the life behind it coming only to the boundary of the skin, to the eye.

He ignored it, and at evening did not tell of things in the indirect respectful way that had been established. What his father wanted to know he could ask.

His mother, uneasy, tried to cover up the situation with a show of naturalness. Let her!

"When are you starting the harvest?" she asked, though she knew already.

"Monday," he answered shortly.

He saw his father's hand grip above the quilt. It looked ungainly at the end of the gaunt wrist bones.

"Is that a way to answer your mother?" The voice, so long silent, came like a blow.

Tom paid no attention.

"Answer me!" The voice behind a whip.

Tom pushed his plate from him, got up and walked out.

He would not eat there again. Bedamned if he would.

When he returned late that night, he found a glass of milk and a buttered oatcake by his bedside. He tried to eat the oatcake but it stuck in his throat. He drank the milk.

In the morning, he took the oatcake with him in his pocket and did not go into the kitchen for breakfast. Around one o'clock his mother appeared. "Aren't you coming in to your dinner, Tom?"

"No." He did not turn round to look at her.

His mother brought him food, potato soup in a small milk pail, with a couple of whole potatoes and a knuckle of meat from a lean bone in the midst of it, oatcake and a spoon.

When he thought she was going to talk, he frowned intolerantly. As she turned away, he saw her look up towards the road. She would keep guard over the public decencies!

His brain was not working very well; it was tired, and could not be bothered hunting an immediate decision. There was no particular hurry. He was not running away all at once, not before he had said and done a few things.

As he went down to the barn to inspect some harvesting gear, including the scythe which needed resetting, he saw his father standing on the little path by the corner of the oat field. He looked taller than in ordinary life, and somehow appeared to be there by a miracle. As if suddenly he was there!

But Tom knew why he was looking at the field of grain so silently and so fixedly. It was ripe enough for cutting to have started that day.

In the dusk of the evening while Tom was still in this state of mind, Alec and two or three of the lads came drifting into the shop. They were very early and Alec said, "Hallo, I see the bicycles are out?" as if they had intended going a run. Tom replied that they would be in shortly, and Alec said it didn't greatly matter for it would be dark soon now anyway.

While they were talking, William Bulbreac appeared in the door and in an instant Tom knew that Alec had staged his master "argument".

"Ha, so here you all are in the academy of learning," William greeted them in a dry but not unpleasant voice.

145

Tom looked at him, but did not answer, waiting for what might be the business purpose of the visit.

Against this silence, William entered, crooking his hazel staff over his arm. "You don't happen to have a round-headed five-eighths bolt?"

"I believe I have," said Tom, turning to the back wall.

"Yes," said William, looking about him, "so this is where you congregate for the new learning?"

"Do you feel like joining us yourself?" asked Alec in a hearty off-taking voice, a pleasant smile on his face.

"In what branch of knowledge do you think you could instruct me?" inquired William, still looking about him.

"Oh, you'd wonder," replied Alec, with a sideways nod. "You'd wonder."

"I have no doubt," said William. "I have no doubt."

"Is this what you want?" asked Tom, quietly concerned with his business.

"I believe that's it. I believe it's the very thing. Yes. And how much is that?"

"One penny," said Tom.

"A whole penny," declared William. "Well, I wonder if I have that large sum," and from his trousers pocket he took a dark leather purse.

Alec winked to his friend Ian Fraser. William, glancing up, caught them before they could wipe the knowing smile away.

"Thank you," said Tom, taking the penny.

"So this is where you are taught manners and all good things," declared William evenly but getting in his reference to their wink.

"What's wrong with our manners?" Alec asked.

"That you know best yourselves," answered William. "And if all I hear is true, you would be advised as young men to mend them."

"That's going a bit too far," declared Alec, shifting to his other foot. "I don't like to be accused of something without being told what it is." He sounded a bit hurt.

"Do I need to tell you?" inquired William.

"Certainly," answered Alec. "How are we to know if we're not told? That surely would be a miracle."

The word miracle came through the surface talk, stood out with all its biblical implications. William's face, with its short dark-brown beard, concentrated on Alec's. "And do you not believe in miracles?"

"That's not the point. The point is you expected me to perform a miracle."

"I? *You* to perform a miracle?"

"Yes. You said I should know a thing without being told."

"Young man," said William solemnly, "this is not a matter for trifling, not a matter for the use of slyness and deceit. You think I do not see what is going on in your mind. I see it, and it is not a pleasant thing."

"I won't take that," said Alec, "from you or from anyone. I have said nothing that anyone could object to. I did not say one word against you or against anything. I don't mind a fair thing, but——" Alec's voice was rising. He half turned away, restless on his feet.

"You have said nothing, have you? To how many men and young men have you said nothing? Do you think I have not been told of your impious questionings and blasphemy? Do you think the whole countryside is not aware of the kind of talk that goes on here? Do you not think it is my duty as an elder of God's church to search out the evil and destroy it from our midst by showing you the perilous errors of your ways? Will you tell me all that is nothing?"

"That's not the point," mumbled Alec.

"The point! Young man, I know your father, and your mother. I know the parents of you all. They are respectable and godly folk. Have you not even concern for their good name, if you have none for your own immortal souls? Would you not only take the road to hell, but also at the same time bring grief and shame and sorrow upon *them*?"

Alec still managed a small toss to his head, but he had no words. His face was flushed, his body awkward.

Tom had gone back to the drawer from which he had taken the bolt and now, having checked its contents, he closed it. He opened and examined the next two drawers. The clinking sound of the small bits of metal as he raked them over thoughtfully with his fingers became an extreme annoyance to William, whose voice hardened in anger, and rose, and pointedly included Tom in its denunciation. But not until William had wheeled and addressed him personally did Tom face round.

"What are you talking about?" he asked coolly.

"Do you deny it?" cried William.

"Deny what?"

"Do you deny that you make a mock of God's holy Word in this shop? Do you deny it?"

"Certainly," answered Tom. "But if you mean do I question the logic of certain matters as related in the Bible, then I do."

"You! You stand there and say you do? You!"

"Yes, me," said Tom.

"*You* question the logic? The *logic*! *You* set yourself up to question the logic of the inspired word of God?"

"I doubt if it's the inspired word of God."

"You *doubt*?"

"Well, perhaps not. In certain respects I feel sure it's not."

William glared upon him as upon a strange and ominous viper. His voice had already gone husky in consternation. As he glared, his head nodded slowly, the eyes hardened, and a faint "Yes" hissed in his mouth.

The other four lads were stiff as ramrods.

"In certain respects," echoed William, the meaningless words sounding like a preliminary to some dark and devastating rite.

"Yes," answered Tom. "In certain respects I consider the whole account of the creation, the whole Pentateuch, as a Jewish tribal story, self-contradictory in parts and in other parts fairly foul."

"Foul!" William, who was normally a voluble man and distinguished as a fluent elder in prayer, could do little more than breathe the word. Clearly he had never anticipated anything so terrible, so terrifying, as this, and even yet could hardly believe his ears.

"By the Scriptures, nearly all the Kings of Judah were a lecherous blood-thirsty lot, and if they were living now you wouldn't allow them inside your church door. And that's the truth," said Tom, in whom the quiver of excitement was now rising, for he knew why William had come and it angered him bitterly.

"Are you speaking of Solomon and David and——"

"Yes, the whole lot," cried Tom. "Butchery and treachery and idolatry wherever you look. Even Solomon, who had seven hundred wives and three hundred concubines, murdered his brother Adonias because he asked for one of them. Or Ehud, who hid his sword under his cloak and went into the king, saying God had given him an urgent message for him. And when the king

148

stood up to receive the message, Ehud drove his sword into his belly and God approved the act. Or David, who ravished the wife of Uriah and then had her husband slain, this David whom the Scriptures praise!"

"David!"

"Yes, David. Look at his life. Mixed up with evil men and burdened with debt. Didn't he sack the house of Nabal, the king's servant, and a week later marry the widow? Didn't he offer himself to Achish, the king's enemy, and then spread fire and blood over the land of those who were the allies of Achish, sparing neither sex nor age? No sooner is he on the throne than he gets himself new concubines. And these concubines are not enough, but he must also take Bathsheba from her husband and then foully slay the husband. And it's from this Bathsheba, this adulterous woman, that, according to the biblical account, Christ himself is descended. That was David—a man we are told, after God's own heart——"

"Silence!" roared William. "Silence!—you blasphemer. Have you no fear that the Almighty will strike you dead where you stand, stiffen you to one of your own boards, as He stiffened Lot's wife on the plain before the cities of Sodom and Gomorrah, which He destroyed with fire and brimstone?"

"Why did God turn Lot's wife into a pillar of salt, merely because she looked back? Why did the two daughters of Lot then make their own father drunk and commit incest with him, when they had the whole town of Zoar to take men from? And the way the two angels behaved before the town was destroyed, and the way Lot offered to make prostitutes of his own daughters——"

"Silence, I say!"

"It's all very well shouting 'Silence'. But can you answer?"

William answered. William thundered. But no sooner had he made one of his biblical allusions—and it was impossible for him to proceed far without doing so—than Tom took him up. Tom's voice was louder than he knew. It rose piercing and intolerant. Now that the issue was joined beyond redemption, he hit out, not blindly, but with the will, the desire, to pierce and destroy.

They went through the Old Testament like a furious whirlwind, Tom picking up Abraham and his wife Sarah in Egypt, Moses married to an idolater's daughter and writing his books ("how? on what?—and beyond the Jordan when we are told he never crossed the Jordan!"). the just man Jacob ("who deceived his father Isaac and robbed Laban, his father-in-law!"), the Hebrews and the Midianites, the harlot Rahab ("ay, but who is descended from her through incest and adultery?"), Joshua and the sun and moon that stood still in the middle of the day ("why the moon in the middle of the day?"), Jonah and the belly of the whale ("do you know how far it was from Joppa to Nineveh?—four hundred miles! *four hundred!*").

They shouted together, Tom trying to pin William to that which he had already overleapt and proceeded beyond in his righteous wrath, one now with his human wrath.

Alec stood in a hypnotic bliss transcending anything he had hitherto experienced.

Boys came down the green and gathered gaping round the door. Elderly passers-by paused and drew near.

Backwards, in loops and circles, whirled the combatants, the thundering Goliath, and the pale-faced piercing David, until they landed in the garden of Eden.

"The tree of the knowledge of good and evil!" cried Tom. "Why should God want to keep knowledge from man? Why? . . ."

" . . . of good and evil, so that man would know good from evil, and choose the good and repel the evil—repel the evil. Do you hear me? Repel the evil—repel the evil from your evil heart, you . . ."

"But He didn't! He didn't want to give them the chance! And without . . ."

" . . . and not nurse it like a viper. But you have chosen the evil, and I say unto you that God's hand will come in its wrath and smite you, as it smote . . ."

"And without the knowledge of good and evil, what would man be? He would be no higher than the brute beast. Why is it a brute beast?—because it still cannot tell good from evil. If God . . ."

" . . . And the Devil took the shape of a serpent, for the Devil can take any shape, even your shape—even your shape, you impious blasphemer, and the Devil spoke to them saying, 'Ye shall not surely die', but we know that at that moment not only did evil enter their hearts, but death, *death* . . ."

"But it doesn't say it was the Devil. The account says it was a serpent, a 'beast of the field', and who ever heard a serpent speak? Did you? Did you ever hear a serpent speak?" cried Tom in shrill mockery.

But William was now not listening to Tom. He was preaching the wrath of God and damnation upon the sinner. Approaching his climax, he rose to visionary and prophetic heights: "For I see the serpent within you, I see its evil coils twisting in your body and in your brain, and I see that you have delivered yourself to the serpent, and I say unto you that if you do not repent, and cast yourself down into the ashes of abasement and humility, and pray to the Almighty to be delivered of the slime and horror of the serpent, I say unto you, *and it will come to pass*, that you will be devoured of the serpent and your final end will be the eternal torment and punishment of the damned."

Folk knew William, and sometimes one or other might smile behind his back, for they felt in their hearts that William wanted to be an important man yet had not within him that sure authority of body and spirit which is recognised in silence by all men. But now William had risen to the height of prophecy which moved them in the secret and fearful places, and they were silent in a deep stillness. Through this stillness went a sudden shiver of movement.

Tom, apprehending the effect that had been created, with eyes blazing on William, shouted: "I can look after myself. I'm not afraid of your Jewish tribal God or of any mythical serpent. 'Almighty!' you cry. You do not even know the meaning of the word. If you did, you would know that there are things even the Almighty cannot do."

A movement went through those at the door.

"What things?" asked William, almost in a small voice now, waiting for the final blasphemy as a man might wait at an execution.

But Tom was far beyond metaphysical consideration of absolute opposites and cried, "He couldn't do what even you could do. You can commit suicide. God the all-mighty can't."

There was a shuffling of feet in the doorway. Tom turned and saw his father before him.

The grey face, the grey beard, the blazing eyes, the silent pursuing face—it had come at last. The power of the father created in the image of God. The tribal power, the unearthly power. Each felt it, and Tom could not move.

The father gazed upon his son with a fixity of expression more terrible than all words. In silence he groped for William's staff. He took a slow step nearer to his son, and, in the short pause that followed, the intention of chastisement gathered in a concentration horrible to behold. Then the hand with the staff went up, not quickly, but with deliberation. It rose, until it rose high above his head, then all in a moment the stiffness of the arm slackened, the stick fell, bouncing off Tom's chest, the arm wavered down, the body sagged, and with a deep soft grunt it collapsed upon itself, pitching forward slightly before Tom's feet.

No-one moved for what appeared a long time. Then William was on his knees. "Adam?" But Adam did not answer. William stretched him out. The unwinking eyes stared upward, glittering. There was no breath in the mouth. No movement in the heart.

Through the door came Tom's mother. She gave a wild look at her son and saw the outstretched body. In a moment she knew her husband was dead and, crouching by his side, her head falling low over him and lifting, she let out a high keening cry.

"We'll carry him down," said William gravely to those about him.

"Will I go—for the doctor?" muttered Alec in a low desperate voice.

"Go," commanded William.

They carried the body out, and the mother, weeping and keening, ran before them. It was growing dark: Alec took one of the two bicycles which were now leaning against the outside wall. Those who had hired them did not venture in to pay, and Tom was left standing alone in the shop.

Chapter Thirteen

The Philosopher withdrew his eyes from that far distant scene to the world about him, and in his sight were the bushes, the tumbling curves of the close-cropped grass, glittering specks of mica in a grey boulder, the yellow broom and the wild roses below him, and, lifting to the blue skies, the wide uninhabited spaces of the air.

The shepherd had probably seen him for he was coming slowly along the hillside. They would have a talk together in the freedom of the day and that would be pleasant. The Philosopher's eyes fell on his home and steadied there under the compulsion of the past now upon him like a dream.

And those days leading up to and immediately following the burial of his father had now a dreamlike quality about them, as if lifted out of an older age, wherein folk moved under the hand of destiny.

His father's body was laid out and coffined in "the room", where he himself had slept. There was a small place, a closet, between the two main rooms, which his mother now cleaned up for a shake-down bed. But he did not sleep there, and when he withdrew it was to a bed of shavings in the shop.

In accordance with custom, folk came and kept watch through the night. William Bulbreac was like one who had a special mission laid upon him, and prayed fervently, and read in the Bible, and read aloud the metrical version of one of the Psalms of David before leading in its singing. There was food and drink for all, and to this his mother attended with hospitality, rising through the sadness and the sorrow, the keening memories of the dead, of a just and a kind and an upright man, remembered now by the poor widow whom he had helped, rising through the hidden good deeds to offer food and drink to those who watched with her through the dark hours of death, to press food and drink upon them.

And because of the way in which death had come, there was an added fervour in devotion, a deeper feeling amongst them, a warmth of sorrow, an apprehension of God's grace with the terror of God's grace around it, like a strong hand around a fragile cup, a hand that had only to close in imperceptible motion for the cup to be shattered.

Outside this community of worship what was there in the world, the world of strife and vainglory and fleeting material things? Outside was the unreality that passed like a dream, like a coloured bubble that floated and burst upon the thin air, like a tale that was told and died in the mind. And there—there—stalking through that outside world, seeking whom he may devour, subtil as the serpent, crashing like a dark beast through forests, the Devil, the destroyer, the blasphemer.

They greeted Tom quietly, not looking at his face, on a gentle even tone, expressing their sorrow, one by one, at the first meeting. When he tried to avoid them, they made no effort to meet him. They came and they went, and he knew that they thought him cold and unrelenting, stone-faced and hard-hearted.

The burial service was held at the house in the usual way. Some of the old friends of the dead, like Sandy and Norman, gathered in the room around the coffin, while the bulk of the mourners, all men, crowded around the door outside, their hats in their hands as the minister's great voice rose so that God would hear and look down upon them and into their hearts.

In the kitchen, with the widow of the dead man, were gathered a few women of her own age, her nearest friends, to keep her company and sustain her in this last trial. They were apart from the men, in their own world of women and women's ways and thoughts.

Tom bore up, expressionless, under the long prayer and under the minister's spoken thoughts that came at him like spears. For he was not spared. Not that the minister spoke at him directly. In the house of death the minister spoke to God, interceding for His servant, who had borne his trial with a patience and long suffering, a belief in God's goodness and in His inscrutable wisdom, that was as an example set before them, even unto the last moment of his mortal life when, his powers failing and the darkening upon him, he yet strove to counter the ways of evil and the tongue of blasphemy. For the tongue was deceitful above all things and most desperately wicked. Yet behind all was the saving power of God's grace, the promise of redemption, even for the most abandoned and depraved, through the suffering of the Lord Jesus Christ.

When the body was buried, Norman and Sandy and one or two others came and shook hands with Tom. But not many came, for Tom did not want them and they sensed this.

By the time he had come back into the middle of the village he was alone. Most of the blinds were still drawn, and he walked past the silent houses like one in a nightmare, visible to the unseen, so that he had difficulty in keeping his feet to an even pace on the deserted way.

When he came by the shop and house where dark-clad figures had so recently gathered and slowly moved away in the black river of death, silence lay on roof and ground. The sky was overcast and from the stillness of the autumn day descended a sadness that pressed against the eyeballs. He stopped at his shop door and looked about him. No life moved. Entering, he locked the door quietly and stood for a moment before the window. But the blinded light hurt as though his eyeballs had got distended. The sadness was of uncountable Sabbaths, and the silence was the silence of the head that is bowed after the last whisper.

Turning from the window, he went and sat behind a kitchen dresser not yet finished, and leaned his back and head against the wall. His body slumped in a weak quivering and a faint moan passed his lips. He sank into a slumberous state, his mouth fallen open, his breathing heavy. Down in the depths, his mind slowly thinned to a clarity so fine that all was seen.

The outcast moving apart from his own people, wandering in desolate ways through the horror of silence. The communal warmth in life and death. Cast out, bitterness in his soul, not giving in, cast out. And this he comprehended not in thought but in visual picture, seeing faces and eyes and the massed movement of bodies going away, seeing them with his own eyes—and seeing himself going from them, cut adrift like a criminal, white-faced upon his own empty road.

Voices coming up from the house. The women going home.

". . . Poor woman. She's had a hard struggle."

"Ay, she was not helped much. There was a hard heart in him and a flinty face. I don't know how he could have done it."

"What could you expect—thinking as he thinks? The like of it has never been known in this place."

"He was bold. I don't know how he could have done it. A judgement will come on him . . ."

They spoke mournfully, awe in their voices, but with a core of hardness, of anger.

They had described his face exactly as he felt it: gone thin and hard, the air whitening it. He knew the women well—decent kindly mothers of grown-up families.

His face creased of itself in a furtive humour. Then he groaned. God, he was tired.

Soft footsteps, heavy, padding round the shop. The knob rattled. "Are you in, Tom?" His mother's hushed voice.

He did not answer. No women ever accompanied a funeral to the cemetery. She would be wondering where he had gone, wondering and fearing.

When he thought she would be back in the house he got to his feet, dusted his Sunday clothes, cautiously unlocked the door. Then he walked down to the house.

She was not in the kitchen, and through the silence he lifted his voice: "Are you there?" The table was spread for guests. The iron soup pot steamed above the fire. To invite relatives, close friends, the old men who had to go a long way, to partake of a meal after the funeral was the honourable custom. He should have spoken to the men and taken them home. Sandy had a long distance to walk, nearly three miles, and half of it was a steep hill. Round the meal elements of the community gathered, and where death had been, life started again. "Are you there?" he shouted. Going to the door, he met her coming in, breathless as if she had been running. She gazed at him. "Oh," she said. "Where were you?"

"Nowhere," he answered, turning back into the kitchen.

She followed him and they both stood at a loss.

"You have brought—no-one?" she asked, turning her eyes on him.

"No," he answered, breaking out of his stance.

Her eyes wandered over the soup plates in a dumb stupid way. She could not realise the emptiness that had come upon the house, its desertion.

They were forsaken.

"Why—didn't you?"

"I didn't get much chance," he replied.

It was no excuse, not even a lie; the bitterness of truth was in it. Yet not the whole truth, for, had they been asked, in duty they would have come. But how could he have asked? Couldn't she see?

But she couldn't see anything. Her small eyes were round and stared as if they were blind. She leaned with her left hand on the table, overcome it seemed by the sudden weight of her body. Her head bowed and she drew in a shuddering breath. Standing there she wept in harsh whining sounds.

As he was going out the door, she called to him: "Tom, don't leave me."

He muttered that he would be back in a minute.

When he came back, she was composed and spoke in a quiet voice. "Sit in to your food."

She pretended to eat to keep him company. He forced the food down his throat. They never spoke. At night his bed was ready in the room where his father's body had been laid out.

The humiliation of that night, the moments of ugly abject fear, when the mind became as the mind of a child, acquired knowledge of no avail, futile and swept away. At twenty-three youth can be more positive than age, but there is a sensitiveness, a capacity for pain and horror, for sheer formless apprehension, that age forgets.

Next day was Sunday, for the father had died on the Wednesday and been buried on Saturday.

Tom was not going to church. When his mother realised it, she sat down. So this, too, had come upon her.

"I don't want to go to church—to be preached at," he said in a cold voice.

She did not speak. But presently she asked in a quiet pleading way, "Will you not go, Tom?"

"No, I'm not going," he answered and walked out.

He saw her set off alone.

The sermon preached that Sunday was of extraordinary power. It had a whelming effect on the people. Even the young men who had heard Tom's arguments were overborne and glad to be able to withdraw in silence into the old ways, secretly recognising the luck by which they had not been found out. Clearly William Bulbreac had reported the matter of his argument with Tom, and the minister, awakened to the profound need of denunciation, had prepared himself for battle and no mercy. Even years afterwards, when a man might speak of that sermon in composure, he found it difficult to remember with any precision what had been said. But the incommunicable effect was remembered powerfully, as of a spear of light stirring the dark ancient sinful roots of being. Each man in the congregation, each woman, knew in the secrecy of the heart how he and she had sinned. And God knew all. God had known the sins of men mentioned in the Old Testament. That was not hidden. That was made clear. At each moment man was on the brink of eternity. At each moment, at this moment now, he could draw back—as the men of old, who had sinned, had drawn back, and been forgiven, and had even found favour in the sight of God, whose mercy was infinite. At this moment, now. But for the one who did not draw back, stiff-necked in his pride, treacherous as the serpent in his blasphemy, for that one—Satan waited in the abyss.

As the preacher warmed, he did not merely argue. He spoke in parables and drew pictures, pictures of gargantuan myth that came from inside them and lived upon the air.

They saw the coils of the serpent.

In all ages, men of all creeds had seen the serpent, had used the serpent as a sign. Why?

The devil had only needed to speak once through the mouth of the serpent. Never again. Once was enough, because from that speaking and man's disobedience, sin had come upon us and death. The coils of the serpent—the coils of sin—the glistening constricting coils of living death.

To fulfil his further purpose, the Devil had to speak only through the mouths of men. Many say they have seen the Devil. Many have described him, in all tongues, in great poems, in terrible tragedies. Great and learned men, Christian and heathen alike. But you may not have seen him, and I may not have seen him, but—we have heard him speak. We have heard him speak—and we have seen what has befallen.

Mounting, step by step, the preacher came at last to his climax of denunciation, each terrible strophe beginning, "Woe unto ye" ... And because of one metaphor which he used, it was to the secret mind thinking of Tom—and which mind was not, even while also thinking of himself?—as if the serpent had uncoiled itself inside Tom and had sunk its invisible jaws in his throat.

When his mother returned from the sermon Tom saw that she was defeated at last, and broken. The small lids of her eyes were red. She had been weeping in church. They would all have heard her weeping. The smothered sound of her weeping amid the awful silence of the congregation.

He had attended to the soup pot—yesterday's plethora of broth heated up—but his mother sat down, she was so weary.

Tom dished two plates of broth.

"Won't you take something?" he asked.

"No," she answered, gazing at the fire. She sighed, and suddenly began weeping. "I did my best," she cried, to no-one. "I could do no more." She wept, and with the quivering breaths her stout body twisted and shook. The thin sounds she made were sounds of pure anguish.

Tom deliberately ate through his soup, got up, and went out.

When he came back in the evening, she was sitting where he had left her. In the deep gloom of the kitchen, she had the forsaken look of the dead. But she stirred when she heard him, and got up, and went silently about her household tasks.

That night he heard her from his bed, to which he had retired early, making strange broken speaking sounds. By a queer intuition he knew she would not take it upon herself to speak to God. And the Bible was not for her. She was speaking to the invisible No-one.

Next day he started on the scythe. She came and worked behind him, gathering and binding the sheaves. The weather was still dull and looked like breaking, but no rain fell.

He worked into the darkness, stooking the sheaves, while she went home to prepare supper. None called that day. Towards noon on the following day it started to rain. When he had set up the sheaves she had bound, he hung his scythe in the barn and presently went in for food. When he had eaten, she broke the silence, asking, "Have you been to the shop?"

As he opened the shop door a draught blew in his face from the window, which had been smashed with stones. The stones had also damaged some small things displayed on the shelf before the window. He picked up the stones, looked at them, stared through the vacant window with incredulity and a slow gathering and narrowing of understanding and hate.

While he was nailing boards across the window outside, the two women, whose voices he had overheard on Saturday, came down past him. He kept his back to them and they did not speak.

After their visit his mother started sighing at odd moments in a vacant way. What mind she had was getting clouded over. This sighing sadness would become her mode of life henceforth. Mindless and sighing and sad. All at once she was aged, a dumb beast, the quickness and the bustle gone.

Before he went to bed, she said, "Alec is getting on."

"Alec? What Alec?"

"Alec Wilson. They say he will live now."

"Live?"

"Did you not know?" she said sadly. "When he was going for the doctor, he ran into Peter Grant's dog. The dog had to be destroyed. But Alec is getting on, it seems. His collarbone is broken."

The news appeared old to her. She turned away from it.

But the news for Tom had an edge of infernal humour. For the first time in many days he smiled, sitting on his bed. Then a thought struck him and he went out and up to the shop. The bicycles were always wheeled into a corner which he had built for them, with wooden racks to hold the front wheels. There was only the one bicycle. The other would have been badly damaged and cleared off the road. No-one had brought it back.

And Alec—he had not asked about him. He dare not go and ask. Alec's parents would . . .

He let the thought die, with the infernal humour.

The wind was strong, with stinging raindrops. It was pitch dark. He turned his face to the hill path, but up there the wind was a mournful howl, ridden by hounds. Beyond the byre it staggered him, and he had to feel with his feet for the path. He thought of Janet, and before he knew it a yell of defiance at the hounds had ripped from him, a harsh tearing yell that emptied and silenced him. His body, like a thin husk, shuddered in the rain-spitting cold wind.

Shortly after daybreak the wind died and by the forenoon the sun was shining. The standing corn and the fallen stooks were bone dry from the high wind, and after an early midday meal they were setting out for the harvest field when a shout made them turn round. The town policeman was coming from the road towards the shop and as they looked he raised his right arm.

No policeman had been stationed in the village since the liquor licence was taken from it many years ago. At intervals, a policeman from the town met here a policeman from the village of Cardin, which lay inland beyond the Glen where two roads merged in the one road to the west. They could sometimes be seen standing by the roadside talking together, often for nearly an hour, before they parted and returned each his own way. Only once or twice in all Tom's memories had the police had any official duties to perform in the Glen. Crime, as the word was understood in the cities, was unknown.

The uniform and the commanding arm sent a shiver over Tom's body, and it was only when he heard his mother's broken intake of breath that he got his legs to move. He went to meet the policeman, who, before opening his mouth, gave him a long and searching look.

"Are you Tom Mathieson?"

"Yes."

"Is that your bicycle lying by the end of the post office?"

"Yes."

"Why haven't you removed it?"

"I—I was going to. The harvest—we're at the harvest." He could hardly speak.

"It's strange that you didn't retrieve it?"

"I'll go just now," said Tom, starting away from the policeman.

"Wait a minute," called the policeman, who joined Tom and proceeded with him towards Peter Grant's shop.

"How did it happen that the bicycle is there?"

"My father—a fellow used it to go for the doctor. He ran into a dog."

"What fellow?"

"Alec Wilson, from the Heights of Taruv."

"I see. Your father was ill and he was going for the doctor?"

"Yes."

The policeman gave a sidelong considering look at Tom. He obviously knew the whole story. That there was no case could now be taken as corroborated.

"And what do you mean by leaving your damaged goods on another man's property?"

Tom did not answer.

"Have you nothing to plead?"

"My father died," said Tom.

As the policeman looked at him again, a cold anger tautened Tom's muscles.

"Did Grant object?" he asked.

"That's my business," answered the policeman.

"It's all right," said Tom.

He breasted the village with the policeman, and folk stood back into doors and at windows. The front wheel of the bicycle was buckled. Tom lifted the frame over his head and bore it away on his shoulder, the policeman, with authoritative legs apart, looking after him.

He saw his mother waddle down from the road as he hove in sight. Locking the bicycle in the shop, he went to the harvest field, and she joined him there. For a while the physical effort of swinging the scythe brought out sweat on his weakened body.

In the days that followed he grew thin as an eel. Had he not known this himself, his mother's actions would have told him. There were eggs and meat when previously there had not been. But he ate without relish. Sometimes a fresh egg had a repulsive taste, slimy as mire and tainted with a certain midden flavour. That this was purely imaginary he knew, but that did not make it the less difficult to swallow the stuff. His mother remained solemn and resigned, and the way she had of sighing at an unexpected moment got on his nerves. Even her half-hidden concern for his bodily well-being irritated him. And when he had worked himself stupid with fatigue, it often happened that it was then his brain came abnormally alive with a feverish and ferocious activity.

It was easiest to bear these mental bouts when he was completely alone, shut up in the barn or shop, for, unobserved, he could gnash his teeth or make his body writhe against clenched muscles, and so free himself from the momentary but appalling stress, which came upon him often without any very clear conscious cause.

Sometimes, too, a quite simple affair, like that of Peter Grant and the policeman, would induce an extreme violence of agitation and desire for revenge. Even if he worked out that probably Peter Grant was not to blame for the disgrace of the policeman's visit, it made no difference. Perhaps the policeman had observed the bicycle, questioned Peter Grant, got the whole story, and promptly acted on his own. But Tom saw into Peter Grant's mind. Saw that he wanted the bicycle removed—and knew why, knew the wordless effect he would create on others, on himself, and on the atheist Tom. Oh, he knew!

But of all these early and horrible bouts, the most horrible occurred on the hill-top where he had gone to spy on the manse. The craving to go had come upon him quite suddenly, but with such overpowering force that he not only had to give in to it but in a moment was actuated by a feeling of ruthless cunning.

When he got amongst the hollows of the hills, he ran, grabbing at the heather, pulling himself up, his heart pounding, a slaver at his mouth, not waiting a moment except now and then to look warily around, lest he be late for what he had to see.

It was October and Donald must have gone back to college. But Tom felt he had not gone back.

Tom had just flung himself down when he saw Janet come out from the manse, walk a little way as if going to the village, pause, and then circle back until she was swallowed by the outhouses. Round the off gable-end came Donald and set out for a walk—that circled back, until he, too, was swallowed by the outhouses.

Half an hour later, Janet emerged from the outhouses and continued on her way to the village.

It was simple. So inevitable that it happened often. Nothing particularly miraculous in coming upon it so aptly.

And then the bout got him.

It turned him on his back, and first his body heaved from the right shoulder and his heels, then rocked to the left shoulder and heaved again into the quivering arch, his head crushing back and thrashing from side to side. There was no particular pain; hardly even anguish in the mind; nothing but this terrible straining to get away from himself, from knowledge, from all he knew. Out of it his voice groaned and cried, "God, O God"; crushing and emptying himself, slaying the thing that was in him, that was himself.

When it passed, he slumped over on his face, in an exhaustion so complete that it was a total forgetting, like sleep or death.

But nothing was forgotten for very long. The mood might change, but beneath it, even under long spells of numb indifference, there persisted that which did not change. The lower the form of life the more difficult it is to kill. The persistence was of that kind.

When it seemed his body could hardly bear up much longer to a day's work, when already he knew that its processes were slowing down, and that he was covering this with what might look like a calculated indifference, a deliberate unconcern, he was assaulted by a new and more terrible enemy.

Life does not get slashed at every exit without wanting to hit back. Self-protection is in the bite of the adder, in its poisonous fangs.

Tom began to see what a fool he had been, what a soft self-destroying fool, not to have hit out where it would hurt most fatally. He had not bitten where he might have bitten, not eaten where he might have eaten.

This smouldering vengefulness grew, and like every new mood, each fresh departure of his mind, it circled ultimately around Janet.

He remembered her quiescent moments, the passive fall of her body in his arms.

He knew what that meant now.

As he sat in the dark of the shop, his face narrowed.

He had not been ignorant of what it meant then. But *then* he had been under the glow of love, of responsibility, of tenderness, of the future, of wonder, of beauty, of the customs man had created in weakness and illusion under the guise of hope and social continuance and other futile little dodges and schemes for containing the earnest and the simple so that the cunning might wallow.

He saw it now very clearly.

He saw it through days and nights. The torment grew. Vision slipped from the past into the present, into nights ahead.

Donald was gone.

He had only to meet Janet and appear to be as he had been—quietened a little by the death of his father. His father's death would account for the interruptions in their meetings. Janet must be wondering about him, knew how everyone's hand was against him. She would be waiting, waiting for his next move, her conscience guilty. Could she, with her guilty conscience, desert him, too? She could—that would be her secret and quite remorseless intention—but she could not do it with a hard indifference, brutally. That was not her nature. Her nature was soft. She would want to reconcile him, to part from him in sadness, in tragic sadness, so that her own happiness would thereafter be the greater. Poor Tom—he had been so good to her!

Then it was up to him to play-act as she did. And he would do it, not in obvious ways, not the silly ways of the outraged male, with his rights and wrongs and petty dignities, but with the cunning of the serpent, the "subtil serpent". He would be so good to her, trusting her so naturally, looking forward to some vague future—nothing urgent to frighten her—that her sense of guilt would swell to a suffocating cloud. She might begin to try to tell . . . but it would be child's play heading that off, turning it into some halting thought about her mother. Not that she would tell him directly about Donald. If he knew Donald, then it was certain she had nothing very definite to hold to—beyond their meetings, their passionate meetings. She would want to hint at some change in her feelings, to suggest that perhaps it had all been a mistake. But she wouldn't be able to do that, not if he handled her properly. One night, perhaps the first night, she would collapse, she would give in, particularly if it followed a bout with her mother.

He would make no mistake then.

Such thought lived on itself in endless involution. Its subtlety at times partook of an extreme clairvoyance, so that again he did not think his thought so much as see it in living picture. There was no hesitancy, no movement, no colour in the face or light in the eye, of which Janet was capable, voluntarily or involuntarily, which he could not observe as clearly as if she sat before him; indeed more clearly, because this solid breathing semblance of her held no uncertainty for him, no doubt. He could not only see her face; he could feel her flesh by touch. Nothing was hidden from him; there was nothing that could not take place.

Now it so happened by some curious chemistry of the body that the more tired he was from labour and the deeper his exhaustion, the greater, the more feverish was his responsiveness to this secret visioning of the physical Janet. Almost before he began to think of her he became excited, not only physically but with an elated, poisonous, mental excitement.

All this did extreme violence to his nature. Under his exhaustion, it tore the core of his nature apart, caused a slow disintegration in its fibres, and the fleshly saps that oozed over and into it were poisonous ejections, slow-dissolving and vile.

In moments of recoil he was overcome, annihilated, by this vileness. Then the original Janet, the Janet of his love, withdrew to a distance so remote that she passed from him and could not hear his cries.

But he drew back into himself, and presently his purpose reformed; so the cycle started again, the deadly disintegration of the core proceeded, and the vileness began to spread outward, slowly, over the face of all things.

So concentrated now was this inner life that he was aware only in a dumb heedless way of what went on round about him. His responses to his mother were automatic and perfected. When she tended to some excess of gloom or anxiety, he ignored her, and she quietened in the fatal animalistic way natural to her.

All the same, he was aware—and no doubt his mother in her fashion was aware—that if pressed too far, by only a hair's breadth, he would move or hit with an evil swiftness. Beneath the surface, living there all by itself, the stroke was ready.

Donald, for example, troubled his thought rarely. But once, when he intruded, and was about to smile, with male knowledge in his eye, Tom, in an arc of movement quicker than thought, knifed him. In no time the image had passed, and Tom had forgotten him. He hated Donald, but Donald at this time did not matter. Revenge over Donald, over all life that moved, lay in Janet.

To recall some of the night hours became unbearable. Their clarity was too stark; the night world—a whole world in itself—was too utterly vivid with movement of passion and evil, with hellish triumph—ebbing into paralysing defeat.

He began to dread the lack of sleep, not in active fear but in a bitter smouldering anger.

One early November afternoon, in a small rain, he went up the hillside to the mountains, to get away from himself and his surroundings, to breathe the high free air that might induce sleep. As he climbed upward, his breath quickened distressingly and his heart began pumping with audible thuds. His weakened condition amused rather than alarmed him. To have to give himself time, like an old man, had its oblique humour. He went on until he saw the mountains. On his way back his legs started to tremble, and, coming among the juniper bushes, he had to rest.

Looking about him for the least wet spot, he saw the bushes and the green grass and the passage-ways that ran secretively. They did not look back at him but were there in their own slyly passive way. A green veil was over the hidden life, but only just over it. Their patience was friendly but watchful.

All at once a delicate mood of renewal touched him, ran over his body and into his mind. The earth, that old patient mother. But beneath the surface—the hidden heartbeat, that which invigorated and renewed, that which drew his body secretly. His eyes glanced hither and thither.

A craving came upon him to lie down and give himself to the earth, to sink far down, to sleep.

He sat under a bush and at once knew release. The scent of the bushes, of the grass, of the mouldering earth, assailed his nostrils like intimate scents of one long forgotten. He stretched out his legs into the wet grass and lay full length, the small mountain rain falling softly. Then Janet came beside him, wordless, full length beside him, that semblance of her which he had made his own, drawing the earth into and about her, usurping the earth.

There was a moment of passion when the bushes and the grass and all the hillside and the air dizzied into darkness.

When he was a small boy, perhaps about ten, he had gone nutting in the wooded burn which wanders down the steep slope of the Glen just beyond Taruv. Johnny Munro, the blacksmith's son, a boy of about thirteen, had been with him. Johnny said that the best trees were near the top of the wooded stretch. There the nuts came out of the clusters a deep dark brown and had a rich flavour—"a whisky taste", Johnny called it. They wandered, and filled their pockets, and cracked the nuts with their teeth, and ate them during long hours on a Saturday in October. When their jaws ached from cracking the nuts, Johnny led the way clear of the last trees to the ruins of an old croft house, where they each searched out a suitable boulder and began cracking the nuts with a stone. Nettles grew about this deserted place and all kinds of weeds and rushes, and here and there, so that you had to watch where you put your feet, were broken iron pots and bottles, rusty, bottomless tin pails, and other bits of household gear. Tom did not care much for the place, and when he got, besides, a faint but filthy old human smell, as if his foot had trodden in something, he cared for it even less.

Still, this was adventure, and his senses were alert.

"Do you get a smell?" asked Johnny with his good-natured grin.

"Yes."

"Do you know what they call this place?"

"No."

"The Devil's Croft," said Johnny. And while Tom was looking about him so that everything became very clear and vivid, Johnny added, repeating what he had been told, "Every place has its Devil's Croft."

No doubt after that he had dreamed about the place. Anyway, in his vision he saw it in a still twilight, dominated by a beast. Except for its full face, he saw this beast with an extreme clearness. It was about four to five feet high as it sat on its hind quarters—he never saw it standing—exactly like a cat. Its hair was rat-coloured, about two inches long, lying smoothly against the body, fine in texture and rather thin. The sweep from the root of the tail up to the back of the neck was a perfect arch, like a young full-grown cat's on a large scale. And this sweep made a smaller arch up over the head, and continued the line down the side of the face in a sort of sleek whorl. The beast was very slightly turned away from him.

The emotions of this beast seemed to find expression in the tail, which was its most remarkable feature, for it was not only long and supple, but had two tufts of hair, bushy tufts, equally spaced between tip and root. When the tail slowly whipped from side to side—and it did this after being stared at for a little while—it brushed the earth, passing over broken nettles, rusty tins, flattened stones, while the tufts gathered about them some of the old filthy stuff which Tom had smelt.

Not only did this vision begin to come back to Tom now, but he became haunted, in these moments of extreme horror and disintegration, by the fear that the beast would turn its face, and look at him.

Often in bed moments of such sheer exhaustion beset him that he lay full stretch on his back, arms extended by his sides, face tilted upward, in the posture of one laid out in death. Thought and feeling would lift from him and pass away. With returning self-consciousness his hands, flat open, would in an aloof way slowly pass over his thighs and find them smooth as marble. Sometimes they would fall limp, before continuing their strange journey up over the cage of the chest. There his open hands and forearms crowded together, grown large as ungainly wings.

Yet through all these experiences there remained the final core that was himself, something beyond his moods and visions, beyond his nature even. It was a small core, sometimes little more than a cry, but it remained—until at last it, too, began to be menaced.

He entered the next terrible phase of his suffering.

Images now did not require to be seen completely. Before a thought had time to form he was already wrestling with it, fighting it back. One night, for example, his imagination produced the figure of a man before his bed, a few paces distant. This figure, cut off at the chest, was wearing a dark morning coat. It no doubt had a face, but Tom's eyes dare not rise above the bare hands, which were hanging loosely, nearly touching, in front of the dark coat. A city man's figure. Quite normal. Yet there was such menace in its quietude as no physical horror in hell could equal. It was dark, and Tom's eyes were shut, of course.

During these days—days and nights that were to Tom two aspects of the one eternity—no-one came to the shop on business. Boys now and then lurked in the distance, with courage not equal to their desire for a bicycle. Their parents had doubtless spoken to them with threats of a punishment beyond the breaking of collarbones. The old Gaelic image of eternity was the wheel made by the serpent when it put its tail in its mouth.

But nothing now could bring Tom back. He did not go near the shop in daylight hours lest the boys might venture to the door. To avoid meeting a human being—and an occasional one, male or female, did call on his mother—he would have walked any distance.

The time came at last, when, even in the daylight, he began to be afraid lest the ultimate centre in him, that which had been Tom as child, as boy, as young man in Glasgow, that continuing essence, that known cry, would itself get broken and be no more.

Lost now in an immensity so vast that it transcended terror's utmost bound, an immensity that could not be inhabited, that could not be borne, from which one turned to escape, running in madness, while the immensity swelled behind, and above, and slowly but surely reached over to engulf.

Again, his last hope was Janet.

One Friday afternoon—it must have been late in November—he was up on the hillside. The day was overcast but quite mild. One of those days that have in them a thought of spring. Small birds were chirping, whisking about in short energetic flights. Towards the Taruv wood the air was alive with rooks, blown about like burnt-black fragments from a fire. A faintly perceptible blueness as of smoke lay against distant land and hillside.

He would have to see Janet.

The very nature of the day affected him with such need for urgency that it excited him and sapped his strength.

There might not be much more time, not if any strength and direction were to be kept.

But now it was going to be a struggle, an immense deliberate struggle. For he knew the weakness that swirled in where strength had been.

He might want to throw himself on Janet, to weep, unable, utterly unable, to struggle. The very thought of it could make him tremble now in bitterness, could make the tears wet his eyes.

But, oh, if that happened it would be worse than time's last nightmare; it would be the end. Coming away from Janet's pity would be a degradation too deep ever to rise out of.

That would not happen. He would fight her, physically and brutally fight her, to get strength out of her. There was no other conceivable hope for him.

He would fight her, to get the primeval strength out of her which his body and soul needed. Not sexual lust now, but the last lust of life itself, life that needed the act of sexual lust in which to be renewed. And because his need was so desperate, he knew that it would seek satisfaction of itself, whatever emotions were brought into play by his own fevered being.

He worked out his scheme in the end with sure coolness and considerable cunning. It was Friday, the night on which they used to meet, and he had come away deliberately to plan for this night.

He would intercept her in the darkness on the way home from the manse. If anyone were with her—and it would be extremely unlikely now—he would follow until Janet was alone and overtake her before she disappeared into her home. A few natural words, pleasant, saying he would like particularly to see her—in an hour or whenever would suit her—just for a little while. Don't worry—come.

There was no way out of it for her. None.

In the first faint smother of dusk, he got up and shivered. The dead bracken glowed like hot rust on a steep patch beyond the little burn. A blackbird scolded in a bush, and the sound sent icy winter over the mild land. The hunter and the hunted alight in his eyes, he followed the track, down past the salley bushes, and his legs stumbled and his body was delicately airborne. His decision had put a stillness on the quiescent land, translating it very slightly into a new aspect. As he came by his own fields, this translating quality increased, and for an instant he was invaded by a strange lightness and happiness, before it turned into an apprehension that grew swiftly into fear, into a clutch of terror. Moving his head half round against the weight of an immense compulsion, he saw his father standing by the corner of the stubble field.

He was standing where he had last seen him on the afternoon he died. He was exactly the same as he had seen him then. But instead of looking at the growing corn he was looking at Tom.

Tom was still perhaps forty yards off. Now the appearance of his father was so natural that Tom behaved—and this might well appear an astonishing thing—as if he actually were alive, as if all in an instant things were as they had been. The grip of terror had him (a quivering and melting of the skin inward in a weakening flush of heat), but not, in these first moments, a true supernatural terror. Tom dropped his eyes to the ground and made a slight detour round his father.

Only as step followed step, and he could not look back, did supernatural terror come behind him, gaining on him. The short distance to the house was an endless journey. Only his will lived. But he made the door and turned blindly for his own room. As he crossed its threshold, invisible waters came about his feet, his legs, swirling about his thighs. He could not push his legs through the flood and fell softly in it and was drowned.

Chapter Fourteen

"You seem lost in thought," the shepherd greeted him.

The Philosopher blinked and looked up. "Oh, it's you," hes aid and a welcoming smile slowly crept over his face.

"It's a lovely day. I saw you sitting there and I thought to myself: he's enjoying it!"

"And when I saw you over there a little while back I thought: the good shepherd leadeth his sheep. But you don't lead your sheep in this country: you drive them. Sit down."

The shepherd sat down, the warm smile on his face making it appear modest and mannerly. "Yes, I have seen them lead the sheep when I was out East in the Great War, but we have different ways here."

"And why wouldn't we?" remarked the Philosopher lightly. "Each land to its own customs. It makes for variety anyhow, and that's something. The pity it is that our best customs die."

The shepherd's thin face and intelligent hazel eyes liked this sort of talk. "I was standing round the corner over there, looking across at the Heights of Taruv. There are only three crofts now. It's sad to look at the ruins."

"I can remember at least thirty. And then there were crofts all along the top, right to Braelone. I can remember stealing off as a lad on a summer evening to see the young fellows at the sports, jumping and putting the shot and throwing the hammer—on the green strip, you know, just by the Taruv Wood."

"Yes, I've been there. I used to enter at the Games for the high jump myself."

"You did, I suppose. And the cycle race. I remember."

"Not the cycle race. I practised one year, but I didn't go in for it. I felt I wasn't good enough. I hadn't the time for the road."

"What I remember best was the warmth of the life up in that crofting district. A ceilidh there of a night was thick with life; singing and dancing, you would think they hadn't a care in life. And neither they had. They drowned care periodically."

The shepherd laughed. "Faith, they did," he said. "And the wild ploys! I have been in a few myself, but Alec Wilson was telling me not long since about a splore they had once with a goat."

The Philosopher smiled. "I was there," he said.

Old days came alive as they remembered this incident or that, one person or another. An elder of the church, who had tried to stop dancing, was accosted one night on a dark road by a tall figure wrapped in a white sheet . . . The wasting away of the Factor and the little clay figure found in the burn of Taruv . . . Donul Macallister, the all-round athlete from the Heights of Braelone, who had thrown the mad bull with his bare hands . . .

The shepherd was forty-five and his memories went back into the early nineties, but Tom had been in Glasgow before the shepherd was born.

"When I was a lad," said the Philosopher, "twenty to thirty women came from the Heights of Taruv to the harvesting on the great farms below. Women worked then for eightpence a day. What a swarm of life was there! The harvest field—and the harvest home. A merry crowd they were, and each as full of character as an egg of meat. And all Gaelic amongst themselves." The Philosopher's eyes glimmered.

"And now not a single woman coming down at all," said the shepherd. "What an extraordinary change there has been in less than a lifetime!"

"Machinery," said the Philosopher. "First the reaping hook, then the scythe, and now the binder."

"Ay, and the land is not cultivated as it was. It's cattle and sheep now, stock-rearing, and you don't need the same hands for that."

"Machinery again," said the Philosopher. "The Clyde builds great steamships; the ships take grain across the seas; and you look at the ruins on the Heights of Taruv."

"It will never come back, the old life," said the shepherd thoughtfully.

"Yes, it will come back, but not in the old way," said the Philosopher. "We are in the period of the great decline in the country here. A period like that will cover a hundred—two hundred —years. We have not reached the end of the ebb yet. But we will, and then the tide will slowly begin to flow again."

"In what way?"

"Life will come back—not merely in numbers—but with the old warmth. You have seen a place swarming with rabbits. Then in a few years you have seen it deserted. Then one day in another few years you see the rabbits have come back."

"But surely we're not just like the rabbits?" said the shepherd, smiling doubtfully.

"I don't know," said the Philosopher, "that we should despise the rabbits. Many a pleasant half-hour I have spent watching the young ones playing together. If you ask any man what is the reason for the decline in our land, he will tell you that folk will not live on porridge and milk as they used to do; in short, he'll tell you that the causes are economic. It's the same with the rabbits. Too many of them, not enough grass, liver disease. It will be time enough for man to despise the rabbit's economics when he arranges his own in a more intelligent way."

"And do you think the resources are here?"

"We have hardly touched them yet. What do you think all these big fellows are trying to get hold of Highland hydro-electric power for? The machine is finding out our land. The machine has taken away, the machine will give, blessed be the machine!"

As the Philosopher smiled, the shepherd did not know quite what to make of him. The Philosopher always excited his mind, for about him there still lingered a memory of strange deeds, of the coils of the serpent in mystery and prophecy.

"And it's more than economics, in the sense that we are more than economics," said the Philosopher. "There is the super-structure of thought, especially, say, of religion. Just as the economic life ebbed, so did the religious. Science, with freethought, was the machine there. When William Bulbreac called me the Serpent he wasn't so far wrong. In my own small way, I was Antichrist. And the awful thing about the Antichrist is that he has nothing to put in the place of that which he destroys. For every personal problem is more than a personal problem: it is a com-munal one."

"I never rightly understood—about that," murmured the shepherd, poking the point of his stick in the grass.

"Who does?" replied the Philosopher. "After giving more years to it than I can remember, my own thoughts have become a little clear only to myself. You read one philosopher and in your young enthusiasm you acknowledge him master—until you read another. In my early days in Glasgow, socialism, as we saw it then, solved everything, socialism and freethought. But socialism soon began to need a philosophy and so developed its materialist interpretation of all history, and as for freethought—what exactly was "free"? How sure we were in those days that the atom was the final indivisible particle of matter! You just couldn't get beyond it. That was that settled for all time! Then the atom disappeared, like the old Devil, leaving an electric swirl behind him. Take even this business of the Serpent. How that, too, has changed!"

"Yes, folk are not now so religious as they were. I mean they're more tolerant now to a man with a point of view of his own. In the old days some of the ministers and elders were real tyrants! And how they liked to use their power! I suppose they believed so strongly themselves that they were sure they were doing what was best for everyone else."

"Yes; power. They loved to exercise their power, particularly when they could link it up with the power that underlay and explained and upheld everything. In this way they became, as it were, larger than themselves; they became part of the company of the sons of God; the executive power on earth. Much the same thing is happening at the moment with the new communist religion in Russia. The ministers and the elders there are behaving in the same way: the same certainty of rightness, the same profound belief that their way is the way of the ultimate good of mankind; the same intolerance of criticism, and a more ruthless way of liquidating the heretic than you or I knew here—though not more ruthless than in the far times of the Covenanters or the Inquisition. That is not to condemn Communism or Christianity as a barbarous creed. It is merely to understand how man acts in a certain set of circumstances —perhaps necessarily acts. He has done it often in history, and each time, in his own mind, he has been certain that he was right in a final eternal way. Without that belief, that faith, he might have accomplished little. However, that's another argument, if a long

174

one! That's not what I was thinking of when I mentioned how our attitude to the Serpent has changed."

"I thought you were a keen Communist," said the shepherd.

The Philosopher smiled. "I couldn't be anything unless I was extreme, could I? How a man's reputation will stick to him! When I was a young socialist in Glasgow we used all the jargon of the time with just the same ease as the young do now. A man had only to use a phrase or quotation for us to "place" him at once—Robert Owen, Henry George, the Communist Manifesto, and so on. But of all these tags that floated about the one that stuck most strongly in my mind was one by Bakunin the anarchist. This is it: 'Liberty without socialism means privilege, socialism without liberty means slavery and brutality'."

The shepherd's eyebrows crinkled thoughtfully as the Philosopher turned his head and looked at him, apparently awaiting some expression of opinion.

"That about hits it off, I think," said the shepherd slowly. "Only," he added, troubled, "I thought anarchism meant—meant——"

"Chaos?"

"Yes."

"Apparently not," said the Philosopher, and quite suddenly and merrily he laughed, tilting his head and looking around on the bright world, and it seemed to the shepherd in that merry moment that the bright world laughed back. "Extraordinary the effect a man's early environment can have on his mind," proceeded the Philosopher. "When I try to work out how it is that always, at the back of everything, I have been a natural anarchist, do you know to what I am inclined to attribute it?"

"No," said the shepherd.

"Precisely to the old days in the crofting world on the Heights of Taruv as I knew it when a boy. Then—and back for centuries and centuries—they were all anarchists. Anarchism was the working basis of their lives, both their economic and mental lives. Think it out and you'll see it for yourself. In my boyhood, I never actually remember seeing the laird in person, the owner of the land. He was an absentee, as you know. Once a year the men put on their Sunday suits and went to the place where the Factor was having his sitting for the collection of rents. They paid their pound or two, got their dram, and came away. After that each man was his own master, worked his own land, having no boss or bureaucrat over him to drive or direct him. Accordingly in the community as a working or going concern, all were equal in social status, or rather the idea of class distinction amongst themselves could not arise, simply because it did not exist. The farther back you go the clearer that becomes because you recede more from the power of money. Then almost everything was, as we say, 'in kind'. Even what tribute was paid to the chief as a leader was paid in kind, just as in Russia some who now work the nationally owned land pay Stalin in produce, in kind. But the crofting country, through long centuries, had reached beyond an active bureaucracy and leaders. True, the chiefs at intervals stirred up the clansmen to fight for some power-scheme the chiefs had on hand, some dirty business or other, but actually for generations on end whole regions of the country lived in peace, cultivating the land and rearing their cattle and sheep. The individual bits of dirty business are remembered. History has so far been a remembering of the dirty business rather than an understanding of the arts and the way of life of the peaceful generations. I remember Alec Wilson getting a hiding in school one day because he couldn't remember all the high-up intrigues behind the bloody Massacre of Glencoe. The history of the Highlands to us as boys was a sort of enlarged massacre of Glencoe, and we had to remember the bloody bits or get walloped."

"That's right!" said the shepherd, laughing softly. Presently, when they had swopped one or two schoolboy memories, the shepherd came back to the word anarchism and its difference from communism, for he had a curious mind in such matters.

When the Philosopher had in a somewhat elementary way explained the difference, he went on, "In Taruv in those days—for there were, of course, no big farms in the Glen then—you had the individual responsible for his own bit of land, while at the same time he was an active member of the community, abiding by its customs and laws, just as his own bit of land was part of the communal land. In fact in the old run-rig days the men used to cast lots every year for the various portions of land. Then each worked the portion he got for that year. They naturally helped one another and at certain times—say, at the peat-cutting—they voluntarily joined forces and worked in squads, and these were usually the happiest times of all. In short, you had a true balance between the maximum freedom of the individual and the common welfare of all, and at the same time—and this is where the anarchism comes in—they had no bosses, no tyrants, no bureaucrats, no profit-drivers among themselves. You see what I mean?"

"Yes. I believe I see what you're getting at now. But do you think folk would go back to that to-day?"

"No. We are dealing with what anthropologists would call a primitive society. What I am trying to show to you is that the society worked. You and I *know* that. When we use the word communism or anarchism, we have something real to go on. Our minds quite naturally take the next step and say: if we could get our society to-day, *with* the machine, working after the old pattern —if we could evolve the old into the new—then once more the life of the folk would be warm and rich and thick. For remember, they were primitive in the old days only in so far as the absence of the machine was concerned. They had their way of life, their religious attitude to life, their arts. Take what is considered the highest manifestation of art, namely, music. Look at the music our forefathers produced. One of the finest folk musics in the world. Do we in the Highlands produce music of any kind now?"

"Man, some of these old Gaelic airs are lovely," said the shepherd fondly. "Do you know, sometimes when I am on the hill by myself, one of them will keep me company off and on for hours. And as it comes and goes it will bring into mind all sorts of strange things." His eyes shone, amused and reticent.

"And all from the anarchists of Taruv!"

They laughed, enjoying the friendly talk and looking upon a wide world that also seemed to enjoy the leisured hour.

"This feverish fascination in the discussion of politics!" remarked the Philosopher. "Odd to think that in another century or so it will have passed. To us now it is nearly everything. I couldn't begin even talking about the Serpent without landing straight in it!"

The shepherd smiled but said nothing.

"My point was simply that in those old days, when they had a settled way of life, when politics and economics had no meaning for them as they have for us they had a special way of looking even at the Serpent. Folk swore here in our country then, not by god or devil, but by the earth. Their bible for swearing on was the earth. You took a little earth in your hand and swore by that. The Serpent was the earth spirit."

"I didn't know that," said the shepherd.

177

"The Serpent was the symbol of wisdom," said the Philosopher. "By the way, have you never used the serpent-stone?"

The shepherd hesitated. "To tell the truth, I have," he confessed. "It's been in our family for a long time. About the size of the palm of your hand, with a hole in it."

"And you put it in water, and the water cures?"

The shepherd nodded. "The last time I used it was for a ewe that got stung by an adder on this very moor. Whether it was the stone or not, the ewe got better." The shepherd smiled through a certain embarrassment.

The Philosopher nodded in turn. "Possibly your serpent-stone is the symbol of the ancient sacred python, of the belief that death came by the woman, whose type is the serpent, and that through the same source life comes again. Just as the sun destroys—and is the source of life. The Babylonians put a serpent round the heavens. But I like the idea of swearing by the earth. It is the ultimate thing; the mother of all life. And to-day she is good to look upon. What?"

"She is," said the shepherd, looking around.

"She is pretty nearly my philosophy, my religion, and everything now. But she has taken a lot of knowing."

"I suppose so," murmured the shepherd, never quite sure of a certain fine light that came into the Philosopher's eye at times.

"For at the end of the day, what's all the bother about? Simply about human relations, about how we are to live one with another on the old earth. That's all, ultimately. To understand one another, and to understand what we can about the earth, and in the process gather some peace of mind and, with luck, a little delight."

"The understanding of one another—that is often very difficult."

"Very difficult," repeated the Philosopher.

"And sometimes," said the shepherd, "you think you have got hold of something, something bright and fine, and then when you try to tell about it, I mean, when you try to bring it into life and make it work—it's like the fairy gold."

"How the fairy gold?"

"Don't you know the legend of the fairy gold and what happens to it when, after finding it, you bring it into the light of the common day?"

"I have heard of the fairy gold but not what happens to it when you bring it into the common day." The Philosopher looked expectantly at the shepherd.

"It turns," said the shepherd, simply, "in your hands into withered leaves or horse dung."

The Philosopher continued to look at the shepherd, the light brightening his eyes, then he looked away over the valley, his head nodding to the rhythm of an inner delight, as if he had been presented with an unexpected gift.

"Wisdom," he murmured. "No wonder Christ had to talk in parables." He began to laugh in sheer tribute, quite friendly chuckles, in which the shepherd joined.

As the Philosopher arose and took a step or two up the hill, his heart began to knock and his breath to labour. "I'm not so young as I was," he explained, smiling to the shepherd. "I also find," he added, thus gaining time to stand still, "that when I have been sitting for a long time in thought, the first move afterwards should be a careful one—but rarely is! And that parable of yours was worth coming a long way to hear."

"Take it easy," said the shepherd, with friendly concern. "If you're along the hill burn, I may see you later on."

"Very good," said the Philosopher.

"So long, then, just now." Saluting with his stick, the shepherd moved away along the face of the hill.

Every few yards the Philosopher had to pause for breath, but this was no hardship, for it gave him time to look at what lay about his feet or flew through the bright air or wandered in the blue field of the sky. The story of the fairy gold was in his mind like a tune or like a gift that he could not help looking at every now and then. He knew the value of such a gift, appreciated the chance circumstance of its presentation, was in no hurry to pass away from it. Life was not so lavish with such gifts but that one should pause and smile as the fairy gold gleamed in the mind, gleamed with a cunning brightness that was the very laughter of gold. More subtil (that biblical word!) than coined gold, this gold of vision, of wisdom, this final medium of exchange between all minds. And not expressed abstractly but with so visible a gleam that even the child mind was held. Particularly the child mind! The dismay of the child mind at the withered leaves, the horse dung! The child mind—coming from where—that it should be so dismayed?

Next time the Philosopher caught himself smiling, he was over the crest and saw the brown heather moor before him, and, upon a knoll at some little distance, the four grey standing stones.

These massive stones were prehistorically old, but age was about them in other ways. The peat had grown up past their waists; they were grouped closely together, tilted slightly, so that they were like old men, like the shoulders of squatting bodachs, held for ever in a last moment of meditation. He sometimes made a fifth in this eternal séance and, after the labour of the climb, became as mindless as any of them.

To-day it was particularly pleasant to sit down in the shadow of the western stone and cool off a bit, for his body seemed rather light on its legs, probably because his mind was so active. And always he liked to look abroad upon the immense prospect of near moor and hidden glen, of vast visible hollows and low hills, until along a skyline stretching over two counties ran the peaks of great mountain ranges. If he were sent to sleep over a long period of time and then were wakened at sunset beside these stones, he would not only be able to tell the month but very nearly the day of the month. On the shortest day of the year the sun set in a small dip below the peak of a mountain in the south-west. He had stared at it with his naked eye when it looked like the end of a half-molten axle revolving in the dip which exactly contained it. It never went farther south than that. From there to the north-west the peaks told the months with a certainty which the prehistoric shepherd never found at fault. Whether the year was marching to high summer or receding through autumn to winter was written on the ground. The fixed mountains and the moving ball of the sun made an impressive calendar!

Perhaps the local folk then gave to short divisions of time the names of the peaks? "Ah, the sun's in the Dip to-day! He'll start travelling north to-morrow." Or, "No, you'll find no real growth in the grass until Sgurannich."

The Philosopher's mind began to speculate amusedly, and in a little while vision drew in about him the prehistoric ones who herded their flocks and hunted over moor and mountain, through glens and forests and across streams. Any folk who saluted the sun and evolved legends about fairy gold must have had a warm human way of looking at things! And what a vantage point this knoll provided, not only for study of the sun but for seeing the folk approach, from strath and corrie and upland. How vastly important was this knoll in the ancient days!

In about him they came; and over there was an old woman

bending down and doing something; whispering to a small boy she was, for the boy was a little frightened on his first visit to this place of worship. She was just the sort of woman who would be doing something, even to understanding a little boy's private needs at such a moment. She seemed strangely familiar to him in this simple day-dream, and then as he looked more closely, he saw that she was his mother.

Chapter Fifteen

The feeling of falling softly into the swirling tide in his room was no doubt a delusion. He had probably fallen full length with a crashing sound. Anyway, when some sort of consciousness returned and he felt the fumbling hands about his body, he was fighting in an extreme, instinctive terror. The first clear picture was of his mother staggering back from a blow, her hair in lank wisps over her forehead and blood at one corner of her mouth. This picture paralysed him, his legs gave way, and he sat heavily on the bed, staring in horror at his mother's drunken face. She brushed the hair back from her forehead in a slow characteristic gesture with her left hand, gulping heavily for breath, and in a lifted quivering voice cried, "Oh, Tom!"

The appeal in the voice was utterly beyond bearing, and now behind it, in an instant, uprose the memory of having seen his father a moment ago in the field. As his mother took a step towards him, he cried "No! No!" in a frenzy of denial, leaping at the same time to his feet, staggering, and then he was gripping the pillow in both fists, tearing at it, collapsing over the bed and smashing his face into the pillow, still shouting "No!" out of clenched muscles.

But the blindness of the pillow was a treachery from which he swung round, for his father would now have had time to come into the room. Everywhere he searched for the bearded face, looking through his mother, his whole body shaking ungovernably, his jaws clicking.

His mother was moving towards him and speaking, shutting out his vision. "No!" he screamed at her. To be touched was to be trapped. Premonition of the familiarity of touch revolted him with such fear and hatred that his whole chest felt like vomiting up. But he lived now beyond physical reaction in an unquenchable agony of fear.

"Hush, Tom, it's only your mother."

She was standing two paces from the bed, afraid to draw nearer.

Her solid body, her voice like tears turned into profound, yearning, hopeless sadness, made a maddening distraction. It would smash his defences, it would break him down. "Get out!" he yelled at her.

But that momentary concentration on her, rather than on his father, pierced him inwardly so that something in him gave, and in a renewed frenzy, with the inward pieces flying asunder, he smothered voice and eyes in the pillow and shook in a fit of dry mad weeping.

But he was still wary, some part of him was still listening, and suddenly swinging his head round he glanced about the room. "I saw him," he gulped. "He's out there."

"No, no," she answered. "He's not there." She turned, however, and looked about the room, now in the eerie gloom of late twilight.

It was that instinctive action on her part, that human weakness, that joining-in with his fear, which helped him to defeat the madness whose mounting wave might else have broken clean over him. In an instant, not by design but by belief, she became in some measure an ally.

At that, an extreme trembling weakness came over him, so extreme that he rolled on his back. It was now as if dissolution was to come through the physical breaking up of his body. He felt her hands on his legs but could not keep still. He felt her fingers at the laces of his boots but he had to kick her hands away. Irritation at the return of her hands mounted to torture. But the pulling off of the boots was like the pulling of his legs out of a quagmire. She turned the patchwork quilt up over him. And by degrees he subsided into an exhaustion whose approach he felt like a delivering death.

In the days and nights that followed he fought a long battle against the figures and forces of unreason. The battle had all sorts of extraordinary turns and phases, but what was ever present, and varied only in degree of intensity, was the feeling of extreme apprehension. In quietened daylight moments he could say to himself, for example, that the appearance of his father in the field had been a hallucination arising from the overwrought condition of his nerves. In such fashion he could reason out many of his more monstrous delusions. But . . . the twilight hour . . . a creak in the woodwork . . . a soft noise outside . . . and he was listening in a mounting agony of apprehension. The room, the still pieces of furniture, the grey light in the window, the appalling swelling silence beyond the window. Everything was "translated" in an ineffably sinister way. Yet "sinister" was not always the right word, for the translation sometimes had in it the approaching majesty of God, the terrifying, august, slowly gathering, invisible Presence of the Almighty God whom his father, and his forefathers, had worshipped. At such a moment even the chance sounds his mother made in the kitchen were cut off from him, softened and enigmatical, so that he strained to hear and understand them, to bring them back to known sounds and movements. When defeated in this effort, he would let out a shout. She would hurry into his room; the tension would pass from the muscles of his neck. Moving his head normally, he would say in a literal voice, "I'm feeling very dry."

"The kettle's on the boil. I was just thinking of making a drop."

"That's fine."

Off she would go then.

He would drink the tea, though it had for his palate a vile taste. He had always liked tea, but the sickliness of its flavour was at times now almost more than he could stomach. In particular the cream with which she was specially careful to enrich it—there was nothing too good for him—gave it an oily taste that was like an offensive smell.

By one means or another he would keep her moving about until the blind was drawn and the lamp lit. From the shop he had got her to bring down the round-wicked lamp and had himself made a fixture for it by the head of his bed. This lamp flooded the room with light.

He was certainly weak and often woke out of a nightmare sweating profusely, but in himself he knew there was no real reason why he should not get up. But he did not want to leave the room; above all he did not want to go out and see people moving. The thought of being stopped by someone could induce a fear, a revulsion, that momentarily blinded him.

During all this time his attitude to his mother was largely one of forbearance. She was naturally there, but the life he had to deal with was secret and beyond her. Often, too, she appeared not only tactless but stupid in a way that all but made him shout at her. She could ask if he was feeling a bit better in a gross hopeful manner that made his nerves scream as he put the brake on them. He would turn his face away in silence. But not always in silence.

Then there was that other appalling mood when her voice gathered a sort of dumb despair, a sheer unintelligence, that yet might have been borne were it not that she managed to import into it that sighing mournfulness straight from the religious world. O God, this was utterly beyond bearing.

The very first night she had asked, "Will I send for the doctor?" The sweat breaking out on him, he turned upon her like a madman.

One definite thing, however, had happened to her: the mood of settling down into dumb witless resignation, which might easily have been her portion to the end of her days, was killed stone dead. The need to look after him had brought all her working energy back into full play. From early morning until the smooring of the fire she was continuously on the move. There was nothing too much for her to do. And when she lapsed into the mournful mood, it was probably not so much due to exhaustion of body as to the feeling, induced possibly by his restrained anger or snapping savagery, that in herself she was unable to understand him, was bewildered and terrified by the malady which she saw was sapping and wasting him before her eyes.

And she never knew the right thing to say. Never. But she kept on, kept on working, with an endurance that nothing could break. Never had she answered him back. Her highest reward was to hear him speak a few words normally. And in time she even learned not to go beyond them and ask any question.

Meantime his capacity for apprehension kept growing or at least refining itself, until at last he did really seem to have an extra quality added to the eyes of his mind. They saw instantly with a perfect clairvoyance, not so much through the opaque, but as if the opaque was turned to glass or a thin mist. At such a moment his own body thinned into nothing around the concentrated power of vision.

This affected at times even the faces he saw—and he was continually seeing faces, faces of every normal and abnormal kind.

For example, the faces sometimes would be thin as pale blown bladders, delicate as toy balloons with a suffusion of light inside, or pale and watery, with a simplicity of features that might have been drawn by a child. These faces could, in a negative almost comical way, be very horrible, but they were not menacing, until, all in an instant, their objective lack of menace became, on a plane beyond all known planes, in a manner beyond all words, inconceivably menacing.

There came back to him also, at this time, one or two faces which he had known in nightmare as a child—particularly one, dark-skinned as a south-sea cannibal with all the features crushed into lines and curves by a smile that was not a smile but an expression of paralysing anticipation of that which was about to happen—to happen to the little boy. There wasn't even a neck to this face. Just a round creased face, round as a football, utterly vivid, with the darkness of night all about it.

None of these had the purely physical menace of such a figure as the one in the morning coat with the hands hanging loosely in front. The head and neck were cut off, not straight across, but at a slant upward from below the right shoulder. Perhaps the head and neck were there. After the first involuntary vision he had never dared to look.

Now the utterly awful thing about a vision of this kind was not merely that it came into focus against the will, against every desire, but that when he used his will to banish it, it remained waiting until he had finished jerking his physical eyes about.

In this capacity of his creations to remain waiting was contained, perhaps above all else, their most demoralising power.

After a time he felt himself slowly getting the upperhand of the disruptive forces, cunningly and gradually getting stronger in that region where the fight went on, until in the small hours of one morning he realised that all along he had been growing weaker and that suddenly, now, at this moment, he was going to break.

Hitherto there had been at one end, as it were, of his creations the figure of his father—rarely menacing him directly, but indirectly of an extreme menace—and at the other that smooth animal-demon of the Devil's Croft. This night—he must have awakened to the intensity of the vision—the demon was at some little distance, beyond a moving formlessness of unfocused figures, and the face was turned towards him. The face was covered with the same fine ratlike hair as the body but quite short and smooth, except where it ran in two raised circles about the eyes like continued eyebrows. The eyes were perfectly round and flat, and the fine skin over them was delicate and charged with a light that was a glimmer of pain, pain that might have come from a scratching of the eyeballs, though manifestly that was not its source. They were looking directly at him across and between the other figures, watchful in a manner impossible to describe because they knew what was going to happen and he in the bed did not. But apprehension was now drawn out to so exquisite a tension that when he realised his father was about to appear in a commanding action that would be final, he knew at last that he was going to be beaten, that he could not hold the tension. As it snapped and he collapsed inwardly into the dark chaos of himself, he began to scream.

His mother came running on her bare feet, in her nightgown, without a light. As she bent over him in the dark, crying his name, he gripped her with all his might and clung to her.

He clung to her like a child wakening out of a nightmare, conscious of her body as a shield against the convoluting hell behind him.

Her arms were round him. "No-one will get you!" she cried. She hit his back with the broad of her hand in firm tender slaps. She pressed him to her. His fingers dug into her loose flesh in a way that must have hurt. She cried soothingly, her voice tremulous and breaking, but fighting for him.

As the wave of horror ebbed, he became aware of her great bosom and the broad planes of her shoulders, and from them there passed into him a slow suffusing sense of physical reality, quietening and strengthening him. He clung to her like the drowning man to his spar, the swirl of the nameless ocean of horror falling away from him.

When at last, fully conscious, he let go his hold and lay back exhausted, he said, "Don't go yet for a little while."

His quietened tone of acceptance, of natural dependence, moved her to a depth of compassion and love that brought a quivering, flowering assurance into her voice and the mothering actions of her body. "My own boy!" she murmured, and her arms went over him, tucking the clothes around him; all in a practical capable way, with no intrusion on the terrible sensitiveness she had come to know. "Wait you now, and I'll have everything all right." She lifted his head firmly and set the pillow straight.

It was an exquisite relief to give in to her, to care no more, to feel her near him. Never had his pride broken like this before anyone; but now that it was broken, his acceptance of his mother was the acceptance of a natural ally who spoke and behaved validly in her own right. That she was not the figure his secret pride and egoism had desired was now all the better. The qualities in her that formerly had made him impatient with her were the very qualities of endurance and patience which he now saw were the only ultimates against the cruelties and inexhaustible resource of fate.

As though she sensed she could not just sit beside him there in the dark but must distract him, she said, "Would you like the lamp lit?"

"Not yet for a little," he answered, realising how much the darkness had helped him.

His friendly tones must have been a song in her ears, for always her questioning had been wrong. It had been wrong this time, but now in an instant she knew why.

"I'll blow the fire up in no time and heat some milk for you. It's good for putting you to sleep. I'll light the candle." She did not wait for him to say anything but, still talking, went into the kitchen. Soon there was a flicker of light coming into his room, and now her voice was ordering the cat off the chair. He could distinctly hear her breath like a bellows blowing the peat embers. She came in with the candle. "I'll leave this here so that I'll see my way in," she said, giving him a look. "You're feeling a bit better now?" she asked, almost as if he had been suffering from a pain in the stomach.

"Yes, much better," he answered.

Off she went again, nearly running.

The sight of her, waddling away in such eagerness, was too much for his terribly weakened condition. There was something in it of love that was too much, and suddenly the tears burst from his eyes and he was choking his mouth against sobbing.

He was certain that, hearing him—and she was bound to hear—she would come running, and to cope with her now was beyond his power. He just could not bear it if she came in. But she did not come. And when the spasm exhausted itself and he listened, there was a great quietness in the kitchen. No sooner was he composed than she entered with the milk in a bowl.

"It's not hot," she said, setting the candle on the small table by his bed. "You take it now. Take it all. It will do you good." She set the pillows behind him with sure strength.

He could hardly hold the bowl and she helped him to balance it. After he had drunk a couple of mouthfuls she took the bowl from him and placed it on the table. "Take your time," she said. "There's no hurry."

He lay back against the pillows and closed his eyes, breathing heavily.

"It's good nourishing food you need to bring your strength back. You haven't been eating nearly enough. But I'm going to see to it, and you'll *have* to eat. Now, come, drink some more."

He gulped most of it and then pushed the bowl away. She set it on the table.

"I'm a great bother to you," he said, lying back.

She began straightening the bedclothes. She could have withstood anything but this tribute in his voice. She shook her head, her hands busy. Then she turned her back to him and stood quite still. He knew she was fighting her tears.

"I'm sorry, Mother."

"No, no," she said. "Oh no." Her voice choked. "Don't say that." She drew in a deep breath that broke. "I'm foolish. Don't mind me."

"Mother——"

"No, no," she cried, and started off, but stood again, then blindly came for the bowl, to carry it away. But she turned her face to him for a moment. How ghastly his own must have been could be read in the compassion of her eyes. It was a moment of pure communion in which a feeling of her own insufficiency, now that he was kind to her, must have risen like a ghost within her.

She stood, bereft of intention and movement. Then she groped for the quilt to set it straight again, her head bowed. But she could not deal with her emotion, and leaned on her hands, and then with a queer culminating cry of shame for her weakness, her breast fell on the bed and she buried her face in the quilt, weeping horribly.

"Mother!" He leaned forward and stroked her head, the tears running hot down his throat.

"No, no, I'm no use. I'm no use to you."

"Don't say that, Mother."

"Oh, my son," she cried, "if I could give my life to make you well —how gladly I would give it!" Her head crushed down again from side to side.

But she fought down her emotion, and he felt her head press against the touch of his hand.

"You have been good to me, Mother."

She got up and wiped her eyes. "I couldn't help it," she muttered to herself.

She went away and came back; she busied herself about the house.

"Do you think you'll go to sleep?" she asked when there was nothing more she could pretend to do.

"Yes. You go to your bed now."

"Very well. I'll leave your door open so that you can call me if you want anything."

An hour later, he heard her coming on her bare feet to the door. He breathed evenly, and she had hardly gone away when a drowsiness began to settle down upon him.

The following afternoon he tried to get up and found he could not stand. Sitting on the bed, however, he got his clothes on and was making an effort again to get to his feet when his mother came in.

He sat down and smiled to her. "I thought I would like to go through," he said and his whole body wavered.

"Do you think you should try?" she asked through her amazement, grasping him at the same time by the arm.

"I think," he murmured, "it would do me good."

She put her arm round him as he stumbled and all but carried him into the kitchen, where she padded the wooden armchair with her bed quilt and set him comfortably to the fire.

But his head was swimming and he felt like an empty husk. The faintness grew and in a few moments his mother was carrying him back to bed.

The humiliation of this did not worry him.

In a few days he was making the afternoon journey to the kitchen fire on his own and lengthening his stay each time. There was a haste in his mother's actions like an overflow of happiness. It was not only that she could not do enough for him—and all she did was practically suited to the occasion—but also that some overflow of well-being suffused her acts. Even the articles of furniture and the fire were in this pleasant conspiracy. Inside the four walls of the kitchen everything was friendly.

Now and again he would see his mother glance through the window. Without a word having been spoken between them on the subject of possible callers, she was keeping watch! One afternoon she said on a breath, "There's Big Ann coming!"

At once he got up and retreated to his own room. She followed him. "Lie down and put the quilt over you," she said.

"No, I'll do fine here," he answered, for she had a fire in his room. At first he had harshly repudiated the notion of a fire, but now it added to the intimacy and security of his room and of the house.

He saw her dismissing him from her mind as she arranged herself for the meeting with Big Ann, and as she left him he smiled.

After a time he stole to the door to listen to their talk.

"Yes, he's coming on fine. He's a little weak yet, but I'm hoping soon to have him up."

"It's a weakening thing, the pleurisy," said Big Ann. "Had he much fever?"

"He'd a good bit, but I kept him warm and gave him a hot drink when he needed it. He's weak enough now but the fever's left him and that's a blessing."

"He's on the mend in that case. It would be a wetting he got maybe?"

"It was," answered his mother brightly. "But now if you'll excuse me I'll just put on the kettle."

"You'll not make any tea for me."

"Indeed and I will."

As his mother lifted the wooden lid off the bucket of well-water, Tom went back to his chair by the fire.

So it was pleurisy he had!

For the first time in months a feeling of the old natural humour spread over him.

There was a period of quiet even happiness, like a period of normal convalescence, which lasted over many days. He could still recall the figures of his visions but they had grown thin and lost their power. His mind could wander away from them as a body by its own volition could wander back from a cliff-head into green fields or small birch woods. Often indeed his mind did wander into a sunniness of braes and woods and singing birds.

This was an intimate world of his own, and all that had happened before was outside it. Even his old desires were outside it and had lost their force, much as the horrible visions had.

He tried to read some of his agnostic books but somehow did not care for them very much. They slightly excited him and so tended to tear the delicate peace in which he lived. A paragraph or two at a time was enough, for the spirit that informed them was an earnest fighting spirit, and he was finished with fighting for the time being, and craved something more in accord with this intangible harmony and sheer wonder of being alive.

As he grew stronger he would often have long thoughts into the outside world. Memories of Glasgow came back to him frequently at this time, as if Glasgow were a distant place of refuge in the factual world much as his own home was in this present intimate life.

Then one night when he awoke and found the fire dying, he decided not to make it up and fell into a reverie. He was wandering back from his visit to Bob and Dannie, and in the cavern of the street experienced again that peculiar sadness at being separated from his old friends. His contacts with Dave and Tim, the new direction of his thoughts, the inspiration from the feeling that at last he had found the true meaning and reality of existence, made a return to the old-fashioned world of Bob and Dannie impossible. Unless he had experienced it, he would not have believed that the sense of division could have been so absolute.

In his reverie, the persons and scene changed, and now he was understanding the mood that moved Janet, the reluctance upon Janet, the meaning and reality of existence for Janet, that made it impossible for her to turn back from the new burning love to the old-fashioned friendly liking.

She could not do it. It was beyond her human strength to turn back from Donald to him.

So clearly, so utterly, did he understand this that he was moved to a profound sympathy and held as it were in his hands her beating heart.

Slowly an infinite sadness darkened his tenderness, and his love which now gleamed brightly (gleamed as never before for it was at last seen and comprehended against eternal loss) slowly faded, and the vivid gleam of Janet's face and the beating of her heart faded, and the fingers of each hand closed and writhed against one another with the dry rustling sound of withered leaves.

Chapter Sixteen

A dullness came down upon him after that, an even shadow over the mind, like the shadow over the land on one of these December days when the ceiling of cloud hung low and grey. The gleam of convalescence had gone, but in its place physical strength had come and presently he was adventuring out to the byre to see the beasts and into the barn where he would stand idly until he grew cold and shivered.

Sometimes, as his eyes cast about to make sure there was no-one near, he experienced the criminal feeling of one in hiding. His fear of encountering a fellow being was such that if he heard behind him, or outside beyond the barn door, a soft sound like a footfall, his heart at once began to race and his mouth dried in the moments of listening.

The inside of his home was now like a burrow, a secure bolt-hole from the outside world. Sometimes he caught his mother's eyes on him when he happened to lift his glance from the fire into which he could stare for long blank periods. He knew that she would have liked him to be more active, not for the sake of doing real work, but for his own good. Yet she, too, in some measure was affected by him, was getting used to this secluded life, and was a jealous part of it.

They spoke little to each other, for he had no desire to know what was happening among the neighbours. But where he could help her he did, and when she found the byre cleaned or the two buckets filled with well-water or a pail of potatoes beside the iron pot, she was obviously pleased. Soon he was giving such help regularly and more than once forestalled her in some special task.

These days toward the end of December were very short, outside duties few, and the evenings long. He tried to read again, but could not get back the old enthusiasm. It did not seem to matter to him very greatly whether the God of Abraham was this kind of god or that. Disputation for its own sake gave him no pleasure. And if the answer to the riddle of the universe was so-and-so, well, it was hardly a matter for excitement. Materialistic certainty had the air of finality which might be satisfactory but gave no thrill—unless possibly to the man who was having the fun of proving his theory. But the earnestness of such a man seemed to Tom strangely remote at times, like the noise of a December bluebottle, galvanised into action against the window-pane by a blink of sun. In the case of the bluebottle, its concern to lay its eggs was at least imperative. It could not help it.

On New Year's eve they heard footsteps passing the window. It was about nine o'clock and pitch dark. At once Tom got up and tiptoed past the knocking to his own room. His mother opened the door but could not see the visitor.

"It's me, Andie Gordon. We were wondering how Tom was. How is he?"

"He's getting on fine, thank you. He's lying down just now, for he's not very strong yet. Will you come in?"

"Oh well no, we won't be bothering you in tha' case. No. We were just going our rounds, an' we thought of Tom, and as we were going our rounds we thought we would jus' call round to see how he was. But if he's lying down—tha's fine. It's all righ'. I hope you're quite well yourself, Mrs. Mathieson?"

"Yes, thank you. I'm sorry——"

"It's all righ'. Just to wish you both a happy New Year. Goo'-night. Goo'-night, Mrs. Mathieson."

"Good-night, and a happy New Year to you all. I'm sorry we have nothing in."

"Goo'-night," called the departing voice.

She closed the door and as Tom joined her in the kitchen she glanced at his face. Her invitation to Andie to enter had hardly been pressing. But Tom looked relieved—and suddenly stood still as if he had heard another footstep in the night. Then he sat down.

"That was Andie Gordon, with a strong smell of drink off him already," she said.

"They'll be going the rounds of the houses," he answered. "If they call back when we're in bed, don't answer the door."

They did not call back and Tom felt that their house was shut away from all others and, behind many odd memories covering the wild jollity and singing and drunkenness of New Year's eve (most of the lads would not go to bed to-night, for even farm workers were on holiday to-morrow), this feeling of being shut off was full of relief, at moments almost pleasant.

He found it difficult to go to sleep that night, however, and though he tried to read in bed under the bright light of the round-wicked lamp, he could hardly get any meaning out of the black-lettered words that crawled over the page like insects. A deep sombre feeling gradually invaded him, and his loneliness came about him like a darkness of the pit. When at last he put out the light and turned over, he fell asleep at once.

In the early weeks of the new year, he set himself all sorts of tasks. After talking to one or two persons whom he had not had time to avoid, for he was often now in the shop though doing most of his carpentry in the barn, he developed a cool, distant, polite method of dealing with such personal encounters. He knew, by the response and look of the person who talked to him, that folk would say amongst themselves that Tom Mathieson had gone "queer",nodding at the same time in recognition of "a judgement", nodding solemnly.

So long as it kept them to themselves, he did not mind.

But with his physical strength restored, he did occasionally feel a vindictive flash of anger, at the solemn-faced approach of someone he knew quite well. He began deliberately to turn his back.

February gave way to the windy weather of March, and the prospect of the heavy spring work on the land was making its appeal when chance brought a piece of news that shattered the personal frame-work he had so slowly been building.

At Big Ann's approach, he had gone into his own room. She was a large ungainly woman with the strength of a horse, slow in her movements, working her own croft single-handed, and finding social relief in gossip, not ill-natured gossip but personal news about folk. She was good-natured and, with discrimination, kind-hearted. Moreover she had always an excellent chance of being the first bearer of special tidings to the lonely Widow Mathieson. Tom gave her time to settle down, and was stepping quickly to the front door when her voice, slow and firm as a man's, stopped his feet dead. The door between the small entrance passage and the kitchen was not quite closed and her words were perfectly distinct:

"Yes, the lassie Janet was coming and going to the manse as usual, for though Williamina had recovered a bit in the autumn, she had taken to bed again with a chill on the kidneys. She is a sharp one is Williamina, and lying in '   does not make one any the less sharp seemingly. Anyway, she told Peter Grant's wife that she had been a bit uneasy for some time. However, she said nothing, but she kept her eye on the lassie for the last month or two, until from one sign and another she was sure at last. She is a well-set-up bonny girl as you know, with good colouring, and when that sort of lassie goes white as a sheet it's very noticeable on her. At last Williamina asked her if there was anything the matter with her, but the lassie said no, naturally enough. Williamina asked her if she was sure. The lassie did not confess. She would be terrified of Williamina and the minister. But it would seem there can be no doubt about it: the lassie must be all of six months gone."

"Dear me! What a blow that will be to her mother!"

"And not only to her mother. For the question now arises: who can be the father?"

"Is anyone mentioned?"

"Well, no, for it seems she was not keeping company with anyone in particular for a long time—not since last autumn."

"And who was it then?"

There was a short pause. "Don't mistake me, Maria. If I would tell you anything it's only to prepare you. Because of things that happened, many might be willing to believe anything against your son. They might like to have a pick against him."

"Tom!" It was an intense whisper. As he heard his mother get to her feet, Tom stepped quietly outside. The door to the kitchen was opened and shut. Quietly Tom stepped back. The voices were now muffled but still distinct.

"Don't you take on about it, Maria. I only thought it would be friendly to warn you, and I wouldn't do that same if I thought it was true. Trouble comes home to roost all too surely. And it may come home to roost nearer to the manse door than Williamina dreams of. I'm saying nothing."

"You mean——?"

"I'm meaning nothing. I admit it may not look like it. The minister's son was home for his Christmas holidays and he'll be home again in a week or so, and you would say that that could hardly be if he was to blame in any way. And I may be all wrong. And indeed maybe I am and doing the young man a sore injustice. It looks like it. And to no-one would I ever mention it but to yourself. But one day I saw a small thing between them. It was nothing much, for the young will be young, but it stuck in my mind."

"Was Tom and her—keeping company?"

"So they say. But that must be a long time back as you know. And surely if there had been anything in it, you yourself would have had some idea?"

"As far as I know, she has never been near this house, and surely if——"

"Surely," said Big Ann.

Yet in the silence that followed, Tom felt the enormous doubt swell in the kitchen. His feet began carrying him down to the barn.

Janet! By God, Janet!

His mother and Big Ann and all the world was wiped out.

Janet! So it had come to Janet! By God, it had come to her! A silent savage laughter twisted his features. His groping hands lifted a lump of wood and smashed it down on the old ramshackle bench. He threw his head back and chuckled harshly. Instantly his features narrowed in a vindictive murderous expression. He cast about him for something to grip, for something to destroy, and stood very still.

So it had come to Janet.

He sat down on a pile of straw, clutched it slowly in his hands, turned over and buried his face.

A fortnight later he waylaid Tina on the Glen road. It was almost quite dark and she was hurrying home. She smothered her cry when she saw it wasn't his ghost and remained uneasy.

After greeting her, he asked, "How is Janet?"

"All right," she answered involuntarily, not looking at him.

"Does her mother know yet?"

"I—don't know," she answered.

"Do you think she knows?"

"I don't know."

"Has Donald Munro come home?"

"No."

"Weren't they expecting him some days ago?"

"I think so."

Tom looked steadily at her. Tina was pale and clearly distressed and could not meet his look. She was like one held in a vast fear.

"Good-night," said Tom.

She hesitated a moment as if about to cry her terrible fear to him, then turned and hurried away.

The following night Tom said to his mother, "I have been thinking of taking a trip down to Glasgow to see Dougal Robertson.

With the year coming on, I'll have to do something with my business, or it will fall through."

She did not speak for a moment. "Perhaps the change might do you good," she said.

"Yes, I think I would like a short change," he answered calmly. "And I could see, too, about a new model bicycle that's come on the market. Anyway, I thought I might take a few days before the spring work."

"Do you that, then, if you feel you would like it."

"Yes." He nodded. "To-morrow is Wednesday. I might as well go to-morrow and get any little business done before the week-end."

She was looking into the fire, her hands gripped in her lap. She obviously wanted to say something but dare not. "What about money?" she asked.

"I have plenty," he answered.

"There's the money in the kist," she said, "and at the bank. I have always been wanting you to look into that."

"That will be all right," he answered reasonably. "It's good to have it behind you."

"It's not only mine. It's yours when you want it. And I don't know about the bank."

"Is it in a bank book?"

"No, it's just on a paper."

"Well, if you would like me to look at it." He got up and followed his mother into his room.

She set the candle on a chair and, getting to her knees, removed the coloured cloth which draped the old wooden chest, unlocked and opened it. After fumbling among dark clothes that emitted a strong camphor smell, she asked him to hold the candle nearer. In a narrow boxed-in shelf, she found the money, mostly in gold, and showed it to him. She did it somehow with a mournful air, as if the gold coins were being unearthed like the dead years. Then she found "the paper". It was a deposit receipt for seventy pounds.

"It's all right," he said. "It's in both your names. So it can be drawn any time on your own signature."

This was what was usually done, for in practice it meant that the woman had no control over the money until the man died, but that then it went to her without legal trouble. The banker always advised this.

She put the deposit receipt back where it had been but seemed reluctant to close the chest. "I would like it to be yours, too," she said.

"Don't worry about that just now."

"But what if anything happened to me?"

"It would come to me then. I know about it."

She slowly closed the lid. "You know where the key is always," and she put it back in the coloured cream jug on the mantelpiece. "I'll have to see about your clothes." She suddenly got busy, and dropped an iron heater in the heart of the fire.

As he was leaving early in the morning for the bus she came to the door. They shook hands. "Take care of yourself," she said. "You're——"

As he glanced at her face he knew the words which she had held back: *You're all that I have.*

He gave a smile and walked away quickly. For a few moments he wondered what was in her mind. Plainly she did not think of him as one going on holiday. What, then? Had that display of the money been an invitation to him to take what he wanted? She had asked no questions. And Big Ann's story, with heaven knew what trimmings, lay unresolved in her mind.

As he entered the village street, he at once forgot her. Only those were about who had business with the bus. Peter Grant, after a steady astonished look, nodded shortly and turned to his mail bag. He glanced at Janet's house, but it was dead.

At the booking office in town, he bought a return ticket for Glasgow, and in the long daylight hours as the train went over the Grampians, he tried to think out his plan once more but could not. He had thought over it too long already and was now committed. He left the train at Perth and bought a single ticket for Edinburgh.

His one difficulty lay in getting Donald's address. That had been absolutely impossible at home, for the only place where it could be got was at the manse. Or from Janet! Besides, it might be very essential that no-one at home should know he had gone to Edinburgh. His hope lay in the knowledge that not all the university classes closed at the same time. There was bound to be some head office of the university where the students and their addresses were registered. And when it came to finding his way about a city, he had little to learn.

Easter was early that year, but Tom was not too late, and the following morning, directed by a policeman, he entered an archway, turned to his left, and came before a long desk with a somewhat pompous but affable man asking him his business.

"I would be obliged to you if you could give me the address of a student who's here. I forgot to take it with me from home, and I said I would call on him."

"The name?" asked the official, smiling to this young country man with the Highland accent who was trying to look as if he wasn't embarrassed.

In a few minutes Tom was back on the street, with the address written down in pencil, and the information that his friend had probably already gone away for the Easter recess.

For the rest of the day he hung about the end of a street that ran off the Meadows, but caught no sight of Donald. He did not want to call, however, until it was dark, for part of his plan was to get Donald to come with him out into the country in the darkness. To do that would be quite simple. He knew exactly how to go about it. "I have a lot to tell you from home. Let us get away somewhere on to a country road where we can talk." No more would be needed. No more would be said, for Donald, consumed by his own unease, would lead the way.

Tom felt perfectly calm and assured. And he knew that when it came to the final decision, he would be coldly calm. Tom's intention would gradually grow on Donald. Donald would see it coming like fate. In a quiet spot they would face each other in the dark. Donald's temper, his excuses, his difficulty with his father, all would be cleared to one side and the issue would be stark. There would be no evasion in that final moment.

As the lamps were lit he turned into the street, hesitated as he saw a girl enter at the open door to the tenement building, stood for a little while scanning the four small brass plates on each side of the entrance, read the name Cowan for the third time on the top right-hand plate over the bell-pull, then walked into the stone passage and began mounting the winding stone stairs.

Two flights above him he could hear the girl's feet still ascending slowly. A young man came out of a door on the first landing, slammed it behind him, and rushed downstairs. The stairs were swept clean and small gas jets illuminated the well dimly. It was a very much better style of lodging than anything he or his friends had been able to command in Glasgow.

When he started on the fourth flight, the girl's footsteps had died away. He slowed his own steps in order to have command of his breathing. He stopped altogether when he heard a door open and the girl's voice ask, "Is Mr. Munro in?"

"No, he's left here," answered an old woman's voice.

"Oh." A short silence. "When?"

"Yesterday."

"Will he—will he be back before he goes?"

"No. He's gone away."

"Has he—did he leave any message for me, for——"

"No, he left no message."

"Thank you."

The door shut and the girl came slowly away. Tom saw her hand grope for the stair rail and heard a small convulsive sniff. As she descended slowly, he stood back against the wall. If she saw him as she passed, she gave no sign but kept her head up. She was obviously profoundly stirred, holding her sobs in with all her strength. She was a slim fair girl, and in the dim well of the stairs looked to Tom at that moment an intensely tragic figure. His heart quickened knowing so intimately the bitter suffering that shook her.

He listened to her footsteps in the hollow well. They descended slowly, and once, for a few seconds, they ceased altogether.

She, too, had been waiting for the dark.

A bitterness withered his features and his thought; a spasm of hatred for Donald cut more sharply than the edge of any knife. He had gone—but where?

He mounted a step or two, paused and stared at the shut door, then on impulse turned and began going down. As he neared the foot, he saw the girl outlined in the doorway. From the movements of her elbows she was plainly wiping her eyes and getting command of herself before meeting the street. At the sound of his footsteps, she moved out and turned down towards the open space of the Meadows.

He followed her at a little distance, her upright forsaken figure gathering the vacancy of his mind to a living point. She was an ally in the night of the world and he felt the warm flush of blood hang heavy in the cells of her body.

She crossed the main thoroughfare, passed between some bushes, and entered one of the broad paths heading in the direction of the Infirmary. His stride quickened and lengthened, and here he was now close behind her, by her side.

"Excuse me," he said, "but were you looking for Donald Munro?"

At the first sound of his voice, her body grew taut, her footsteps hurried on—then slackened, and she half-turned, regarding his face with a startled, searching expression.

"I don't know you," she replied, vaguely walking on.

"I think you come from Muirton," he answered companionably, falling into step beside her as if they were walking on a country road. "I know Donald very well."

After a few more paces, she stopped and turned her face full to him. "I don't know you," she repeated, getting control of herself. "Are you a student here?"

"No. I merely come from Donald's own country, as you might tell by my voice." He smiled, hardly looking at her.

"How do you know—I was looking——"

"I was behind you on the stairs and heard you ask his landlady. I was on the same errand myself."

"Then you don't know where he's gone?"

"I thought I would catch him before he went home. But apparently I'm too late."

She did not answer, but he felt her eyes searching his face. He looked full at her. "Why do you think he has not gone home?"

She glanced away, but did not answer.

"Please tell me," he said gently.

She moved on a step or two and paused again.

"I don't know," she answered, her emotion threatening her again.

His sympathy for her, the kindness in his heart towards her, was such that she must have felt it. It obviously irked her terribly, but she could not leave him.

"Tell me," he said, "I wish you would tell me."

"Do you know Alastair Chisholm?"

"I know his father, James Chisholm, the wood merchant, better. My father did business with him." Then he added, "Don't be afraid to tell me anything. If I can help you, I will."

He did not look at her face, making it easy for her, because it was clear that he had stumbled on her secret trouble and this knowledge was now between them.

"Alastair told me Donald might not be going home," she said "—he might be going to Canada." She looked at him, searching for his denial.

But Tom nodded slowly. "I—see," he said.

"You don't believe it, do you?"

He looked at her. "I don't know," he muttered.

He saw her lips press in between her teeth, saw the quiver go over her body. She turned from him and walked on.

He stood where he was, looking after her. Before leaving the green meadow, she paused and looked back, then drifted across the thoroughfare. He watched her until she had gone from his sight.

Through Toll Cross and down Lothian Road he went until he came to the West End. Almost unconsciously he was heading for Leith and the sea. But as he walked along the garden side of Princes Street, a cavernous train whistle drew him up, its sound indescribably forlorn down there in the black shadow of the rock. His eyes lifted to the outline of the castle and so clearly was it silhouetted against the sky that somewhere the moon must have risen. He saw the outline through the tall iron railings, and for a moment had the shudder of a mediaeval prisoner looking on an eternal fortress.

Through the cab rank and across the wide street he picked his way until he came amid the lights and the sauntering throng. There was a slight touch of frost in the air and the wide pavement seemed gay with distinguished faces over tall, fashionably-clothed bodies. Drifting like a waif, his loneliness came about him. Opposite the Mound, he stopped.

In this sea of life he was lost; forever in the tides of life he was lost. He turned up to his left, and as he passed a corner of Rose Street a woman invited him from the shadows.

He looked at her and she approached, but he kept walking on and as she drew by his side, he turned his face. "Nothing doing to-night," he said in so natural a voice that she stopped as if a brother had spoken, and with a small upward nod of understanding fell back.

When he got on to the ridge of George Street, he saw the rising moon, nearly at the full. It held him arrested for a long time, and slowly from it, against his will, there trickled into his mind the memory that it was round about the full moon that Janet's mother had usually had one of her bouts. For an instant the memory was a country superstition remote from him in time and place, a necromancy of the past—that advanced and closed upon his mind like a fist. He shook his head and staggered where he stood.

The geography of the world settled about him in vast oceans

and continents. Canada—if going to Canada, Donald would have taken train to Glasgow. Tom stared at the moon, at the gleam on its face, the serene unearthly pale gold gleam of the moon-woman.

Turning, he made back for Princes Street and the railway station. He would take the first train for Glasgow.

So weird a night he spent in Glasgow that it had for him long afterwards the quality of one of those dreams in which, amid new scenes and new faces, one hunts and never finds.

His impatience to discover whether a ship was leaving or had left for Canada drew him to the docks. All offices, of course, were closed, but he learned in time that a steamer had left the previous day from the Tail of the Bank, passengers having gone to Greenock to join her. He had no desire to see Dougal Robertson or any of the lads he had known so well, and with a strange outlandish feeling stuck by the half-drunken company he had landed amongst. He was accepted as a country lad, the inevitable Highlander, anxious to flee the poverty of his native heath. His knowledge of socialism and agnosticism soon drew him into argument. He was utterly without care now, without vanity, without hope. Nothing could offend him, and the thick warm oaths came upon his ears like echoes from some ancient inferno. With what complete liberation hell lets loose the desperations in man's mind! He had some shillings in his trousers pocket, and he offered the money for drink. Though all the pubs were closed, no difficulty was experienced in buying whisky.

The raw spirit went fierily to his head for he had eaten little that day and he spent the night in the room where the liquor was drunk. A tow-haired strident-voiced girl had made a pet of him and taken his head on her knees. The drink had had the effect of letting him see through surface talk and gesture to what appeared to be the essential human nature of his companions, and for a time he was conscious of an almost fantastic feeling of human understanding and liberation. At one point there was a fight and a lean cantankerous man was thrown out, and the meaning behind that fight partook of the nature of revelation.

Under a growing feeling of illness the scene became blurred and the girl bent her head over him.

In the morning his instinct was to slink away, but the same girl gave him some scalding hot tea. What was he going to do now? "I'll have a hunt around," he answered, hardly looking at her or at dim corners of the ill-lit dingy room. There was a strained pain in his eyes and his head was throbbing. But as he left he turned, and with Highland manners, thanked her for her hospitality. She was going to have laughed, but didn't. Her loose mouth came adrift in a jeering expression that her eyes belied. He was glad to get away.

His belt was still round his waist under his shirt, for he had never lost the countryman's fear of being robbed in the city. In a latrine he opened the small leather pocket in the green canvas of the belt. It had held three pound notes. It now contained one.

Even a surge of anger was enough to bring out cold sweat, but as he stared through his dismay, a dry smile wrinkled his features. Why hadn't she taken them all?

He could not have accused her or anyone—even if he were mad enough to dare accuse them.

Why had she left him one?

In a sudden flurry his fingers dived into a top waistcoat pocket. The return half of his ticket from Glasgow was still there. He breathed heavily with relief.

He started for Greenock and on the train thought that if he had gone to the head office of the steamship company in Glasgow he might have been saved the trip. If Donald had booked as a passenger, his name was bound to be on a passenger list. He could present himself as one who had arrived from the far north with something which Donald had left behind, and so would be glad to know if he, Mr. Donald Munro, had been in time and had actually sailed. He felt, however, that Donald, who could not have the money for the passage, must have signed on as an ordinary seaman or steward. He had probably been trying to arrange this for the last month. If not in the steamship office, then in some Custom House or Board of Trade office his name was bound to be among the names of the crew.

Something which Donald had left behind!

That night, in a sudden revulsion of feeling against the city, he retrieved his small bag from the left-luggage office and caught the train for the north.

He had got shaved for the first time in his life by a professional barber. His face felt thin almost to vanishing point. His body was so exhausted that it, too, had attained a light incorporeal feeling. Donald's departure for Canada as a steerage passenger induced a sense of finality. There was nothing more he could do. It was a relief to be free of the murderous burden of what he had intended to do; sheer relief, and he cared no more.

He lay slumped in his corner with his eyes closed. In this attitude he could let time pass for ever. Vaguely he dreamed, though he knew he was not asleep. But the drifting figures in his dream had no power over his emotions. Nothing came to a point of feeling. Somewhere in the Perthshire highlands the carriage lurched and his eyes opened. Through the window he saw the moon, full in the sky. He gazed at it for a long time with some of its own detachment. Slowly an austere quality in its serenity touched him with a shiver of cold. The bare outlines of the near hills, their dumb shoulders, their endurance, their darkness under the living gold of the moon, affected his body to a slow writhing. His lips moved and his head fell back.

Chapter Seventeen

He got home on Saturday night. The absence from his mother had somehow estranged her in his mind, and as he approached the house he had all he could do to force himself to enter. But he spoke to her in a friendly even way, and soon he began to feel the security of his home about him. He answered that he had found everyone and everything pretty much as they used to be. "Any news?" he asked casually.

"No, nothing very special. Indeed no-one has been here since you left. I was down at the shop this morning with the eggs. There's not much price for them now. And that's all I have been out. Did you enjoy your journey?"

"Yes, fine. It was a change."

"I thought you would be staying for a few more days when you were at it."

"Well, I thought of it—but ach I got tired of the city. It's all right if you're living there."

She was very busy with the table, making excuses for not having proper food ready, obviously pleased that he had grown tired of the city. He could not but feel her pleasure in having him back. Perhaps she had thought he might never come back!

That night, however, he slept badly, and it angered him for he knew how desperately his hot body needed sleep.

Breakfast over and the soup pot on the fire, his mother began to dress for church. When she had gone, instead of the relief he had expected to find in the empty house, he was pursued by an extra virulent restlessness.

When his mother returned, she was subdued. At table she said, "Donald the minister's son was not in his place to-day. He has not come home."

"Oh. Why?"

"I met Mrs. Maclean on the way to church. She was telling me that Mrs. Grant told her and she got it from Williamina that Donald wrote his father saying that he found the church was not for him, he could not go on with his studies. So he left and has gone to Canada."

"To Canada."

"Yes. Poor man, it's been a terrible blow to him. If only Donald had come home and told him; anything but going away like that. His voice was wrung to-day. You could see sorrow on him."

Clearly his mother had much more on her mind, so as soon as the meal was over he went out.

There would be the new startled whisper that perhaps, after all, there was more in Donald's disappearance than his having found he had no vocation for the church. Though how unwillingly they would shift suspicion from the serpent-atheist who had killed his own father to the son of the minister of the gospel!

Tom might have enjoyed the bitterness of this, were it not for the implication of fatherhood, which he had hitherto kept from really entering his mind. The irony of it in his case was so annihilating that it could not be allowed to enter. It was hardly the sort of thing to brood upon!

That afternoon, when some of the old spasms of violence began to possess him again, he took to the hills.

Damnation! was there to be no peace for him for ever? He would have wept in his rage had there been tears left in his dry hot eyes.

The hills had only loneliness for him, not peace. Nothing had been solved. He was going to have made Donald marry Janet under threat of death. Donald would have understood him. For there would have been no escape for Donald. If Donald made a false promise to gain time, Tom would pursue him. Tom would pursue him, if need be, over the earth, once the position had been made clear and final between them. There would be no let-up after that. It had taken a week for him to achieve this certainty of death in himself. But he had done it. He would not emotionally threaten Donald. Calmly, clearly, he would show Donald his duty. This calmness would penetrate all vanities and evasions, until Donald would perceive that in Tom *was* death. There had been days when Tom had known a strange peace, when the killer, death, had walked with him as a quiet companion.

But Donald was gone and no word had been spoken between them. Peace was broken. The hours and the hours ahead would press in on him, ever more heavy with what could not be avoided.

He came back through the dusk and the bird-singing, looked at the corner of the field where his father had stood, saw the near dead ground and the outlines of the low hills far away, and, as once before, there was a blueness on the hills, but now in a moment it held as in a remote memory the promise of spring, of distant summers. Their shining days ran on youth's feet over the land.

About nine o'clock he got up to go out, for he had communicated his own silence to his mother and suddenly became afraid that she would speak.

There was a strong wind blowing. The sky was dark in colour but clear of cloud, and he could see well enough to know that the moon had risen beyond the hill which he began slowly to climb. His feet took him to the hollow where Janet and himself had met so often.

For a moment his heart rose into his throat, but when he had stumbled down he saw that the bent back was no more than a low salley bush. That weakened him, and for a while he lay down on the damp grass.

But the illusion brought Janet very near to him, so near that he realised how she inhabited his mind. His bitterness was suffused by a sensation of tears, of an extreme weariness, of irrevocable loss.

Moving up out of the hollow, he came presently on to a shoulder and saw the moon. Its circle was flawless. It looked over the hill ridge down upon the Glen. The intensity of its stare whitened its golden face. Its withholding serenity was ominous. Its calm sinister. Suddenly Tom was struck by a primeval ghastliness of fear. In the moon's light was a dread more terrible than any darkness knew.

He turned away and began hurrying down. Without hesitation he went straight along the base of the hillside until he stood above Janet's home. He saw the light in her kitchen window. From the house to the left of it rose the muffled singing of a psalm. It was the hour for Sunday night family worship, and everyone was within doors.

To go down there was worse than futile: it was betrayal of himself; it was a maddening advance against his own loathing. Not though his life depended on it would he have touched Janet with a finger-tip. There had been times when he had wished with a sick hatred that he could let her see how much he loathed her, as a desperate man might desire the only medicine that would cool him.

But now he knew that nothing could keep him back. After the first few steps he hardly thought, indeed, of what he was doing. It was nothing of any importance, it meant nothing. By the time he reached the henhouse wall, he was like a cool stranger to himself, the invisible one who can't be seen.

He had no sooner reached the wall than he heard high voices beyond the yellow blind. At once he stepped across to the window and in a moment his skin ran cold.

By their voices, he had plainly come on the scene as it was reaching a culminating point.

"But I will make you tell me. Do you hear me?" The voice was shrill, but not out of control. It was charged with the horrible menace of one who, however mad, would fulfil her words, and fulfil them now. "Who is he? Will you tell me?"

"No," answered Janet in shrill defiance.

"You won't tell me, won't you?" There was a clatter of fire-irons. "You won't tell me!" screamed the voice. "You hussy, you impudent, brazen, dirty hussy. I'll make you tell me! I'll smash in your pretty face for you, you whore. I'll teach you how to go with men, you low bitch!"

"Mother!" yelled Janet. "Mother!"

Tom sprang to the back door. It was on the latch. He stumbled over a bucket of water against the wall in the small dark porch, and as he pitched against the door to the kitchen it burst open before him to the sound of a scream from Janet, the upsetting of the kitchen table, and a spilling roar from a drawer of cutlery.

The woman was standing with hair wisps over her brows, her eyes, blazing with an insane light, now concentrated on Tom with such speechless, motionless intensity that he could hardly draw his own eyes away from them. The table, tilted over on its side, lay across Janet's thighs. In its shadow he saw Janet's pale face, streaked with blood. Her chest and shoulders squirmed slowly, her head tilted, giving a low moan.

"My God, what have you done?" he breathed.

In an instant he forgot her, going towards Janet. He was stooping to lift the table back, when he heard her yell and turned. He knew he was too late; in the fraction of an instant he realised, with a sense of prolonged dismay, that he was too late. Almost indeed it seemed to him that he waited for the blow. Possibly he could not have moved more swiftly. But that was not how it seemed. And when the heavy fireiron struck him, he still had the feeling of standing and looking at her and waiting.

Later his bruised forearm showed that it had taken part of the blow, and his head must have dodged to one side, for the heavy end, shaped like a huge soldering bolt, of the long iron poker struck him across the side of his face from above the right ear down to the jaw.

He was conscious of a crushing of his face rather than of pain. His physical strength ebbed and his sight dimmed. He made a supreme effort to keep to his feet, but the darkening thickened. Through it he heard her savage cry, small as if shouted from a great distance, and saw her draw back to swing the iron once more. The squat brown-painted tin lamp, with its bright reflector behind the glass funnel, sat on the mantelshelf at the level of her ear, glowing from a trimmed wick fully turned up. The end of the poker caught the metal bowl of the lamp and swept it from the mantelshelf. As his consciousness faded out he saw the moving light flare up violently in the funnel behind her head.

He came to with a not unfamiliar feeling, though the first gropings into consciousness never lost their freshness of terror. He was not in his bed, however. He fought back the panic. Where was he? cried his silent fear as he cunningly lay still. The pain in his head became real. He sucked in a deep breath and choked on the paraffin fumes. He moved and, his face coming away from the shield of the upturned table, saw the smouldering glow of the peat fire.

Memory now returned but still in an unreal way. He scrabbled at the table and heaved it round. On his knees—he saw Janet.

Janet! On hands and knees he approached her. Janet! "Janet!" he cried.

In the dim glow from the flameless fire, her face was still and ghastly white. He saw the dark blood-streak on her temple.

For a little while he lost his head. "Janet, speak to me!" he cried, like a frightened child. "Janet, my own love! Janet!" He touched her cheeks, caught her face in his hands, and turned it to him to make her speak. He kept calling her name, moving and fondling her, stretching her out, so that it would be easier for her to answer him. There was a cry behind. He started back, a wary enraged beast, and saw Tina.

He must have continued to glare at her, even when she had stepped past him and was on her knees beside Janet.

Presently Tina turned wildly, and looked up at him.

He nodded. "I'll get my mother," he said. "Stay here."

He fell many times before he rattled in at the door and came on his mother in the kitchen.

"Mother!" he cried. "Run to Janet's! Quick! She's hurt!"

His mother's mouth, her whole face, opened as she stared at him, at the shaking body, the bruised cheek, dark with dried blood.

"Run, I tell you!" he shouted.

She did not speak, but let out a cry and in a moment was gone.

He drank some well water out of the pail that was always kept in the passage, slapped more of it against his face, and hurried away to the shop. He had to come back to the house for the key, but soon he was on his bicycle, heading for Muirton and the doctor.

It was a wild ride, but he was never once thrown. This was even to him at the time extraordinary, because there was a long spell when he had hardly any bodily feeling or, rather, when his body felt light as cotton wool and it was a marvel how the bicycle kept upright. He suffered, too, what was to him at the time an incredibly vivid hallucination. Some three miles from the village the road turns sharply from the moor to a bridge over the stream. Stunted Scots firs grow about this spot; there is an old quarry on the right by the entrance to the bridge; and here the stream narrows and is noisy over a bed of broken rock. The bridge itself has a three-foot stone wall on either side and a drop to the water of about thirty feet.

Of all spots in the district—and there were a few—it had the worst reputation for being haunted. Varied were the apparitions, but pride of place was held by the woman of the tragic love story.

She could be seen walking from the quarry to the keystone of the bridge, where she disappeared, sometimes silently, sometimes with a cry. Tom himself had explained the legend away by reference to witchcraft, running water, and the probability that there had been a bridge here from ancient times.

So far he had been helped by the wind, which was funnelled by the Glen, but its true direction was such that when he turned sharply towards the bridge, a back eddy, from the steeply banking ground on his right, hit him strongly in the face. Head down, straining on the pedals, he was all but stopped, and as the machine wobbled on some loose gravel he let out a cry of rage, of desperation, at being kept back when every second had a fatal value. As he tugged at the handlebars his head jerked up and there in front of him, perfectly distinct in the bright moonlight, was the figure of a woman, dressed in black, just entering between the walls of the bridge. He saw her ghost-like face turned over her shoulder, and her whole action was that of watching him and at the same time escaping from him. This suggestion in the figure not of haunting the spot but of itself being hunted, was somehow so unexpected, so ominous, that an icy cold drenched his skin. His legs kept the pedals going round automatically, for now he had cleared the high ground on his right and the wind was once more being funnelled downstream. As the figure gained the keystone of the bridge, he heard its unearthly screech above the roar of the narrowed tumbling water and the howl of the wind in the trees. For a moment it hesitated on the wall of the bridge and then went clean over.

He did not look at the spot as he passed, but kept his trembling legs to their task and, when he had got round the off bend, with the wind once more in his back, he began pedalling down the valley in a blind fury of speed, sick with weakness, shaken by soft humps, jolted by round stones, swaying into and out of the middle track loosed by horses' hooves, on the solid rubber tyres of his heavy machine.

As he dismounted before Dr. Manson's door, he staggered badly feeling gone from his knees, but the bicycle supported him.

No physician cares to be called out on a Sunday night, and certainly not one with a country practice as wide as Dr. Manson's. The doctor, who answered the door in person, had plainly been on the point of following the rest of his household to bed, and as he listened to the stammered request, "You're wanted in Achuain at once," he frowned, and peered at the shadowed face.

"What's wrong?"

Tom could not speak.

"Come in," said the doctor, and when he had shut the door behind Tom and led him into the sitting-room, he turned to face the country lad and his eyes at once narrowed on the wound in his head. "What have you been up to?"

The reaction from his abnormal physical effort together with the warmth of the room and the strong smell of tobacco smoke so weakened Tom that he was glad of the chair the doctor offered.

"There's been an accident," said Tom. "It's a girl—she's very bad."

The doctor, sitting down opposite him, looked into his face. "Take your time," he said, "and tell me about it."

"You'll have to hurry," said Tom, anxiety getting the better of him. "It may be too late."

"I see. What happened?"

"You'll have to hurry."

"Keep steady now. If I'm going to do good to anyone I'll have to know what's wrong, what to take with me."

"She was hit. She's unconscious. She may be dead."

"Hit? How?"

"Her mother—they had a row."

"About what?"

"The girl—is going to have a child——"

"Hold on!" said the doctor sharply. He went to a wall cupboard and poured some whisky into a glass. Tom gritted his teeth against the hellish fainting sensation that had gradually been overcoming him. He did his utmost, but could not quite reach the proffered tumbler, and all in a moment passed out.

When the doctor had got him round, Tom's anger at his weakness, and shame, became mixed with his increasing anxiety to have the doctor on the road. But the doctor took him into the surgery, wiped and dabbed at the wound until it stung, and insisted on tying a bandage round it. This delay maddened Tom. "You were lucky," said the doctor.

He heard the doctor talking to someone upstairs—probably his wife. Would he never come? At last his footsteps and his parting words: "No, I'll drive myself."

Tom was eager now to be on his bicycle again. The whisky had revived him and he wanted to tear back through the night in front of the doctor.

"You'll help me to yoke the mare. Sandy, my man, will put your bicycle home on the bus to you to-morrow," said the doctor coolly. He was a man of about fifty and had a son, who would one day succeed him, in medicine at the university. He took Tom's acquiescence for granted and moved round to the stable. Tom soon realized that in his present condition he could not have stood up to the force of the wind.

"How did you get that blow?" asked the doctor as the mare settled to a steady trot on the country road.

Tom did not answer.

"Are you any relation of the girl?"

"No."

There was a pause.

"As a doctor, you know, I have to ask questions. Are you the father of the child?"

"No."

He felt the doctor studying him keenly. "I'm afraid I thought you were. Is the father known?"

"I couldn't say," Tom replied.

"Has the blow on your head any connection with the girl's accident?"

Tom hesitated. "I was passing and heard the noise. I went in. I thought I might help."

The doctor asked more questions. Tom replied with reluctance. About the mother's condition of mind he hinted in such a vague way that clearly the doctor did not trust him. Before relapsing into a long silence, the doctor said, "When it comes to answering the police, I'd advise you to be more direct."

Anxiety at mention of the police hardly touched Tom, so fathomless in a moment became his misery.

The valley lay under the moon, glittering here and there in a barrenness of water and rock, swept by the black wind, the scarified earth of a planet dead before time began. The mare lifted her head and ears and snorted as she crossed the bridge. The doctor caught the reins in a firm hold and, checking her wayward fancy, urged her on with a "Klk! Klk!" She broke into a gallop, round the corner of the bridge, out of the whining trees, and on to the moor.

"She got a fright there once," remarked the doctor calmly.

Presently he asked Tom who he was and where he lived. Tom answered with the minimum of words and once more was aware of a scrutinising look. The doctor knew who he was now, flicked the reins against the mare's back, and settled down to the last lap of the journey. The circumstances attending Tom's father's death would naturally be known to the doctor who had been called in too late. After Alec Wilson's bicycle smash, Peter Grant had gone to the extreme length of sending a telegram for the doctor. Indeed so widespread and distorted became the news of the death that the Procurator-Fiscal in Muirton called on Dr. Manson to see if there was a case for investigation by the Crown. But the doctor had shaken his head: "Pure heart failure." He had known the history of the case.

As they dismounted opposite Janet's house, the doctor said, "Watch the mare, will you?" And walked away without waiting for an answer.

Tom caught a rein lightly near the horse's mouth and stood still in the night, waiting. There was a numbness in his brain, in his feelings. The village looked dead, and life itself, under this burden of anxiety, was only half real, already partook of the nature of death. Time, drawn out endlessly, added its weight to this burden. When thought or feeling started in him, he moved his feet or his head to defeat it. Once the mare grew restless, and by the time he had quietened her he felt exposed, and hot thrusts of emotion pierced him.

With the noise of the opening door, such a weakness came over him that he gripped the shaft and leaned against the beast. The doctor's footsteps were approaching sounds so portentous that for a moment he felt he was going to faint and could not meet them.

The doctor put his bag in the gig and stood buttoning his coat. Tom could not trust his voice.

The doctor looked at him. "She's very low," he said. Then he brought the flats of his hands together as if about to say something further. The hands parted and the gig lurched as he put his weight on the round iron step. "Good-night," he called in his cool voice.

Tom listened for a time to the crisp beat of the iron-shod hoofs as they passed away from this house.

Afraid of the front door, he walked round to the back and stood for a little against the henhouse wall. The light was in the kitchen blind; the same pale yellow light. He leaned against the wall, his forehead on his wrists. "O God!" he groaned and began to weep. He was very weak. He had no strength to do anything. There was no fight in him. There was nothing he could do. Feeling he wanted to lie on the ground, he made an effort to draw himself together. As his right hand went up to push the hair back from his forehead it encountered the bandage. By the time he had taken the bandage off, he felt steadier and approached the door.

His mother, hearing his fumbling feet in the porch, opened the inside door. Catching a glimpse of old Bell the midwife on a chair by the fire, he backed away. His mother followed him and closed the inside door behind her.

"She's asleep just now," she said. He waited for her to go on. "She's very weak," she added in a fatally quiet voice. "The doctor thinks she may not see the morning. She bled a terrible lot."

He thought of her condition, of an internal bleeding, of complications beyond his knowledge, and realised there was no hope. Her sleep had been induced like a pale mask over the physical disorders of death. Death came out of the doctor's words and his mother's quiet manner.

"I'll make Bell lie down and I'll keep watch myself until the early morning. The doctor will be back with the daylight. You go home now and take a sleep. There's nothing any of us any more can do."

As he turned his head away, he heard a voice calling distantly among the hills on the way to Altdhu.

"Some of the men are out looking for Janet's mother. But go you home," she urged him.

He had forgotten Janet's mother entirely. Nor did thought of her, or desire to search for her, trouble him now, as he went slowly up the field and along towards his own home.

Reaction had hit him heavily; he had all he could do to drag his legs. For the first time a pain began to throb in his wound. When he got into the house, he took the bandage from his pocket and started winding it round his head. It was something to do. Then he pressed in fresh peat about the red heart of the fire and stretched himself full length before it and closed his eyes.

His eyes opened on a red point in a mass of grey ash. As he lifted his head, pain stabbed him in the right temple. The lamp was burning low in a deathly silence. He glanced at the bed where his father had lain so long, and in an effort to scramble swiftly to his feet was all but defeated by the cramps in his body. The clock on the mantelshelf said eight minutes past two. He gripped his head and discovered the bandage but forgot himself in a moment when he thought he heard his mother's footsteps outside. O God, that awful sound of human footsteps!

Soon he realised the footsteps could not have been in the night but only in his mind. At a distance he caught a dim reflection of a bandaged head in the small mirror that hung on the wall by the window. The first glimpse of this ghastly visitant shook him; then he approached the mirror and took the bandage off. An urge came over him to clean up his face, hastily, like one in a fevered hurry for an important meeting. With the clotted wound he could do nothing, but drops and trickles of dried blood over his right eyebrow and about his ear he rubbed away with the wetted end of the towel that always hung on its nail by the water bucket. With the comb that was stuck in the brush on the window shelf, he combed back his hair. This final act for some reason slowed up all his movements and he turned round and began to stare and hearken.

Suddenly he started to shiver from the cold and, taking his overcoat from the back of his bedroom door, put it on.

He was now all dressed to meet Janet.

As he went along the hillside the pain from his wound spread through his head in a dull ache and this helped to steady him. But all the time the overcoat was flapping against his knees, and as he came by the henhouse wall he looked down at the dark cloth hanging so still now and strangely upon him. Memory in an instant introduced the headless stranger of his vision. That stranger was not himself, yet never had it stood so near him, so perilously near. Shedding the coat, he dropped it on the ground.

In anger he hissed at this stealthy approach upon him, and with the uprise of his fighting spirit his limbs began to tremble. Panic forces, waiting their chance in their moving wolf-circle, can slash in very quickly.

And all this as by-play around the awful act of going to the door.

His mother opened the inner door and pulled it nearly shut after her. "She's wakened now, but very weak," she whispered. Then after a profound silence: "Would you like to see her?"

He looked up at his mother's face in mortal agony, unable to distinguish her features in the dark porch. "Yes," he whispered.

"Wait till I see"; and, going from him, she closed the door behind her. He tried to listen but could only hear the blood in great threshing beats in his ears.

The door opened and, with a composed smile, his mother invited him in.

He entered, turning from the fireplace to the back wall where the large bed stood with its wooden sides and top. The curtains were drawn completely back, and Janet's great dark eyes were looking at him from her pale face, from the white pillow, from the tumble of her black hair.

They were full of light, of a shy half-startled light, centred upon him in an expectancy so sensitive, so ready for withdrawal, that Tom stood bewildered and immensely awkward. It was Janet—Janet's face—removed from him into a white beauty, living in the glimmer of spirit, of wonder, from the dark eyes, a troubled wonder, alive with the knowledge of what had been between them and had brought them to this strange and final moment. She was holding her defences even now, holding the hidden question in expectancy of what he would say or do.

It could not be borne. His eyes dropped to the white counterpane. His body shifted on its feet. "I'm sorry you are ill," he muttered. His defences began to crash internally. Desperately he choked down the flood of released emotion. He had meant to be quiet and sensible, to tell her that he understood what had happened, that he still thought of her as his old friend. He had meant to make her mind easy on his account, if that would help her.

Her hand came wavering over the counterpane. He drew in a great gulp of breath that made him shudder. He took her hand in his own. Then he buried his face in the counterpane and pressed her hand against his cheek.

While he struggled there to control himself, he felt the light movement of her hand like a spoken word, a delicate tenderness. He turned his mouth on it and kissed it. Before getting up, he crushed it against his forehead.

The expectancy, the wonder that had been troubled with a vague fear, was gone from her eyes, which now smiled to him. But the life that was in her was like a light in a shell, and she remained at her distance looking at him. There was something strangely objective in that look. It was a woman's look that entered into him and, for its own purposes, wandered in the known byways of his mind.

She had not yet spoken to him. Now, to release him, she said, her whole face speaking to him as it had done so often, with its shy charm, "Thank you for coming, Tom."

"Get well," he answered. "Fight—your best."

He could not speak more. And she needed all her strength. He lifted his eyes from her hand to her face.

It was then she gave him that strange white look that haunted him for years. There was loneliness in it, something wild and scared. It glistened distantly from him yet came into him and burned him up. It was more than a farewell in its glistening anguish. And from somewhere in the heart of it she smiled to him.

But the cry, that silent cry of her spirit, remained unuttered.

He blundered out past his mother, who was standing in the porch.

Later, on the bare hillside, he heard his mother coming before he saw her body form in the deep gloom, for the moon had gone under cloud coming up from the west. He heard her slow heavy footsteps and then he heard the low spasmodic sounds of her weeping. Janet was dead.

Chapter Eighteen

The Philosopher sat staring at the distant mountain-tops that told the months by the setting sun. The shadow of the stone, in its slow wheeling, lifted its edge from the earth and cut his hands and knees in a sharp warmth. The ceremonial of the stones, of the doctor and the police and the Procurator-Fiscal, of the whispering of the folk under the shadow of tragedy, of the long funeral cortège that bore the bodies of Janet and her mother to the graveyard beyond the grey church.

For the body of Janet's mother had been found under the bridge. It was no ghost he had seen that night when he had rushed for the doctor on the old solid bicycle. Nor had he mentioned his experience to anyone, for the complications of that wild night enmeshed him too fatally.

First to the door of his home came the policeman with a notebook, the same who had questioned him over the smashed bicycle at the time of his father's death, a big fair man, with a fair moustache, a soft full face and sharp blue eyes.

His mother admitted him to the kitchen where Tom sat waiting.

With a pitiful smile she bespoke him, finding him a chair in an act of natural hospitality that took on the air of a propitiatory rite. Her voice, thick with concern and fear, trembled, and as she moved about, charged with words and cries, Tom looked at her. "You can leave us, Mother."

But she did not want to go. She started to speak, broke down, and, lifting her dark apron to her face, went out.

In a clear important voice, the policeman introduced the occasion of his visit by stating that it was his duty to investigate certain circumstances attending the deaths of Mrs. Marion Morrison and of her daughter Janet. He would take evidence from all those who could in any way throw light on what had happened, and he had to warn Tom that what he said would be noted down and used in such manner as the proper authorities would decide. All he wanted was the truth and nothing but the truth.

Tom admitted his presence in the kitchen on the fatal night and described what had happened. The policeman then took each point carefully, inquiring into Mrs. Morrison's apparent condition of mind, the exact words she used, Janet's attitude. He rehearsed each separate act, until he felt he had a clear grip of the whole scene, pondering now and then, between writing, possible points that he might have missed. All this took a long time.

"Now," said the policeman, "will you tell me how it came about that you were there?"

"I happened to be passing and heard the noise."

"Where were you passing?"

"Near the back door."

"The back door? What were you doing there at that time?"

"I happened to be passing the door."

"Were you going to call on them?"

Tom hesitated for a moment. "No," he answered.

"What were you doing there at that time?"

"Taking a walk."

"Were you going out for a walk or coming home from one?"

"I was going out," said Tom.

"Do you usually go a walk in that direction?"

"Sometimes."

When the policeman had plotted the walk he asked if it was not a curious place to be taking a walk at that time of night, and a Sunday night, too.

"Not for me," answered Tom with a touch of bitterness. "Besides, there was a moon."

The policeman looked closely at him, but his further questions Tom answered shortly. "I've told you how it happened."

Then came the questions about Tom's personal relations with "the two deceased".

"Did you know them well?"

"As well as one knows the rest of one's neighbours."

"No more than that?"

"About that."

"What do you mean by *about* that?"

"Relations vary between neighbours."

"Had you been in the habit lately of seeing much of them?"

"Very little."

"Had you at any time close relations with the daughter Janet?"

"I knew her quite well."

"When did you know her quite well?"

"Since I was a child."

"Had you been keeping company with her within the last year?"

"I had been in her company occasionally."

In such matters the policeman had the countryman's knowledge and all the native cunning. Obviously he suspected Tom of hedging and was determined not to be outdone. But though there was a queer nervousness all over Tom's body, his mind was coldly clear.

"You repeat, do you, that there had been no special understanding or relation between you?"

"I knew her quite well."

"You're not answering my questions."

"I am."

"You're not. Do you refuse to answer it?"

"I have answered it."

"Were you engaged in any way to each other?"

"No."

And then the inevitable question at last:

"Were you courting at any time?"

It maddened Tom. "That's my business."

"So you were courting?"

"I never said so."

"Do you deny it?"

"I have had enough of this." Tom jumped to his feet. "What right have you to ask about my private life?" he shouted.

"I have to inquire into all facts bearing on the case. So keep calm, and answer my questions—or it may be the worse for you."

"What facts?" blazed Tom.

"We'll come to that."

"Well, come to them!" Tom was now quivering all over.

"I'm coming to them. Sit down."

"I will not sit down."

"Were you courting the late Janet Morrison within the last year or less?"

"What has that to do with it?"

"It may have a lot. Answer me."

"I won't." Tom turned away. The policeman put a hand on his shoulder. Tom swung round as if he had been hit. "Don't dare touch me!" he yelled.

The door opened and his mother cried, "Oh, Tom! Tom!"

Tom walked swiftly past her. The policeman made to follow but his mother must have stopped him. Tom found himself alone in the barn.

He was trembling all over and full of a madness of anger. As his mind cleared and he was able to stand still, the real purport of the policeman's questions began to dawn on him. It had been obvious all along that what the policeman had been coming at was the fatherhood of Janet's child. His effort at a cunning approach had been maddening, until at last it could not be borne, and if the policeman had grabbed him again he would certainly have lashed out.

But why was the policeman . . .? Had Janet not told anyone who the father was? In a flash of utter certainty Tom realised that Donald would have held her to silence until such time as he could plan . . . Janet herself would have been silent. The birth was some distance away. Any woman would protect her lover—and Donald was the minister's son!

My God! thought Tom, seeing the significance of his own particular appearance in Janet's kitchen at the fatal hour. The mystery of the mother's dead body in the river. The fight—in which he had taken part, of which he bore the mark. The local whispering that he was the father of the child. Big Ann's words . . .

Tom the atheist who had killed his own father . . . now driven by "the judgement" upon him to destroy the girl whom he had fatally wronged *and* her mother!

Tom's body ran cold, and he laughed.

The completeness of the case would make anyone laugh! My God, it would! Make the whole hellish world rear like a serpent in silent black laughter.

His own body seemed to rear, enlarged, the legs sheathed in frost, awkward, divorced from him, the temples cold as thin sheets of ice.

In Janet's silence he stood condemned before men. Janet's silence—now eternal.

In the silence of Janet he stood condemned before himself. "The author and the finisher"—that pulpit cry!—of death.

The guilt of all mankind, the guilt of the hunted man, the terrible horror of the outcast, "fleeing the wrath to come", now assailed him, and in these moments was comprehended with an unearthly clarity.

Over all the earth it went, from all the byways of the earth it came, down all the twisting years of time, pastoral ages and cities ... the dark pursuing serpentine evil, with its eyes and mouth of sin.

Coming in to him, serpents gathering to their focal point, their central pit.

The policeman darkened the door, stooped and entered a pace. He had one more question to ask. His tidy sense of duty made it necessary that he ask this question. He had to complete his case. "Are you the father of the child in the girl Janet Morrison?"

Tom saw the face in all its soft fat lineaments, looked in at the small glinting windows of the eyes.

"Do you refuse to answer?"

All the movements of the policeman's mind were seen. The policeman. Then Tom's own mind blurred, like water over which a wind blows, and out of the coldness of the wind came a bitter remorselessness. The policeman must have seen the change.

"Very well." He nodded. "You refuse." He stepped outside and in view of the door wrote in his notebook with the official mannerism of menace.

Tom left the barn and went into the hills.

He wandered there for hours, over the dead heath, in the silent valleys, now throwing himself on his face and gripping the heath, now walking in a stupor, his eyes, uncomprehending, on the near and far silent dead valleys and ridges.

The eternal silence.

The far peaks of the mountain ranges drew him. They always had childhood's illusion of being the barrier to a strange country. But Tom was no longer a child, and that strange, half-fearful, half-inviting country he now realised was the country of the dead.

Beyond the barrier, lost for ever, lost to himself, in the quiet sleep of death.

The sun was descending towards the peaks, too strong yet to look at with the naked eye. But presently it could be looked at, when it touched a destined peak, and slowly sank, amid the flowing of colours, of red, and saffron, and pale yellow, of delicate blues and infinitely remote islets of green, sank down beyond the peaks of time into darkness.

As he sat on a ridge, a final ridge it seemed, separating him from the world behind and the world beyond the mountains, a quietening came on him, a premonitory feeling of liberation, and his mind at its core became single as a child's, and he wondered if he would go into that country of the dead.

It was the calm sweet wonder of the mind that is already going. But the mind was troubled in its surfaces, and the wonder as yet no more than its core.

By her silence Janet had shut him out from the world of mankind, and also, and for ever, had shut him out from herself. His was the lonely way into the mountains, a clean separateness, a final forgetting.

A curious treachery there was in women; not so much treachery as a ruthlessness. They would lie, and deceive, and be treacherous to the utmost degree, in order to get their desire. As if their desire was something more than themselves and knew no law. Knew no mercy, no kindness. Their feelings tender and delicate: tentacles searching for their food. More genuinely cruel at the core than anything yet conceived in the realm of life. Poets had seen them as harpies and wantons and tragic queens. On bleak hillsides they hunted their desire with greed, ruthlessness quivering at the heart of their broken tenderness.

Such thoughts were hardly verbal in him, were little more than the pale death-image of Janet, shut away from him, of Janet who had shut him away.

As the sun was touching the mountain, he heard a cry far down the slope on his left, where boulders and bits of scrub littered the ground before it began to rise again. He looked and saw a squat human figure get up and stumble on. Then it stood, and he heard again its forlorn and broken cry: "Tom!"

It was his mother.

She had not seen him, for her eyes went before her up the bottom of the valley. Though she moved slowly she had the appearance of going with earnestness and haste, as a dog seeking the scent of its quarry. Now she leaned with a hand against a boulder, stooping slightly like one drawing harsh laboured breaths. Then on again; but the ground was broken and her exhaustion must have been very great, for, when she stumbled and fell, she drooped in upon herself like one of the boulders, and, listening acutely, he heard the dry whining of her distress.

He got up and slanted down the hillside towards her. But while he was yet a little way off, she got to her feet to continue her journey towards the horizon she had set before her. As he drew in behind her on her right side, she became familiar to him as his mother, in her body and its movements and its laboured breath. The familiarity touched him sharply and in order not to startle her too much he called from twenty yards:

"Mother!"

She stopped as if she had been hit, and, half-turning, saw him. Her left hand went out vaguely seeking support from the hillside, while her mouth opened and the small arched creases appeared over her round eyes. In her face for a moment was disbelief like a stupid dismay. "Tom!" breathed her mouth.

"What are you doing here?" he asked quietly.

But her eyes kept devouring his face. "Tom, you're here?"

"Of course I'm here," he answered evenly. It always took her such a length of time to realise anything.

Then at last her face drooped, and, forgetting that her out-stretched hand had found no support, she sat down. All her processes were slow. She struggled against the weakness that followed the breaking of the long-sustained tension in her mind and tried not to weep. But she could not hold out any more and she wept heavily.

He realised as he stood looking at her that the weeping now was not for herself but for all the tragic events that had pursued them.

She recovered, choking down the outburst that had broken the core of struggle, and mumbled against herself as she wiped her eyes and prepared to rise.

"Rest for a little," he said, and to make it easier for her to rest he himself sat down a yard or two from her. His voice had been kind but firm. She needed strength.

He sat looking before him and gave her time to compose herself.

"I did not know where you had gone," she said.

"It's all right," he answered, nodding to the hillside.

"Don't be angry with me," she said. And then after a short pause, "I told the policeman myself."

"What did you tell him?"

"That Janet told me you were not the father."

She said it naturally, but to him the words had there at that moment a dreadful, an appalling intimacy.

"Why did you not tell him yourself?" she asked.

"Doesn't matter," he muttered shortly.

She had said the wrong thing again, and stirred in her distress.

"I came after you—to tell you," was all she could add.

"You could have waited till I came home."

"Yes. I should have done that. But I got an awful feeling that—that you were going away."

"Where would I go away to?"

"I—don't know."

The sun must now have sunk well behind its peak for the first shadows were in the bed of the valley.

"When you feel rested we'll go," he said, "for it will be dark before we get home."

She arose and they started back down the valley. When they came to its outlet and the ground steepened for a short way, he took her arm. "You'll have to watch your feet," he cautioned her.

She had to pause and say it. "You're not angry with me for coming?"

"No, Mother. I know why you came."

He felt her look on him and heard the breath in her nostrils, but she did not speak and, his eyes searching for the easy way, they went down together.

What Janet had said to his mother was only a mother's evidence. Humanity realises that a mother will tell a lie. Janet had not told the doctor who the father was, nor had Tom's mother.

The Procurator-Fiscal arrived from Muirton to interrogate Tom.

During all this time Tom had no care for himself, no fear. He still lived in Janet's death and was bitterly resentful of all this horrible pawing and sniffing over the dismembered place where love and life had been. He felt its degradation in him, and his instinct was to shut his mouth and let happen what would happen.

But the Fiscal was a lawyer of sensibility and a wide experience in human motive and feeling. He was clean shaven except for a stubby grey moustache, and his brown eyes were intelligent and friendly, not given to any obvious effort at penetration.

"You see," he explained to Tom, "unless I can be sure that no living person was implicated, was the direct cause of what happened, I'll have to prepare for a full court case, and then the whole thing will have to be gone into, in the smallest detail, in public. It may have to be that way, of course, in any case. But that depends on what I learn now. Take this difficulty, for one. Can you throw any light on the condition of the mother's mind? You saw her at the time."

Tom hesitated.

"Was she wrought up, in your opinion, just because she had found out her daughter's condition?"

"It was more than that," said Tom.

"Tell me everything, my boy. This is something that goes beyond you and me. We owe whatever justice we can give to the dead."

Then Tom, his head down, began to speak, and he told the Fiscal what Janet had told him of her mother's periodic bouts.

"Where did she get the stuff?"

"In Muirton. She went herself for it by bus."

"You don't know where she bought it?"

"No."

The Fiscal nodded. He could easily find that out.

"You were friendly with the girl, Janet, then?"

"Yes. We were friendly for a time."

"Did that friendliness change?"

"Yes."

"When?"

"After she had been going to the manse."

"Did it change on your part or on hers?"

"Hers," said Tom.

"When would that be about?"

Tom told him.

"Why do you think she changed towards you?"

Tom was silent.

"Tell me this. Did you have reason to suspect who the father of the child was?"

"It could only be one person."

"Who?"

"Donald Munro."

"No one told you that?"

"No."

"How did you first hear that she was in that way?"

Tom told him.

"How did you feel—did you do anything?"

Tom hesitated a moment, then quietly related the whole story of his trip to Edinburgh, his meeting with the girl from Muirton, his trip to Glasgow and how he discovered that Donald had gone abroad.

"I see," said the Fiscal, nodding slowly, realising that here was detail that could be confirmed. "What were you going to do to him?"

"I was going—to get him to marry—Janet."

The Fiscal was silent.

Then whether because of this man's sympathy or not, emotion touched Tom. He tautened his features but his eyes silently over-flowed.

The Fiscal got up and moved to the window.

Tom got control of himself but felt weak and wretched.

The Fiscal came back to the fire and stood before it, slowly washing his hands in the heat.

"So it wasn't altogether chance that brought you past the back door on that night?"

"Her mother generally was bad about the full moon. It was full moon that night. I began to wonder."

The Fiscal nodded.

When at last he was going away, he stretched out his hand. "Thank you for what you have told me. You were wise to have done it, for your own sake—and for the girl's."

But it was Tina finally who cleared Tom. She confessed to the Procurator-Fiscal that she had always been fully in Janet's confidence—the only one who ever was. She knew more about the outbreaks of Janet's mother than Tom did. She had a multitude of intimate details. Of the relationship between Janet and Donald, she spoke freely. She had sworn to Janet that she would never give her secret away. Donald was terribly afraid his father would get to know what had happened. His father was the minister, and he himself was studying for the Church. It was an awful position.

Then Tina said that Janet, who grew desperate once Miss Williamina began to suspect, had got a letter from Donald begging her to give nothing away until he came home with his plan all ready. Secretly she would then leave with him.

Janet's private belongings were searched and the letter found.

No further Crown proceedings were taken. As far as any public inquiry was concerned, Janet's name was left in peace.

The shadow of the stone had now passed from the Philosopher's face, and the sun was so hot that he blinked and looked about him, and, arising, continued on his way.

Chapter Nineteen

From the knoll of the Stones the ground dipped and then rolled into the outskirts of the moor proper. Here was good rough grazing ground, with sheep nibbling by whin bushes and a swampy flat now dry and full of long rank grass, rushes, and the white flags of the cotton plant. The Philosopher skirted this dry marsh, keeping to the firm ground on his left, where vague ridges or rigs told of an old husbandry.

He could, in fact, remember this ground under cultivation over fifty years ago. The ruins of the croft house lay at some little distance in front of him on the sunny side of a green hillock. The old hairy crofter had been a bard, a satirist of some note, and his topical verses were quoted over the countryside. These ruins were usually the Philosopher's last resting place before reaching the banks of the moor stream.

The wealth of wild flowers was familiar to him and he began nodding here and there to tormentil and eyebright, cuckoo flower and primrose, milkwort, pink campion, lady's mantle, stonecrop, petty whin, trefoil, herb Robert and buttercup. He had a special affection for the plants that grew here, probably because, for some reason that he could not quite explain, he loved the place. It was not altogether because, being shut away from sight of all other human habitation, it had won to its own freedom, a freedom from interference, a freedom to smile and laugh, dance in the wind, to curl up in sleepy daydreams in the sun, to know the grey mist and the quagmire, to shelter from the howling storm, to endure like a stone, to be forever natural and in the fullness of the cycle to salute the blue sky with blossoms.

He knew his Rousseau and many of the nature writers; had penetrated into animism and kindred beliefs. He was not prepared to be deceived or led away easily. Why this definite experience of gladness, of happiness, in this place? It always came to him now. He could think of it from a distance.

It was as if happiness itself had worked and dwelt here. The feet of happiness still moved about the grass and eddied in the wind. The place made him smile, as though he were in secret collusion with it and not just prepared to give it away to anyone! For as its fragrance is to wild honey so to this feeling of happiness was its own subtle humour.

As he plodded on, his eyes saluted by the flowers, to which he nodded—he had seen folk of the older generation when he was a boy take off their bonnets to the sun or bow to the new moon—he began to wonder about the true nature of this gladness (gladness coming, perhaps, before happiness, as the earth before heaven—a theme in itself?)

And then the idea came to him and he stood still . . . went on slowly again . . . and stood still; and when after many stops he reached the green bank by the lower gable end of the ruins where he usually rested, he stood and looked at it for a long time before he at last sat down on it.

For the idea was an interesting one and had already on this remarkable day been pursued in some small measure. Indeed although he had walked very slowly over these last few yards, he now felt the beating of his heart. It did not take much, of course, to make his heart beat. A legacy of weakness from his father? He smiled in a curious distant way, his sight out of focus.

Clearly the vivid manner in which his mind had wandered back into a certain period of his life had been given an unconscious start by the sight of Henry, who was Tina's son, supplying petrol to the passing cars.

But there were other periods of his life—centring perhaps round that period of intense human relations as round a pivot? The period of childhood, of boyhood, of adolescence—that long early spell curiously allied now to his present state, as if the circle were completing itself. That early freshness of contact with nature—in how far was it subsumed in his present attitude, with what loss—and with what gain? For a certain loss there was, but the loss could be fairly estimated, and the gain was tremendous. That should be a fascinating inquiry. To it alone he could take days that would be long intimate excursions. Each point worked out with precision through a delicate analysis.

Yet even this gladness, with its golden freshness of a buttercup, could not be fairly valued and understood without help from still other and later periods.

For example, following on Janet's death and those bitter days of official inquiry, there had descended upon him, after a short interval of curious unreal relief, a state of extreme despondency. It was more than that state of negation in which earth is very earth and mud mud, when such negative realism is seen with final conviction as the only positive, when wild flowers are another and tawdry form of grass and both are pushed up and sucked down in a blind and futile and mindless procession. It did not stop there. Had it been able to do so, things might not have been so bad. It was when he lifted up his eyes from this peat bog and looked at the air, at the grey air of an overclouded day, and in the silence apprehended its stillness as that of ten thousand Sabbaths invisibly distilled, that a dazing and quivering came upon him, an apprehension of menace and sadness too overwhelming to be borne.

In the moment of tragedy, of normal death, a countrywoman would throw up her apron over her face. How simple was this natural act!

To decipher the agony that uprose before that nameless grey immanence . . .

He had run away. Had jumped on his bicycle, with a small bundle, packed by his mother, tied behind the saddle, and pedalled off as hard as he could—up the Glen and on to the West, to places where he had never previously been.

That was a remarkable odyssey, containing some weird and

memorable scenes. It lasted barely five weeks, yet in after thought—even now—it had the air of a journey to another world. Not only the remote deep-winding sea-lochs, the small fishing boats, the tides and currents, but the folk themselves in their scattered cottages, their little townships, as remote from Muirton and a railway train as their story-tellers from Huxley and Haeckel.

At first there had been considerable discomfort in the way of invasion of his privacy and he could have wished he had gone to the solitude of Glasgow. His bicycle was the trouble. Not only did the children rush after him and, when he dismounted, surround him in a wondering mob, but the young men, and the old men, and the girls, and even the old women—ochanee! what is the world coming to!

But he soon learned to deal with that difficulty, and in any case the unpeopled spaces were so much the vaster that often he travelled for the better part of a day without meeting a soul. It took him nearly a fortnight to defeat the need to push ahead, to keep pedalling on tracks that were rutted and dangerous, as if he had an appointment he dare not miss.

White-fishing over the sands off Gairloch in an evening light. A night in a bothie by Gruinard Bay and a midnight expedition for salmon-poaching. How he travelled from Ullapool to Achiltibuie to give John Macleod the following message from Duncan Macrae: "They're here and after you. Clear the hold at once."

The Revenue men found nothing at Achiltibuie and John Macleod threatened to have the law on them for the way they had brought suspicion upon him before his neighbours. Tom had to stay nearly a week with John, who fished lobsters off the Summer Isles and made the finest drop of whisky in these parts. At times wisdom ran so deep in him, in his silence and quiet movements and smiling eyes, that to lie on the heather beside him, or haul up the corked string of the lobster pot, was a rare indulgence in pure life.

That odyssey alone would need a long mental journey to unfold it. For whereas then it had been full of experience, now it was full of meaning. The night he had slept out in those black rock hinterlands beyond Kylescu . . . He had come pretty near facing the grey ghost of his soul that night!

Scourie, and the Laxford River with salmon in the pools. The long eastward trek past the lochs. That wet day by the shore of Loch Shin. Was there a more desolate loch, more desolate moors, anywhere in all the wide Highlands? And then in the midst of that desolation, with the fine rain smothering the view like a clinging smoke, wet and cold and miserable, he had felt so far beyond all mortal care, so stripped of the last vestige of desire, so finally and wholly the outcast, that a rare thin delight, like a wintry sunlight, had for a time lit up his soul and glimmered in his sight.

By the time he came back, the last of the crops were down and everything was tidy on his land. Norman had helped his mother. The neighbours, she said, had been very kind. She was so glad to see him that she lost her wits for a little, and began hunting for the wooden spirtle which was already keeping up the lid of the boiling pot, for he was bound to be very hungry now, she said. More light-hearted than he had known her, she was like one who, harbouring a very special piece of good news, had feared he would never return to get it.

He soon found out what it was. The true story about Janet and himself and Donald had got abroad, and the sympathy of some of his old friends had returned to him strongly. That summer he opened his shop, repaired the damaged bicycle, and got in touch with Dougal Robertson once more.

There would also have to be examined from this time onward the gradually changing social conditions, the emigration of young men to the Colonies, the slow break-up of the crofting townships. When was it—around 1910?—that he had sold the first petrol engine to a croft? An affair of $1\frac{1}{2}$ h.p., that could be hitched on to the old hand-threshing mill and so dispense with the human labour of turning the drum. Three gallons of petrol would thresh the harvest. But it did not really affect crofting conditions. It merely took the place of the strong arms of the young men and women who had gone away. The old folk remained, and the crofts died out.

All this had been accompanied by a psychological change in the folk themselves, not only towards the ways of the world but even in the attitude to religion. It took the form of a tolerance that was not a true tolerance but a vague acceptance of the strength of the outside world, a folding of hands before the inevitable. The minister, however, continued to thunder. His son's betrayal and desertion only increased a certain prophetic, fanatical fire in him. But he became gaunt, his clothes flapped on him, and his white beard grew longer. He died just before the end of the Boer war. Some say that he had heard once from his son, but this remained uncertain and Donald never came back.

During that war Tom had been accused of being pro-Boer and his small business had suffered. He tried to explain that he was no more pro-Boer than he was pro-Glen. How would they like it if Imperialists from the other side of the world came here to conquer and hold them? The Lovat Scouts were formed and young men came riding home in pride from their summer camps. But Tom saw in the motor car and motor cycle the inevitable supplanters of the horse on the public highways. He built a petrol store and inquired into sub-agencies for motor cycles and cars. Clocks and hardware goods he dropped altogether. His main business in these opening years of the century lay in hiring, selling, and repairing various models of pneumatic-tyred push cycles.

A period of social and economic change, a "transition era" from the old self-sufficiency of the croft in work and thought and Gaelic culture to—this world of to-day, itself vastly unstable and heading perhaps for future wars on a gigantic scale.

All that as the background—or foreground—affecting individual action and reaction. For he must never forget again that what was important in social change was the effect on the individual.

That was one of the lessons it took him longest to learn. In youth one is taken up with parties, movements, causes, with vast idealisations of social change. Not that one ever used the soft word ideal. Truth, rather; objective truth. One does not cure oneself: one cures the whole world. One's neighbours are miserable narrow-minded people who do not understand objective truth. Beyond them, beyond oneself, is the vast curative pool which can be scientifically stirred for the lasting good of a blind humanity. The thrill is immense. Like the spectator's thrill in an international football match. One gives of one's best. Everything is outward towards mass movement, mass change.

Against this ideal out-thrust stands "the reactionary". As William Bulbreac stood against him when he had called the Pentateuch a Jewish tribal story, in parts self-contradictory and in other parts foul. It did not matter what sort of real person David was or Solomon or Moses or Bathsheba. Did not matter to either of them. What sort of person William Bulbreac was or himself did not matter. Nothing mattered but the ideal fight. With the mood of contest properly worked up, they were prepared to indulge in cruelty on a fabulous scale, to measure out destruction and death till one or the other—and so till half the world—was destroyed or slain.

Tina, Alec, Big Ann, Norman, his mother—what did such simple country folk signify in this fight? Nothing; almost less than nothing, as if they lived on a kind of sufferance, in a backwash that only retarded the great "movement". Let them be scorched with the earth, as the two opposing movements, locked in the death grapple, swept hither and thither. The "ideals" involved so transcended them that their human sacrifice in circumstances of hellish barbarity was their privilege and only possible offering to society!

So he came back to the individual, and as the only individual he would ever have a chance of knowing was himself, he drifted from his preoccupations with socialism and freethought into a tentative reading of philosophy. For manifestly each individual was born by himself, lived by himself, and died by himself. There was no getting past that. That was central. All the rest was added to it, was superstructure.

Meantime in these early years of the century his little business, particularly on the repair side, demanded a lot of his time. Niggling affairs like punctures and broken spokes were always awaiting his attention. In 1909 Tina's husband died and her eldest child, Henry, left school at the age of fourteen.

After Janet's death, Tina had seemed to be scared of him. Even two or three years afterwards, if he chanced to meet her, she gave him the impression of locking her real self up behind a pale strained smile and of being anxious to make the meeting as short as possible. For a while he felt that she must hate him for something he had done, secretly hate him. Yet he could not say that this hatred showed in her face. It was rather as if she had made up her mind about him and definitely wanted to avoid him. He had been sorry about this and a little irritated, for his bitterness was easily invoked in those days. Moreover Tina was the only girl of his own age whom he could naturally talk to, and he had always liked her. In an effort one day to break down her defence and surprise her real feeling, he twitted her pointedly about George.

"What have you against George?" she asked..

"Against George? Nothing," he answered in astonishment.

"Well——" But her lips closed on whatever she had been going to say and, turning from him, she walked away in the queerest abrupt manner, almost as if she were going to be violently angry— or cry.

He very nearly ran after her.

Next year George and Tina got married and Tom felt he had been a fool. He gave them a clock, but Tina never quite came from behind her masked expression to forgive him.

Though George had a reasonable hope of a share in the business, and ultimately of running the whole business, actually when he died he had no such share, and Tina and her three children were left without any regular support. Her parents were getting on in years and she had been in the habit of helping them latterly with little gifts of food.

Henry had been one of a few boys who could hardly stay away from Tom's shop. He had plenty of self-assurance, a sound head, good hands, and, with some of his father's manner, was inclined to boss the other boys successfully.

When Tom asked him what he was going to do, now that he had left school, Henry answered, "I'd like to be in a job like this."

"Well, what about coming in? I'll give you five shillings a week to start you."

Henry looked at him directly and perhaps a little fearfully. "You don't mean it?"

"I do."

"Will I start now?"

"Perhaps you'd better go home and talk it over with your mother first."

Henry walked up to the road, but when he thought he was out of sight of the window he took to his heels.

Henry was Tom's best business investment. If he had not Tom's persuasive way with metal or his eye for wood, he was on the other hand a far better manager and salesman. The first day Henry had the shop to himself, Tom hardly knew it when he came back. His stock of small materials had got badly mixed up, corners were becoming litter-dumps of discarded stuff, parts of which might come in useful if kept long enough, and much of the floor space was piled up with cardboard boxes.

Henry had set about cleaning up the whole place, and soon the familiar "I know I should have something to fit that somewhere", followed by a ten minutes' search, often fruitless, became a waste of the past. Income increased out of all relation to Henry's wage. For the really profitable business, like selling new bicycles, Henry had a natural genius, and in an uncanny way seemed to get to know youths in neighbouring parishes who were secretly dabbling with the idea of acquiring a new machine. For each such sale Tom gave him a commission of five shillings.

When the Great War broke out Henry, at nineteen, had a fixed wage of fifteen shillings a week and his commission. Tom raised it to a pound, for mechanical repairs to cars and motor cycles and sales of petrol were rapidly increasing as a result of a new "passing" trade.

Then Henry grew uneasy and one day said to Tom, "I'm thinking of joining up."

Tom nodded.

"I'm sorry to go. I hate to leave you alone."

"Can't be helped."

Henry could not look at him. "How will you manage?"

"Oh, I'll do my best."

"I feel it—not joining up, at my age."

"I understand. When were you thinking of going?"

"Willie Grant and Duncan Ross are going to-morrow." Henry began working again on the old bicycle chain which he was shortening by a link. He looked miserable.

"Well," said Tom, "I'll keep your place open for you, if you care to come back."

Henry's screwdriver slipped. "I'll promise to come back," he said, examining his thumb.

"You have done very well by me here," Tom added. "No-one knows what this war will bring us, but one thing is certain: it will mean a tremendous increase in motor traffic. It's not much good making any plans, but if things turn out favourably, I could offer you a share in the business when you come back."

It was the first time Tom had ever seen Henry really moved. His skin darkened with blood and his elbows stuck out awkwardly.

In the third winter of the war his mother sickened. She was now over seventy years of age and he himself must have been over forty-five. She had not lost her stoutness as her age increased, and the doctor—a man of about his own years and son of the Dr. Manson for whom he had once ridden through the night—said after his examination: "I'm afraid it's just a case of the old machinery running down." He folded his stethoscope. "Make her rest in bed for a day or two and I'll look in later in the week."

Tina now began calling on his mother in the forenoon when he was at the shop, cleaning up the house, and leaving her daughter Bessie to finish the cooking of the midday meal or dinner. Bessie was fifteen, dark, serious-faced, shy, and anxious to do her best. At first Tom thought she did not like to be with his mother, as if old age and ill health frightened her. But she responded to kindness in a marked way, and soon she was quite at home, leaving the house spick and span, with nothing for Tom to do when he returned in the late afternoon or evening but boil the kettle. It was Tom's own mother who insisted that Bessie was too young a lassie to stay the whole day with a sick old woman.

Perhaps the doctor knew what was wrong with his mother: perhaps he didn't. Tom was never sure. Sometimes she said she was ashamed to be lying in bed and looked at Tom with a shame-faced expression. He answered her that that was all nonsense and that she must stay in bed until the doctor allowed her to get up. Whereupon she seemed relieved and accepted the position with a quiescence which secretly rather astonished him, for all her life had been one of action, of doing, and now that she was confined to bed he had expected her to fret.

Soon after four o'clock in the afternoon the lamp was lit and he settled in his chair by the kitchen fire for the whole evening. She lay quietly; and often for long spells, two to three hours, he would forget her. At that time he had got four volumes of the writings of David Hume, and the breadth and common sense of that philosopher's mind was an almost perpetual surprise. Every page held some sort of discovery which, after a pause for self-investigation, he acknowledged, sometimes with complete agreement, at other times with a certain doubt or reserve, but always with interest and not infrequently with delight.

The letters that passed between Hume and Rousseau held for him, the deeper he went into Hume, a remarkable fascination. Rousseau's last long letter, with its incredible suspicions and vilifications of Hume, he read several times, and though he favoured

Hume, acknowledging the strong clarity of his male intellect, yet there gradually developed in him a profound sympathy for Rousseau. He had no knowledge of any other writings by Rousseau then, and looked upon that last long epistle as a manifestation, almost perverse in its innate subtlety, of the feminine mind. He felt no essential kinship to Rousseau. The relationship seemed one of extreme interest, brought about by irrational experiences he had gone through, and sometimes, in the contemplative pause of his thought, a pale reflection of Janet's face would, as it were, pass him by. Only gradually indeed did he perceive the existence of that queer irrational world as a realm of experience all its own with even a rationale of its own, particularly where it approached in living essence the feminine mind.

In these penetrative pauses he would get glimpses of the workings of Janet's mind and body. Just as Hume's essential attitude to life, on which his principles were based, was different from Rousseau's, so was the male attitude from the feminine. He began to perceive definitions of justice, beauty, chastity, truth, not as absolutes but as masculine conceptions, often obviously related to economic conditions or to property rights (as in the case of chastity). More than once he glimpsed that pale reflection of the feminine face—it was always Janet's face—flitting by in a darkness, like the darkness of a wood, where also there were caves and solitary tall grey rocks, and each grey rock was like a door, and the feminine face appeared first at one side of it from behind and then at the other, in that darkling world, but could not enter the male clearing where Hume sat or where Tom himself watched. These grey doors were the male categories, the philosophic absolutes, the masculine rules of life.

"What is it, Mother?" he asked once, startled out of his thought.

"Nothing, Tom, I was just coughing."

"Would you like a cup of tea?"

"No, no. Don't you bother."

"It's no bother." And he got up and swung the lazily steaming kettle back over the fire.

She loved these interludes, these little picnics, and it gave him a real pleasure to attend to her. Whether the world outside was a frosty silence or a roaring wind, there was peace inside, the soft lamplight, his books, the need for his presence in his mother's illness.

Rarely did she ask what he was reading or thinking, possibly because she felt she would not understand if he told her or because his peculiar reading had caused such trouble before her husband's death, but to-night—she may have caught some interest or lively expression on his face—she asked him if he liked the books he had.

"Yes," he answered, after pressing the small table with the tray close against her bed. "They deal with philosophy—a big subject! But it's interesting, too. The author was a Scotsman, very famous in the learned world. And do you know how old he was when he wrote this great work on the Human Understanding?"

"No?"

"Between twenty-three and twenty-six."

"Dear me!" She shook her head in wonder. "And did it have any ill effect on his health?"

"No." He laughed.

"He was so young," she explained. "He must have been clever."

"He was, and he became a very famous man even abroad." He went on talking about Hume because he knew his mother liked this friendliness of speech, though the personal detail of Hume's *Autobiography* was slim enough.

She listened and by way of final comment said, with a distant strangely longing look at him, "I wish you could have got a chance for more schooling yourself."

"Nonsense, Mother. I got all I needed. Are you comfortable?"

"Yes, Tom. You're very good to me."

"That's fine."

"I enjoyed my tea. And I like to hear your voice sometimes." There was no hidden reproach here, only explanation, a deep natural gratitude. "You be doing your reading now." She hesitated. "You're not feeling lonely staying in here with me?"

"The very opposite," he assured her. "We haven't had such peace in the house for a long time!"

"Very well," she said, smiling, and her rough hands smoothed the counterpane.

He got back to his reading, but often before becoming completely absorbed in it, his mind would carry on some thought or intuition aroused by perhaps no more than an expression in his mother's eyes or a tone of her voice. Often, too, when he had read to the limit of what he could comfortably absorb for the time being, his mind would wander inward and take up again its hidden problem or preoccupation.

239

And ever more clearly he began to perceive that what at one time he had denounced as instability, as cunning, as treachery, in Janet, only seemed to be so to him. To Janet her conduct would have appeared quite differently. Within her realm of actual experience these acts that to him appeared deceitful were to her a feminine manner of releasing herself from what had become to her unreal in order that she bring herself into contact with the real. And he saw now how vivid a woman's apprehension of the real was. A man could cloud his apprehension with all sorts of rules, categories, principles, theories. Not so a woman. She saw what she wanted, the inner kernel, the thing-in-itself, and went, by some law of her feminine being, unerringly for that. When she did this lightly, without appearing to care in the least for her "deceit", man called her a wanton.

True tragedy began for her when her desire to lay hold of the real was defeated.

But though he worked this out through ethical and other realms until it assumed at last a realisable pattern, he was not then freed from his own particular problem. For now a terrible thing took place in his thought.

Janet's love for Donald having been to her the true reality, an absolute, he, Tom, was forever shut out from that central citadel of her spirit. The curious thing was that this should affect him with a feeling of eternal desolation, though he himself professed not to believe in personal immortality. In these quiet hours, this sense of eternal desolation could become very acute. Not only consciousness but matter itself became a bleakness extending to infinity in time. Death would not end or mend it. Death was but an incident on the way. What had been, had been—and would for evermore be.

And cleansed by this bleakness, he saw how right Janet had been, how true her life instinct to nature, to the phenomenal world, the stars, the dialectic of rhythm and change, all the processes that together make up the sum total of what we know and guess at. And this vision came back upon him with a still deeper sense of loss, of bleakness, and, because he could not get beyond himself, of bitterness.

Then one night, for the first time, he realised that his mother was dying. The realisation was borne in upon him from his mother in a characteristic way, for now that she knew death was at hand she became concerned for him.

"The neighbours have been very good," she said, "especially Tina and young Bessie. They have been very good to me."

"No more than you would have been to them."

"I don't know," she answered, plainly now with something on her mind. "Tina is a good-hearted woman. You must not mind me saying it, but I sometimes wonder who will look after you when I am gone."

"You're not gone yet, Mother, so there's not much good in talking like that."

"I'm not thinking about it sadly. Don't think that. I just wonder away sometimes to myself." She always found it difficult to express herself, and quite impossible when she felt that her men folk were impatient with her.

As he saw her thought being bottled up, he said in a kindly voice, "I can understand that, Mother. So just say whatever is in your mind."

"It's just that I would like to see you with someone."

"Well, I'll always get someone—if no-one as good as yourself!"

But she was exercised in her thought. "Tina is a fine woman and a good manager. But—I would like to think of you with someone younger about the place."

He laughed. "Tina has never cared much for me, Mother, so I'll have to look elsewhere."

She did not even smile, but her eyes were on him. Then they withdrew, and he was left with a momentary uncertainty, as if his mother had a secret knowledge of Tina's feelings towards him of which he had never dreamed, and now shielded the knowledge from him by withdrawing her eyes.

"Very well," she said. "I had to say it. I would like to think of you well looked after, and—and—with someone young. Don't mind me saying that."

"Keep your mind at ease, Mother. I'll look after myself. Don't worry about that."

"All right," she said, with a tired nod of acceptance, as if all this had exercised her profoundly, draining her vital strength. She must have been thinking about it whole days and nights.

So oddly moved was he himself by her utterly selfless acceptance of death, that he wondered what he could do to comfort her. "Would you like me to read to you?"

She smiled, with longing and regret in her face. "I would not understand maybe."

Then his thought brightened with a sudden inspiration: "Would you like me to read out of the Bible?"

"Oh, Tom!" she said, and her eyes filled with tears.

His reading of the Bible was to him a curious revelation. At first he stuck to the New Testament, in order to avoid what he felt were the barbaric embarrassments of the Old. When he had read to her, and laid the Bible aside, he got up in a practical way saying she must now compose herself for the night, and went out for a little while. On his return, he saw the mild happy expression of her face and the ease of her arms over the coverlet. Instinctively she glanced at the fire, anxious that the house should be comfortable for him.

Seeing the Bible, he took it up instead of Hume and now, in silence, turned to the Old Testament.

Revelation first consisted in his realising that he had passed beyond all the early heats and arguments. He was prepared to read with an objective mind, as if here were ancient stories which could not affect him personally or raise any question of belief. And then, secondly, he realised that the stories were in themselves extraordinarily interesting in the sense that they were so absolutely human. Here were real men and real women, love and hate and pride and superstition and humility and boasting. Nothing was suppressed. Goodness was here but so was vice. Songs of praise and gladness, the tribulations of utter misery. And gathered in clusters, amid the buzzing and stinging and slaughter, were the cells that held the golden honey of wisdom.

No wonder such a human record had kept its hold on a living humanity.

Next afternoon the minister called. He was an oldish, humdrum, humming man, and when Tom in the evening asked his mother how she had liked the visit, she said, "Och, well enough. He seems a good-meaning man."

"You'll be saying next you prefer my own reading!"

"Indeed and I do, and I hope that's not wrong of me."

A small note of distress crept into her voice. She was getting weak. "He makes everything seem so—terrible, and I feel—I feel cast out, as if it couldn't be for me."

"Don't feel that, Mother. If you'll be cast out then most of us will be cast out with you!"

But she couldn't fully respond. Some solemn mood had been engendered, leaving behind the dead waters of despondency, whereon she now found herself alone and desolate.

As he set the lamp to its highest point of illumination and, bending before the fire, began to bank up the glowing core with new peat, he continued talking in an easy natural voice. "I know you often wondered why I wouldn't go to church. But the trouble with a lot of these men, like William Bulbreac, is that they're so full of themselves and so sure they're right. They're only happy when they make you feel like a sinner. Is it St. Paul who says that joy is next to godliness? But to them joy is a sin. And if you dare question them, they grow angry and threaten you with the bad place. They're solemn because to be solemn makes them feel important. The last thing they would do is turn the other cheek. No fear! They want to have the power of the lash. And the only real sin is to question their belief and their authority. The world knows all about it, Mother. The world was weary of it in the old days. And in Europe to-day, not in religion now but in politics, the same old hideous thing is working away. So it's no good being upset about it, Mother. Men who have power are like that. Now isn't that a good fire?"

"Yes," she said, turning her face. Her eyes were shining.

He had to go on. So, as he got his books together, walking back and fore and preparing to sit down, he continued lightly: "Christ was so gentle and kind. He never sent anyone away with a sore heart if he could help it. Suffer little children to come unto me. Always that human understanding and warmth. I was watching old Norman in that blink of sun yesterday with his two grandchildren rushing about him. They were swarming over him like two puppies and shouting to beat the band. It would never occur to Norman to cast a stone at anyone. But William Bulbreac would have cast a whole quarryful. Well, why should we worry about people like William? And if the minister comes in about in a doleful solemn way, interceding for us and so on, well, Mother, we're not doleful and sad. We just do our best according to our natures, and there's no more we can do. If anything is going to be understood hereafter, surely that will be. And if Christ was kind, it was because He understood. With Him always it was kindness and

243

mercy." He looked over his shoulder. "Do you think I could have made a preacher myself!"

But she could not articulate, and the tears came again, and in a moment she was weeping heavily, her sobs all the louder for the effort she made to control them.

Tom sat down in his chair and took up Hume, leaving her to herself.

"It's not because—because I'm sad," she tried to explain, as her emotion died down. "It's like lifting a load off me."

"Right you are, Mother. I understand fine. I may as well put fresh water in the kettle. I think it makes a better drop. Don't you?"

"Yes," she said. And as he lifted the kettle off the crook, she murmured, "I'm so happy."

As he stood in the gloom of the passage filling the kettle with the tin skillet, he thought: That so little should make her happy! The smile seemed not only in himself but, with an equal irony, extending into the farthest reaches of life, and the irony was profound, deeper and gentler than he could ever plumb. He felt the faint coldness of its exaltation as something forever inexplicable and beyond him.

On the third night thereafter she died. By a great mercy she died not in pain or suffering but quietly, life sinking away from her like water through sand. Her mind had been clouded now and then in the two preceding days, but with the cloudiness of a dream she had hardly the strength to wake out of. What secret suffering she may have had, she never mentioned, but it could not have been very great or he would have divined it. To inquiring neighbours, he reported her condition as more favourable than it was. The doctor in his frank way had said she might last a little while or she might go any day.

He knew on this night that death was coming by her eyes. They spoke to him and told him. The change is coming, they said, but she herself did not speak. In the lamplight, he moved from his own place and sat on the simple wooden chair, its padded seat covered in bright-coloured knitted wools, by the bedside. "I'll read to you," he said in his normal voice.

He read out of the New Testament many of the things Christ had done and said. He left the Pharisees alone and all uncharitableness. He left Calvary and redemption alone. Because now, at this final moment, he could not raise even as a shadow in his own mind what was contentious or difficult. None of that now, not salvation even, but only this wisdom of act and mind, this penetration, this gentleness, that gave out kinship and lifted the heart into eternal community with all fine hearts, this singing of wisdom, this song of life, down the great ways. For if there was no death, then all is life. And if, at the end, there is death only, then here is life's greatness and its beauty.

The strange reserve—the reserve of the stranger—that always was in him when he read the Bible, he now allowed to leave him, so that his mind was open as the book before him and his voice natural as a hill stream.

He stopped reading aloud and read to himself in the peace of the kitchen, and this peace was somehow about him in a calm strength, even though he was profoundly sensitive to his mother's presence and to her condition.

Glancing from under his brows, he saw her eyes staring in a sightless way and heard her breath in her half-open mouth, short shallow breaths like ghostly sighs.

She stirred and he hid his eyes from her in his book, listening acutely.

Then he looked again and saw that her spirit was struggling with its earthly tie, that it was wanting to come back, to resolve some final difficulty, as if it were not yet ready, and in this struggle there was for a poignant moment, it seemed to him, the final pathos of human tragedy.

The struggle passed and now her eyes looked at him from the midst of the calm.

They had the nameless gleam of intelligence by which she had first communicated the knowledge that her death was at hand. But now the gleam softened and shone in a tender light. The hand nearest him made a tentative movement and he put out his own right hand and caught it.

"I'm leaving you, Tom."

The whispering voice brought a great tenderness upon him, dissolving the hardness of his flesh, and tears came welling up into his eyes and ran down his face.

"You have been a good mother to me," he said, and he caressed her wrist with his free hand.

She took in a breath and he thought she was going to cry, but slowly she smiled upon him in a profound pity and tenderness that was love's last service, and perceptibly moved her head in a negation that knew her love and service had not been enough. Not enough. He felt her fingers grip at his hand.

Now she wanted to say something to him, which yet she knew she could never say. Her strange gleaming look seemed to regard him as if he were not looking at her, but only she at him.

This last effort at communion exhausted her strength, and on a faint surge of emotion she drew in a deep shuddering breath. As the breath ebbed from her life went with it and the gleam faded from her eyes.

Chapter Twenty

The deserted croft came to a focus in the Philosopher's eyes, whose blue was full of a glowing light. It was the sort of croft where shadowy figures like those of his mother and Janet might pass, busy in the sunlight. He looked about him, at the grass, the wild flowers, the tufts of rushes, the white flags of the canna, the shorn sheep nibbling away among the whin bushes. The valley was now hidden from him, the land continuing beyond it, great rolling sweeps of brown heath, with a far crofting township showing up in a quartering of tiny fields like a shield.

He got to his feet, but before leaving that old croft, with its silent stones and half-obliterated rigs, he gave it one long look, and his eyes smiled.

It has a gladness about it, he thought, as he faced the moor. Not altogether the sort of joy that is next to godliness nor yet the solemn tenderness of Christ. But a gladness that is part of the old human gaiety. Pagan is hardly the word, not exact enough. It is the ultimate gaiety that comes from a knowledge of loneliness. It is a gaiety that knows the wind and the grasses and the sunlight and moves with them. It is the gaiety that is lost in the crowd, and lost to oneself when too concerned with the crowd. It is a final individual bubbling up of the spirit of positive life.

Yes, it would be a long inquiry—before he covered all the

ground. In the years that immediately followed his mother's death, he had had many a mixed dealing with the world. Tina . . . there had been that time when he wondered if he would drift into marriage with Tina. That had been an earthy time, long drawn out, tormented. His mind seemed to lose its power to come to any decision, to lose itself in haunting the physical body, in creating physical fantasies that took possession with a sort of horrible inertia. Very little then might have made him marry Tina. But it had to come from the outside in order to overcome the inertia. The inertia was too strong of itself, and Tina lacked something, some directive compelling element. Or was he, unconsciously, even in his physical fantasy with her, fighting against her? Why else had he cleared off to Glasgow for a few days more than once?

By contrast, his occasional reading at this time attained moments of extreme clarity, so that an involuntary memory of them was like silver-bright windows in a dark house. But the house had been dark—dark with that sense of weariness, of frustration, which now and then came to a pitch of bitterness that flared in acute physical spasms and died down into a condition as unresponsive as mire. Yet possibly most of the time passed in an even normality, a sort of grey good nature. Anyway, a period that would require a long chapter to itself—that might prove revealing of a human nature not directed by or towards anything, but living in itself, at the mercy of chance currents and gusts.

Henry came back from the war, grown in body and strength, full of energy and confidence. He took the eager young man's command of everything, including the business and his mother. Tom gave him the promised half-share of all profits, retaining final control himself. Henry had ideas galore and the business began swiftly to open out and thrive.

That was a not unpleasant time, full of Henry's talk and energy and friendliness. Behind Henry, Tina slowly retired.

When Bessie left him at the age of twenty-one to go and get married, he had turned fifty, and found in the loneliness of the house a secret pleasure which he did not feel disposed to give up. Henry said his mother would look in in the mornings and tidy things for him, but Tom said he would rather not have anyone for a while as he wanted to make certain alterations in the kitchen, fix up some bookshelves and other odds and ends suitable for a bachelor.

How many years was it since he had made a will by which the business would be left to Henry and his money divided between Tina and her other two children, Bessie and George? Difficult to remember because from that time when he had first begun to live alone, a new life had opened out.

This would be perhaps the most difficult period to get a clear grip of, for its essential adventures lay in the region of the intellect and the spirit. And what extraordinary adventures they had been! How brilliant a creature was the individual genius in history! How marvellous a receptacle was society which retained the stuff of his genius as a feeding trough retains food! From Hume to Kant. From Kant to Hegel. And the emergence in practice of the bureaucratic concept among those who derived from, however in theory they ran counter to, Hegel. The new formulation of materialism under its three headings: dialectical, historical, and philosophical. Parallels in the physical world. Water changing quantitatively in temperature until the moment of revolution when it is changed qualitatively into ice—or steam. A reasoning that held some of the clear beauty of mathematics.

The opposed school of thought: the ideal, the transcendental, the mystical. Mathematical proof absent here. Adventures now in the realm of individual experience. Ah, this was the difficult realm. Because an individual experience here was insusceptible of "proof" that did not mean its reality was less valid to the one who experienced it. This, too, had its own parallel in the physical world. However brilliant your description of the taste of a blaeberry, it will never evoke the taste in the mind of one who has never eaten the fruit; just as you can never communicate the scent of wild thyme to a man with no "nose", or its colour to a man born colour blind.

This nodding of tall grasses in the wind, with its literary (historical) associations for him, such as the passing of "the lordly ones", how communicate the exquisite gaiety that invades the mind at such a moment?

Literature. He remembered his first vague dissatisfaction with literature because it "proved" nothing. It had taken him a long time to realise that outside mathematics and pure science, nothing was susceptible of their kind of proof. Voltaire was probably the first to give him some idea of the meaning of literature. For very early he made what seemed to him a curious personal discovery, namely, that it did make a difference who presented particular "truths". Obviously a truth was a truth whoever expressed it and the introduction of "difference" was absurd. Still, truth in the living (as distinct from the mathematical) realm had to be phrased and the way in which it was phrased affected as a matter of simple fact the mind of the recipient. He found, for example, that he preferred Voltaire's phrasing in biblical criticism to that of the hammer-and-tongs rationalist or freethinker. He began to feel that the realm of experience of the propagandist rationalist was too confined, too partial. In Voltaire's phrasing there was implicit a wider experience, a profound apprehension of total life. And it was with this experience of total life that literature was forever dealing in all places, at all times.

Let the philosophers and political theorists build up their opposing systems, let science add to the pool of common knowledge its marvellous discoveries, but somewhere somehow the individual has to stand on his own two feet and reckon with it all.

And the proof of this? That here he was a simple individual, a unit of the crofting folk, nameless to the world, wandering across this deserted moor now and trying to bring to a focus in himself, if not the meaning of the whole, at least some coherent apprehension of the whole.

Does not a time come to every man when he walks and thinks, in however different a degree, as I do now, I, the solitary individual?

So literature would seem to prove out of an immense body of evidence that traversed all systems and all times.

Perhaps amid the intellectual and spiritual efforts of man, literature in its detachment from any specific field of effort, as an observer in all fields, had the job of synthesising for and in the individual all the theses and anti-theses, and bringing the result with some coherence to walk on its own two feet amid the tall grasses! The ultimate of what is felt and thought and experienced by all, expressed in terms of life. The living essence of the communal whole. The living individual.

Yes, it was going to take a good few trips, many days and nights, to look into these matters and apply them to some reasonable understanding of the pattern he himself had woven in his days on this old earth and of those, close to his spirit, whom the pattern had touched.

The prospect pleased him, and he set his eyes upon the moor in greeting.

A snipe got up from a marshy hollow in front and he stood watching its irregular flight until it was lost in the far air. Casting his eyes towards the green hillock on the right, he saw a white spot and thought—Ah, a mushroom! No-one in this country ate mushrooms except himself. A mushroom was a snow-white legend in the grass. But when he reached the spot he found it was a sheep's skull. He smiled and examined it curiously, noting, as man instinctively does, the perfect teeth.

As he straightened himself, three peewits took the air from beyond the hillock, but only one cried, and its cry had lost the sibilant urgency of the spring. This was one of his favourite birds and his mind had developed a curious almost esoteric intimacy with its life-cycle and its anxious impatient moods. He often spoke a few words to it. In the spring and early summer: "It's all right—all right—you needn't worry!" Now: "You're not worrying much, are you?" and he observed how they tumbled away from him, in a grace almost sad with distance and fulfilment.

His eyes lit on a small object in front of his feet, black spots on brown, like a tiny circle of tapestry. The tapestry divided into powder-blue wings with a white edging, and the butterfly got up and flew off, with a flitting elegance that neither the snipe nor the peewit had quite achieved.

The roses red and white, the golden broom, the red and the white clover, tall wild flowers of the grassy ditches, gave way now to the dead heather of the moor. But there! the bell heather was in bloom, a deep red glory, an old red with blue in it. That invisible shimmer of blue in the shadow, how lovely and elusive! Why should it make him think of blood?

Bog asphodel! One has to know flowers, year by year, before they evoke the friendly silent cry. And now, almost under his feet, the trailing deer's grass has set up its yellow-green spikes. Everything that crawls will some time lift its spiring thought to the sun! No, not thought, but desire . . . The butterwort, still in bloom, but the leaves now growing yellow and curling up in their old age. They had had a pretty good season . . . Petty whin—but beyond, yes, wild thyme, a whole purple cushion of it.

He squatted by the cushion, pinched a corner with his fingers, and sniffed his fingers. Aromatic, rich. It penetrated through the congested ways of the head, it did the heart good, this living cleansing scent. Let the heart be lifted up: it is gratitude's deepest acknowledgment.

Lord, how would he ever be able to make intelligible his entrance into the kingdom of the earth!

A wild bee came along in a buzzing hurry. A very busy fellow. A little drunk by the look of him and by the way he side-slipped, but holding to his ravaging purpose amid the blossom, with interludes of silence and of song. The Philosopher watched him until all of a sudden he buzzed off.

The Philosopher nodded several times in agreement and in a merry wonder that held itself within the light of his eyes.

The Philosopher was no methodical naturalist; indeed he felt himself like nothing very much at all. And in this nothing much there was a freedom, an acceptance, a participation, a part of everything-in-itself, that had a humour subtly produced as honey. Once he had fancied he had seen a grey boulder hold its sides in this cosmic mirth. But the boulder had outstared him and put him back in his place. It's no good fancying things and making merry with a boulder. It's been longer on the game than you have and your little fantasies are a silly intrusion.

Fantasy-making was no more than the flitting of errant butterfly-wings round the whin-root of being. But it could be amusing—and had . . . perhaps . . . *something* in it!

Amid the after thoughts to such pleasant thoughts he came over the last ridge and saw the stream, the small river winding from the mountains and hiding parts of itself in little gullies. With the sun at his back, he admired the lower reach as a lovely blue, full of light, that for no particular reason always made him think of the belly of an eel or a serpent. He had known he would find this colour, and lo! he had found it.

The river—the names of rivers—rivers of commerce—the rivers of great continents—the veins of the earth. The river the Greeks called Lethe, and the Gaels called the Black River of Death. Blue, a living blue, blue as heaven.

You cannot leave your money to a river, nor your business, not anything but your thoughts and your affection, unless you left it yourself!

He just loved this stream, and that was all.

Love. Well, there was love. Just as there was suffering. Suffering by itself brutalised. But suffering transformed by love—than that man knows nothing more profound. Just nothing. It was the ultimate experience, the ultimate cleansing . . . short of death, that enigma.

He had been thinking so much about Janet . . . and then about his mother . . . The river passed from his conscious sight for a little while. Through the dead heather he went until he came on the last verge and looked down into the water, which was quite clear though it appeared, as always, faintly brown.

The off bank was low and flat, with tall purple thistles holding about their roots the dead grey grasses of the last spate. Golden flecks of the tormentil . . . a cluster of trefoil. And the water; the running water—down from the mountains, over the moor, in many a swirl of adventure, and away to the distant sea.

Often the simplest object would set up a train of thought that would reach astonishing heights or depths, or, rather, would confer upon him moments of illumination that stilled his humble being in a beatified wonder.

Where had he been reading about water? Two volumes of hydrogen gas and one volume of oxygen gas invariably come together to form water. That was it. Why? And the only answer the chemist knows is that the oxygen atom has an "affinity" for the two hydrogen atoms. Of the nature of this "affinity"—the chemist's own word—the chemist has no notion, and the physicist cannot help him out.

Affinity. Odd sort of word to use, denoting a relationship, like a human relationship. Was human love its evolved form? Who was it said that the human being was just matter thinking? Marx. Yes, it was Marx, in the philosophic aspect of his materialism. Was thought, then, potential in all matter? Was affinity, then, not only potential but a recognised constituent—if an unknown one—in matter, and necessary to its "revolutionary" changes?

Were thought and affinity the two supreme active principles in the known universe?

Of the nature of affinity in the human relationship, what was the principal element? Probably a certain tenderness. The tenderness of love.

He had been thinking of tenderness before—yes, the tenderness of Christ—that time, by his mother's bedside. And that time, too, when he had seen the shepherd leaning on his staff at a little distance. That extraordinary pure tenderness which had penetrated the centuries, which nothing could kill, neither torture nor death, neither the hell-fire of authority nor the ritual of its form, importance nor vanity, nothing, not anything. Amazing that it should so persist, from generation to generation, like the scent of the wild thyme. What relationship did this argue in man that he so manifestly craved it?

The affinity of the oxygen atom for the hydrogen atoms . . . in cosmic evolution up to the tenderness of Christ, to love. And what relationship in this vast evolutionary process will be (or may now be somewhere) as far beyond human love as that love is already, in its expressive consciousness, beyond the affinity of the three atoms?

There was a range for thought! How glorious a range, how supreme and unending an adventure for the human spirit! To get a glimpse of it was to feel glad.

So caught up by his visioning was the Philosopher that it exhausted him a little and he was pleased to sit down.

The feeling of freedom, of expansiveness, that came to him on the moor, was always increased, when, having chosen his spot, he sat down, extending his legs, and lay back against a heathery support for his shoulders and head.

There was first the delicious feeling of rest, of sinking down upon the moor and thereby set floating upon its whole varied expanse, with the subdued sounds of the stream running by and the slow curves of the near hills against the summer sky. Then secondly, and in a moment, there was that ancient intimate scent of the old heather stalks. One always forgets that scent and its surprise has the freshness of an original memory. Long lives ago it was here; it is here still; and this element of time in it is an abiding strength.

The Philosopher settled himself comfortably and his heart expanded in tribute. Indeed for a little while his eyes closed under the snout of his bonnet and he floated deep and away. Not wishing, however, to lose altogether this solitary delight, this pagan sensation, he half-opened his eyes, so that he only half-slept, a temporary in-between state which permitted what was heavy to dissolve quite away. Than these moments there were none more pleasant in his life.

Presently not only his mind but his eyes and his ears and the skin inside his clothes came delicately alive. His ear was the whorl of a shell that hears the song of the ocean. His eyes saw the mountains uplifted, singing the song of the earth to the sky, one far cone clear as a pipe. Jocund was the word the poet used. He smiled in divine ease, for if all he heard was the song in his own blood, that blood came out of ocean and earth and sky and would return thither. Not much separated one element from another. Not much—but yet how exquisite the little, the little that separated being from not-being!

The Philosopher's thought, now entering into its ultimate region, assumed the extremely tenuous condition wherein it distinguished subtleties that no pen could record, because the least physical movement, even the speaking of a word, would have dispelled them. And in this experiencing there was no labour, as if by some miracle thought found its true flow and moved like vision.

His chin fell to his chest, his eyes to the heather by his upturned toes, for in this attitude sight went more readily inward, identifying itself with those inner eyes that produced the light by which thought was made visible.

He knew the moment of extreme pause when it seems that the veil which divides being from not-being becomes filmy, verges on complete translucence. Here the last illusion seems to be dispelled and time in stillness completes itself; the beginning and the end are comprehended.

To be suddenly recalled from this pause by the outside world is to experience an extreme almost anguished beating of the heart, with the body putting forth its whole strength in a supreme effort, the breath labouring, sweat breaking on the forehead.

Properly such a pause should fall away into the sleep that is like the sleep of death, until one awakens, not only refreshed, but with a feeling of delight, which cannot be named, of having wandered in a place which leaves no memory.

Just beyond the Philosopher's boots was a small outcrop of quartz before the ground dipped sharply to the stream. In a damp crevice grew a saxifrage whose gold was paler than the spikes of the bog asphodel. The heather about his legs and under his body was springy and comfortable. It was a natural place, with its gentle slope to the south-west, for animal life to enter upon and curl up in the sun.

The Philosopher's eyes were on the heather by his boots, though they did not consciously see it, for all external things were now out of focus. Last year's pin-head blossoms, withered to a delicate ash-brown, still adhered to the dark-brown heather stalks. But already up through this darkness and withered ashen blooms, the new green shoots were sprouting, tipped with tiny pale buds, pale to living white.

Suddenly over from his left boot the stalks began to shiver and pouring through them came the body of an adder from two to three feet long.

This movement brought the Philosopher's staring eyes into focus and a slow swelling started in his chest. The adder slid through the heather towards the left hand, which was extended, palm upward, pale as quartz. Over the root of the Philosopher's little finger the diamond head uprose, seeking warmth. The hand was warm as a rock in the sun, but the head, swaying slightly from side to side, seemed at a loss. Then tentatively it poured some of its cold dark-brown body onto the palm, touched the wrist innocently with its mouth, stopped suddenly as the hand gave a slight convulsive jerk, and quickly slid off over the ball of the thumb and down into the heather where the Philosopher's sleeve lay sunk.

He must be asleep, thought the shepherd, smiling to himself. However, too much sun mightn't be good for him. Instead of shouting again, he decided to go over and wake him.

The snout of the cap shaded the eyes. Frail and done, the old boy looked. The shepherd put a hand on his shoulder and called, "Hi!" From his stooping position, he was astonished to see that the eyes were wide open. He called again and pushed the snout back a little. The eyes were gazing so intently at something in the distance that the shepherd involuntarily glanced over his shoulder at the mountains. Then the shepherd's heart chilled and a coldness ran over his skin. He stared at the set face. By God, the old man was dead! He touched the forehead with his hand. Death has a clammy cold there is no mistaking.

Though the shepherd had handled many dead and half-dead bodies on the battlefields of the world, the death of the Philosopher here on his own moor on a sunny day touched him with the mystery that is quick with the ancient fear. But he got his hands under the armpits, and, calling to the Philosopher as though he might yet awaken him, heaved him up. Whereupon a serpent of monstrous length issued, as it seemed, out of the left arm, out of the very hand, and for a moment so intense was the shepherd's shock of infernal horror that he went muscle-bound. Then as he spasmodically jerked himself away, the cap fell from the Philosopher's bald head and the light body rolled over and lay still in an incongruous heap.

The shepherd turned and ran, and in the first few steps he lived through those years of his youth, the impressionable years of prophecy and curse, with the Serpent that would devour the atheist who had killed his own father.

He stopped, panting; forgot the primal fear, and tentatively returned. Gripping the neck of the jacket, he stepped backward, hauling the body after him. Presently when he had it on a bare patch, where the heather had been burned in the spring, he stood and looked about him. He could not leave the body for any length of time here where the grey crows waited to peck the eyes out of death. An eyeless body for a Christian burial by the old church—by God no! Not for his old friend!

Remembering their recent meeting, he was deeply moved, flooded in a moment by a tenderness that yet quivered like an exalted fear. He got down on his knees and felt the body all over for concealed snakes. He hardly knew what he was doing—until he became aware of the face.

At once all urgency fell from him before that timeless calm, that austerity which yet gathered about the small wrinkles of the skin a profound and nameless gentleness.

As the shepherd put his hands under the body he spoke to the Philosopher as he might have spoken to a boy. "It's all right, Tom, boy," he said reassuringly. "I'll see you home."

THE END